Praise for the novels of Cassie Ryan

"From the first erotic word to the last sensual line, *Ceremony of Seduction* weaves a spell around its reader and doesn't let go."
—*Joyfully Reviewed*

"An incredibly creative read. If you're looking for a sexy escape, you'll find it here."
—*Romantic Times*

"Ms. Ryan creates a bold and beautiful world . . . I highly recommend it."
—*Night Owl Romance*

"An amazing journey between two worlds. Definitely a book that, once opened, won't be closed until the final page has been read."
—*Kate Douglas*

SEDUCING
the SUCCUBUS

CASSIE RYAN

BERKLEY SENSATION, NEW YORK

THE BERKLEY PUBLISHING GROUP
Published by the Penguin Group
Penguin Group (USA) Inc.
375 Hudson Street, New York, New York 10014, USA
Penguin Group (Canada), 90 Eglinton Avenue East, Suite 700, Toronto, Ontario M4P 2Y3, Canada
(a division of Pearson Penguin Canada Inc.)
Penguin Books Ltd., 80 Strand, London WC2R 0RL, England
Penguin Group Ireland, 25 St. Stephen's Green, Dublin 2, Ireland (a division of Penguin Books Ltd.)
Penguin Group (Australia), 250 Camberwell Road, Camberwell, Victoria 3124, Australia
(a division of Pearson Australia Group Pty. Ltd.)
Penguin Books India Pvt. Ltd., 11 Community Centre, Panchsheel Park, New Delhi—110 017, India
Penguin Group (NZ), 67 Apollo Drive, Rosedale, North Shore 0632, New Zealand
(a division of Pearson New Zealand Ltd.)
Penguin Books (South Africa) (Pty.) Ltd., 24 Sturdee Avenue, Rosebank, Johannesburg 2196,
South Africa

Penguin Books Ltd., Registered Offices: 80 Strand, London WC2R 0RL, England

This book is an original publication of The Berkley Publishing Group.

This is a work of fiction. Names, characters, places, and incidents either are the product of the author's imagination or are used fictitiously, and any resemblance to actual persons, living or dead, business establishments, events, or locales is entirely coincidental. The publisher does not have any control over and does not assume any responsibility for author or third-party websites or their content.

PRINTING HISTORY
Berkley Sensation trade paperback edition / October 2010

Library of Congress Cataloging-in-Publication Data

Ryan, Cassie.
    Seducing the Succubus / Cassie Ryan.—Berkley Sensation trade pbk. ed.
        p.   cm.
    ISBN 978-0-425-23684-0
    I. Title.
    PS3618.Y33S43   2010
    813'.6—dc22   2010027827

PRINTED IN THE UNITED STATES OF AMERICA

10   9   8   7   6   5   4   3   2   1

In memory of Anna Smith

ACKNOWLEDGMENTS

Thanks to my amazing agent, Paige Wheeler, and my wonderful editor, Kate Seaver, for seeing promise in my wacky story idea about four succubi in Hell's version of the witness relocation program . . . and not laughing me out the door. You both rock!

Thanks to the entire crew of my local Starbucks. This entire book was written there in my favorite squishy chair. So for all your support, terrible jokes of the day, love, encouragement, laughter . . . and of course all the Chai . . . my undying thanks.

Last and most important, thanks to Jon and Darian for not only enduring living with a writer, but doing it with humor, understanding, and love. I couldn't do this without you guys!

1

"Dinner time, gentlemen," Jezebeth said to herself as she raked her gaze over the many men crowding into the darkened club.

The heavy beat of hip-hop music thumped through the soles of her knee-high lace-up boots and made her heart beat faster as anticipation curled deep inside her belly.

A long mahogany bar ran the length of the back wall, and dozens of men crowded around jostling for their turn to order a drink. In the middle of the room scantily clad women gyrated on four raised platforms while colored laser lights panned over the audience in regular intervals, briefly illuminating the smoky atmosphere. Not that Jez needed the light. One of the perks of being a succubus was being able to see in the dark—not to mention sense and smell the sustenance-giving potential of those beings around her.

Her searching gaze fell on a large human male sitting at a back table with broad shoulders and just the right amount of muscle. A glowing aura of nearly white energy surrounded him like a pulsing mist, and Jez's skin ached with longing—the succubus equivalent of a stomach growl. The size and general health of the man's aura told her not only that he'd feed her well but that taking his energy and tempting him toward good or evil would also give her great brownie points with her boss, Lilith, the succubus queen. Especially since Jez was behind quota this month—again.

Jez concentrated on the man and a slow warm tingling flowed through her as her body shifted to become whatever form the man most desired.

She glanced down to see her now-overgenerous breasts nearly spilling out over a tight-laced bloodred corset, her skin milk-pale and her body fully curved. She wore a tight black miniskirt and short black ankle boots that displayed a winding rose tattoo snaking up her right leg to disappear under her skirt.

This body was shorter than she was used to, and she had to crane her neck and stand on her tiptoes to keep the man in her line of sight over the tightly packed crowd.

Jez reached up and tried to fluff out her hair, surprised to find it short and spiky instead of long and flowing. She shrugged as amusement spilled through her. The preferences of men were wide and varied, and as long as they provided her with what she needed, she didn't care what form she had to take to get it.

Well—that was almost true.

There *had* been forms she'd outright refused to remain in.

She shuddered in memory of some of the more bizarre bodies men had desired her to take and wrangled her thoughts back to the situation at hand—dinner.

Jez started forward, weaving her way through the crowd, her gaze fixed on her target where he sipped his drink and watched the dancer on the nearest platform as she spun expertly around the golden pole using only her muscular thighs.

As Jez neared, the man turned his head, and she could tell the exact moment he became aware of her. His movements stilled and his gaze did a slow and very thorough exploration of her from head to toe and then back again. When he was finished, his lips parted in surprise and the bulge just behind the fly of his jeans grew larger in response.

Jez smiled at him from under her lashes and wet her bottom lip with her tongue, suppressing a small giggle as she tasted strawberry-flavored lip gloss.

His blue gaze burned into hers for a long moment before Jez stepped close and straddled him, making her already short skirt ride up high around her thighs. She sat on his lap and pressed close against his erection. The sensation of rough denim against the sensitive skin of her bare pussy was exquisite. She rubbed herself against him and laid her hand over his chest, noting how his heartbeat thumped a strong pulse under her palm and the energy surrounding him surged higher, tingling against her skin in tiny static electric shocks.

To her surprise, he didn't push her away or show any signs of protest. For someone with such a clean aura, she'd expected a bit of a challenge, but she definitely wasn't going to complain.

She leaned in close to his ear and whispered, "Buy me a drink?"

His strong hand settled against her lower back, the heat from his skin burning through the corset and making her pussy throb in anticipation of what was to come. She pulled back slowly, allowing her breath to feather against the side of his neck until she could look into his eyes.

"Only a drink?" he asked with mischief and lust dancing in the blue depths of his eyes.

Jez smiled and leaned forward again so her breasts pressed against his chest as she brushed her lips over his.

His lips were warm, and he growled deep in his throat and then deepened the kiss, exploring her mouth long and slow.

The tangy taste of Jack Daniel's made her smile. That explained his lack of restraint. A few more drinks would probably make her job all that much easier.

His kisses were a bit sloppy and clumsy, but he made up for that with enthusiasm and the promise of a great energy payoff in the end. With one large hand he cupped her breast roughly, the hot possession making her gasp against his mouth.

She kissed him again, hard, and the familiar tingling and liquid warmth sensation of his life-energy siphoning into her hummed through her veins, ripping a long moan from her throat. Jez sighed against his lips as her clit hardened and slick moisture formed between her labia.

This was only an appetizer, but already her gnawing hunger receded and her skin tingled with vigor. She threaded her fingers into the man's soft hair, capturing him close as she continued to kiss him.

Two sharp taps on her shoulder surprised her and she turned, ready to deal with a bouncer or an angry girlfriend.

Instead, she found a four-foot imp.

It was shamrock green with two tiny yellow horns poking out the top of his knotty head. His glowing red eyes reminded her of twin laser pointers, and he smiled revealing jagged yellow teeth. "Mind if I cut in for official business, Jezebeth?"

"What the hell is that?" The man stood abruptly, dumping her off his lap so she landed hard on her bare ass against the cold concrete floor.

A high-pitched squeak escaped her just before sharp pain radiated up her back from the hard landing. She turned to glare at the imp, who only smirked and shrugged.

Jez pushed to her feet, pulling the short skirt down around the tops of her thighs as she straightened and smiled up at her now-spooked dinner. "It's okay." She gestured toward the imp. "It's leaving." She took a step toward the man, but he held up a hand stop-sign fashion between them.

He shook his head and backed away from her, rubbing his eyes as if he thought he might be hallucinating. "I think I've had a little too much to drink if I'm seeing things already." He took one last longing look at Jez before turning and melting into the crowd.

Jez sighed as the hip-hop song ended and a slow bluesy number started up in its place.

Since no one else in the bar was running away in horror, the imp was probably shielding his true form from all the human eyes—except the man she'd targeted. "Couldn't this have waited another hour or so?" she said loud enough to be heard over the music.

"Lilith sent me to tell you Semiazas has escaped his prison and seeks revenge on you and your sisters."

An icy chill of fear danced down Jez's spine and bile threatened to inch its way up the back of her throat. She swallowed hard before she risked speaking. "How long do I have?"

The imp cocked its head to one side as if considering. "It took me several days to find you. Unknown."

She swallowed back the fear that tried to smother her. "And my sisters?"

"Other messengers have been sent to warn each of them in turn."

The sound of wrenching metal accompanied by an animalistic growl that prickled every hair on Jezebeth's body grated through the air, sending patrons screaming and running in all directions. Sharp, hot anger churned inside her stomach, and she trained her narrowed gaze on the imp.

"You bastard, you led him right to me!" She reached out and grabbed the imp around the neck with both hands, lifting him off his stubby feet.

The imp kicked Jez in the stomach. Pain curled through her as the air was knocked out of her, causing her to loosen her grip on the imp as she doubled over. She rested her hands on her knees as she tried to suck in a new breath.

The imp's smug laughter sounded from nearby. "I fulfilled my promise to Lilith, I delivered the message. And now I've paid a debt I owed to one of the bounty demons as well. It's a good day all the way around."

When Jez could finally draw a breath, the stench of fresh sewage crossed with rotting flesh filled her lungs and stung her eyes. She stumbled backward, trying to put distance between her and the demon, but by the intensity of the stink she knew it was already too late.

The sweeping laser lights showed the crowd of humans still streamed toward the exits. The bluesy music continued to play like a macabre accompaniment to the human screams, sounds of breaking wood, and screeching metal.

Jez dodged around overturned tables and chairs, trying to lose herself in the crowd of stampeding humans.

As she neared the exit door, her survival instincts screamed and her gut clenched, surging adrenaline through her body as she whirled to look behind her.

A flicker of movement was all the warning she had before red-hot pain sliced through her shoulder and left arm and she found herself flying backward. Her back smacked against something hard, and her breath whooshed out for the second time in a few minutes.

She gasped against the pain, even as her brain belatedly told her she'd been slammed against the wall. A few long seconds later, she glanced up into the glowing red eyes of the bounty demon.

Fear and frustration warred inside her belly as she struggled against the poison-tipped demon's claws that were sunk inside her arm and shoulder, pinning her back against the wall. Her movements were sluggish, which told her the poison had already begun to affect her.

"Jezebeth, follower of Lilith. Finally, we meet." The demon's hot, rotten breath huffed against her face with each cultured word. It towered over her, the laser lights flashing off its thousands of jagged sharklike teeth. Mottled black skin covered every inch of the demon and maggots and worms crawled along its flesh in a constant sea of putrid motion.

A pestilence demon.

Jez tried to ignore the shiver of revulsion as some of the maggots slid off the demon's hands and crawled onto the bare skin of her shoulder.

She shoved aside her fear, glared up into the demon's glowing red eyes and raised her chin. "You'd better hope Lilith never finds you. She'll rip you into tiny little shreds to send back to your master."

The demon laughed. "The size of the reward that Semiazas has on you will go a long way toward protecting me from the anger of the queen of the whores, little one. Besides, you'll be dead long before that." He opened his mouth revealing ten rows of razor sharp teeth, and Jez tensed as she waited for the deathblow.

A sizzling sound drowned out the music, and the stench of burning flesh filled her lungs just before the demon's jaws snapped closed like a deadly animal trap just an inch from her nose. The demon let out a high-pitched squeal and wrenched his claws out of Jez's flesh.

White-hot pain sliced through her, and she crumpled to the floor as she was freed from the demon's grip.

"Run!" shouted a very deep voice.

Not about to argue and waste her chance to escape, Jez scrambled toward the door on all fours, trying to ignore the sudden rush of warmth down her arm as blood gushed out of her wound.

Another loud squeal from the demon made her glance back as she pushed to her feet.

A human male nearly as tall as the demon stood holding a Super Soaker toy gun Rambo style in front of him. There was no trace of fear in his gaze as he pumped the gun and then shot a stream of liquid toward the demon.

A sound like a thousand skillets of frying bacon filled the air along with another keening sound from the demon. The demon convulsed as plumes of black acrid smoke rose toward the ceiling in lazy curls.

The man turned his head toward Jez as if he sensed her scrutiny. Their gazes locked and Jez jumped like a guilty child caught eavesdropping. "I said run, damn it!"

The terse command jogged her out of her reverie, and she turned and stumbled out the door along with the last few straggling humans.

Cold night air hit her blood-soaked clothes, and Jez gritted her teeth against the sudden round of gooseflesh that marched across every inch of her skin. She envisioned herself whole and healthy and wearing long sleeves, tennis shoes, and jeans.

When no familiar warm tingling signaled her body changing forms, Jez huffed out a breath as frustration churned inside her belly. "Damn."

As a succubus, blood loss and cold alone wouldn't kill her, but those would make her more vulnerable to those who *could* kill her. Besides, it was her fault the human was inside facing off with a pestilence demon. But she couldn't do anything to help him in her present condition.

Jez stumbled out toward the rapidly emptying parking lot happy to find two men sitting in the bed of a large pickup truck, bottles of beers clutched in their hands. Since their truck was blocked in by the exiting traffic, they seemed to be making the best of it.

She picked up her pace, jogging toward them, cursing the tight corset and the larger-than-life breasts that bounced painfully with every step.

Both men's heads swiveled toward her and she slowed to a brisk walk, smiling at them. She hoped they'd had enough beers and were distracted enough by her oversized boobs to make them look past the gaping shoulder wound and her bloody clothes.

"You need a ride, miss?"

Jez couldn't tell which of them made the offer, but at this point, it didn't really matter. She reached the truck and scrambled up into the bed, shivering as her bare legs hit the cold metal. "Actually, I'm freezing and hoped you boys could warm me up."

The men smiled at each other and then back at her, not bothering to move from their seated positions on opposite sides of the truck railing. "What did you have in mind?"

In answer, she stepped toward the first man and straddled him just as she had with her dinner. She grabbed his face in both her hands, the slight stubble scraping against her palms as she kissed him hard.

He opened his mouth and she took the opportunity to slip her tongue inside, using several thousand years of experience to keep him fully engaged. He returned the kiss, and his beer bottle clattered loudly against the bed of the truck as his arms came around her holding her close.

Jez didn't have time for a slow surge of energy, she was losing blood fast, and the human who'd helped her could already be dead. She ground against the man beneath her, kissing him hard and deep, allowing his energy to flow into her in a quick rush.

When he swayed against her and his hold on her loosened, she pulled back and stood.

He blinked hard as if coming out of a trance and then slid down into the bed of the truck like a rag doll. "Damn," was all he managed to say past the wide grin on his face.

Jez rotated her arm and winced at the pain still there. Although, she was glad to note she could move the arm at all and that the rush of blood had slowed to a trickle. Her fingers were still numb from the poison, but nothing she couldn't heal totally if she had more time and some full-on sex.

"Hey, what about me, beautiful?" asked the second man in the truck.

Jez flexed her hand and shrugged. She could definitely use a little more energy, and the man would experience less of an energy hangover from her than he would from drinking a case of beer. She leaned forward, giving him a full view of her over-impressive cleavage and allowed him a quick look before she cupped his cheek and pressed her lips to his.

He opened for her immediately and stood to pull her against him, dropping the bottle just as his friend had.

Jez stood on her tiptoes as his energy flowed into her. In only a few seconds he swayed against her, and she guided him down to the bed of the truck where he flopped over, smiling up at her.

"Thanks," he slurred with a smile as his eyes slipped closed.

"No, thank *you*." She rolled her injured shoulder noting the improved healing and the reduced effects of the pestilence demon's poison. Not fully healed, but good enough to go back and save the Good Samaritan's ass.

Not bothering to waste her siphoned energy to change form, Jez hopped down off the truck, wincing as it jarred her still-injured arm. A quick jog took her back to the door she'd left just a few minutes ago, and she took a deep breath for courage before she stepped back inside the club.

Sounds of battle told her the human still lived. She breathed a sigh of relief as she used the darkened interior to her advantage and kept to the shadows along the side wall until she could sneak behind the long mahogany bar. From there, she was able to kneel on a box of clean bar towels, which put her at the perfect height to peek above the bar to see the action unfolding in between the dance platforms.

The human stood facing off with the pestilence demon just as she'd left him, making her wonder what other tricks he had up his sleeve besides the obvious holy water in a Super Soaker trick.

Movement behind the man caught Jez's attention, and she turned to look just as the imp head butted the back of the human's legs, making him lurch forward to land hard on his knees with a loud curse.

The pestilence demon laughed and straightened, even though his hide still sizzled and smoked. "I'll eat your soul, human!"

Jez bit back her cry of warning since it would only get her caught. Instead she rolled off the box and landed hard on her ass as she racked her brain for any way to help. As a succubus, she was the definite example of lover, not fighter, but she had to do something. The human had saved her, after all.

More sizzling sounds and one definitive "fuck you" from the human told her he was still alive, but she didn't have much time.

Her gaze landed on the bottles of liquor filling the mirrored shelves behind the bar and a slow smile spread across her face as she glanced back at the box of bar towels.

She grabbed a half-filled bottle of Jack Daniel's and twisted off the top before stuffing the edge of one of the bar towels inside it far enough to begin to soak up the liquid. Working quickly and listening for any sign she'd been found, Jez grabbed all the bottles she could reach from her hiding spot and filled them with bar towels.

She risked being seen by standing and grabbing two of the still-lit table candles that sat on the bar and pulled them down onto the floor with her.

"Please let this work like it does in the movies." With her hands trembling, she grabbed the first two bottles and held the protruding end of their bar towels over the flames.

When they caught fire and the flame began to spread, she stood and threw first one and then the other in the general direction of the demon, but as far away from the human as she could.

For a long few seconds, nothing happened except the crash of splintering glass, and then the flame met the liquid and there was a satisfying flash and fireball.

Jez resisted the urge to pump her arm in the air in victory and instead grabbed two more bottles as another satisfying high-pitched squeal sounded from the pestilence demon.

She lit the bottle bombs in her hands, stood, and with her good arm, chucked them one after the other in the same general direction.

The man had regained his feet and stumbled back closer toward the bar, bringing the pestilence demon with him, their battle still ongoing. She winced as she noticed a few bleeding wounds where flying glass from the bottle bombs had hit him.

The second bottle bomb hit a few inches away from the imp, and the resulting fireball lit the small demon like a Fourth of July sparkler.

Its scream of gurgling anguish was cut short when a loud pop drowned out all other noise as the imp's physical form was destroyed and he was sucked back to Hell.

"Serves you right, you little bastard," she muttered as she grabbed more bottles, prepared to keep up the barrage until she could either do the same to the pestilence demon or figure a way out of this mess.

She lit another two and tossed them between the human and the demon. When the fireballs exploded, she gave in to the urge to whoop as she lit another two bar towels.

In her peripheral vision, she noticed the human pull out a small gun from his backpack and take aim at the pestilence demon. Over the music and the demon's screaming, Jez never heard the retort of the gun, but five pink darts hit the demon in quick succession, protruding from his skin like odd piercings.

Jez watched in fascination as the demon's form sizzled and slowly expanded as if he were doing a remake of the blueberry girl from Willy Wonka. She definitely didn't want to be around when he "popped."

Movement caught her attention, and she glanced up in time to see the human jump onto the bar in front of her.

"You gonna throw those?"

Jez jumped when he grabbed the two already-lit bottle bombs in front of her and tossed them toward the demon before he dove over the bar, nearly knocking her on her ass.

She scowled as she realized she'd gotten distracted and almost let the bottles explode in her face.

The sound of two explosions one after another rent the air and startled Jez. She sat frozen for a long moment, sizing up the human. Up close his eyes were the soft gray of storm clouds, and they alternately sparked with intelligence and curiosity.

He picked up two more bottle bombs, lit them, and tossed them blind over the bar in the general direction of the demon before he grabbed her around the waist, dragging her with him as he rushed toward the end of the bar and along the shadowed edges of the walls.

"Hey," she protested as she scrambled to try and gain her feet. "I can walk, you know. Put me down."

"Fine." He let go and dropped her, nearly dumping Jez on her ass again as he continued forward. "Stay down, and run like hell," he hissed over his shoulder as he ducked through the exit doors, just a second before the two bottle bombs exploded.

2

Noah shook his head at the annoyed expression that slid across Jezebeth's features when he'd nearly dropped her on her ass. After all, he'd risked his neck to save her back there; she could at least be appreciative. Hadn't he told her to run?

She came back for you, his conscience reminded him, making him scowl.

That had surprised him. From everything he'd learned about succubi in the past few weeks from the imp Lilith had sent to give him this assignment, he'd figured Jezebeth would cut and run and he'd have to track her down once he'd killed the demon.

Although since the imp who had given him the information was the same one who had just tried to help the pestilence demon kill him, Noah wasn't sure how much of its so-called information he could trust.

He had to admit, he'd been impressed with Jezebeth's quick thinking in making the bottle bombs. Succubi had to be smart to survive as they did, so maybe this assignment would be quick and easy.

Yeah, right.

Noah adjusted his backpack on his shoulders and winced as the shards of glass still embedded in his arm and side from the first of the bottle bombs moved inside their wounds. Once the first one had exploded he'd kept his distance and let the demon take the worst of the debris.

He mentally shoved aside the pain and glanced around. It wouldn't be too long before the pestilence demon recovered enough to come after them, and they needed to put some distance between them and it as quickly as they could. He doubted they'd been lucky enough to destroy its earthbound form—mid-level bounty demons were supposed to be very hard to kill.

Noah edged around the building and breathed a sigh of relief when the pickup he'd stocked with supplies still sat unharmed in the parking lot. The way the last few weeks had gone, he wouldn't have been surprised if the truck mysteriously disappeared and he had to walk the damned succubus to the final rendezvous.

He looked over his shoulder to find Jezebeth peering past him toward the parking lot. Her ridiculously large breasts nearly spilled out of her corset as she leaned forward to see around the corner. Noah resisted the urge to roll his eyes. "By the way, I'm Noah. Lilith sent me here to bring you back to her lair." The words sounded inane, even as they spilled from his lips, but he couldn't think of a better way to broach the subject quickly.

A furrow appeared between her dark brows, and she looked him up and down as if seeing him for the first time. "Seriously?" From her tone, her disbelief was obvious.

A spurt of irritation sizzled through him and he said through gritted teeth, "Yes, seriously."

"Prove it," she said before edging past him and walking quickly toward the parking lot. "And do it quickly," she called over her shoulder. "I've got to get out of here."

He caught up to her in a few quick steps and grabbed her arm, spinning her around to face him.

She winced and cried out, the sound lancing guilt through him like a sharp knife. He'd forgotten that was her injured arm, and now he felt like an ass as he dropped his hand.

She glared at him, the venom in her gaze stopping him as if she'd slapped him.

"I'm sorry. I didn't mean to hurt you."

When her glare turned to surprise, confusion swam through him. She wasn't quite what he'd expected. True, the short, spiky hair combined with the over-generous curves made her look like a bad caricature of what he'd envisioned a succubus to be. But what did he know? She had survived for centuries before this, so men obviously liked the look.

He mentally shrugged and raised his free hand to eye level to show her the sterling silver ring the imp had given him from Lilith but had warned him not to remove until his assignment was complete. "This is the only proof I have to show you."

At her dubious expression, doubts spilled through him.

Had the imp given him something that would tell her to kill him instead of believing him? The sterling silver ring had faded ancient Hebrew characters inscribed on it that roughly translated to the current-day equivalent of "Temptation"—fitting and ironic for a succubus. But would that really convince her he was here to help?

Jezebeth's brow furrowed, and she reached out tentatively to touch the ring with just the tip of her index finger.

Noah had the impression she was afraid the sterling silver might burn her. He racked his brain to see if he knew anything about the effects of silver on succubi, but came up blank. He had just opened his mouth to suggest they get out of here first and save the "proof" for later when Jezebeth gasped and her lips opened in a tiny "o."

She gave no explanation of her reaction before she raised her gaze to his and nodded once, her face suddenly serious. "Good enough. Let's go."

Before she could walk off again, he grabbed the wrist of her uninjured arm and pulled her after him farther into the parking lot toward his truck. He made a mental note to ask her about the ring as soon as they were out of immediate danger.

Jezebeth followed behind him until they were nearly to the truck, then she slowed her steps. For a long moment, he worried that the effects of her injuries were finally catching up with her. He'd seen how deeply the pestilence demon's claws had penetrated her shoulder, so her words surprised him.

"Please tell me they aren't with you."

Noah frowned and glanced back at her trying to figure out what she meant. He followed her line of sight to find a large pickup parked just next to his in the now nearly deserted parking lot. Two burly good old boys were sprawled in the bed of the truck as if they'd passed out before everyone had fled the building. "No, I came alone. Why?" He glanced back at her, and she smiled, just a small, sardonic curve of her lips.

"I had to take some quick energy from them to be able to come back inside and help." She shrugged. "Would've sucked if I'd just exhausted your entire escape plan."

Noah glanced at the men, who didn't look as if either of them would be waking any time soon. Shock and revulsion spilled through him, and he frowned down at the succubus. "You came out here and had sex with both of them?"

Jezebeth yanked her wrist from his grip and glared at him with a clearly irate expression. "If I'd had full-on sex with two men in the parking lot, don't you think I'd be fully healed and not walking around in this hooker getup?"

Noah had no idea how the succubus/energy thing worked, but filed away that bit of information to study later.

A roar shook the building and shot a new dose of adrenaline through Noah in a sudden surge. He fished in his front pocket for the truck keys and pressed the alarm button to unlock the doors. "Run!"

The command turned out to be unnecessary as Jezebeth had stayed so close on his heels that when he opened the driver's side door to the truck, she jumped in and slid across the bench seat to the passenger's side.

In a quick motion, he shrugged out of the backpack, ignoring the lancing pains up and down his right side from the shards of glass, and tossed the pack to Jezebeth before he jumped in the truck and slammed the door. He started the truck and peeled out of the parking lot as he fumbled for his seat belt.

A quick glance over at Jezebeth showed him her struggle with her own seat belt, her injured arm not working quite like it should. "Hold on tight and as soon as we're clear, I'll help you with that."

She glared over at him as she grabbed onto what his family referred to as the "oh shit" handle just over the passenger window. Then she kicked off her shoes, bracing her feet against the dashboard since her legs weren't long enough to reach the floor. The movement edged her tiny excuse for a skirt up around the tops of her thighs and Noah got a quick eyeful of the smooth, clean-shaven skin that covered her mons.

His cock swelled to life, and he swallowed hard as he ripped his gaze away from Jezebeth and back onto the road.

She's a succubus!

And she'd just fucked two strangers in the parking lot—or did something close enough to take all their energy and make them pass out. How in the hell could his body be responding to that?

Succubus glamour?

He swerved out of the parking lot and glanced up into the rearview mirror in time to see the slow-moving pestilence demon limping after them, its still-misshapen form visible in the harsh lights from the club. Noah cleared his throat, praying his voice sounded normal. "Looks like it's injured enough to stop it from following us, at least for now."

"Look out!"

He glanced down and instinctively swerved as a glowing bright red demon that looked like it had stepped out of a nightmare appeared in front of the truck, lighting up the dark road in front of them with an eerie red glow. The tires squealed as they found traction and the truck fishtailed, smacking the demon aside with the back quarter panel of the truck.

A loud wrenching noise of metal grinding against metal made Noah grit his teeth and wince as he stomped down on the gas pedal and they shot forward.

"Its claws are hooked into the tailgate dragging it along behind us." Jezebeth had unbuckled her seat belt and turned in her seat. She stood on her knees and looked out the back window.

Noah glanced over his shoulder just as the bumpy red hand of the demon curled over the tailgate, its long black talons digging deep into the metal of the truck bed. "Damn." He glanced over at Jezebeth. "Do you know how to drive?"

She rolled her eyes and turned around in her seat. "Give me a minute."

Irritation at her calm tone snapped through him. "I'm not sure we have a minute," he told her as another demon hand appeared over the edge of the tailgate, the claws digging in and pulling more of the demon into sight.

Jezebeth's form shimmered and although she still looked the same, she was suddenly much taller, allowing her feet to reach the floorboards.

He stared for a long moment, swatches of light strobing over her as they drove past light posts.

Noah frowned and resisted the urge to rub his eyes to ensure he wasn't hallucinating. "The imp never mentioned succubi could change forms."

"They normally can't." She turned to look at him, and he could just make out the dark circles of fatigue under her eyes and the lines of strain etched across her pale face.

Concern and guilt twined inside his gut. She'd said she needed the energy from the men to come back inside the bar and help him. She'd obviously used most of that energy up to help him and then change into a form where she could reach the gas pedal and brake. And he'd been a judgmental ass.

Way to go, Noah.

He'd known she was a succubus when he started on this mission, so he shouldn't be surprised when she acted like one. If she didn't, she'd die, or whatever the equivalent was for a succubus.

"Do you want me to drive, or not?" she snapped, making him realize he'd fallen silent.

Noah glanced into the rearview mirror to see the demon hooking one leg over the tailgate and pulled himself back to the present. "Yes. Slide over close to me."

As if she'd done the maneuver a million times, Jezebeth took the steering wheel in her left hand and slid one long leg over Noah's. She braced her left foot on the floor mat near the driver's door. When she pulled her weight up with her left arm, she winced but made no other protests.

Noah slid to the right on the bench seat and waited until Jezebeth nudged his right foot off the gas pedal, keeping an even pressure as he slid out from under her. Her short spiky hair brushed across his face and he inhaled a lungful of a combination of pomegranate, honey, smoke, and sweat from the club. Then she was driving, and he found himself free to move in the passenger seat.

"Hold on!" she said just as he reached for his backpack on the floorboards.

Noah braced one hand on the dashboard and one against the door as the truck swerved hard to the right and the sound of something large thunked as it rolled around in the bed of the truck.

Noah winced as he thought of all the supplies he'd strapped down back there. But having them destroyed this way was better than becoming a late night snack for a demon and letting Jezebeth get captured.

He started to turn his head to see where the demon was when Jezebeth yanked the steering wheel hard to the left, wrenching his neck and making him grab tight to anything he could to avoid being shaken around the cab like dice in a cup.

The loud thumping from the bed was now accompanied by an angry-sounding roar.

Noah braced his feet as Jezebeth swerved again. He grabbed his backpack, fumbling inside for some type of weapon to use against the demon.

His hand closed around two balloons filled with kosher salt and he yanked them out as he tried to figure out how to hit the demon without endangering Jezebeth. After all, she was a demon too; would the rabbi-blessed salt harm her as well?

A large crack filled Noah's ears, quickly followed by the sound of a thousand marbles being dropped onto concrete as the back windshield shattered, raining him and Jezebeth with tiny rounded cubes of glass. Noah instinctively shielded his face as the truck swerved erratically again.

He wasn't sure if he should be frustrated or impressed with Jezebeth's creativity in trying to dislodge the demon since it might kill him as well if she wasn't careful.

He twisted on the seat and lunged forward to put himself between Jezebeth and the demon. He stopped short as he found himself face-to-face with the snarling, lava-colored nightmare. The stench of sulfur surrounded him as the demon's heated breath seared against his skin, the glistening fangs looking larger than life this close-up.

A sardonic smile twisted the demon's scaly lips as it opened its mouth wider, probably in preparation to take a large bite out of Noah.

Noah raised his hand, shoving the salt-filled balloons into the gaping maw and then jumped back, slamming against the dashboard, hitting the steering wheel and causing Jezebeth to swerve once again.

The demon's jaws snapped closed, bits of salt flying out in a spray around them.

Pain radiated up and down Noah's back as he curled forward to try to avoid hitting his head. He slid down until his ass was wedged in the space between the dashboard and the seat, his feet trapped at eye level on the seat in front of him, his body pretzeled in a painful angle.

Jezebeth remained quiet, the salt bouncing harmlessly off her back, which relieved at least part of Noah's fears as she continued to keep them on the road and moving.

Noah snapped his gaze toward the demon to find it melting like a wax figure under a blowtorch. Before its facial features melted entirely away, Noah thought he saw a quick expression of surprise. Then a loud pop echoed through the cab, and the thing disappeared back to Hell as its earthly form vanished, plunging them into near darkness.

"Are you all right?" Jezebeth's voice was soft and filled with exhaustion.

Noah unwedged himself from between the seat and dashboard and turned to find her slumped in the seat as she continued to drive.

He glanced through the broken window, noticing the cold night air for the first time since he'd entered the club to search for Jezebeth. "I'll be fine. What about you?"

"I need to stop and find sustenance, even if it's only a quick fix." She swallowed hard, as if the effort to speak cost her more energy than she had to spare.

After witnessing her in action, he'd expected her to give a stoic response and tell him she was "fine" or some other equivalent. Her matter-of-fact honesty surprised him.

"The other demons can track the place where that one was sent back to Hell, so we need to keep moving and get as far away from there as possible." Each word became softer and more slurred as she continued.

"Pull over."

She didn't argue and, instead, slowed the truck and drove onto the shoulder of the road, shifting it into park.

Noah glanced around them, glad the club was on the outskirts of the small Texas town and the road was currently deserted. He hopped out of the truck and circled around to the driver's side to find Jezebeth already scooted over and slumped against the passenger door. He pulled the door shut and turned toward her. "Is there anything else I need to know?"

She nodded, weakly. "Wherever we go, I need to find someone who will be attracted to me in this form. I don't have enough energy to change into another one."

Noah's cock surged to life again, as if to say *it* was very much attracted to her in this current form—not really for the ridiculous form itself, but for her bravery back at the club, for how calmly she'd handled their near death-by-demon encounter, and for her sense of humor through the whole ordeal. Her driving skills didn't hurt either.

He smiled at his last thought and shifted in his seat as he tried to ignore his body's blatant reaction to her.

She was a succubus, for God's sake, and had probably slept with millions of men in her long lifetime. He didn't have any desire to be the newest notch on her bedpost—even if she needed an energy fix. Not to mention he really wasn't into the overdone curves and short, spiky hair on a woman, regardless of his body's reaction.

His sense of chivalry and honor prodded him to offer her some of his energy, but he swallowed back the words before they could form. "We'll find you something. Hang in there." As the words left his lips, he felt like an utter and complete ass for the second time in the span of less than an hour but couldn't bring himself to take it back.

Instead, he guided the truck back onto the road and let silence fall between them as they drove through the darkness. It was past midnight on a Friday night. Where was the best place to find a few men willing to offer themselves up for a wounded woman who looked like she was about to pass out?

A soft glow of light in the distance caught Noah's attention, and he grinned as he pressed the gas pedal down harder. "I think I have just the place. Sort of a succubus smorgasbord, if you're willing."

3

As Lilith, Queen of the Succubi, materialized in the deep shadows outside the large brick three-story, she expanded her senses and sniffed the night air. The salty tang of ocean mixed with the astringent scent from the weeping willow just behind her left an almost metallic taste on the back of her tongue. The sharp ocean breeze stung her cheeks and ruffled the long hair around her face.

Other than small animals and a few ocean birds, no one and nothing lurked nearby.

She stepped out of her hiding place, her soft-soled shoes silent as she made her way across the perfectly manicured lawn as a soft aura of moonlight bathed her in its warmth. After all, she'd been a creature of the night since Adam had chosen Eve over her in the Garden of Eden all those many centuries ago.

Only kindness from a surprising source had saved her.

Adam's rejection still stung, more from her pride after all this time, but she shoved it aside and let anticipation curl inside her belly as she stepped up onto the porch and rang the bell. Chimes that reminded her of a grandfather clock echoed through the foyer before the large front door swung silently open.

Lilith stepped inside and pulled the tie at her neck to undo the fastening of her flowing black cape. She shrugged the sensuous material off her shoulders and hung it on the coat rack as the doors swung gently closed behind her.

"Uriel, I'm here." The sound of her voice echoed in the entryway, and she took a moment to let her gaze linger on the silk paneling, the hardwood banister, and the priceless pieces of artwork tastefully on display. As if drawn by a magnetic force, she stepped forward toward a life-sized marble statue of Uriel done by Michelangelo during the Italian Renaissance.

The statue stood on a three-inch platform, nearly seven feet tall from top to bottom. It captured the Archangel in a fighting stance holding his twin deadly daggers, the promise of swift justice in his expression. He was completely nude, and Lilith let her gaze drink in the delicious sight of him—the broad shoulders, smooth, hairless chest, trim waist, corded thighs, and long, thick cock that laid against his thigh, his heavy sac hanging just underneath.

Blood rushed through her body, pooling in her breasts and between her thighs, leaving her skin achy and her pussy empty and wanting. She needed to feed, but knew that even had she been fully sated, her reaction would be the same when it came to Uriel.

And the statue was nothing compared to the real thing.

She reached out and brushed the tips of her fingers over the statue's thick cock, tracing down the shaft to the head as vivid mental images of when she'd touched the reality flashed through her mind. Even flaccid, Uriel was impressive.

A sensual growl sounded just behind her and made her jump like a guilty child.

"The smell of your sweet arousal is like ambrosia, my beautiful *nassah*." Uriel's warm breath against her cheek and the heat of his body just behind her sent a quick rush of silky moisture between the swollen lips of her labia.

Uriel inhaled deep and pulled her back tight against him. The instant she felt his hard erection pressing against her, she gasped.

"I didn't realize you had such an interest in art."

Unable to speak through her suddenly tight throat, Lilith tilted her head to the side, an invitation that he readily accepted, skimming his lips down the side of her neck and gently sucking at her skin. Arousal shot through her veins like liquid fire, and more silky moisture leaked from her body as she melted back against him.

With a feral growl, Uriel bit down on her neck hard, the pain sharpening into an exquisite torture as a light wave of vertigo slapped at her, making her sway.

Uriel held her tight against his body until the dizziness passed and then . . . he was gone.

Lilith wasn't surprised to see he'd materialized them straight up to his bedroom—she always had that slight slap of vertigo when she wasn't in charge of their destination. She also wasn't surprised he had disappeared . . . again. But she couldn't help the familiar disappointment that slid through her like a black cloud. From the way he'd greeted her tonight, she'd dared to hope.

But she should've known better.

Uriel had interceded for her back at the Garden of Eden and vowed before God that he would keep her supplied with sustenance so she could survive. His intervention had been necessary since once humans fell from grace, their energy was no longer strong enough to sustain her—only another supernatural creature could. And without God's approval, no supernatural creature would even speak to her, let alone feed and sustain her. Many of them still blamed her for Adam and Eve being kicked out of the Garden of Eden, even though she was only doing what she had been created to do—tempt humans so they could grow and evolve.

Lilith still didn't know why Uriel had saved her. She wasn't privy to God's plans concerning her, but assumed without Uriel's intervention, she would be long dead and all the incubi and succubi that currently populated the earth and the other realms would have never existed.

To further complicate matters, Archangels were forbidden to have relationships—with each other or with other high-level supernatural creatures. God meant them to help the humans, and the temptation for His "executive staff" to become too familiar with each other and leave the lower angels and the human race to their own devices was a very real threat to God's plans.

But that didn't mean God expected the Archangels to remain abstinent, only to choose their partners from among those beneath them in the hierarchy. After all, He had made sex for the enjoyment of all His creatures, and the Archangels were no different—although they had a lot less sexual hang-ups than the humans. But then, who didn't?

Lilith still wasn't sure why she counted as a high-level supernatural since she and her minions were considered the bastard stepchildren of the supernatural world—neither demon nor angel, but something in between. And yet, somehow when Uriel had taken responsibility for her, her status had been set.

It had been difficult for Uriel to reconcile his two sets of vows until he'd found a loophole. He facilitated sexual sessions between Lilith and others including humans, demons, succubi, or incubi. He watched and pleasured himself but didn't participate. The sexual energy he gave off from his completion was more than enough to feed Lilith, and he still technically stayed within the boundaries of his vows.

She sighed. There had only been once that Uriel had given in and taken Lilith himself. She'd been hopelessly in love with him long before that, but she'd spent the millennia since longing for another night in his arms. Tonight's greeting had given her hope, and his dis-appearance had cruelly dashed it all over again.

"Damn it, Uriel." She turned in a circle looking for him.

The large custom bed big enough for six full-grown men took up one wall. A large vertical dark cherry log sat at each corner—the side braces for the intricate wrought-iron headboard and footboard that graced the huge bed. The comforter was deep purple, the satin sheets and pillowcases black, matching the theme of the rest of the room.

But no much-too-gorgeous Archangel.

On the wall to the right of the bed stood two glassed-in French doors that led out to a balcony that ran the entire length of the back of the house. The wall to the left of the bed held an antique cherry chest of drawers, dressing table, and the door that led back inside the house.

Lilith slowly turned around to look behind her.

Uriel sat on a large black leather couch dressed in gray slacks and a white button-down shirt open at the collar. She sucked in a breath as she let her gaze roam over him, only then realizing she'd stopped breathing as she'd searched for him.

His large erection tented out his trousers and a small, round wet spot had formed from his pre-come against the cloth. His multicol-ored hair hung straight over his shoulders, the golds, reds, and browns blending together so no matter how many times Lilith saw his hair, it always looked different. It was silky and soft under her fingers, she knew from past experience, and she had loved feeling those strands sliding over her naked body.

A shudder quaked through her at the vivid sensual memory, and she raised her gaze to meet Uriel's silver one, his eyes reminding her of mercury—the silver constantly moving and all seeing.

"Still as beautiful and enchanting as ever, *nassah*." His voice was strained as he smiled up at her.

"Still as beautiful and *stubborn* as ever, *ahuvi*." She gritted her teeth against the hurt she heard in her own voice. She always called him "beloved" and he always referred to her as "temptation," when she knew the damned Archangel returned her love.

A sad smile curved his lips. "Let us not fight, *nassah*. You know my feelings, and that will have to be enough. Come, our time grows short."

The familiar arguments rose inside her throat, and she swallowed them back. After all, countless millennia of rehashing the same things ensured pretty much every avenue had been explored. And Uriel was right, she didn't want to waste what precious time they had together. Although frustration churned into anger inside her gut—at the situation, at his easy acceptance of it all, and at her own complicity. Her eyes stung, and she blinked away the tears that tried to form.

"What shall it be tonight, *nassah*?"

Instead of answering she reached up and pulled the tie at her throat. Her crimson dress loosened around her until it slithered down her body to fall into a silky puddle at her feet. She stepped out of her slippers and stalked forward to stand naked between Uriel's open knees, careful not to touch him. An exquisite torture for them both.

His nostrils flared as his silver gaze devoured her naked form like a possessive caress, expressions of longing and pain slashing across his beautiful features.

Her nipples hardened into tight peaks and she narrowed her gaze, daring him to come closer, to take her as she wished.

But as he had since the last time he'd broken his vows and given into her temptation millennia ago, he swallowed hard and raised his gaze to hers. "What that I *can* give you do you wish for tonight, Lilith, Queen of the Succubi?"

She stared down into the swirling silver depths of his eyes as hurt and pain welled up inside her until she thought her chest might explode from the pressure. She wanted to scream, to hit him, to rail against her fate, to go back in time and let God end her existence with that first step out of the Garden.

Instead, she swallowed it all back and raised her chin. "I wish for whatever would hurt you most to watch, my lord Uriel." Her voice came out hard and flat, and she was glad it betrayed none of her pain and churning emotions.

Uriel's blond brows furrowed and he frowned, the tension in the room skyrocketing until it felt like static electricity nipping against her bare skin.

He slowly stood, their bodies so close, Lilith could feel the heat pouring off him, betraying his own churning emotions. She held her breath when he reached out to cup her face in his large palms, his thumb feathering over her bottom lip and sending waves of goose-flesh marching over her bare skin.

"You cannot wish for this, Lilith. Please . . . do not."

"Will you take me, then?" she countered. "Will you put aside your fucking Archangel pride and vows and all the rest and love me as you wish to? Without guilt, without remorse, and without torturing both of us for another eternity afterward?"

"It is forbidden."

She swallowed back her anger enough to bite out, "And yet, you've not been punished for our previous indiscretion."

He met her gaze and pain sliced through her chest as she clearly read the answer in his eyes. "I cannot," he said, confirming what she'd seen. "Lack of punishment doesn't make it right, Lilith. As much as I wish it could be otherwise . . ."

She took a deliberate step back from him and squared her shoulders. "Then fulfill your promise, my lord. Fulfill the promise you made to me before God." She reached up and cupped her breasts in her hands, tweaking the nipples and watching as his cock twitched inside his pants. She gritted her teeth, holding back the building ache of tears that had taken up residence in the back of her throat. "I wish for whatever will hurt you most to watch. And on your honor, I expect you to deliver it." She sounded like a shrew—bitter and angry—and didn't care.

Uriel swallowed hard, but then bowed his head as if unable to look at her. "So be it . . . *ahuvati*," he whispered almost too softly for her to hear.

The endearment she'd yearned to hear for so long choked her, and she turned away, hoping to hide the tears that had finally escaped to run down her cheeks.

The temperature in the room flashed—like a blast of heat that dissolved into a blessed coolness across her bare skin, and then the hair on Lilith's nape prickled.

She slowly turned, swallowing hard against the certainty of what she would find.

Two too-beautiful-for-words Archangels, a female and a male, light and dark, stood on either side of Uriel, who sat stiffly on the black couch, his expression unreadable.

Gabriel was the epitome of the female form with full but gentle curves perfectly matched with long, strong limbs and a sense of grace that Lilith had always envied. Silver blond hair spilled over her shoulders, and ice blue eyes made her seem even more ethereal in her white form-fitting pants and shirt.

Raphael was her polar opposite—short, spiky, dark hair and hazel eyes that darkened to black when he was angry. He stood nearly as tall as Uriel with wide shoulders, a powerful form, and a reputation for being a very inventive and generous lover. He wore black leather pants, steel-toed boots, and a simple black T-shirt that made him look more like the grim reaper than the Archangel with a reputation for being the soft-spoken fun-loving one of the bunch.

"Are you sure this is your wish, Lilith?" Gabriel's ice blue gaze ran shamelessly over Lilith's naked flesh before the Archangel met her gaze. "Raphael and I are more than happy to accommodate you separately or together, but you must be sure. Your being with us is using something of a loophole since Uriel's directive to protect and care for you was given directly by our Father." Gabriel pushed her long, silver blond hair back over her shoulder.

Lilith stared at Uriel as he and the others exchanged a significant glance, leaving her feeling as if something big was being left unsaid. But when all three returned their gazes to hers, she ground her teeth as anger flashed through her.

Fucking Archangels with their secrets and politics!

"This is my wish, and Uriel has vowed to grant it." She brushed away her tears and noted the slight tightening of Uriel's lips when she said the word "vowed."

Uriel's silver gaze rose to hers, and she saw a quick flicker of sadness and regret before the familiar blank mask he showed the world slid back into place.

"Both of us?" Raphael's gentle voice brought her gaze to his and she forced herself to smile.

"Yes, both. Together," she said anticipating his next question.

Raphael's hazel eyes darkened to black and he exchanged a quick, knowing smile with Gabriel before they both turned back to Lilith.

The knowledge of what she was about to do both excited and repelled her. Her body ached for sustenance, and yet her heart ached for Uriel.

She refused to look at him as she beckoned to Gabriel with her index finger.

The angel came forward, unbuttoning her shirt with quick, graceful movements as she closed the distance between them. As the white, fitted shirt parted, it revealed pale, bare skin along with full, firm breasts tipped with wide peach-colored areolas and thick nipples that puckered as the air hit them.

Lilith's own nipples tightened in response as she imagined what it would feel like to have her bare breasts pressed against Gabriel's while they kissed. Lilith shuddered and let her gaze follow the Archangel's movements as she slid the shirt down her arms and dropped it to the floor.

When Gabriel's hands reached for the button of her pants, Lilith reached out to stop her. "Let me."

Even without turning to look, she felt Uriel's gaze burning into her, but she ignored it and instead met Gabriel's gaze as she stepped close.

As soon as her breasts brushed against the plush, softness of Gabriel's, arousal shot through Lilith's veins like a sudden hit of heroin, and four distinct scents of arousal perfumed the air like dark, spicy musk.

Lilith closed her fingers over the front button of Gabriel's pants while she leaned slowly forward to press her lips against the Archangel's. Gabriel opened her mouth and energy poured into Lilith like water onto sand. She drank it in as she swept her tongue inside to taste the cool, lemony flavor that was Gabriel and enjoy the soft textures that went with kissing and caressing a woman rather than a man.

Gabriel slid her hands into Lilith's hair, capturing her close, their breasts pressed between them, their nipples rubbing together in a soft slide of female flesh.

Lilith tilted her head to the side and let Gabriel take control of the kiss as Lilith finally slid the button on Gabriel's pants free and made quick work of the zipper before hooking her fingers in the waistband and sliding the material down over Gabriel's trim hips.

Lilith slid her hands down over Gabriel's silky soft skin and around to cup the firm globes of the Archangel's ass, pulling her tight against her own sex.

Whereas Lilith's mons was totally smooth and bare, soft feathery hair at the apex of Gabriel's thighs tickled against Lilith's skin, making her gasp.

A groan broke from Gabriel's lips and Lilith swallowed it, exploring the soft skin under her fingers, tracing Gabriel's waist, spine, and back as if memorizing them. Then she slid her hands up into Gabriel's hair and sighed at the sensation of plunging her fingers into soft, warm feathers.

Gabriel broke the kiss and stepped back, leaving them both panting as she kicked off her pants and shoes. "You taste of dark, forbidden spices, Lilith." The angel's ice blue eyes had darkened to the deep gray-blue of the sky before a storm. She glanced back at the two male Archangels.

Lilith followed her line of sight, her entire body still buzzing from the quick taste of Archangel energy. Uriel sat on the couch, his jaw clenched, the tent in his pants still very obvious.

Raphael pulled off his shirt and dropped it on the floor, catching her attention and diverting it from Uriel. Raphael grinned as if he'd read her thoughts and then toed off his steel-toed boots and peeled off his leathers to reveal an unbroken expanse of golden-brown skin and a long, thick cock that jutted out from his body.

He was an impressive specimen—one of God's best representations of the male form—but still not half as beautiful to her as Uriel.

Lilith shoved the thought aside and smiled at Raphael as she motioned him forward as well.

He wasted no time as he strode across the room and pulled Lilith flush against him, his hard body pressed against hers as he captured her mouth and plundered, leaving her feeling as if she were being battered by an erotic hurricane.

She had the fleeting sense that he tasted like Irish coffee before

she received the first burst of his energy—hot, quick, powerful—
and her knees weakened. His large hands were everywhere, holding
her up and locking her against him as his hard cock dug against her
stomach.

Cool softness settled against her back just before her long hair
was brushed aside and Gabriel began to nuzzle the sensitive area at
the back of Lilith's neck.

Gooseflesh marched over every inch of her and she moaned into
Raphael's mouth as both of the Archangels captured her between
them, assaulting her with sensations that threatened to overwhelm
her reality.

A steady flow of energy seeped into her from the skin-to-skin
contact, and she felt like a balloon—slowly stretching to capture
it all.

Raphael loosened his close hold on her, and Gabriel's cool fingers traced around Lilith's rib cage to cup her breasts and roll the
nipples between long fingers. The combination of Gabriel's fingers
and Raphael's coarse chest hair rasping against the sensitive tips
sent fire shooting straight to Lilith's clit. The tiny nub throbbed
with the need to release and Lilith's hips began to buck against
Raphael faster and faster.

Gabriel nipped a path up Lilith's neck, and her cool breath
feathered against Lilith's ear as the Archangel whispered, "I want
your mouth on me, while Raphael fucks you and Uriel watches.
Can you picture that, Queen of Temptation?"

The mental image flashed into her brain so vividly that Lilith's
body exploded, the orgasm catching her off guard, the contractions
flowing through her like a row of tsunamis hitting every shore.

She was dimly aware of being carried to the bed and laid on her
stomach. When she gathered the strength to raise her head, she
found Gabriel sitting in front of her, the Archangel leaned back
onto pillows propped against the headboard, her legs spread wide,

her pussy covered with downy silver blond hair, the swollen folds already glistening with her arousal.

Lilith smiled as she met Gabriel's gaze.

Lilith had been with countless women since her creation, but she wanted nothing right now except to taste what Gabriel so freely offered.

She crawled toward Gabriel and laid flat on her stomach until she could hook her arms under Gabriel's thighs and lean her face in close to nuzzle the downy hair that covered the Archangel's sex. Just like the hair on Gabriel's head, these soft curls reminded Lilith of feathers or goose down. She nuzzled the hair with her nose, smiling when Gabriel squirmed and made an impatient noise deep inside her throat.

"Patience, Gabriel," Lilith whispered against the swollen folds just before she swiped her tongue along the glistening slit in front of her.

A groan broke from Lilith's throat, blending with Gabriel's sharp gasp.

The taste that burst inside Lilith's senses reminded her of a ripe plum, sweet and tangy, with soft juicy flesh under her lips and seeking tongue.

Gabriel leaned back, cupping her breasts in her pale hands, lightly pinching the nipples as she relaxed back and opened her thighs wider for Lilith.

Lilith chuckled at the Archangel's eagerness before she buried her mouth against the Archangel's sweet slit to taste her in earnest. Gabriel's labia were soft and swollen under Lilith's tongue, the wet flesh hidden by the nether lips slick with the Archangel's arousal.

Lilith concentrated on exploring and finding each sensitive spot that made Gabriel's thighs quiver or pulled a gasp or moan from her lips, and then ruthlessly exploited them. She ignored the Archangel's clit and instead, dipped her tongue inside Gabriel's pussy, exploring the textured walls of Gabriel's sex, as her own hips bucked against the bed, her pussy aching to be filled.

Gabriel's breaths came in short, urgent pants and Lilith's entire body slowly tightened until it felt like she was about to explode. Lilith pulled her right arm from under Gabriel's thigh and traced the Archangel's slit with her fingers before slipping two fingers deep inside the tight, slick heat.

Gabriel arched, her hips bucking, her body wordlessly begging for release.

Lilith smiled as pure, heady feminine power spilled through her. She sucked Gabriel's clit between her lips, swirling her tongue gently over the tight nub, enjoying the way Gabriel's body quivered and the Archangel's thigh muscles tightened under her grip. Lilith pressed her fingers deeper inside Gabriel's pussy and then curved them up toward the pelvic bone, searching for the woman's G-spot.

Gabriel's hips continued to buck against Lilith's face, and Lilith sucked Gabriel's clit hard as her fingers brushed against the slight rough spot inside the Archangel that signaled Lilith had found her target.

Gabriel stiffened and cried out as Lilith mercilessly massaged the spot she'd found and continued to suck and swirl her tongue over the clit between her lips.

A hard slap of energy surged through Lilith as Gabriel's orgasm poured over both of them, triggering Lilith's own release and ripping a scream from her lips.

The orgasm and energy influx went on and on until Lilith thought she would shatter from the exquisite torture of it. But finally, the wave of sensations lessened and receded leaving her body with a warm hum of afterglow.

Firm hands on her ass reminded Lilith that she and Gabriel

weren't alone—nor were they finished. Lilith raised her head from Gabriel's pussy and glanced behind her to see Raphael's cock hard and ready, his gaze so black, his eyes didn't look real.

She smiled as her pussy clenched in anticipation of his thick length pushing inside her. Movement just beyond Raphael caught Lilith's attention and she glanced past him to see Uriel still sitting on the couch, his slacks open, his hard cock in his hand, his expression filled with an equal combination of lust and self-loathing.

"You could join us any time you wish, my lord Uriel," she said loudly enough so she was sure he heard her.

His gaze found hers, but he made no move to join them, which sent renewed hurt and anger spiraling through Lilith. She raised her gaze to Raphael's. "I want you inside me, hard and fast. No holding back. I'm not a fragile human—I can take whatever you have to give."

Uriel's deep growl sounded through the room, and Lilith ignored it.

She turned back to face Gabriel, who scooted down the bed so she lay flat on her back. Lilith smiled and crawled on top of the woman, lowering her weight so she lay in the cradle of Gabriel's hips, their breasts pressing together, so they were soft female flesh against soft female flesh. Lilith lowered her lips to Gabriel's, slipping her tongue inside to let Gabriel taste her own essence on Lilith's tongue.

Raphael grabbed her hips and lifted her until she was on her knees, her upper body still lying flush against Gabriel, her tongue still exploring Gabriel's mouth.

The blunt head of Raphael's cock nudged against her pussy as he settled himself behind her, the crispy hairs on his legs against the back of her thighs a definite contrast to the soft, smooth female beneath her.

Raphael traced the head of his cock up and down her slick slit before he slid just the head inside her.

Raphael's thick cock stretched her opening, teasing her with what was to come. She groaned into Gabriel's mouth and arched her hips, wordlessly begging for him to thrust inside her, to fill her. Instead, he slid inside slowly, inch by inch until her entire body quaked with need and she panted too hard to continue her kiss with Gabriel.

Gabriel tucked Lilith's face into the crook of her shoulder and nibbled her way over Lilith's neck as she skimmed her cool hands over Lilith's back, which only contributed to the quaking need rocking her body.

What seemed like an eternity later, Raphael pushed forward the last little bit, stretching Lilith wide, his pelvis pressed tight against her ass, the heavy sac of his testicles resting against her labia.

"Are you ready?" he asked, his voice tight with control that Lilith hoped to weaken.

"Fuck me. Hard."

As if the words snapped the last of Raphael's control he began to pound inside her, holding her in place with his two strong palms, stretching her sheath wide, the swollen head of his cock pounding against her cervix faster and faster as energy and arousal tightened inside her like two hurricanes joining forces. He was rough and hard, sparing her no quarter with attentions that would've damaged or even killed any mortal woman, and yet, Lilith reveled in it—even if she wished it were Uriel's hard cock filling her instead.

Lilith held on to Gabriel like a safe haven in a storm and rode out the sensations that pounded against her as she sped toward her peak.

Each time pre-come would leak from Raphael's cock and touch her inner flesh, her body would absorb it and a flash fire would erupt through her veins, speeding outward along every nerve ending in a breath-stealing rush. Gabriel's cool fingers continued to skim over Lilith's back and sides before dipping into her hair and massaging her scalp, while the Archangel's teeth, tongue, and lips suckled at her neck.

Her body steadily tightened until her overtaxed system hovered on the fine line between pain and pleasure.

It was Uriel's hoarse cry and the sudden scent of his come as it hit the air and not Lilith's pussy where his essence belonged that pushed her over the edge.

She screamed into Gabriel's neck as her orgasm slammed into her, the walls of her pussy squeezing Raphael's cock as it continued to pound into her.

Mere seconds later, Raphael grunted as his cock convulsed inside her, his come shooting forward to set off a bright white explosion of energy behind her eyelids as if she'd been suddenly plugged into an electrical socket.

Dimly she was aware of Gabriel stiffening beneath her, the energy from the Archangel's orgasm adding to the churning maelstrom inside Lilith while Raphael continued to pump inside her through his release.

An undetermined amount of time later, awareness trickled back into Lilith's mind and she realized she was warm and more sated than she'd been in much too long. Strong arms held her close, the musky scent of nighttime deep inside the forest surrounded her, and she blinked open her eyes to find Raphael staring down at her.

"Lilith?" The steely concern lacing his voice was obvious.

She pushed away from his hold at the realization of what she had done, and what Uriel had watched—two of his fellow Archangels, who were closer to him than any family could ever be, had taken her together—and she'd enjoyed it. In fact, she felt more alert and alive than she had since the night she and Uriel had . . .

"Are you all right?" Raphael tried again.

She nodded and glanced past him looking for Uriel.

"He's gone."

Pain slashed through Lilith, squeezing her heart until she was surprised it still beat. She swallowed hard, pulling her composure around herself like a protective blanket before she raised her gaze to look into Raphael's intelligent hazel eyes. "I think the energy from three Archangels at once was a little ambitious after surviving on less for so long." She forced her lips to curve and hoped Raphael saw a smile rather than a grimace. "I think next time I shall ask Uriel to only watch me and one of you."

Raphael's gaze darkened, and he seemed about to say something, but then his lips firmed and he nodded once. "I shall return if asked in order to help Uriel meet his vow." He stood, and as he dematerialized Lilith resisted the urge to cry.

4

As Jezebeth glanced up and realized what Noah had suggested, she couldn't help but giggle. A truck stop could very well be a Succubus Smorgasbord.

The sound of her amusement came out weaker than she'd like, but the fact that she still had enough energy to laugh gave her the freedom to wait and choose who she took sustenance from.

Noah had already made his disgust of her and her survival needs very clear back in the parking lot—even though she could smell the musky scent of his arousal that wafted through the cab of the truck. Her skin ached with longing in response to the scent. It was too bad he felt that way because the glowing aura of nearly white energy that surrounded him like a pulsing mist looked as if it could totally heal her even with minimal contact like a deep kiss.

He was attracted, but also repulsed.

Interesting, but definitely irrelevant.

Jez had never been ashamed of what she was and what she had to do to survive. That would just be a waste of time since there was nothing she could do to change it. But for some reason, Noah's distaste as he'd looked at the two men lying in the truck had stung. He'd risked his life to help her, and for that she found she wasn't willing to broach the subject of taking Noah's energy unless she was near death and didn't have any other choice.

She was used to seeing men only as a means to an end—survival. For the most part they were predictable, easy to manipulate, and totally uninteresting. But so far Noah was a puzzle that intrigued her.

She mentally shrugged and concentrated on conserving her energy for the task ahead.

"What's so funny?"

Even in the near darkness, she could make out his small scowl of confusion.

"You said the truck stop is a Succubus Smorgasbord if I'm *willing*. There's no 'willing' to it. I'll take whatever we can find at this point." Her words were still weak, but she was glad to hear an underlying thread of strength that hadn't been there before. Pure stubbornness might help her hold out long enough to find more energy.

When the next exit loomed, Noah took it and drove toward the large truck stop that sat on the side of the freeway—a halfway point between nowhere and nothing.

Jez tipped down the visor and checked her appearance in the tiny mirror. Dark circles rode under her hazel eyes, which looked too big for her pale face. She looked like she'd had a hard night of partying and hadn't recovered yet.

A large sigh escaped. She'd been in worse forms and still found those willing to offer her their sustenance. She combed her fingers through her hair and used most of the rest of her energy to remove the blood from her arm and clothes until she slumped back against the seat, wishing she could just close her eyes and sleep.

Noah pulled around to the back parking lot and parked among the large semitrucks scattered in the extra-long parking spaces. He turned off the ignition and pulled out the keys before glancing toward Jezebeth. "So, how should we do this?"

"We?" She gave him her best sardonic smile. "You've already made it quite clear how you see my need for energy." Her words came out more cutting than she'd intended, but she was surprised when Noah winced. But when she glanced again, his expression was haughty and unforgiving, convincing her she'd only imagined it.

"Yes, *we*. I promised I'd take care of you and get you back to Lilith safe and sound. You're nearly out of energy, so the least I can do is help you . . . find some."

Jez huffed out a breath of sarcastic amusement. "Don't go all noble on me. I'm sure the night of hot sex with Lilith was well worth everything you'll have to go through to pay for it." She reached for the door handle. That was usually Lilith's side of the equation, and got the succubus queen whatever she wanted in return.

"I didn't have a night of hot sex with Lilith." Noah's words were defensive and low.

Jez popped open the door and glanced back at him. "Don't worry, when Lilith gives her word or makes a deal, she keeps it. You'll get your night when this is done."

Noah frowned as he studied her. "Why would I want to be just another fuck among billions? This is my payment for *not* spending the night with Lilith."

Jez frowned trying to understand the meaning behind his cryptic words. She was tempted to ask him for clarification, but she was already light-headed and needed to find energy fast. Besides, the distaste in his voice was obvious, and his words echoed through Jez's mind like an accusation.

Why would I want to be just another fuck among billions?

She winced as anger burned through her. Who the hell was this guy to judge her and her kind? He was a mere human, and while his aura was distractingly clean and white, she was sure he hadn't taken any vows of celibacy or morality. "Then you'll be relieved to know that I'm a bit more discerning than my mistress. You'll never get any type of offer from me."

Noah snapped his mouth shut as if she'd surprised him, and she enjoyed a small surge of satisfaction as she slid out of the truck and closed the door behind her.

The cold night air hit her from all sides, stealing her breath and slowly leaching her low reserves of energy. She leaned heavily against the truck as she gathered her strength for the walk into the truck stop.

Noah cursed as he jogged around to her side. She thought she caught the words "stubborn fricking woman" within his mumbles as he stopped in front of her. "Let me help you get inside. You're still weak." He took her arm in his and pulled her close against his side.

His body was warm and firm, the muscles of his torso flexing against her as he moved.

Why would I want to be just another fuck among billions?

She stiffened and pulled away from him. "I'm fine. It's time for me to go look for one billion and one, so if you'll excuse me."

Noah recoiled as if she'd slapped him, an expression of surprise flashing across his features.

"Miss? Do you need any help?"

Jez turned to find a tall, lanky man in his mid-forties wearing a thick flannel shirt, jeans, and boots approaching them, his keys jangled in his right hand. He had dark hair, piercing blue eyes, and a kind expression. But even more important, the hazy mist surrounding him was thick enough to call to her like a dark promise, and yet dark enough to show her that he might not take too much convincing to give her the sustenance she needed right here in the parking lot.

She didn't look back at Noah, but instead willed her legs to hold her weight as she walked carefully forward toward the newcomer. "Actually, I could really use some help, if you don't mind." Jezebeth smiled up at him. "Maybe a ride?" She let her meaning show clearly in her gaze as it traveled down his body to center on the growing bulge just behind the fly of his jeans.

"Jezebeth . . ." Noah's voice was a low warning behind her, and she ignored it, hoping he took the hint and shut up.

The man's gaze flicked past her to Noah, and she could sense his primal protective instincts kicking into high gear. Humans were very territorial—especially about women. "Don't worry about him," she soothed the newcomer. "He just can't accept that I'm not interested."

Jezebeth could've sworn she felt a blast of cold air coming from Noah's direction—an outward sign that her mark had hit home. But she knew that was only her own fancy at work. After all, he was only human.

The man held Noah's angry gaze for a long moment before he said, "Of course, darlin'. My truck is right this way."

"Actually, the lady is just fine." Noah stepped forward placing his body between Jezebeth and the newcomer, wrapping a possessive arm around her waist.

Her mind sent a signal to her body to object and pull away, but her body refused to respond. Noah was warm and pulsing with energy, and before she could do anything further, he'd pulled her close, cupped her cheek in his large, warm hand and lowered his head to kiss her.

The shock of his warm lips against hers rocked her system, and she froze.

He continued to hold her, kissing her gently but firmly until Jez's traitorous body melted against him.

The parking lot and the entire world fell away as her lips softened under his attentions, and he slipped his tongue inside her mouth.

He tasted like dark, warm spices and the taste only increased in intensity as his energy seeped into her and pulsed through her system like tiny explosions that did nothing to help her light-headedness. Liquid heat seeped through her body, energizing and arousing her until she slid her arms around his neck, thrusting her fingers into his hair and holding him close.

He expertly kissed her, coaxing her body to respond and arch against him until a low moan escaped from her throat and she pressed greedily against Noah's growing erection.

When he gently reached up and grabbed both of her wrists from around his neck and stepped back out of her embrace, Jez fought not to stumble against the sudden lack of sensations.

After a few long moments of her mind reorienting, she glanced up to see him watching her carefully, a small furrow between his blond brows.

The world came crashing back like someone had tossed a cold bucket of water over her and heat burned into Jez's cheeks as embarrassment warred with the arousal still skyrocketing through her system. So much for her controlling herself and showing Noah she didn't need him and his condescending, bossy ways.

Noah continued to gently hold her wrists until she was steady on her feet, and then she pulled out of his grip to glare up at him, gathering her scattered dignity around her like a cloak of protection. "What the hell do you think you're doing?" She nearly cursed as her voice came out shaky and soft.

Noah swallowed hard before speaking.

At least it looked like she wasn't the only one affected here.

"I was giving you energy. You shouldn't be going off with strange men."

She couldn't help the laugh that welled up from inside her throat at his statement. "You do realize that's the bulk of what I've done for countless millennia, right? I'm a succubus, Noah, not a virginal debutante."

He continued to study her with an intensity that nearly made Jezebeth squirm. "I'm here to take you back to Lilith safely, so there's no need for any of that. I have the ring to protect me—"

"So that's what this is about? Protecting the population from the big, bad succubus?"

Noah huffed out a breath, irritation plain in his expression. "That's not it at all. I just—" He stopped midsentence and paced away, running his hands through his hair and leaving it to stand up in sexy tufts before he paced back to face her. "Damn it. Has anyone ever told you how frustrating you can be?"

His comment seemed to deflate her anger, and she stared back at him. "Not recently."

He sighed. "Well, they should." He shook his head. "By the way, do you realize you've changed forms again or have I totally gone insane?"

*   *   *

Gabriel materialized between two large trees inside Central Park and smiled as she looked out over the Lake. Moonlight dusted the calm waters and a cool breeze ruffled her hair until it latticed across her face. She brushed the white blond waterfall back and tucked it behind her ear.

The scent of sulfur and scorched flesh filled her senses and she slowly turned to face Semiazas. He stood seven feet tall, his skin cherry red, his talons sharp and black. Two thick black horns grew out from his forehead and his leathery lips were curved into an evil leer.

She laughed as she looked him up and down. "Apparently the costume shop ran out of all the good ones before you got there."

"You don't approve my form?" His voice was deep and cultured—everything his form was not.

Gabriel didn't bother to answer and instead cocked her eyebrow at him and waited.

A long moment later, his form shimmered and reformed into the one she was familiar with since the time of their creation. He stood a few inches taller than her own five foot eleven, his dark hair tousled by the gentle breeze, his piercing blue eyes too shrewd to make him handsome, although as a fallen Archangel, he still retained his grace and beauty.

"Better." She resisted the urge to hug him as she'd done each time they'd greeted one another before he had followed Lucifer in the rebellion against God. Instead she stepped back as the scent of cinnamon and sex twined through the air. She frowned and glanced around them, but only animals were nearby.

"Your form is luscious, as always, Gabriel." He slowly circled her, his blue gaze raking over her blatantly. He stepped close and sniffed her hair, not bothering with subtlety. "And freshly fucked from the smell of it." He finished his circle and faced her. "Although not by a cock." He leered at her and stepped close. "It's been a long time for me. How about a nice thick cock to tide you over until you meet your girlfriend again?" He cupped his own large erection while he stared into her eyes.

The faint scent of burnt cinnamon and female arousal that still clung to him told Gabriel he was definitely exaggerating his claim to "a long time." With relief she realized the burning jealousy that used to assault her barely even registered. She'd mistakenly given into her urges where Semiazas was concerned once he'd rebelled. After all, by definition, a fallen Archangel was no longer bound by the rules of the faithful. What a mistake *that* had turned out to be.

She raised her chin, refusing to step back or let Semiazas's theatrics make her uncomfortable—probably the reason he kept at it. "How did you break out?"

He squeezed his cock once more and then pressed himself against her stomach. "No answer to my generous offer?"

When she stood stock-still giving him no reaction, he finally stepped back, a flash of irritation marring his calm features. "Your loss, my sweet. I've been building up quite the stamina while caged these last seven hundred years."

"And since your punishment was for ten millennia and not just under one, I'll ask again—how did you break out?"

"You don't think they let me out for good behavior?"

She let all the derision and disbelief she felt show in her face. "No, I don't."

"Pity. You and I would get along famously if you were more gullible."

"Get to the point, Semiazas, or I'm leaving. I only agreed to meet you because you were once very dear to me."

He snarled, the animalistic sound coming from his mouth seeming at odds with the superficial beauty of his true form. "Don't speak to me of that time. You betrayed me! If you and the others would've supported us, Lucifer would be on the throne, and—"

Anger flashed through Gabriel, and as if her body was on auto-pilot, she grabbed a handful of the front of Semiazas's designer button-down shirt and slammed him against the nearest tree. "Don't you dare speak of betrayal to *me*." Her gaze burned into him and she let all the anger she'd harbored over the eons show in her expression.

"Still angry over that, pet?" He smiled, but whereas before his betrayal of their Father, his smile could brighten her entire world, now it was empty and made her feel the same way.

All the fight and anger drained out of her, leaving only sadness and resignation. She loosened her grip and paced away from him. "What do you want?"

He stayed leaning against the tree, looking like he'd chosen to lean against it rather than being slammed back against it. "Your help."

The laugh bubbled up before she could stop it, the ironic amusement spreading through her body in a cool wash. "My help?" She shook her head as she faced him. "Why would you think I would help you in any way?"

His knowing smile and confident gaze sent dread curling inside her stomach. "Because it's in your nature, Gabriel. You believe good will triumph over evil, you still have a conscience, you're still naïve. *That* is why I know you will help me."

She frowned as she tried to puzzle together what Semiazas referred to before he could twist things around to suit himself—something he'd always been a master at, even before Lucifer's fall from grace. Gabriel ensured her face remained a placid mask as she returned his stare. "Sorry. Can't think of a single reason in the universe why I would help you." She turned away and started walking, ignoring the sensation of his blue gaze burning into her back.

"What if it would save Raphael?"

Shock froze Gabriel midstep even though a tiny voice inside her warned her not to listen. "What have you seen?"

He chuckled.

Gabriel clenched her jaw as she forced herself to turn back toward Semiazas. He may be untrustworthy and a traitor, but his visions were always accurate. "Tell me what you saw."

The demon's sensuous lips curved at the edges, and he studied her as if she were his next meal. He pushed away from the tree and stalked forward, beauty and grace in motion until he stood so close Gabriel could smell the subtle spicy scent of bergamot and coriander that she remembered so well from their time together. He slowly leaned forward, his eyes darkening just like they used to before he kissed her.

"Look into my eyes and tell me what you saw." She tried to stare inside his soul, but there was too much inky blackness to give her much clarity.

Her strident words stopped his forward motion and his dark brows furrowed before he straightened. "I saw Raphael on his knees near death, the sword of Michael skewered through his back and protruding from his chest. A succubus stood just behind him with her hands on the hilt. She was one of the four who conspired to cage me."

Fear licked its way through Gabriel, leaving behind an icy cold that made her bones ache. Losing one of the other Archangels was one of the worst things she could imagine. And Michael's sword one of the only ways to kill them. But that didn't mean she trusted Semiazas. That was a mistake she planned on never making again.

"All I ask is for you to help me find one of the four succubi. I don't even care which one. After all, what's one little demon to you?"

"You know very well succubi aren't demons."

"Semantics?" Semiazas's sarcastic tone and condescending smile grated against Gabriel's nerves.

"Demons had a choice. They chose to rebel against God." She glared at him pointedly as an example. "Those who serve Lilith have made no choices other than to exist."

The demon shook his head. "I disagree. Those four little succubi sisters chose to betray me to Lucifer. *That* was their choice, Gabriel. And for that, they will pay, with or without your help. I just thought you might like a chance to save Raphael in the process."

Gabriel sighed, suddenly weary. "Your visions are always accurate, so me helping you find the succubi doesn't help me prevent the outcome."

"No, but it will help you avenge his demise," Semiazas growled. "For once, Gabriel, our aims are the same."

She shook her head, realizing that she'd held out hope that

someday Semiazas would change, would return to her as he had been. But that last hope had finally been shattered. "If that's what you truly think, then you never knew me at all."

The last thing Gabriel saw as she dematerialized was his beautiful face contorting with rage.

5

Noah took a deep breath in an attempt to calm the hot arousal that still pumped through his veins as he stared down at the woman in front of him.

Even though she looked totally different from just a few minutes ago, he knew this had to be Jezebeth. But something about this form she'd taken sucker punched him in the gut. She was pretty in a girl-next-door way with large, milk chocolate brown eyes framed with impossibly long lashes. Her long chestnut hair was pulled back into a ponytail leaving some wispy bangs in front to frame her face.

In place of the ridiculous caricature body he'd first met her in was an athletic frame of about five-seven with subtle curves that made Noah's cock harden further inside his jeans and his mouth go bone-dry.

Jezebeth looked down at herself and blushed. "Damn, I didn't realize I'd shifted." She seemed more annoyed with herself than him as she glared up at him. "You scared him away, you know."

Noah frowned as he tried to keep up with the quick subject change. "Who?"

"The trucker who was more than willing to offer me his energy." Her words sounded unsure and she didn't meet his gaze. "I know how you feel about . . . who I am and how I survive. You didn't have to . . . offer your own energy. I'm perfectly capable of finding my own in the future."

Noah's system was still humming from the aftereffects of kissing Jezebeth, and he was surprised his brain could even make sense of words, let alone form them himself. But at the same time, he found himself drawn to her like a magnet to metal, which disconcerted him. "I didn't 'offer,' I gave. I'm here to get you safely back to Lilith, and I can't do that if you're starving to death or injured."

She raised her chin as she stared at him. "Fine. We'll chalk this up to a learning experience, but just remember next time that I'm perfectly capable of taking care of my own needs."

His body tightened at her defiant expression. Not only was she lovely, her chocolate brown eyes expressive, but he still remembered how her soft curves felt pressed against him while she met his kiss with a hunger of her own.

Her lips lifted in the corners as if she knew his reaction, the smile lighting up her entire face and making a dimple flash in her left cheek.

Noah swallowed hard, realizing from his reaction that he was in deep trouble.

"Are you ready?" Her voice was pleasant, the timbre of it vibrating through him like a resonant string had been plucked inside his body.

When she raised her brows a few very long moments later, he finally managed to croak out, "Yeah. Let's go." He turned away, heading back toward his truck, taking the time to try to collect himself and pull himself back from the brink of idiocy.

"How about I drive? You're still bleeding."

Noah stopped and glanced down at his right side, surprised to find his shirt soaked with blood, sticking to his body from the still-embedded glass shards. He suddenly felt the cold night air licking at the wet cloth, chilling his body, as if the discomfort had waited for him to notice to spring to life. He fished inside the front pocket of his jeans to grab his keys before he tossed them to Jezebeth.

A second after they left his fingers, he winced, wondering if she could catch. Keeping her safe included him not breaking her nose with a handful of jagged metal.

Jez plucked the flying keys out of the air easily before she clicked off the alarm and slid inside the driver's door of the truck, leaving him standing outside the passenger's door staring after her.

"That'll teach me to underestimate her," he muttered under his breath as he slid inside and buckled his seat belt.

She started the truck, adjusted the mirrors to her liking, and then pulled out of the parking lot. When she glanced over at him, a questioning expression on her face, he realized he'd been staring.

She returned her attention to the road and guided them back onto the darkened freeway. "Don't like this form? I can change it." She shrugged, her posture stiff, closed, and defensive. "This is the form I'm most comfortable in when I'm not . . ." She trailed off and silence fell between them as if she were searching for the right words. "Well, when I'm not hunting."

"Hunting?" Noah resisted the urge to laugh as he glanced over at the harmless-looking woman beside him. "Other than the need to siphon off sexual energy from willing men, am I missing some piece of understanding about what a succubus does?" The long string of words seemed to aggravate his injuries, the pain in his side blending together to become a constant throbbing ache.

"Unless you count tempting people into sin, then no. Although

I have learned some basic self-defense through the centuries purely for self-preservation."

At the word "tempting," Noah glanced down at the sterling silver ring he wore. "Temptation," he said under his breath as he traced the ancient Hebrew characters that spelled out the word on the wide face of the ring.

"Yes, temptation," she said with an air of impatience. "We can't gather sustenance or quotas from unwilling humans. But our job is to tempt them using pleasures of the flesh. As they make decisions using their free will, their soul gains experience and knowledge." Her tone lost some of the defensive edge as she continued. "When under a tight deadline, we can combine and double up temptation to reach our quotas, but that usually requires up-front research and setup, but not always."

Noah's mind reeled as he tried to understand what she described. "Double up?"

"Yeah, you know. A guy who has anonymous sex is committing fornication, and depending on his lexicon of belief, that will decide how much experience his soul takes on from that act. But someone who is married and knowingly cheats on his wife isn't only committing adultery. He's also breaking a promise to his wife from their marriage vows, lying, risking her health and well-being since he doesn't know succubi can't carry or pass disease, and he's also lying to whomever he is having sex with since he most likely doesn't admit he's married."

Noah frowned and shook his head. He'd wrongly assumed this was a much more straightforward process. "Wait, you mentioned that all of this was dependent on the person's lexicon of belief, right?" When she nodded, he continued. "So, if they don't believe that cheating is wrong, there's no sin attached to it?"

"It's not as simple as that. That might work for fornication, but if he's married and cheating, he's affecting others, and those effects will also have consequences. We are all interconnected, and our choices therefore affect the whole. Succubi aren't out to damn anyone; we have to have energy to survive. But temptation is the best way to get humans to use their free will, to make decisions and gain experiences that will refine their soul."

Noah's thoughts chased around in circles exploring what she'd told him and trying to make sense of it from every angle.

They passed under a lit highway sign and the silver ring he wore flashed. "What about the ring made you realize I was telling the truth?" He glanced down, turning the ring around and around on his pinkie finger as he waited for her to answer.

"When I touched it, it was imbued with Lilith's essence."

Noah's head snapped up and he stared at her. "What?"

She sighed as if impatient with his lack of understanding. "Lilith has four pieces of jewelry that were given to her by Adam before he was expelled from the Garden of Eden. He'd made the pieces himself and embossed each one with his pet name for her—*nassah*, which means temptation in Hebrew. After so long a time of Lilith wearing them, her energy has imbued them. When I touched the ring, I could literally *taste* Lilith's energy signature inside it."

Noah's writer nature perked up as story ideas swam inside his mind and excitement curled inside his gut. "So Lilith and Adam in the Garden of Eden . . . that all really happened?"

"Of course." She changed lanes to avoid a slow-moving camper. "I'm surprised you even recognized that form of the story. The commonly accepted events as depicted in the Bible have been gender biased toward males. Lilith has been sanitized out of them, placing all the blame on Eve. When in fact, it was Lilith who refused to share Adam with Eve—Eve was perfectly content with the threesome arrangement."

"What?" Noah stiffened in his chair and then groaned when

pain lanced through his right side from the movement. "A Garden of Eden threesome?"

"Sex was very open back in the beginning, as it was meant to be. There was no ownership of each other and no puritan barriers. God created sex as a pleasure to be enjoyed by His creations. When He created Adam and Eve, He also created Lilith. They lived happily as a trio for a millennia, but then tensions began to mount and in the end it was Lilith who demanded Adam give up Eve, not Eve who tempted him into sin like the stories say. That's when God kicked all three out of the Garden of Eden. He'd made it as a paradise, but with all the discord, that sacred place was beginning to wither and die. At the same time, tensions were heating up in Heaven. Lucifer and his followers went before God and demanded He choose them over the humans. In the end, Lucifer and his followers were cast out of Heaven and Adam, Eve, and Lilith were tossed out of the Garden of Eden and told never to return."

"Why isn't any of this in the Bible or other documents?"

Jezebeth shrugged. "The church had its own political agendas and made sure their documentation reflected what was best for them, including making women subservient to men, even though God had created both sexes as equals."

"Wow." Noah was sure if he weren't so tired and leaking blood like a cracked garden hose he would have a thousand more questions. But instead, he just relaxed back against the seat, letting these new facts percolate through his mind as they shifted the reality he'd always known—or thought he knew. He'd gone to Sunday school as a child and later in college he'd studied more in-depth in his literary classes.

As a writer, he'd even used stories from several different religions for his own purposes within his work, but Jezebeth's few sentences had totally thrown off his equilibrium.

"Are you a demon hunter? Is that why Lilith picked you for this job?" He could tell from the way she rushed the words together she'd wanted to ask him for a while and had finally worked up the nerve.

A laugh escaped before Noah could stop it. "No. I'm a horror writer."

Jezebeth's gaze snapped to his and the truck swerved slightly before she corrected the movement and they were safely moving down the highway once more. "A horror writer?" The implied *what the fuck?* communicated clearly through her tone.

"Yeah, you know, novels that after you read them make you want to hide under the bed with every light in the house on? The scarier the better." Noah grinned. He was used to the surprise and even the disbelief when he told people what he did. But unfortunately, he had a feeling Jezebeth's reaction was more about her lack of faith that he could keep her safe. Too bad that made two of them.

"A horror writer," she repeated softly as if pure repetition would make it more palatable. "But you probably have experience fighting demons, right?"

He didn't miss the hopeful note in her tone. "Only in my stories. Mr. Pestilence bounty demon back there was my very first."

She glared at his backpack. "Then what about all the hardware? The holy water, the kosher salt, and the bag full of other toys? I mean those darts—"

"I'm a writer." He cut her off midrant. "I'm good at research. The darts had a combination of holy water, peroxide, and pesticides. I had to experiment until I found a combination that didn't degrade or react badly with each other, but figured that would damage the pestilence demon and it did."

"So in other words, you know only enough about demons to be dangerous?" Her knuckles were white where they gripped the steering wheel. "How the hell did you get roped into this?"

He sighed and pinched the bridge of his nose as a headache

pierced behind his eyes like a persistent ice pick. "I was researching ancient demons for my next book when I found an incantation that supposedly summoned Lilith the succubus queen." He sighed as the memories swam back fresh and bright. "I dictate as I write and then transcribe later, so when I said the words aloud, all hell broke loose. When things died down, Lilith was standing in front of me."

He scrubbed his hands over his face as he remembered his shock and disbelief when the most darkly delicious woman he'd ever laid eyes on had materialized in front of him. His cock had hardened so quickly he was surprised he hadn't come inside his pants just from the friction of his skin against his jeans. But his logic told him his physical reaction was off and nagged at him until his cock had softened, his intense craving for sex draining away until it was a mere background hum.

Dazed, curiosity had taken over, but changed quickly when Lilith told him to take his due—as in *sex* . . . with *her*.

"You said you were doing this so you *didn't* have to take Lilith." Jezebeth's words were a whisper as she glanced over at him, this time keeping the truck moving smoothly forward before she turned back toward the road. "Wait. Which incantation did you use?"

He grimaced as he remembered. "The one that traded a night with Lilith for an eternity of damnation and torture."

Jezebeth whistled long and low, the sound slicing through the truck like a sharp knife through butter. "And she let you turn her down? You're lucky to be alive, human."

"Noah," he snapped. "My name is Noah. Not human. Okay? And I didn't think it would really work. I thought it was fiction."

"Yeah, sure. Don't get testy. I was just surprised, that's all." She cocked her head to one side and mouthed the word "wow" silently.

"I saw that."

She shrugged. "Well, *Noah*. Even succubi have pride, and Lilith's is legendary. She never does anything without a reason."

"Are you trying to convince yourself that it's not a bad thing you're stuck with me?"

She shrugged. "I think you're missing the bigger picture. We're stuck with each other and all that entails, for the duration."

"And you don't think I have any idea what that entails, right?"

"Pretty much."

Noah sighed and tried to ignore the persistent throbbing from the wounds in his side. "Look, normally I wouldn't mind bantering with you. And under other circumstances, it might even be fun, not to mention that I have a million questions I'd love to ask you for future books. But right now, I'm fading fast." He swallowed hard and rested his head against the edge of the broken truck window behind him. "Why don't we find someplace to rest and recover a bit and then we can pick up where we left off?"

Jezebeth turned those milk chocolate–colored eyes toward him as she studied him with a frown.

"What?"

"I expected you to avoid the discussion entirely or do the male thing and just tell me to be quiet."

Noah chuckled. "Where's the fun in that?"

A slow smile curved Jezebeth's lips as she turned her attention back to the road.

6

Jez drove for hours, checking on Noah periodically after he fell asleep to ensure he wasn't in mortal danger from the loss of blood or other injuries he'd sustained while defending her from the pestilence demon.

Guilt bit at her for not stopping immediately and tending to his injuries, but if they were caught, he'd end up dead. She preferred the risk of painful injuries, which also by definition meant she hadn't gotten him killed.

It had been several hours since Noah had poofed the last demon back to Hell with the kosher salt balloons, and she was confident they hadn't been tracked. If they had, they'd be dead by now.

She winced as she realized all her thoughts led back to that outcome tonight. "Get a grip, Jez. You've stayed hidden for this long, what's a while longer?" A nearly hysterical chuckle threatened as she reminded herself that now she had a human companion to protect.

What had Lilith been thinking to send such an inexperienced human to accompany her? But then Lilith never did anything without a reason, and in the queen's own way, she did care about her subjects.

Jez sighed. She'd just have to trust that there was more to Noah than she could readily see.

A billboard up ahead advertised gas, food, and lodging two miles ahead. She had no idea what town they were in, or even what they were close to. She'd been busy taking every odd interchange and unlikely road she could to lose the demons, and in the process, she'd gotten herself good and lost. She had no doubt they were still somewhere in Texas since she hadn't seen any "welcome to a new state" signs.

Which unfortunately meant all the portals to Lilith's lair even remotely close to Texas were out of the question, since the demons would be waiting for her there. She'd worry about where they could cross after she got Noah cleaned up and they both had some rest.

The exit to the gas, food, and lodging loomed ahead, and she slowed and steered the truck onto the off ramp. She followed the signs and found herself on the main road of what appeared to be a one-stoplight town. A large sign that simply said MOTEL caught her attention. She headed toward it, pulled off into the gravel parking lot, and shut off the truck.

The motel was a small one story that couldn't have more than fifteen rooms. The office/restaurant was on the far end and the sign over the door boasted the best chicken and dumplings for five hundred miles.

"Guess we'll see about that." Jez pulled a jacket over Noah's still-sleeping form and hopped out of the truck, clicking on the alarm behind her. She scanned the area around her for any signs of demons or even a human threat as she approached the front door of the office. Other than a stray cat nosing around near the Dumpster, the night seemed quiet.

Jez hadn't materialized a watch, but from how long they'd been driving, it had to be nearly four A.M.

She glanced in through the front window of the office and saw a thirtyish blond man at the front desk with his boots up on the desk and a black cell phone clutched in both hands, his fingers flying over the keys.

Jez concentrated on the man and a slow tingling marched through her. When she glanced down at her hands, they were petite and definitely female. She breathed a quick sigh of relief. Sometimes when she plucked their most desired mate out of someone's mind, she ended up in male form, and she'd never quite gotten comfortable in male guise. It was like walking around in clothes that were several sizes too big.

Jez caught a quick flash of her reflection in the glass and jumped to the side of the window before the man noticed her standing outside.

"Damn it." Apparently, the man wanted Kate Beckinsale, and now Jez resembled the gorgeous actress in every respect. Although she was a little more Kate in *Van Helsing* than Kate in *Underworld*.

Under normal circumstances, Jez wouldn't think twice about using someone else's form to get what she needed to survive. After all, that's exactly where most of Hollywood gained the worst of their reputations and the appearance of never taking responsibility for their baser acts. Jez might be the only succubus or incubus who could change forms since each of her kind had a different talent, but demons and the other supernatural denizens such as Djinn, vampires, were-creatures, and the like could and often did. And celebrity forms were *très* popular.

Which meant it was usually others in the guise of the rich and famous who performed the more sensational acts that were splashed all over *TMZ* and *E! News*. Well, except for a choice few, who tended to get into plenty of trouble without any help from Hell or any of its inhabitants.

Jez glanced at her hands again and shook her head. The last thing she and Noah needed was a rumor in a small town that they were traveling with Kate Beckinsale. They needed anonymity, and just a touch of forgettable—which Kate could *never* pull off.

Jez concentrated on morphing her features—just enough to leave a slight resemblance to the things the man was most likely attracted to, but enough so no one would ever mistake her for Kate Beckinsale. She added a few inches in height, reduced down a cup size, and added simple jeans and a V-necked top.

When she was satisfied, she took a deep breath and headed inside.

As soon as the door hit the bell stationed just above the door frame, the man dropped his feet to the floor and sat up straight, tucking the cell phone into the front pocket of his jeans.

Jez smiled and hoped she'd guessed right with the softening of her current features. "Morning." Jez smiled wider at the sound of the very different voice that emanated from her own mouth.

The man's hungry blue gaze raked up and down over Jez before he sat up straighter, flexing his muscles under his tight black T-shirt and blatantly meeting her gaze with a small smile. He was cute in a nerdy sort of way, but Jez would bet he spent more time thinking about women than actually being with one.

"Morning," he finally managed in a breathless rush. "You looking for a room? The restaurant doesn't open up till six A.M."

Jez made a mental note as she glanced up at the large clock on the wall, which confirmed her guess: 4:14 A.M. "A room, please. I'll have to come back to try out those chicken and dumplings." Jez winked and leaned her elbows on the top of the desk, leaning over just enough to reveal her now-reduced cleavage.

The man's gaze was drawn downward as if she'd had magnets

installed on her nipples and then his head bobbed back up, a blush
flowing up into his cheeks as he realized he'd been caught staring.

"Will it be just *you* in your room?"

Jez gestured toward the truck sitting outside. "No, my . . .
brother and I. He's pretty beat, so I figured it was time to stop and
let him get some rest."

"Brother? Cool." The man smiled and nodded as he stood, easily
towering over her five-foot-nine form. "I'll just need some ID, beautiful, and I'll get you two all set up." He gave her a clumsy wink and
Jezebeth almost felt embarrassed for him, until his words penetrated her brain.

Jez's temples began a slow throb. She'd forgotten all about the
humans' love for identification. In more recent times, it was becoming harder and harder to get around this restriction. But maybe she
could work something out. "We were mugged back in San Antonio
and haven't been able to replace our ID yet. But I have plenty of
money." Jez smiled, turning on the charm, dropping her voice to a
sexy, husky whisper. "I can assure you neither one of us is a criminal
or dangerous. At least not in a bad way."

The scent of the man's arousal wafted through the room like
thick, heady cologne and satisfaction curled through Jez's gut.

"How about you and I work something out?" The man smiled
and held her gaze with mischief sparking inside the blue depths of
his eyes.

Normally Jez would take him right here on the floor, get the
room, and not give it another thought. But the idea of having sex
with this man while Noah lay injured in the truck just didn't sit
right with her. However, that still left them without a room. "What
exactly did you have in mind?"

He gave a nervous laugh and held a hand up between them. "I
didn't mean anything like that."

Jez cringed at the thought that she'd sounded reluctant enough to give away her thoughts. "Will you be around here for a few days? Maybe we could go for a drink sometime?"

Jez smiled and tried not to look too relieved. After all, she was supposed to make him think she was interested. "We'll probably only be at the motel for a night, but we might be in this area for a while. We're traveling on business." *Well, we are . . . sort of.*

He grinned and studied her for a long moment. "You don't look like a criminal to me. You actually look a little like Kate Beckinsale."

Jez forced a smile. "Really? I've never heard that before. Must be my new haircut."

The man laughed and grabbed one of the hotel's business cards off the desk, turned it over, and scribbled a name and number on the back before handing it to her. "I'm Jim. I always work the graveyard shift, so I'm available earlier in the evening. Give me a call. Any time."

Jez took the card and dutifully looked at the back while Jim pulled the room number four key off a hook set in the wall and laid it on the counter between them.

"Eighty dollars for the night and I can set a wake-up call for you if you'd like."

Jez pulled a hundred-dollar bill out of her pocket and slid it across the counter. "Thanks for your help. I look forward to that drink." She winked as she picked up the room key and made her way out toward the truck and to Noah.

* * *

Sharp pain lanced through Noah's side, ripping him out of a very deep sleep. He winced away from the pain, snapping his eyes open, to find Jezebeth sitting next to him on a bed.

"Hold still. I have to get all the glass out before you bleed to death."

Her touch was cool and gentle against his bare skin, and as full awareness returned, Noah realized they were in an older motel room, and he was currently lying faceup and naked on the bed. Blood rushed due south and his cock swelled to life, which at least gave him hope there was enough left inside his body that Jezebeth hadn't meant she was literally afraid of him bleeding to death. He reached for the sheet to cover himself, and Jez batted his hand away.

"Hold still." Her tone was gentle but firm.

Another sharp pain sliced through him, followed by a tinkling sound when she dropped the piece of bloody glass into one of the tumblers provided by the hotel. "I'm a succubus, remember? I've seen naked men before."

Noah did remember, only too well. He was a confident man, but wasn't sure he wanted to have a comparison between himself and a host of millions going on inside her head. "Can't a guy have a little privacy?" Noah inwardly winced when his voice came out sounding more defensive than he would've liked.

Jez straightened and frowned down at him. She reached over and pulled the sheet over him, just enough to cover his erection but leave the area she was working on bare. As her fingers brushed his shaft through the sheet, Noah stiffened as lust pumped through his veins, making him even harder.

"Sorry, I'm not used to worrying about things like that. Usually when men are with me, they're more worried about *not* getting hard." A hint of pink colored her cheeks and Noah frowned as shock and surprise warred with curiosity inside him.

He'd embarrassed a succubus? Could this day get any more strange?

He was afraid he'd just jinxed himself with that thought.

A sharp sting shot through Noah's hip as she pulled another piece of glass out, and he sucked in a quick breath, gritting his teeth until the pain passed.

Jezebeth held a towel near his side and poured peroxide over the wound, causing a warm bubbling sting to radiate across his skin. Noah concentrated on the perfect lines of Jezebeth's face and the long sweep of her lashes to keep the pain at bay.

"If it's any consolation," she said conversationally, "you have a very nice cock. So you have nothing to be embarrassed about."

Noah stiffened and grabbed the sheet as if she would rip it away at any moment to reexamine him. He cleared his throat, not sure how to react to her blatant observations. A change of subject seemed terrific right about now. "How long have I been out? And how did I get in here?"

Jezebeth's dark brows furrowed as she glanced up at him and a look of confusion chased across her face. "I didn't mean to offend you. Really. Usually men are very happy to hear that they have a nice—"

"I'm not offended," Noah cut her off before she could start talking about his cock again. What was it about this woman that made him feel awkward and embarrassed? He wasn't a naïve virgin by a long shot, but her invasive and blatant attitude toward his male parts threw him off balance.

"For someone who isn't offended, you sure do look pissed off." She wiped off a pair of bloody tweezers that Noah realized she'd been using to pick out bits of glass from his skin.

He loosened his grip on the sheet, but left his hand in place to weigh the material down as he scrubbed his other hand over his face. "I'm sorry. I barely know you and I wake up to find myself naked and wounded in a strange motel with you talking about my body parts as if I were a prize stallion you were evaluating for breeding."

She nodded once as if his hurried words explained everything. "I apologize again. I'm not used to spending time with people I'm not trying to have sex with."

Noah's pride prickled and he stiffened again.

What was wrong with him that she didn't want to have sex with him? Hadn't she just said he had a nice cock?

He pinched the bridge of his nose as he sternly reminded himself she was a succubus, and he had no interest in having sex with her. Which meant her opinion of him in that regard shouldn't matter anyway.

Liar! his subconscious accused as vivid memories of how Jezebeth had felt in his arms when he'd kissed her surfaced as if they'd happened only seconds ago.

For some reason, his ego still stung even after that rationalization, so he remained silent, unsure of what to say next.

Jez smiled, but her expression remained guarded. "I guess my small-talk skills need a bit of work too." She kept her gaze down as if studying his injured hip. "Can you turn onto your side so I can get these last few large pieces of glass out? I can cover your ass if that makes you feel better."

He scowled at her and held the sheet tight to his belly to cover his raging erection as he rolled to his side, exposing his bare ass for her view. "No need," he bit out, as pain lanced down his side, twined with irritation with himself when curiosity burned through him to know what she thought of his ass. Given that he'd just scolded her for such blatant observations, he doubted he'd find out unless he asked. But he'd be damned if he allowed that question to pass his lips, so he tried to relax and stare at the stained flower wallpaper and the open door to the tiny bathroom.

When Jezebeth's cool touch landed on his ass, near the painful area on his hip, he jerked as arousal shot through him like a geyser. "Sorry," he mumbled.

"I'll try not to hurt you, but we need to make sure all this glass is out. Especially since it's my fault you got peppered with it."

Noah breathed a silent sigh of relief that she thought she'd hurt him, rather than driving him crazy with lust. He smiled as he remembered Jezebeth in her ridiculous club-hopping form with her huge breasts spilling out of the tight bustier as she chucked bottle bombs over the bar. "That was pretty quick thinking, by the way, with the bottle bombs. I haven't had much of a chance to tell you, but I was impressed."

Her hands stilled on his skin for a quick second as if he'd surprised her, before she began to move again. "Thanks."

An awkward silence fell between them punctuated by sharp slices of pain as she removed more glass from his hip, and even sharper curses from Noah that had less to do with the pain and more to do with her innocuous, cool touch. Not to mention the fact that he was mostly naked and his cock so hard it could drive nails.

Which reminded him that he still didn't know how they'd gotten here. "How long have we been here?"

The bed moved and he glanced back to see the last movements of Jezebeth's shrug. "A few hours."

He pushed up on his elbow and laid his head in his palm, turning his head so he could watch Jezebeth work. She leaned over him, her face so close to his hip, he could feel her warm breath feathering over his skin as she pulled his skin taut with one hand and gently pulled out chunks of glass with the other. Her movements were quick and efficient and, for some odd reason he couldn't quite fathom, made him want to roll her beneath him on the bed and peel her out of the conservative sweater and jeans she wore, to unwrap the girl next door beneath.

She's a succubus!

He ground his teeth at the tiny voice inside his head. She was definitely a succubus, but she fascinated him, and he couldn't pinpoint why. "So how does your succubus glamour work?"

She glanced up, confusion swimming in her hazel gaze. "I'm not sure what you mean by succubus glamour."

"You know, the supernatural ability that allows you to tempt humans."

She glanced back down at her work. "It's different for all of us. My ability is shape-shifting. I can change into the form that person desires most."

"And those you hunt are supernaturally drawn to it? Like an aphrodisiac in the air, or something like that?"

She frowned. "It's different for everyone. But mine is purely the change in form. There's no compulsion for them beyond that. It's up to them to give into the temptation or not."

Noah looked away as the meaning of her words hit him square in the chest like an accusation. In other words, his reaction to her wasn't chemically or supernaturally induced, it was his own damned reaction! He ground his teeth and forced himself to adopt a casual tone. "So, give me an example. What form would I desire most?"

She shrugged, never looking up from her work on his side. "Since you're wearing Lilith's ring, my ability wouldn't work on you. But I'd leave it on; extended time spent with a succubus, even in a nonsexual manner, can drain your energy, and the ring keeps you immune."

He filed that information away for later, not sure if he was disappointed or intrigued, considering her present form drove him crazy as it was. But it wasn't just her form. She was easy to talk to, and she was a writer's dream—information and research all wrapped up in an easy-on-the-eyes package. "So how does the changing form thing work? Is there an incantation or something?"

She poured more peroxide over his wounds and he winced. "The wounds in your arm are all small, but I'm going to have to stitch the longer gash in your side. All I have for pain meds are some aspirin and a bottle of Jim Beam." Jezebeth dabbed at his wounds with a towel and Noah peered down to see a long, jagged gash refilling with blood. It definitely needed stitches, and he hadn't thought to pack anything beyond basic first aid items.

"A little of both would be great." He glanced away from the wound, willing himself to man up for the pain to come. In all honesty he was scared of needles and would've taken all offered pain relief had they been in a hospital. But his male pride refused to let him show fear or weakness in front of Jezebeth, so he swallowed hard and chased back two aspirin with a few long swigs of Jim Beam while Jezebeth ran the needle through a flame to sterilize it.

The whiskey burned its way down his throat and a few long seconds later, sent a warm flowing sensation along every nerve ending. He waited for the soothing heat to soften his cock, but with Jezebeth's continued close proximity, apparently his body refused to let down its guard.

Damn.

"Ready?" Jezebeth gently prodded the wound and Noah winced.

"Do it." Noah took a deep breath and closed his eyes, trying to concentrate on anything except what it would feel like to have a needle pierce his skin repeatedly.

The first sharp stab of pain caught Noah by surprise and he clenched his fists and clamped his teeth together to keep from wincing away.

"I just concentrate on someone and my body changes."

Noah opened his eyes and glanced back at Jezebeth just as the needle bit into his skin a second time and the slow drag of the thread sent shooting pain through his side. "What?" he gritted out.

"You asked me how changing forms worked." She flashed a quick smile before returning to her work. She was trying to distract him to help him get through the stitches.

He turned away again before he gave in to the temptation to look at how far she still had to sew and instead turned back to his view of the yellowed wallpaper. "Can you give me an example?" His last word nearly ended on a very unmanly squeak when the needle bit deep again, followed by the long drag of the thread through his skin.

"To get us a room here, I concentrated on the male clerk to see what form he would be most receptive to."

"And?" he asked on a long exhale as sweat began to bead on his brow and bile began to inch up his throat from his body's reaction to the pain.

"And, I found myself in the form of Kate Beckinsale."

Shock slapped at Noah and he glanced at Jezebeth to gauge if she was serious. When her features showed she was, a laugh bounded through him. "Seriously? As in the hottie who was in *Pearl Harbor* and was Selene in *Underworld*? *That* Kate Beckinsale?" His last words came out weak and he blinked slowly as a sensation of light-headedness swam through his brain.

She smiled. "That's the one."

"Too bad I missed it," he slurred.

She studied him critically and then stood and crossed the room to rummage inside a duffel he recognized as one of those he'd packed in the back of the truck. When she returned, she held up a purple Tootsie Pop. "Here, eat this. The sugar will help with the pain endorphins. Not sure why it works, but it does."

Noah had never heard of painkiller by lollypop, but since he had nothing to lose, he unwrapped the treat and popped it inside his mouth. Rich, grape flavor burst over his tongue and a few long moments later, the clammy skin, the dizziness, and even the roiling inside his stomach receded. "Thanks," he said as he saluted her with the Tootsie Pop. "How did you know that would work?"

She shrugged as she settled beside him again. "I've seen a lot of beings get tattoos, and that's something they've done to keep the side effects of the pain at bay. Has something to do with blood sugar, I think. Figured it couldn't hurt." She picked up the needle again, and Noah quickly turned away as the now-familiar sharp stab of pain lanced through his side.

"So what happened?"

"With Kate Beckinsale?" she asked on a laugh.

"Yes. You can't leave me hanging after a story intro like that. I'm a writer, remember?"

She laughed again. "I do remember hearing that somewhere." Jezebeth continued to work, and although Noah was peripherally aware of it, he focused his attention on the story.

"I told him you were my brother and we were traveling together. I didn't think it was a good idea for us to have a Kate Beckinsale sighting when we are trying to stay under the radar, so I changed some of my features just enough so I would resemble her, but not look like her, if that makes sense."

"I assume it worked?"

"I guess so, although he did say I reminded him of her." She tugged against the thread and he concentrated on the grape flavor inside his mouth and the sound of her voice.

"Since I didn't have any ID, I had to do some finagling, and here we are."

"What?" Noah sat up, ignoring the sharp protest of pain from his injured side as he turned to face Jezebeth, who still held the needle between her fingers. "While I was out cold in the car you were having sex with the hotel clerk in Kate Beckinsale's body?" As the words tumbled from Noah's lips, they sounded insane, but he shook his head as he tried to wrap his mind around them.

Shock followed by anger flashed across Jezebeth's features. "Technically it was my body with a slight resemblance to Kate Beckinsale, and it's none of your business who I have sex with or not." She met his gaze calmly.

"Is the clerk all right?" A vivid image flashed through his mind of the two men in the truck back at the parking lot of the club.

"He's *more* than all right. Which means you and I have a room until checkout time at eleven tomorrow." Her words dripped with venom, and he thought he detected a note of hurt underneath, which didn't make sense at all.

"But I don't understand . . ." Noah trailed off as he realized he couldn't even begin to put what he was feeling into words. It just seemed wrong somehow to trade sex for a room. Jez wasn't a prostitute.

But she is a succubus, he reminded himself and then winced.

Anger and impatience flashed across Jezebeth's features as she glared at Noah. "If you're asking for clarification, that's fine, but if you're asking me to defend my actions, you can go to Hell." She grabbed the thread still attached to Noah's body and held it tight long enough to pull the needle free and gather up the other first aid supplies off the bed.

Noah bit back the words that threatened to bubble up his throat. Why was he so surprised that she'd traded sex for what they'd needed? She *was* a succubus, and he *had* been injured and out cold in the truck. Would he really have preferred she take his definition of the moral high road? That would've left him injured or eventually bleeding out in the truck, or worse, in police custody when they couldn't explain to the hospital staff how he'd been injured. The details of the altercation at the club were probably all the buzz on police scanners right now.

He scrubbed his hand over his face before dropping it to his lap, where it bumped against his finally softening erection. "Look, Jezebeth . . ." He trailed off as he searched for the right thing to say. "I'm sorry. You did what you had to do. You took care of me when I was injured, and I really do appreciate it. I have no right to judge you or your actions."

"You're right. You don't." She laid the needle and other medical supplies she'd used on him on the chest of drawers and whirled to face him. "I'll let you handle room arrangements next time. I'm going to take a shower." She turned away and stopped with her back to him. "For the record, I didn't sleep with him. I flirted and agreed to have a drink with him. That was all."

The door to the bathroom snicked closed behind her, and Noah sat dumbfounded as he realized what a total and utter ass he'd been over the last few minutes. She never said. He'd just assumed.

He laid back against the bed with a sigh. "Way to go, Halston. Way to go."

7

Jezebeth let the hot water pound against her bare back and shoulders, her anger at Noah still spinning inside her chest like a growing hurricane. He'd apologized and sounded sincere, but his obvious shock at her methods had shown her his true feelings. Besides the fact that for once she hadn't even done anything!

Humans could be so puritanical in their views, and judgmental too. She wasn't sure why Noah's reaction bothered her so much, but the pain inside her chest showed her that it clearly did.

What the hell had Lilith been thinking when she'd chosen Noah for her protector?

An oppressive presence suddenly filled the small space of the bathroom and Jez whisked aside the thin plastic shower curtain. She instantly recognized the energy of an Archangel and cringed as far back against the cracked tile wall as she could, the spray from the showerhead still pounding against her shoulder.

As the warm smell of a campfire surrounded her, she glanced outside the tub, aiming her gaze toward her visitor's feet so she wouldn't accidentally look directly into his eyes. She might be trapped in the small room with a being who could crush her with a thought, but she refused to look into his eyes and let him see inside her soul. That was an invasion she'd let happen only once, and the sensation of that experience still haunted her.

Besides, since succubi weren't demons and definitely not one of the heavenly realms, Jez had no way of knowing if this particular Archangel was friend or enemy.

"Good evening, little one." His deep voice reverberated softly throughout the room, and she allowed her gaze to travel up high enough to see the thick shoulder-length hair that shifted colors the longer she looked at it.

Uriel.

"You recognize me." She thought she detected a hint of amusement in his voice, but his words were a statement and not a question. "Won't you raise your gaze and look at me?"

"No, my lord. I don't wish to share a glimpse of my soul."

His soft laughter twined around her like a soft, warm blanket, relaxing her muscles and loosening her fists. She recognized the reaction as a natural byproduct of the angel's proximity, but her mind refused to relax along with her body.

"Honesty. Something I very much admire and don't see often enough." He shifted, the ends of his multicolored hair changing from red to black to brown as she watched. "Raphael didn't mean to leave such a lasting impression on you with his glance. We sometimes forget the power within our gazes." He sighed. "Raise your gaze to mine, little one. You have my word I will not look at more than the lovely color of your eyes."

Jezebeth released a slow breath. Once an Archangel gave his word, he had to keep it. She wasn't sure what happened if they didn't, but suspected they'd end up as a fallen angel like Lucifer and the others. Jez raised her gaze, taking in Uriel's broad shoulders, the chiseled features of his face, and finally the liquid-silver eyes that reminded her of molten mercury.

His unique eyes unnerved her, but the rest of him was beautiful. Not handsome, not gorgeous, but absolutely beautiful—male perfection standing in front of her.

"Lovely." He smiled, his entire face lighting with the movement. Jez's brow furrowed as she scrambled to figure out what he'd meant.

His laugh bubbled around her, soothing her again but not bringing her any closer to understanding. "Your eyes, Jezebeth. They are lovely." He shook his head. "After all these millennia of men, women, and beings of all types telling you how beautiful you are in all your forms, you still don't believe it?"

She raised her chin, amused at the irony of his question. "I've never had cause to believe it. First, I can take whichever form they desire most. And second, most of them thought it necessary to tell me so because they mistakenly believed it would influence my decision to have sex with them."

He snorted, something she hadn't known Archangels did—purely on principle. "I can see why she likes you."

"She?"

"Lilith."

Jez frowned as she turned off the shower and grabbed one of the thin, scratchy towels off the flimsy metal rack. Not that she'd ever thought the queen disliked her, but to hear otherwise was somehow surprising. "Is that why you're here? Did the queen send you?" She slowly dried off before attempting to wrap the towel around her body and giving up when she realized it was so small and threadbare, she might as well not bother.

Uriel crossed his arms and leaned his ass back against the tiny excuse for a bathroom counter. Jez expected his gaze to roam over her breasts or down to the curly chestnut hair that sat at the apex of her legs in her true form, but his gaze stayed trained on her face. "Lilith doesn't even know I'm here, and I'd prefer to keep it that way, if you don't mind."

Jez cocked her head to the side as she studied him. "No offense, my lord, but then what could you possibly want with me? There are many others you could ask for sex besides me, and I can't think of anything else I could offer an Archangel."

He reached out to cup her chin in one strong hand, his thumb absently feathering over her skin as he studied her. His aura of power buzzed against her, not unpleasant but a throbbing prickle of pure unadulterated energy.

There was no spark of heat or surge of attraction like she'd just experienced with Noah inside the bedroom, so if Uriel was waiting to smell her arousal, he'd be sorely disappointed.

Slowly, a smile curved his lips, and he dropped his hand and leaned back to cross his arms again. "Have you ever wished to do something besides be a succubus?"

It was Jez's turn to snort. "Like what? Become a flight attendant?"

He grinned, and it turned his dark features almost boyish. "No, I meant other than quotas and temptation and sex with an endless array of beings?"

She shrugged and began to dry her hair, more for something to do with her hands than anything else. "I am what I am, and I can't change it."

He pursed his lips. "But what if you could?"

She frowned as she hung the towel over the flimsy, metal towel rack. A life doing something other than what she'd always done? It was oddly intriguing and yet frightening at the same time. "Are you offering?" Jez wasn't sure if that was even within the Archangel's power, but it couldn't hurt to find out.

"Not exactly. Let's just say I like to stay well informed. And Lilith's interests are in some ways my interests, as well."

Jez huffed out a laugh as she reached around him to grab a brush off the counter and run it through her long, wet hair to coax out the tangles. "The only interests of Lilith's I'm privy to are my individual quotas each month and my current need to get back to her lair and meet my sisters before Semiazas finds us." She didn't bother to hide the truth from Uriel; he could sense lies, and besides, maybe he could help.

"My retreat also serves as a portal point." He fell silent as if waiting for her reaction; when she frowned, he continued. "The earthly location it appears in shifts every week, and only those with my express permission can find it."

She didn't pretend ignorance. Uriel's retreat would be a portal the demons wouldn't be watching and that she and Noah wouldn't have to fight their way through. "And how would we find it?"

"It will remain in Yuma, Arizona, for two more days, and will then be in Greece."

"Yuma? Seriously?" She tossed her brush on the counter and propped her fists on her hips. "As in the armpit of the Southwest? You've got to be kidding."

Uriel smiled. "My property exists on the other side, and merely appears in the earthly plane to those whom I've allowed to see it. The location rotates—it's been just about everywhere by now."

"And how do you give that permission?" Jez had dealt with Archangels for too long not to think there was more involved than just his word.

"Get dressed and I'll meet you out in the main room. I'll extend my permission to both you and your human." Uriel opened the door and stepped outside, not closing it fully behind him.

Jez concentrated and after a quick round of tingling was dressed in jeans, tennis shoes, and a simple V-necked top, her long hair still damp over her shoulders.

"Who the hell are you?" Noah's panicked voice was followed by an odd sound like sand hitting a wall.

She rushed out into the main room and stopped short at the scene in front of her.

Noah stood naked, the thread she'd not bothered to snip still streaming down from the freshly stitched wound in his side. He held another kosher salt–filled balloon in his hand, cocked back and ready to throw while he stared at Uriel with curiosity and determination.

"Stop!" Jez rushed to stand between them and grabbed Noah's hand that still held the balloon and lowered it. "Noah, this is the Archangel Uriel. Uriel, this is Noah, the man sent to bring me back to Lilith's lair."

Uriel brushed kosher salt from his hair and clothes, the white crystals falling around him like solid snow. "I suppose I should've announced myself, but I'm not used to humans attacking when Archangels come calling."

"I'm not used to men jumping out of a bathroom that only held one woman." Noah shrugged. "Although if you'd looked like Kate Beckinsale, I wouldn't have panicked."

Uriel frowned. "The actress?"

Jez huffed out a breath. "Long story." She turned to look at Noah. "Uriel has a house that will be in Yuma, Arizona, for two more days, and if we can get there, we can use it as a portal."

"That's real?" Noah tossed the balloon on the bed before he stepped around Jez. "Your retreat that moves locations every week?"

A flash of annoyance darkened Uriel's silver eyes until they appeared gunmetal gray. "How do you know about my property?"

"I'm a horror writer. I do a lot of research."

"What does horror writing and research have to do with a human knowing about my retreat?" Uriel's voice rose—not the volume, but the intensity—until it shook the walls of the tiny room.

Jez grabbed the front of the Archangel's white button-down shirt and yanked until he dropped his gaze to hers. "Can you tone down the kick-ass Archangel effects?" She gestured around them and the quaking stopped suddenly. "Thanks."

Uriel stepped back and ran a hand through his long multicolored hair, mussing it and leaving it in sexy disarray. "I apologize. I had thought that information was better hidden."

"It's considered a myth . . . a legend," Noah supplied. "But there isn't much known about it beyond that."

Uriel shook his head. "Then I guess we should all be thankful for small blessings. Hopefully none of the demons chasing you have that same information, Jezebeth." He caught her gaze and held it until she nodded once, in the manner of the succubi and incubi.

"Do you really have art treasures from the Library of Alexandria and even a few originals from Michelangelo?" Noah's soft question was filled with curiosity and excitement and after glaring at him with no visible effect, Uriel sighed.

"Yes, I do."

Noah grinned. "When we make it to the portal, can we see inside the house?"

Uriel's glare returned, and he finally glanced at Jez in what appeared to be amazement.

"Noah," Jez warned under her breath.

"What?" He held his hands wide. "I read that information at the same time. I didn't think it was a big deal, but I'd love to see the place for myself. I could set some amazing stories there—"

Uriel stalked forward to stand toe to toe with Noah, who was still very naked. "What other information did you read about my retreat, human?"

"Noah," he said simply. "My name is Noah, not human, and other than that there was a mention that Lilith sometimes visits the house." Noah snapped his fingers. "That's it. That's where I read it. I was researching Lilith for one of my novels and a private collector had an open house and allowed people in for two hours to look at his collection. The information was in a small burgundy journal, handwritten in ancient Hebrew. I recognized Lilith's name. I'm pretty rusty without a translator, but was able to snap a picture of that page with my phone and take it home to translate later."

Uriel stepped back, but not before Jez had seen a stricken expression flash across his face and then disappear. "Do you still have that picture?"

Noah nodded. "Jez, where are my jeans?"

Jez grabbed his blood-soaked jeans off the chair and handed them over.

Noah reached into the left front pocket and pulled out his phone. After clicking several buttons he showed the phone to Uriel, whose face suddenly drained of all color. "Who is this private collector?"

Noah shrugged. "I don't know off the top of my head. I have the information at home in my notes though."

"That won't be necessary." Uriel grabbed Noah's chin and leaned close to lock gazes with him.

Noah stiffened, his fingers falling open so both the phone and his jeans fell to the floor.

Jez had to look away as a chill ran through her. She rubbed her arms as she pointedly stared at her shoes.

She still vividly remembered when Raphael had unwittingly gazed inside her soul. All the darker places inside herself had been ripped open and left raw and aching. It wasn't physically painful exactly, but was a sensation she had absolutely no desire to repeat.

Finally Uriel cleared his throat. "Thank you . . . Noah. I have the information I require. And here is your permission to enter my property." Jez glanced up just as Uriel stepped toe to toe with Noah.

Noah tried to step back, but Uriel's hand on his chin held him in place. A golden mist spilled from between Uriel's lips, crossed the several inches separating the men and filtered in through Noah's nose and open lips.

Noah stumbled back and sat down hard on the bed, his expression dazed.

"Your turn little one." Uriel turned to Jezebeth, and she closed her eyes just in case the promise not to look inside her soul had only been inside the bathroom. She sensed him step closer and then his warm lips pressed against hers.

Invisible pressure parted her lips and she opened for Uriel as he lingered over their kiss. Something tangible passed between them from him into her—most likely the same golden mist she'd seen enter Noah.

When Uriel stepped back, Jez's equilibrium swam and she stumbled backward, her calves hitting the bed so she ended up sitting down hard right next to Noah.

When she blinked open her eyes, Uriel was gone.

8

Noah's insides were raw and aching, and he still wasn't entirely sure what had just happened.

As his mind cleared, he realized he still sat on the end of the bed next to Jezebeth, totally naked. His body reacted predictably, and he grabbed the edge of the sheet and pulled it over his lap while heat seared up his neck and into his face.

"Wow," Jezebeth said softly from beside him.

After glancing over to make sure she meant the situation and not his sudden return of shyness, Noah nodded, not sure he trusted himself to speak just yet. He swallowed hard and cleared his throat as he glanced over at Jezebeth, who seemed lost in thought. "What the hell just happened?" His words came out soft and dazed-sounding, which was a pretty accurate indicator of how he felt right now.

"Oh, sorry." Jezebeth shook her head and sucked in a breath. "I've never been kissed by Uriel before—talk about intense." She turned and touched his arm. "Are you all right? I had no idea Uriel was going to look into your soul."

"My soul?" Noah stiffened as he shifted experimentally, wincing when his aching insides and not his external wounds protested.

Jezebeth nodded as she studied him critically. "Archangels have the ability to look through someone's eyes to see inside their soul. There's nothing you can hide from one of them, and the only beings who are safe are other Archangels and other supernaturals who are at that general level."

Noah shuddered as he remembered the sensation of meeting Uriel's liquid-silver gaze. "Is that why I feel like someone took a blowtorch to my insides?"

Jezebeth nodded once. "Yes. It's not a comfortable experience."

"What was with that gold mist? And why did he kiss you?" He frowned. "Don't get me wrong, I'm glad I didn't get the same treatment. But I felt that mist go inside me."

She smirked. "You haven't done much research on Archangels, have you?"

Noah cleared his throat. "Not much. I haven't written a lot of Heaven's minions as characters." He pinched the bridge of his nose against an oncoming headache. "For some odd reason I'd always pictured them as fluffy cute cherubs who flitted around spreading cheer and healing."

Jez snorted. "Welcome to another fat slice of reality. I have a feeling during our time together you're going to get a much bigger dose of it than you want." She stood and paced across the room before she turned back to face him. "Uriel needed to give us permission to enter his property where the portal is, so he passed it to us with that mist. As for the kiss, he probably knew you wouldn't be comfortable with that same delivery method."

"Are you saying if I would've been comfortable I would've gotten the same 'delivery method'?" He scrubbed his hands over his face as he raced to find mental footing in a world made entirely of quicksand.

Jezebeth laughed, which made Noah stiffen and frown. "You just had an Archangel look inside your soul and you're worried that he might've kissed you if you'd been up for it? No offense, but we have bigger things on our priority list right now." Jezebeth's features softened as her smile died away. "Uriel is an Archangel, who was most likely present for your creation, so that's why you weren't shy around him—he's seen it all before, and he isn't really male, so he doesn't have the normal human box of safe sexual definitions."

"He sounded and looked very male."

"He's an Archangel, not a human. They can choose whatever form they are most comfortable in to appear to humans. Their true form is pure energy, a ball of beautiful light so bright that humans and even most supernaturals can't look upon their form without being blinded."

"How do you know? Have you ever seen it?" His writer curiosity kicked into high gear as he faced Jezebeth.

She opened her mouth to retort when two quick knocks sounded on the door, interrupting what she'd been about to say.

Noah exchanged a quick glance with Jezebeth before he stood and pulled on his jeans, zipping them quickly before he crossed to his backpack and pulled out a small water pistol filled with holy water, and a Ruger loaded with custom-ordered hollow points.

Jez grabbed the kosher salt–filled balloon he'd dropped on the bed earlier and then nodded that she was ready.

Noah cleared his throat. "Who is it?"

"It's Jim from the front office. I just wanted to bring you two some breakfast."

Jez glanced back over her shoulder and sighed. "I'll get rid of him. He's the guy I agreed to have drinks with sometime."

Noah blinked and a different woman stood where Jez had been a split second before—a woman who held a passing resemblance to

Kate Beckinsale. Noah frowned as the woman tossed a wink in his direction.

"Just a second, Jim."

The husky, sexy voice complete with a British accent that came from the near-Kate surprised Noah, and he chided himself as he tucked away the Ruger inside the backpack but kept the water pistol in his palm. Of course when Jez changed forms, the voice would have to change too, or it wouldn't be a very effective disguise. But it was still disconcerting.

His thoughts were cut short when Jez unlocked the door and opened it to reveal a pretty, petite blond girl standing just in front of a tall man wearing boots and a tight black T-shirt. The girl held two plates with napkins draped over them while she raked her gaze over Noah as if he was on the dessert menu. He shifted uncomfortably as he realized he was still shirtless.

Jim cleared his throat and smiled at Jezebeth with definite interest sparking in his eyes. "Morning. How'd you two sleep?"

A male protective instinct rose so quick and fast that Noah had to clench his fists to keep from glaring at the man while stepping forward to warn him away from Jezebeth. Jim thought they were brother and sister, Noah forcefully reminded himself as he stayed in place and tried to keep his expression neutral.

Unaware of Noah's internal struggles, Jez leaned against the edge of the open door and smiled. "We slept great, thanks. Are those for us?"

The girl nodded, her tongue darting out to moisten her bottom lip. "Yeah. I'm Sadie from the restaurant. Jim thought you two could use some breakfast." She handed the plates to Jez, who passed them to Noah.

The tantalizing scents of eggs and bacon made Noah's stomach growl. Jim laughed as Noah set the plates on the tiny end table next to one of the twin beds. "I see your friend is hungry." He looked between the two of them. "How long before you head out?"

From his hopeful gaze it was obvious he wished it wouldn't be too quickly.

Jez gave an apologetic smile. "Actually we have to get going. But we appreciate you bringing by breakfast."

The girl's bottom lip poked out into a pout as she looked past Jez toward Noah. "Hey, what happened to your side?" She pushed past Jez and into the room before Noah realized what she meant.

Jim followed her inside and Jez softly closed the door and shrugged behind their backs as Noah sent her a "what do we do now?" look.

Cool fingers touched his side and then slid down to trace around the waistband of his jeans before Sadie looked up at him from under her lashes—apparently one of her practiced moves. "Is that real? It looks cool."

Noah glanced down at his side to find his skin perfectly healed around the neat black stitches Jez had made in his side. The row of thin black threads disappeared into his jeans after the first few inches of tiny stitches. His skin wasn't even red where the thread entered. "What—"

Jez cut in. "It's the new piercing rage in California; he's just trying it out."

Sadie dipped a finger under the waistband of Noah's jeans, and pressed her body against his. "Care to show me the rest of that, handsome?"

Before Noah could figure out a way to turn the girl down without offending her, Jim stepped forward and gently peeled her away from Noah and guided her to the door. He sent an apologetic look toward first Jezebeth and then Noah.

"Enjoy the breakfast. Sadie's got to get back to the restaurant."

He sent the girl a stern glare before turning back to Jezebeth. "But don't forget, I'd love to see you on your return trip."

Jez smiled as if she was genuinely looking forward to drinks with Jim, and Noah ground his teeth. Surely she was just a great actress. Right?

She made some kind of farewell too soft for him to hear and then waved to Jim before gently closing the door. Then she surprised him by muttering, "Damn, talk about persistent."

Noah wasn't sure if she referred to Sadie or Jim, but he swallowed that question back and ran his fingers over the stitches in his side. "Any idea how this happened?"

Jez shrugged, the motion looking decidedly Jez-like in her borrowed near-Kate body. "I'm assuming it's from Uriel. He's the only thing we've come into contact with that could've healed you, although that's not usually his thing."

"That's right. He's something of a warrior for God, isn't he?"

Jezebeth nodded as she crossed to the first-aid kit that still sat on the chest of drawers. "All of them have some inherent healing abilities just because of who they are, but you're correct. He's usually in the thick of the battles and enforcement, not healing the aftermath." She pulled out a pair of tiny scissors, snapping them open and closed a few times in the air in front of her face. "Why don't you pull those jeans back off and I'll get rid of the stitches?"

Noah reached for his fly and then paused. "Can you change back to your other form?" Men from around the globe lusted after Kate Beckinsale, himself included, but he was still getting used to Jezebeth and all her forms, and he longed to look into her own chocolate brown eyes again.

"If I do I'll have to recharge my energy again before I leave. And since both Jim and Sadie are expecting me to leave looking like this, I figured I'd retain this form until I can recharge."

Without realizing what he planned to do, Noah stepped forward and pulled Jezebeth against him, capturing her lips with his.

She opened her mouth to protest, and he delved inside, determined to kiss away all thoughts of Jim. He realized the oddity of the urge since he and Jezebeth were purely traveling companions, but some things were just instinctual, like the heady sensation of kissing the handful of woman in front of him.

Jezebeth started to push him away, but he held her tight, kissing her until tingling power sparked between them and Jez moaned deep inside her throat.

He spun out the kiss, coaxing little sighs from Jezebeth until the urge to do much more rolled through him like a wave. Realization came like a slap of ice water, and he broke the kiss and stepped back suddenly, leaving Jezebeth, now back in her own form, to sway against the sudden change.

Tense silence hung between them until Noah forced out, "Will that be enough energy?"

When Jezebeth flinched he realized she'd taken his clipped words for something other than him fighting off the effects of the arousal she'd ignited inside him. Before he could think of something to say, she glared up at him and pointed at him with the scissors she still held.

"Don't do that again. Wearing Lilith's ring doesn't give you permission to manhandle me any time you want. If I need energy, I know where to get it, and it won't be from you."

Her cold words sparked his anger, and he glared down at her. "No problem. I'm sure Jim will be more than happy to be your guinea pig. Just be careful or you'll leave him passed out like the men back in the truck at the club where I found you."

As soon as the words left his lips, he wished them back.

Why did this woman drive him so insane? He wasn't looking for a relationship with her, so he had no reason to be so possessive or territorial. And beyond that, he wasn't a jerk who yelled at women and found words to hurt them. "Jezebeth . . . I'm sorry."

Jezebeth stepped forward into Noah's personal space, her face a mask of nonchalance. "We have things to do. Drop the jeans, and let's get the stitches out."

He searched for something to say, but when nothing came to mind and she continued to watch him calmly, he sighed before unzipping his jeans and shoving them down around his knees. When his cock hit the cool air both it and his balls tightened against his body.

When Jez dropped to her knees in front of him, Noah's cock surged to life. He closed his eyes and glanced toward the ceiling instead of watching her kneel in front of him where her mouth was so close Jez could easily suck and lick him.

Noah breathed deep and tried to concentrate on the stained yellow-flower pattern on the walls and the dirty gray popcorn ceilings—anything but the uncomfortable situation. After all, hadn't she just told him she didn't want any energy from him? And that's what sex equated to with her.

She's a succubus, he reminded himself for the millionth time.

At Jez's first gentle touch Noah jumped and then murmured apologies.

"Are you all right? Did I hurt you?" Jez's deep voice was filled with amusement and Noah gritted his teeth. The damned succubus was playing with him! And unfortunately, after how he'd treated her earlier, he probably deserved it.

"No. I'm fine."

"Just checking." Her touch was gentle, the tips of her fingers lightly tracing a path over the sensitive skin of his side and then lower down his hip.

Noah bit back a curse as she snipped the exposed edges of the threads and then with a quick yank pulled out the first piece of thread with only a tiny stinging sensation. After a few more, she leaned close to get a grip on the small thread and her warm breath feathered against his skin sending a shiver flowing through him to pool in his now rock-hard cock.

Noah tried not to be too self-conscious in his very exposed position, but what really put a dent in his male pride was that Jezebeth didn't even seem to notice his aroused state. He shoved the thought aside reminding himself that they had to get moving.

He cleared his throat and tried not to fidget as she yanked the last few threads out of his skin. "I'm really sorry about earlier. I was an ass."

She laughed. "Yes, you were. But I know you're not used to dealing with supernaturals, so I'm trying to give you the benefit of the doubt."

Noah huffed out a short laugh as Jezebeth traced one fingertip over his skin. "This is going to take me a while to get used to, that's all."

She stopped and Noah glanced down to see her staring up at him. Her chocolate brown eyes held a very familiar glint of amusement as she dabbed a peroxide-soaked cotton ball over the tiny pinpricks left in his skin. "You realize that as a succubus I can smell arousal even if there wasn't a very nice, erect cock in my face, right?"

Feeling suddenly overexposed, Noah jerked away and yanked up his jeans before he stalked across the room to grab a fresh shirt out of one of his duffel bags and pull it on.

"I guess it's my turn to apologize." She picked up the tiny threads off the floor and stood. "I know you're struggling with all of this, and I guess teasing you was my way of getting back at you for the comments before I stormed off to take a shower." She threw away the thread scraps and replaced the scissors and peroxide back into the first-aid kit.

Noah stopped and glanced back at her, not sure how to respond.

"I'm not sure if this will make it easier or not, but it's just a fact that whether you like it or not, you're attracted to me, regardless of the form I'm in. It's biological, not a choice, so get over it." She raised her chin and crossed her arms over her chest as if daring him to deny it.

"That was blunt." He couldn't help the small smile that curved his lips.

"I figured blunt would save us some time since we need to pack and get out of here. We don't have time for you to start doubting yourself. It could get us both killed."

"Fair enough."

9

Lilith sank into the heated water of the underground hot spring that ran through the corner of her suite—a perk of having her lair underground. The fact that it wasn't in the human realm reassured her that the water was pure and fresh and that it contained the healing properties that had been lost to the humans when Adam and Eve were kicked out of the Garden.

Hopefully the hot, bubbling waters would soothe away the aching pain that still tightened Lilith's chest from her time at Uriel's. A sob caught inside her throat and she hiccupped as fresh, hot tears streamed down her face to mix with the swirling waters.

At the quick flash of memory of her time with the three Archangels, a slow ache began deep in her pelvis and spread outward. But as always, her thoughts returned to the few hours forever embedded inside her memory—when Uriel had broken his vows and taken her.

Vivid memories flooded back and the swirling water against her sensitive skin became Uriel's hands as they feathered over her skin.

That night had begun like all the others, except when he'd materialized them up to his room . . . he hadn't disappeared. His arms remained warm and firm around her as he stared into her eyes as if searching for something.

"Uriel?" The word came out as a mere whisper as hope swelled inside her.

"*Nassah*, do you know why I saved you? Why when my Father sent me to expel Adam and Eve and to kill you that I begged Him for another way?"

Her stomach tightened at his husky words, and she held her breath, afraid to hear what would come next, even as anticipation skittered through her. She shook her head.

"You enchanted me," he whispered against her lips before he brushed his warm mouth over hers. "You were beautiful and graceful, and so intelligent and sure of yourself that I couldn't imagine a world without you in it. I couldn't bring myself to destroy you."

Lilith swallowed hard, not sure what to answer.

"I petitioned my Father for mercy, and He smiled and told me that temptation could have a place in this world. Then He made me responsible for you." Uriel laughed as he brushed another kiss over her lips. "And He was right as He always is. You've tempted me every day since, my beautiful *nassah*." He leaned his forehead against hers and closed his eyes, while Lilith slowly traced the muscles of his back with her fingers. "Sometimes I feel I'm as weak as the humans when it comes to you."

"God gave us free will just like the humans, Uriel. Those urges and emotions swirling inside us both, those are from Him as well." She brought her hands to his face, meeting his raw gaze. "I love you, Uriel. I have for ages. You've taken care of me and befriended me when the rest of the world would have gladly tossed me aside. You take the weight of the world on your shoulders and are never satisfied with anything less than perfection. I would do anything for you."

Uriel met her gaze, searching her face for a long, charged moment before he swallowed hard as if it took great effort to speak. "May my Father forgive me, but I'm afraid I would do anything for you, as well, *ahuvati*."

No sooner had joy at Uriel's words registered inside Lilith's mind than his lips came down on hers like a dark command.

She opened for him, reveling in the surrender she read there as her body melted against him.

He growled deep inside his throat, crushing Lilith against him and lifting her until her feet dangled off the ground.

Lilith clung to him, reveling in the intensity of the passion that exploded to life between them. Millennia of yearning for Uriel left her surprised that he'd finally given in, if even for a moment.

Uriel never stopped kissing her as he carried her toward his large bed. He set her down gently and drew back only long enough to strip off her dress before he pulled her tight against him once more.

The erotic sensation of her bare skin against his clothes swept through her and her body tightened in response. She worked at the buttons of his shirt, eager to feel his firm skin under her fingers.

Uriel made an impatient sound in the back of his throat and suddenly he was entirely naked and tipping her backward, following her down onto the bed until he covered her. His hands were everywhere, his tongue mating with hers, dipping and tasting her lips, her teeth, every part of her mouth.

She arched against him, offering herself, begging for his touch.

He captured the sound in his mouth as his hips thrust against her hot core, mimicking what she wished he would do in reality. She moved with him, each movement rubbing against her aching clit just the way she liked. He gently rolled her nipple between his thumb and forefinger and she gasped. When his mouth replaced his hand, she released a moan. Moist heat closed over her sensitive peak and lava burned from the tip of her breast straight to her pussy, liquid heat pooling between her legs.

Uriel turned his attention to her other breast. She ran a hand over his hard cock and he shuddered and groaned. She cupped the hot length of him, stroking him as he suckled her breast harder, teeth scraping over her nipple until she thought she would explode.

She dipped her fingers into Uriel's thick hair. "Please. I need you, now."

Uriel kissed his way up her chest and skimmed his lips up the column of her throat sending gooseflesh marching through Lilith until she gasped and writhed under him.

He shifted and slid inside her in one long, slow stroke.

Lilith gasped and then moaned as he filled her, stretched her.

When his cock was fully seated inside her, he paused for a moment, allowing Lilith to savor their kiss, as the tip of his swollen head bumped deep against her core.

He raised his face to look down at her and the breath caught in her throat at the wonder she saw reflected in Uriel's eyes, which had turned a gunmetal gray.

"*Ahuvati*, you're so beautiful," he whispered as he moved inside her and her body slowly tightened around him.

The first hard slap of energy from Uriel's arousal surged through her body, ripping a hoarse cry from her throat and it was absorbed.

Urgency built between them, their bodies heating with the deliberate pace. The musk of their joined arousal perfumed the air, and in between drugging kisses, Lilith inhaled the heady scent into her lungs to memorize for all time.

The only sounds in the room were the little gasps of need that escaped from her every time he filled her, along with the shush of the sheets sliding with each movement.

Lilith pulled him down tight against her and captured his lips with hers. Her tongue delved inside his mouth, mimicking the purposeful movements of his hard cock claiming her body.

His movements became more deliberate as the vortex of arousal tightened inside Lilith, until it exploded outward.

Uriel stiffened over her as his hot essence spilled inside her, triggering another hard orgasm as her body welcomed the energy he offered.

The memories sailed back quick and bright, and it was almost jarring for Lilith to realize she still sat in the hot springs in her quarters millennia later, her body still aching for him.

When she'd woken that night he'd been gone, but he'd left behind the jewelry set that she'd given the companions of the four sisters.

She sighed as she trailed her fingers down under the water to trace her slick slit as she savored the memory of Uriel's taste, his scent, and the sensation of having his long, thick cock thrust inside her.

Arousal zinged through her, and she gasped at the intense sensation. With her free hand she cupped her breast and then lightly pinched her swollen nipple, enjoying the rush of answering liquid heat that shot straight to her clit.

Lilith slowly stroked her first two fingers over the tight, sensitive nub, arching her hips with each stroke as if rising up to meet Uriel's thrusts inside her. She let her head fall back as her eyes slipped closed, the swirling hot water caressing her sensitive skin as it teased the long tendrils of her hair that had escaped her hastily fastened barrette.

Her pussy slowly tightened around Uriel's remembered width as Lilith continued to give herself up to the memories of that one exquisite night.

A gasp escaped her as she vividly relived the sensation of Uriel's soft multicolored hair brushing against her breasts and neck as he thrust inside her faster and faster, as he stared into her eyes, linking them soul to soul. She still remembered the smoky campfire scent of him and soft scrape of his whiskers against her skin as he nipped, kissed, and licked her.

Urgency drove her and she rubbed harder and faster against her throbbing clit, widening her thighs as she sucked in each labored breath on her race toward impending orgasm.

A vivid mental image of the cry that ripped from Uriel's throat as he came inside her in searing jets flashed across her mind's eye and pushed her over the edge of her own release.

A hard slap of ecstasy engulfed her, radiating from her clit along every nerve ending until a euphoric numbness settled over her, enticing a long sigh from her throat.

"Lilith."

The sudden sound of Uriel's strangled voice made Lilith bolt to her feet, the warm water sluicing down her bare skin to join the swirling waist-high waters.

As if she'd conjured him with her thoughts, Uriel stood before her in the same clothes he'd worn the last time she'd seen him at his home. Fresh pain welled inside her, tightening her voice. "Uriel?" She continued to stare at him, waiting for him to turn out to be a figment of her oversexed imagination. "Why are you here?"

He stared at her for a long moment, his eyes darkened to gunmetal gray—the same color they'd turned when they'd made love all those millennia ago.

Lilith bit her bottom lip, the sharp pain helping to remind her not to run into his arms and risk him pushing her away again.

Finally he shook his head as if pulling himself out of a deep trance and reached into the front pocket of his slacks and pulled out a small, burgundy leather journal worn with time.

Confusion swirled through Lilith as she glanced up to search Uriel's face for answers. Hurt and anger now tightened his handsome features, but anyone who didn't know him as well as Lilith wouldn't be able to read anything from his expression.

Whatever was in the journal, it wasn't good.

"The letters I wrote you . . ." His voice trailed off as anger tightened his last few words.

Icy cold dread scratched up Lilith's spine as she rushed out of the hot spring, the cool air sending a rush of gooseflesh marching over her naked, wet skin. She brushed by Uriel and headed toward the six-foot marble chest that sat at the end of her bed.

She knelt, the soft fur rug sticking to her wet skin as she raised the lid of the chest and dug under layers of memories to the very bottom. When her fingers closed over a hard wood box, she yanked it out and flipped open the lid. She blew out a slow breath when she found the hide scrolls inside still weathered with age.

These were the letters Uriel had written to her just after the episode where he'd broken his vows. The ancient Hebrew symbols were weathered and faded with time, but every word was emblazoned across Lilith's memory for eternity.

Uriel's gaze burned against her skin and she slowly turned to face him.

"You told me they'd been destroyed." Hurt and betrayal lined his flat voice.

Lilith rose and then slowly closed the lid of the marble chest before picking up a red silk robe off her bed and slipping it on. She picked the box up off the bed, caressing her fingers over the smooth dark wood as she spoke. "They were all I had of you after you shut me out. I couldn't bear to give them up."

A heavy silence fell between them, and as each second ticked past, bile inched its way up her throat to sting the back of her tongue.

Finally Uriel slowly walked forward and laid his hand on her shoulder.

Lilith gasped at the sudden unexpected touch and raised her gaze to his, offering him the opportunity to look inside her soul if he chose. But when his eyes remained constantly moving liquid silver, Lilith clenched her fists, waiting for Uriel to speak.

"I can't break my vows again, Lilith. Not even for you." He took her hand in his, laid a gentle kiss on the palm, and then laid her hand on the box containing the letters he'd written so long ago. "This is all of me I can offer."

Glistening moisture filled his silver eyes as he dematerialized.

"Uriel, wait! What's inside the journal?" When the Archangel didn't rematerialize Lilith cursed and gently replaced the wooden box inside the marble chest.

*　*　*

Uriel materialized inside the makeshift field hospital tent. A few of the injured and dying turned their faces in his direction, but none seemed to be able to see him.

He could appear to humans when he chose, but most often they wouldn't be aware of him at all, or he would strike them as something similar to déjà vu. Only those humans most sensitive to shifts in energy would be able to sense his presence directly.

He easily found Raphael kneeling over a dying soldier whose forehead showed a gaping head wound. The man's soul hovered half in and half out of his body, the gauzy sheet of energy already eager to return to the other side and begin again. The human's chest rose and fell in a choppy rhythm as he struggled to breathe, even with the help of the oxygen mask covering his face.

Raphael knelt next to the man's cot, his eyes closed, concentration etched across his handsome face as he laid his large hand gently over the wounded man's forehead. A golden glow erupted under Raphael's fingertips and sweat broke out on the Archangel's brow as he worked.

Uriel stood silently watching, but not interrupting. He'd always been fascinated by Raphael's healing abilities. All Archangels could heal humans to some extent, but Raphael could bring them back from the dead if God's plan required such an event.

By contrast, Uriel was known as the Fire of God, which basically meant he was God's enforcer. Not to be confused with His right-hand general, which was Michael. That's why Uriel had been the one sent to evict Adam, Eve, and Lilith from the Garden of Eden.

He sighed as a thousand memories assailed him—especially those involving Lilith. He'd often thought how much easier life would be if one of the others had been sent in his stead to the Garden. But then Lilith would be dead, as God had originally ordered.

A cold spear of pain pierced his heart at the thought of such a possibility.

Raphael's eyes opened, his hazel gaze locking with Uriel's for a long moment before the large Archangel leaned down, moved aside the oxygen mask, and set his lips against the soldier's to literally breathe life back inside him.

The man's chest expanded with the force of Raphael's life-giving breath. The soul snapped back inside the body and his labored breathing eased as he sank into a deep, healing sleep.

"Live. You have much left to do in this world." Raphael replaced the oxygen mask and ran a gentle hand over the soldier's short hair like he comforted a small child.

Raphael stood and stretched, his vertebrae making a series of pops after the long time spent in one position.

Tension rose between them thick and oppressive. Raphael was most likely waiting for Uriel's reaction from the session with Lilith.

Uriel had hoped to avoid the subject, but he should've known Raphael's sense of empathy and honor wouldn't let him ignore it as Uriel had hoped.

Uriel mentally squared his shoulders and waded in to confront the pink elephant in the room as circumspectly as possible. "I've always enjoyed watching you work. I suppose I'm a bit envious of your ability to restore life rather than just mete out punishments." He smiled, a silent peace offering for Raphael.

Raphael's lips curved, but the action was still short of a full-fledged smile. "And here I've always been jealous that I never get to kick ass like you or Michael."

Uriel stepped forward and hugged Raphael in a quick bear hug before releasing him and stepping back. He kept his hand on the angel's shoulder and met his hazel gaze. "Lilith asked for what would hurt me most, and I had no choice but to honor it. I bear no ill will toward you or Gabriel." He forced his lips into a small smile, even though the pain of watching the two beings closest to him with the woman he loved still ate at him like acid. "God meant for us to enjoy the pleasures of sex, even though our options are limited. I would've done the same in your situation. Sex with only humans and those below our station in the supernatural realm can be very limiting since we can never truly be ourselves with them."

Raphael studied him closely, but Uriel knew not much made it past his very observant friend. "The situation sucks, and for that I'm sorry. I won't return for—"

"No." Uriel held up a hand to stop Raphael's continued denial. "If she asks for you again, please return. Lilith needs sustenance, and in a warped way, this does allow me to be with her through you and Gabriel."

Raphael sighed and then slowly nodded. "If either of you need me, I'll be there."

Behind them, a doctor checked on the soldier Raphael had set on the road to healing and quickly called another doctor over to consult. An excited murmur flowed around the medical staff and Raphael slapped Uriel on the shoulder and stepped back with a satisfied smile. "Why don't we go elsewhere? My work here is done, and I don't think you came to find me just to make sure things were still good between us. God only knows you would've ignored it until the apocalypse if I allowed it."

Uriel snorted, unsurprised with Raphael's bluntness. "Ouzo?"

"Meet you there."

Uriel held a picture inside his mind of where he wanted to go and dematerialized. A quick second later he rematerialized on a balcony in Santorini, Greece, that looked out over a hillside dotted with colorful buildings and beyond to the turquoise waters of the Aegean.

A cool breeze ruffled his long hair and he tucked it behind his ear as he breathed deep the scent of the salty air. So much history here, and so much that must remain buried. But the beauty of the place made up for all that, he supposed.

Raphael materialized next to him and they sat on either side of the small table reserved only for high-level supernaturals. The tiny establishment was staffed both by low-level angels and demons alike, as well as everything in between. But then only in the Bible and in history was good versus evil as clear-cut as the humans thought.

A snow-white Wendigo demon bustled to the table, its long yellow claws and fangs glistening in the afternoon sunlight as it set a bottle of ouzo on the table next to a platter filled with feta cheese, Greek olives, hummus, and fresh-baked pita bread.

The spicy scents teased Uriel's senses, and he sighed as his stomach churned from the stress of recent events. Archangels technically didn't need to eat, but Greek food was one of his favorite pleasures.

"Thanks." Raphael accepted the two tall, thin shot glasses the Wendigo produced from thin air.

The demon nodded and disappeared back inside the house.

"Here." Raphael filled Uriel's glass to the top with the clear-colored liquor. "You look like you could use it. Then you can tell me what's going on." He filled his own glass and set the bottle aside. "I sense something much worse than just the situation with Lilith."

Uriel raised the glass to his lips, inhaling the pungent scent of black licorice before toasting Raphael and downing the ouzo in one swallow. The slow burn down his throat seeped out into his limbs, and he sighed and relaxed back in his seat as Raphael downed his own drink. When Raphael refilled both glasses and popped a green olive into his mouth, Uriel pulled the small journal out of the pocket of his slacks and laid it on the table between them.

Raphael cocked his head to one side, his brows furrowed in question. "What is it?"

Uriel took a deep breath, glad to finally share this burden with someone else who would understand its significance. "It's a journal of poetry and supernatural myths—most of which are absolutely true, and known only by a select few."

Raphael froze with his glass partway to his lips. "What kind of myths are we talking about here?"

Uriel didn't want to mention his love letters to Lilith. Raphael and Gabriel knew about his broken vows, but after Lilith's most recent visit to his house, his emotions were still raw and aching where she was concerned. Besides, the very explicit letters were only one small part of what was inside the journal. It was the embodiment of something he'd hoped would stay trapped forever.

Uriel refilled his own glass and downed it, letting the burn spread for a long moment before he spoke. "There's information about my house, references to places where all of us spend our time, what we do, who we interact with and when. Not to mention the true histories of several events such as the flood, Atlantis, Pompeii—"

"Atlantis?" Raphael demanded as he set his glass down on the table with more force than necessary. He glanced quickly out toward the blue Aegean and then back toward Uriel. "No one except God Himself, the Archangels, and Lucifer knows about Atlantis. That's the one story that can't ever get out."

"It's a little late for that apparently." Uriel flipped the journal open to a page he'd marked and held the book out to Raphael.

Raphael took the small book, his gaze scanning the page as Uriel downed another shot of ouzo.

"Fuck me. These are Armageddon prophesies. The herald to the end of the human realm."

A bitter laugh escaped Uriel. Raphael rarely used human curses, but that was his favorite when the situation called for it. "We're pretty much all fucked if all these secrets get out into the mainstream. The faster the human consciousness accepts it as fact, the faster the end of the world will speed toward us."

"Lucifer?"

Uriel shook his head. "Lucifer stands to lose the biggest if the fast-forward button is pushed for Armageddon. But it would be easy to convince all the so-called human scholars that he has the most to gain. They're all convinced that whoever has the most souls in the end wins the big battle between good and evil. They have no idea that it's a much more complicated system than that."

"Which means . . ."

"Which means there's a traitor among us." Unfortunately, they had no idea which side the traitor was on, or even how to begin to find him.

Raphael tossed the journal back on the table between them before he leaned back in his chair, staring off over the balcony at the sea for a long moment. "Any other joyous news to share today?"

"Actually, yes. Look at the inside front cover of the journal."

Raphael scowled and leaned forward to open the front cover of the journal where it lay on the table in front of him.

Uriel leaned across the table to place his finger just over a notation on the bottom of the page. "This is journal one of four. There are three more out there, and I have no idea where to find them."

10

Semiazas straightened and experimentally moved the arms and legs of the borrowed elderly librarian woman he'd just possessed. The old bat was still in here somewhere with him, but her consciousness had been pushed aside when he'd taken over. Thanks to her little habit of smoking joints on her lunch hour in the back alley, he'd been able to slip past her normal defenses and borrow her for a little stroll.

Lucky for him, she'd just think she'd dozed off and had a very odd dream. That's why he loved borrowing substance abusers, they were so gullible and ready to explain away anything out of the ordinary.

He adjusted the old lady boobs more comfortably inside the bra that rivaled Fort Knox and then tucked the tiny blue journal inside the generous cleavage. He'd be surprised if anyone strip-searched this form, and if they did, he could play the sweet, innocent old lady card.

Humans were so easy to manipulate!

After making sure everything was as it should be, he draped her gaudy polka-dot purse over his forearm and strolled around the front of the building to the entrance to the British Library.

Semiazas passed the thirtysomething male security guard, who nodded politely. Semiazas fluffed his salt-and-pepper hair playfully and tossed a saucy wink in the younger man's direction before he lifted his cleavage with both hands as if making sure the man hadn't missed the display.

When the man's face paled and he suddenly became very interested in reading the magazine in front of him, Semiazas chuckled. Being an Archangel was never this much fun—other than the time he'd spent in Gabriel's bed. Now *that* was something worth crowing from the rooftops about. Not only was the very delectable Gabriel very inventive and uninhibited in all things sexual, she was also insatiable. Too bad she hadn't loved him more than that poor excuse for a deity she'd betrayed him for. After all, they were already breaking God's rules by having any relationship between them; was it that much more of a leap for her to follow Lucifer when he did?

He shoved the old anger aside and concentrated on navigating through the dusty corridors.

How interesting that when he'd seen Gabriel in Manhattan she'd just come from fucking a woman. His curiosity burned to know who it was. Maybe when his work here was done, he'd do some spying. Heaven knew he'd enjoyed some voyeuristic tendencies over the ages. But to watch Gabriel's glistening pussy be licked and sucked by another woman made his cock hard.

Well—he didn't have a cock in this form, but he was definitely horny as hell now. As soon as he placed the journal, he'd find a way to take care of that. He didn't think he'd enjoy sex very much in this current form.

Semiazas smirked and tossed the tacky purse onto the librarian's desk before making his way to the back rooms where the serious researchers spent time poring over dusty tomes to piece together their so-called expert opinions. Humans were so egotistical, thinking any part of the universe revolved around them. But then, that's what made them so fun to screw with.

"Excuse me, Miss Shelly?"

Semiazas turned toward the voice to find a small boy tugging at the long flowered skirt this form wore. "What are you looking for, little man?" He balanced his fists on the ample hips of this form and smiled down at the boy. "Something to read that offers a little excitement?"

"Yes, mum. I have to write a book report for school on a nonfiction book." He scrunched his nose, clearly showing what he thought of anything nonfiction. "I'm not sure where to start."

"Oh, that's an easy one. Follow me, my boy." Semiazas headed toward the back wall where the research rooms were located. On the way, he stopped and scanned the shelves until he found a particularly gruesome book outlining the torture methods pirates employed during the 1800s. That ought to keep the boy entertained.

He handed it to the boy and grinned. "Here's something you'll find fascinating, and I can tell you from firsthand experience that every word is true. A particular favorite of mine is on page forty-four."

The boy flipped open the book to page forty-four, his eyes widening until Semiazas thought they might pop out of his face and roll around on the ground like sticky marbles.

Page forty-four showed a particularly detailed and full-color illustration of how pirates strung up men by their testicles until their body weight ripped off their family jewels—or they talked. But more often than not talking wouldn't stop the progression of the torture.

Semiazas hadn't invented that particular method, but he'd enjoyed watching it being employed.

The boy swallowed hard and closed the book. "Uh, thanks."

"Another satisfied customer. Now, shoo. I have work to do." Semiazas turned away and did a little dance step on his way to the back research rooms. If the boy read that book and came back for more, he might actually be interesting. He shrugged and pulled out a large silver key to unlock the main research room.

As soon as he entered through the thick, wooden door, the musty smell of old paper assaulted him, and he wrinkled his nose. "The things I do for my job." He fished inside the bra cup that held his left breast and pulled out the journal, wiping the sweat off the tiny book onto his skirt. "There we are. Now, where to leave it?" He glanced around at the stacks of books left on the tables, some open where the readers would most likely pick up next time.

He found one book written in ancient Hebrew open to a section discussing the history of the origins of Christianity and grinned. "Perfect." He laid the journal on top of the open book and headed back out into the main library to have some more fun and possibly find some way to work off his lust over Gabriel.

He headed into the loo, as they called it here in Britain, and sat on the toilet inside a dingy blue stall. He released the woman and stepped out of her body, enjoying his first breath of air in several hours through his own lungs.

The old woman moaned and slumped back against the wall. He'd heard that demon possession left a raging hangover, but it was no more than she deserved for toking up in between her shifts.

Semiazas left the stall and stood in front of the mirror to ensure his dark hair was perfect. He adjusted his tie and brushed a few stray wrinkles out of his dark blue button-down shirt before he left the bathroom in search of a woman.

Not just any woman—preferably one who looked a lot like Gabriel. Brownie points if they were smart enough to spar with him mentally.

He could have a demoness take her form, but he preferred to have his sport with the humans. After all, those little meat sacks were the reason his kind had been reduced to mere servants. And that after an endless time of serving God faithfully. As anger flashed through him, his fingernails snapped out into razor sharp talons and he scraped four perfect furrows in the spines of a shelf full of books as he walked past.

The destruction only banked his anger; it definitely could never remove it. But if things worked out, revenge would be his soon enough.

He made his way upstairs and walked silently up and down the endless aisles of old books, stalking his prey. There were only a few people here and there as he passed, but then he turned the corner and found exactly what he'd been hoping for.

A young woman with silver blond hair pulled back into a ponytail stood on tiptoes trying to reach a book on the top shelf. She had to be nineteen or twenty, her body tight and firm, but yet not fully developed as she would be once she matured. Human women in their thirties and forties were so much more fun to seduce than the young ones, but today he wasn't after sport, he just needed to come inside someone he could pretend was Gabriel.

He quickly stepped behind her, pressing his body against hers and easily lifting the book off the shelf she'd been reaching for.

She made a noise of surprise deep in her throat and whirled to face him as he stepped back, pasting a confused yet innocent expression on his face.

"I didn't mean to startle you. I just noticed you were having trouble reaching this book." He held it out to her with his best "I'm harmless" expression.

Her full pink lips curved into a smile, revealing teeth a little too large for her face. No matter, he could fuck her from behind.

"Thanks. I just wasn't expecting anyone up here." Her voice was high and scratchy, not low and smooth like Gabriel's. He sighed. Well, she would have to remain silent. No talking or witty verbal sparring with this one.

He lowered his voice and whispered like a conspirator. "There are only two other people up here and they are both on the far side of the floor." He held her green gaze and glanced inside at her soul just long enough to find the insecurity and the yearning there that he could exploit to get what he wanted.

She glanced around to confirm his words and then looked up at him.

Victory surged through him, and he pulled her roughly against him while he captured her mouth with his. He expected her to protest, at least a little, but instead, she curled her fingers into the material of his shirt as he plundered her mouth, trying to pretend she was Gabriel and failing badly.

"What's the meaning of this?" The angry and distraught words were from the elderly woman he'd taken over earlier.

Semiazas didn't stop but instead bent the girl backward, kissing her hungrily in a last attempt to relive his past.

"Sir! This is a library."

He smirked at the woman's outrage—especially since he'd been inside her and knew her darkest secrets.

"What better place to look for a piece of ass on a beautiful Sunday afternoon, Miss Shelly?"

When she sputtered, her mouth opening and closing like a fish, he stepped past her and slapped her ass as he made his way toward the stairs. "Don't be jealous, darling. I've already been inside *you* today."

At her indignant shriek behind him, he laughed as he walked slowly away.

*   *   *

Noah strapped the last of their gear into the back of the truck, careful to avoid the jagged metal edges left from the demon claws. He glanced up to watch Jezebeth back in her near-Kate form scanning the horizon with nervous alertness.

"You see anything?"

She shook her head, Jez's familiar mannerism at odds with the form she currently wore. "No, but that's what scares me. There's no way Semiazas has given up. I'm sure he's got everyone he can out looking for me and my sisters." She slid Noah's backpack off her shoulder and laid it inside the cab of the truck before jumping in and closing the door behind her.

Movement from the front office caught Noah's attention and he glanced over in time to see Jim watching them from inside the office window. Jealousy snapped through him and he immediately glanced away, pretending not to have seen him as he jumped inside the driver's side of the truck.

He started the ignition and peeled out of the parking lot, his tires kicking up a wall of dust behind them as irritation at himself burned inside his gut.

"So much for trying to stay below the radar." Jezebeth glanced over at him and then cocked her head to the side. "What's with the look of death? I thought I was just stating the obvious."

"A minute ago you were talking about how half the world is gunning for you, and now you're questioning why I'm in a hurry?" As soon as the angry words left his lips, he wished them back. Just because his reactions had been screwed up since he'd first laid eyes on Jezebeth was no reason to take it out on her. After all, he was a big boy and could be responsible for his own jealousies. "Look, I'm sorry. I'm just trying to find solid ground here."

She seemed ready to say something, but then fell silent. "I wonder why Uriel was so upset about that information you read."

Noah let out a slow breath as relief flooded him.

Jezebeth was going to let him off the hook with a subject change, and at this point, he was coward enough to take it. "I'm not sure. I wish I'd had more time with the book, but I only snapped a picture of that one page because it related to my research."

"Do you still have the picture?"

Noah pulled his cell phone out of his pocket and handed it to her. "Do you know how to . . ." He glanced over at her, his words trailing off as she expertly found the picture file and brought it to the full-screen view. "I guess succubi don't have an issue with cell phones?"

She grinned. "I don't have one myself. I always thought it would make me easier to track down, but that doesn't mean I'm not tech-savvy—or at least that I've hunted enough tech-savvy people to pick up a few things."

He laughed and wished she was back in her normal nonhunting form. It still disconcerted him to be attracted to her in this new form, although since she seemed to shift forms a lot, he might have to get used to it for the duration of this assignment.

She stiffened in her chair. "Wow. No wonder Uriel was pissed. Now I'm surprised he stayed long enough to give us passage to his place."

"Why?" Noah changed lanes and took the interchange to the freeway that would take them toward Yuma, Arizona, and the portal to Lilith's lair.

"*Har magiddô.*"

"Armageddon?" A cold chill settled firmly in the pit of Noah's stomach and he grabbed the phone out of her hand and scanned the picture. "I would've recognized a reference to that. Where do you see that on here?"

A honking horn made Noah snap his gaze back on the road in time to swerve the truck back into his own lane.

She grabbed the phone back from him and pointed toward the road. "You pay attention and don't get your research panties all in a twist. This discussion will become moot if we're both dead." She watched him pointedly until he stared straight forward toward the road. "It's the symbol that appears at the bottom of the page. It's not common knowledge to anyone in the human realm."

Noah remembered the intricate swirling design, but figured it was just decoration since he'd seen the same thing on every page. "So just having the symbol there says that anything written on those pages refers to Armageddon?"

She nodded. "The notation of the symbol classifies all of these as Armageddon prophesies. Or simply put, the things that need to come to pass in order to trigger the end of the human realm."

"Shit."

"Yup. Totally agree." She closed the picture and handed him back the phone. "Did you notice the style or age of the book binding on the journal you got this from?"

Noah frowned as he pictured the small journal inside his mind. "I'm guessing it can't be more than a few hundred years old. The handwriting was faded, especially around the edges and the leather cover was worn with time. But it was a modern binding style." He glanced over at her, careful to keep them on the road this time. "Why?"

"Armageddon is one of those prophesies that's triggered by certain information making its way into the human consciousness. Since this is a more recent book, Armageddon may not be too far off."

"Wait a minute, what about Revelation in the Bible? That's obviously been around for quite a while."

Jez laughed. "That's actually a long poem about a dream one of the prophets had about the end of the world." She flipped her dark hair back over her shoulder. "Lots of metaphors and imagery that can be used to mean many things, but it was more a work of literary masterpiece of the time than a handbook to the end of the world." She spread her hands in front of her. "I wouldn't be surprised if the author got some of it right, after all, it was probably an inspired dream, but prophesy should stay hidden until it's needed for a reason."

"What reason?"

"Words and ideas have power. That's just the way the universe is built. If all the nuances of prophesy were made common knowledge, there are those who could twist it to their own purposes. In other words, bring about what was written in their own time frame and for their own purposes."

Noah barked out a laugh. "Sounds a lot like human politics."

"Only without the term limits. Just think of those same human politicians in office for eternity."

"Ouch." As the possibilities of that scenario spilled through his mind, he winced. He couldn't even begin to imagine what type of power trips those who held power for eternity started to build up, and he wasn't sure he wanted to.

Silence fell between them as Noah digested what she'd told him. He'd never thought much about the end of the world. Regardless if the reason was science or religion or both—he'd always figured he'd be long dead before that became an issue.

Now it looked like he'd been optimistic.

He glanced over at Jezebeth, who seemed lost inside her own thoughts. "If the human realm ends, what happens to the succubi? Are you stuck in Hell?"

She cocked her head to the side. "To be honest, I'm not really sure. The succubi and incubi are sort of the black sheep of the demonic realm. We aren't truly demons, we're descendants of Lilith, but not in the sense that she gave birth to us. After the fall of man, God created us as a family to Lilith, and also to help teach the humans about temptation and the responsibility that comes with free will. It's said we're descended from the triumvirate of those who inhabited the Garden."

Noah frowned as he remembered their earlier conversation about the Garden of Eden. "Do you mean you're all descendants of Adam, Eve, and Lilith?"

Jezebeth nodded once.

"How is that possible? People are descended from two parents, not three."

Jez smiled. "You're thinking in human terms. God can make anything possible, and did."

Noah whistled long and low as he let the ramifications of that information perk around inside his brain. Vague story ideas started to take shape inside his mind and he wished he wasn't driving so he could jot them all down before the wispy ideas floated away from him. "So what do we do now?"

Jezebeth frowned over at him. "You mean other than make it to Yuma as quickly as possible and get back to Lilith's lair?"

He shook his head and sent her a lopsided grin. "Yeah, besides that. If Armageddon really is looming, then aren't there bigger issues at play here?"

"Possibly. But Semiazas has been caged for seven hundred years on a several millennia sentence. I think his sense of revenge is going to win out even over the demon-jazzing subject of Armageddon."

"I never did ask you what exactly happened with that. I know you and your sisters helped put him away, but that's all I know."

Jezebeth sighed and ran her hand through her long hair, fixing him with an expression that Noah recognized from the movie *Van*

Helsing. "Semiazas started the Black Plague in the 1300s, and then used the fear and paranoia to expand the amount of souls who would go to Lucifer. We aren't sure if that was his overall goal, or if he was just enjoying wreaking havoc on the world, but he had to be stopped."

"I wouldn't think having mass deaths would be of too much interest to demons, even with the added soul factor. From my research it seems like they have more fun twisting events here in the human realm."

"True, but that would mean Semiazas thinks ahead, which he doesn't. If the plague was allowed to run unchecked the human population of the earth would've been seriously in danger. And as you said, can you imagine thousands of bored demons gallivanting around messing with the very small human population that would've been left? And even by the time all those souls chose a reincarnation, there has to be an age ratio within the population."

"Wait a second. Reincarnation?" Noah had always thought multiple chances made better sense than just one shot at life, but hearing it confirmed from within the framework of Heaven and Hell brought up too many questions to count.

"Yes. I know most humans who believe in God, Lucifer, Heaven, and Hell don't believe in reincarnation, but reality is more a hodgepodge of most of the religions combined. No one organized religion has gotten it all right, and there are several who didn't get anything right, unfortunately."

Noah blew out a long breath. "Wow, talk about a wasted incarnation if you're led to believe in all the wrong stuff."

Jezebeth shrugged, her near-Kate lips quirking up on one side. "Being led is only part of it. Every human is reincarnated with deepdown knowledge of the truth. It's fear that holds them back from recognizing it, and it's fear that most organized religions use to keep their followers in line. An incarnation is supposed to be used to learn and grow, but those who only know hate, fear, and bigotry don't end up doing much of either." She laughed. "And they call *us* the ultimate temptation. Succubi and incubi are pretty straightforward compared to all of that."

Noah knew it would take him a while to process all the ramifications of this new information, so he filed it away for another time. "So how did you guys stop him? Semiazas, I mean."

"It's a long story, but Lilith heard of the plot and asked us to go before Lucifer to present it. Due to where we all fall in the hierarchy of things, Lilith couldn't be seen moving against the demon directly, so she sent the four of us to petition Lucifer to stop Semiazas."

"Wait, so you've met Lucifer?" Unease made him tighten his fingers on the steering wheel. "Face-to-face?"

She nodded once. "It's not something I'd relish doing again, but it looks like I don't have much choice. If Semiazas finds us before we petition Lucifer for protection, let's just say an excruciating death would be preferable to whatever he has planned for us."

So just like in the human world, the worker bees got sacrificed in the name of the higher good. Sounded like a universal tenet. "Okay, I've got to ask. What's up with the whole nod once thing?"

A surprised look flowed across her near-Kate features and she pursed her lips. "To be honest I've never thought about it until now, but as far as I know all succubi and incubi nod only once, the same as Lilith. After all, she is our queen."

Noah chuckled. "So I've heard."

The ground quaked under the truck, the road bucking and shaking them as Noah swerved to try to stay on the road. Ahead of them, a fireball shot into the air like a giant firecracker had been set into the middle of the road. Smoke billowed up and out until a shape solidified, looking like a large gray genie straight out of the cartoons.

The thing laid a large hand on the hood, instantly stopping the forward motion of the truck and killing the engine.

Noah was thrown against the seat belt and felt like his head would snap off his neck from the sudden stop. He reached out for Jezebeth to make sure she was all right and his hand closed over hers in a tight grip.

Jez grabbed his backpack and thrust it into his hands as she fumbled to unhook her seat belt.

"Hello, little succubus." The voice seemed to come from everywhere and nowhere and sent a sharp tang of fear shooting through Noah and freezing Jezebeth midmotion.

"Shit." Jezebeth's husky near-Kate voice barely reached him, but he could only nod and agree with her sentiment.

11

Uriel materialized in the foyer of his house and immediately sensed the energy of other Archangels. Gabriel, Raphael, and . . . Michael?

He hadn't seen Michael in nearly five hundred years.

As the leader of the Archangels, Michael tended to only show up when something bad was going on, so either Raphael had summoned him or things were about to get a whole lot worse.

"Great. Another fun day." Uriel walked down the hallway through his spacious kitchen and out onto the patio where the three Archangels sat enjoying the hardwood deck that overlooked the flowing waterfall and lush gardens no matter where in the human realm his house appeared.

As Uriel closed the patio door behind him, Michael raised his glass in a mock salute. "Uriel. Come join us. We're drinking your wine, so you might as well."

Michael still looked the same, not that Uriel was surprised. Most Archangels retained the same human-type form, although they could instantly recognize each other in any form they took.

Michael stood an inch taller than Uriel's own six foot seven with mocha skin and the most piercing green eyes Uriel had ever seen. The combination tended to be both surprising and intimidating to most beings, which Uriel supposed was one of the reasons Michael preferred it.

Uriel accepted a glass from Gabriel and nodded at Raphael in greeting. "Welcome, Michael. It's been a long time."

Michael sipped his wine before setting the glass aside and facing Uriel. "It has. Which only means you've been staying out of trouble." He grinned, flashing even, white teeth.

Uriel took a seat between Raphael and Gabriel, directly across the table from Michael. "So are you here about what I found, or is there something else going on?"

"Let's just say that as usual, everything happens at once." He stretched out his long legs in front of him, crossing them at the ankles and threading his fingers together over his chest.

Uriel had always envied Michael his unshakable calm no matter what was going on around them. Even when Armageddon came, he expected to see Michael calmly stopping midbattle for some wine or an unhurried meal.

Raphael cleared his throat. "I hope you don't mind that I summoned him." He gestured to Michael with his glass. "Once Gabriel told me her news, I thought we might do this all at once. He's already up to speed on everything. We were just waiting on you before we discuss what we can do from here."

Uriel frowned, setting his own wineglass on the table next to Michael's. "Gabriel's news? What did I miss?"

Gabriel filled Uriel in about her conversation with Semiazas and the vision he'd seen involving the sword of Michael skewering Raphael, and then added the part about one of Lilith's succubi with her hands on the hilt.

Uriel's disbelief grew as he listened, and when Gabriel finished, he sat forward, taking her hand in his. "I can't believe you met with him. After everything that's happened, you can't possibly still believe Semiazas can be brought back, do you?"

She sighed and dropped his hand before leaning back in her chair. "I suppose I had hoped. But he was all about manipulation and getting what he wanted. And right now he wants those four succubi to the exclusion of all else, and I'm not sure why."

"You don't think revenge is enough of a motivator?" Michael asked quietly, but there was something in his tone that told Uriel he wasn't telling them everything. Which was typical Michael.

"No." Gabriel bit her lip as if trying to put her thoughts into words. "Don't get me wrong, he's all about revenge, but he has to know that Lilith and not the four succubi was truly behind his incarceration. Semiazas is many things, but stupid isn't one of them."

"So what's so special about these four succubi?" Uriel glanced at Raphael, then Gabriel before he asked the question he hoped would pry some information loose from Michael.

Michael smiled. "What indeed. All I can tell you is that my sword is safely with me at all times and I don't plan on using Raphael as a shish kebab anytime soon." He winked at Raphael. "Just don't tempt me too much, all right?"

Anger snapped through Uriel and he slammed his hand down on the table, making the glasses jump. "Damn it, Michael. We're not humans, you can drop the secretive bullshit and let us in on what's going on."

Michael's smile drained away, but his calm demeanor remained unruffled. "There are things that can't be known, or outcomes will be changed unnecessarily." Michael breathed deep and met each of their gazes in turn. "There are things I must know to be effective. But believe me, the knowledge is more of a burden than it is a blessing. Part of what I do is protect others, even all of you, from a wealth of knowledge that would be more harmful than helpful."

Uriel thought he saw a flash of pain and weariness in the piercing green eyes before Michael forced a smile. "All I can tell you is that as of right now, we must not interfere in the paths of those four succubi."

Raphael snorted. "Officially? Are you giving us a hands-off order?"

Michael shrugged. "No."

Silence fell as they waited for more elaboration from Michael. When none came, Uriel clenched his teeth.

He understood Michael's reasoning for being secretive and mysterious, but that didn't stop it from pissing him off. He sighed, glad he'd already given passage to his property to Jezebeth and Noah. Michael had said no interference from here forward, so Uriel hadn't violated any orders.

Uriel glanced up and his gaze locked with Michael's, the intense green gaze burning into his as if the other Archangel was trying to communicate something, but Uriel wasn't sure exactly what. He opened his mouth to ask when Michael glanced away and stood in a lazy, graceful motion. "But it would behoove us to find the other journals as quickly as possible. Even Lucifer agrees on this point."

Uriel frowned as he realized Michael had just admitted that he'd spoken to Lucifer—something they'd all suspected, but had never had confirmed until now. Michael and Lucifer had been best friends before the fall, and many had wondered how much of that continued even afterward.

A quick glance around the table showed Gabriel and Raphael were just as surprised as Uriel.

When Uriel glanced back toward Michael, the Archangel was gone.

* * *

Jez stared out the window at the giant gray Djinn and sighed. "Terrific. Him again."

"You know him?" Noah squeezed her hand and she returned the pressure, trying to offer reassurance she didn't feel. Djinn were hard to read, and she hadn't run into this one in centuries.

The Djinn smiled, his booming laugh sounding inside her head, as Djinn communication tended to. *"I'm flattered you remember me, little one. Who is this human you travel with?"*

Noah stiffened in his seat and Jez glanced at him willing him to remain silent until she could gauge the situation. "He's my guide. Tasked with getting me back to Lilith right away."

Careful to conceal her actions from the Djinn, she took Noah's cell phone off the seat where she'd left it, and with one hand typed a text that said, "Trust Me" and laid it on the seat for Noah to see. She just hoped she really knew what she was doing.

The Djinn's smile was only a hint of shadow in his smoky face. *"So I've heard. Semiazas is offering quite a bit to ensure that doesn't happen. I was lucky to recognize your energy signature and come out to investigate."*

"What do you want?" She mentally held her breath, waiting to see what the Djinn was after.

"What I've always wanted, Jezebeth." His voice had dropped to a silky whisper inside her skull, like a cat chin marking its territory. *"You."*

Jezebeth sighed and hoped he didn't sense that it was in relief rather than frustration. She'd avoided this Djinn for several centuries, but apparently her time had run out. "What are your terms?"

"Jezebeth," Noah hissed. "You can't mean to—"

Jez cut him off with an impatient gesture and tapped the cell phone with their joined hands. They could've run into a million other creatures who would kill them on the spot, but this was one they could survive the encounter with and possibly still make it to Yuma on time.

Noah glanced at the cell phone display and closed his mouth, but he didn't look happy.

The Djinn's large form rippled, giving Jez the impression of eagerness. *"One day with you changed into my current Djinn form."*

"I don't have a day." She crossed her arms over her chest and stared at him. "One hour."

He grinned like a child who knew he was about to receive a long-awaited toy.

The Djinn had fixated on her because she was the only shapeshifting succubus in existence. All the other beings who could change forms would have nothing to do with him, and until he completed his service—the Djinn equivalent of an internship into full Djinn warrior—no other Djinn would associate with him either. The Djinn valued strength and individual accomplishment. Jez had no idea why they thought thousands of years of alone time was character building, but it just made her glad succubi didn't share the same beliefs.

As for the Djinn, if he couldn't complete his service on his own, he wasn't considered worthy to join their ranks.

His form wavered as a breeze blew through him. *"Twelve hours."*

"Two hours." She shrugged. "I'm on a tight time frame here."

"Not my problem. You've turned me down for years, purely because you can't tap my energy and it wouldn't count toward your quota. Now I have something you want—safe passage—and it's going to cost you."

Jez thought back over the several times she turned down the Djinn—sometimes rather rudely, and hoped those past actions didn't end up biting her in the ass. He'd always seemed to find her when she was in the middle of something urgent. "If you kill me and collect the reward from Semiazas, even if he does hold up his end of that bargain, that means you'll have seven thousand more years of long, lonely service to complete with no hope of reprieve."

His brows pinched and a twinge of guilt wormed through her. She couldn't imagine spending a millennium cut off from her own kind, living out that time in solitude with only those humans or supernaturals who stumbled upon her prison to pass the time with. But that was the way of the Djinn.

"Three hours, and even that will put me in danger of not making it back to Lilith's lair on time. Which, if I don't do, will mean that same seven thousand years of lonely service for you."

His lips thinned into a hard line. "*Four hours. I'll accept no less, Jezebeth.*"

She studied him skeptically. "And afterward you'll let us go and forget you ever saw me?"

The Djinn nodded once and Noah rolled his eyes and huffed out a small breath. "Him too with the one nod thing?" He turned to her. "Jezebeth, you don't have to do this. We'll find another way."

Jez ignored Noah and concentrated on the Djinn. "And Noah will remain safe before, during, and after?"

The Djinn nodded once and Noah threw up his hands. Jez wasn't sure if it was because she continued to ignore him, or if it was because of the Djinn's nod.

"*He will have my extended protection. None will harm him or you during those four hours.*" The Djinn's smoky form floated closer. "*Although afterward, once you're beyond my range, I can't promise any protection.*"

"Fair enough," she said, short-circuiting Noah's attempted objection. "I accept your terms."

"Jeze—"

Noah's words were cut short when the world fuzzed out and then refocused. Jez shuddered as she let her molecules recover from the Djinn method of dematerialization. This was her first experience with it, and one she didn't look forward to repeating.

Her eyes slowly adjusted to the dim light that was able to filter into the cave where she currently sat on the cold, hard ground. She had excellent night vision, so suspected her body was still throwing off the effects of the travel. The walls were reddish brown and the tang of mold rode on the thick air.

Noah groaned from beside her, their fingers still twined. "What the hell was that?"

The Djinn's booming laugh echoed inside her skull. *"That's the Djinn method of travel, human."*

"Noah. My name is Noah," he croaked out as he pushed himself up to sit, leaving the backpack he'd been clutching when they transported lying at his feet.

Jezebeth smiled as warmth curled through her stomach, chasing back the cold from the cave as she squeezed Noah's hand.

She'd been a supernatural all her life and had endured being called succubus, whore, and an endless litany of other labels. By supernatural terms, Noah was even lower on the power totem pole than she was, and yet he stood up for himself each and every time someone called him by his species and not his name. He reminded her of one of her sisters.

"You've found an arrogant one, here, Jezebeth. Maybe I should remind him what his place is—"

"You promised safe passage for both of us before, during, and after," she reminded him.

The Djinn's features morphed giving Jez the impression of pouting. *"I wouldn't have hurt him, Jezebeth. I was just going to play with him a bit. It tends to get boring and lonely here."*

"I'm sitting right here." Noah pushed to standing and pulled Jezebeth up next to him. "There's no reason to talk about me in the third person."

Jezebeth smiled as Noah pulled her close in a protective gesture. She turned in his arms and laid her palm against his cheek not sure how much he knew about the Djinn. "I made a pact with him."

He sighed and nodded. "Since the penalty for breaking a Djinn pact is death, I know you have to go through with it." He glanced past her toward the towering Djinn. "I trust you. But I don't have to like it."

Jezebeth smiled and leaned forward to brush a kiss over his lips.

Before he could react to the kiss, she pulled back and turned to face the Djinn. "I'm ready." She concentrated on the large gray form of the being in front of her and within seconds, the familiar tingling that signaled her change flowed through her body.

Jez waited for her form to solidify, and then remembered that as a Djinn, that wasn't going to happen. She felt as if her body were in a zillion tiny parts, all her molecules constantly bumping against each other, but somehow loosely retaining a general form.

"Whoa!" Noah stumbled back away from her and she glanced down noting how tiny he was in relation to her current form.

"It's all right, Noah."

Noah bent over wincing, his hands over his ears. "Stop shouting!"

Jezebeth concentrated on a quiet whisper instead. *"Sorry."*

Noah cracked open one eyeball and glanced up at her before standing straight and facing her. "Better. You okay?"

She smiled and nodded once. *"Fine. We'll talk again in four hours."*

Noah frowned, his jaw clenched hard, but he returned her single nod.

Jez turned back toward the Djinn. *"So how do we do this?"*

Djinn didn't have sex until they were fully initiated, so unlike what Noah feared, that's not what the Djinn wanted from her.

"Just relax and trust me to keep my promise that I won't hurt you."

She resisted the urge to giggle. Jez couldn't count how many times she'd heard that in some form or another over the years when it *did* apply to sex.

The Djinn floated forward until the edges of their forms touched and then his molecules slid between hers, stretching them apart. A quick spurt of panic arrowed through her when her molecules stretched to accommodate, but she battled her fear back and forced herself to relax and just let it happen until they completely over-lapped.

When it was finished, their floating forms slowly sank until they pooled against the floor like two vaporous beanbags curled to-gether.

The Djinn sighed and relaxed against her—the Djinn form of cuddling and comfort, and something they were denied until initia-tion. Jezebeth had always thought it a cruel and unfair practice, and most likely what made the Djinn so vindictive and cruel, but then, they saw those as qualities of strength.

She reached out with her mind, wondering if it was true that Djinn could read each other's minds while merged. Her energy eas-ily reached inside the Djinn's mind, but she found only peaceful oblivion.

The damned Djinn was asleep!

She shook her head and smiled. She mentally shrugged as con-tentment slid through her making her eyelids droop as a heavy, languorous sensation crept over her.

"Jezebeth?"

Noah's soft question jarred her to alertness and she glanced down to find him staring up at her with concern and strain etched across his handsome features.

"*I'm here.*"

"What's going on?"

"*He's a child Djinn, and this is their way of comfort. In order for them to come of age, they have to spend a millennium alone and tethered to one location. He wanted some comfort and cuddling.*"

Confusion flashed across Noah's face. "So, he doesn't want sex?"

Jezebeth shook her head. "*No. Just this. He's asleep.*"

Noah blew out a long breath, his lips curving into a smile. "You scared me there. I'm glad you're okay, and I'm glad I'm not going to have to watch you have sex with someone else." He stiffened as if he realized what he'd said. "I mean, it would be weird to have to watch you have sex. You know . . ." He shrugged, not meeting her gaze as he ran his hand through his hair. "I'll be over here taking a nap when you're done."

"*Noah.*" When he glanced back at her, she smiled. "*You can lay on us. Djinn forms are very comfortable, and it'll save you from lying on the hard ground.*"

"I won't wake him, will I?" Noah's expression was dubious as he walked nearer and slowly reached out to press a hand against the bottom edge of the combined Djinn form as if he were testing the softness of a mattress.

She grinned. "*You can't hurt either one of us. The molecules will shift to accommodate your weight.*"

Noah climbed carefully onto them and Jez could sense him somewhere near her thigh as he relaxed onto his back. "Wow, this would be a great bed if there wasn't a volatile Djinn attached." He laughed.

"*For what it's worth, Noah, I don't think I'd be very comfortable watching you have sex with someone else either.*"

A blush crept up into Noah's neck and face and he nodded, but didn't turn to look up at her.

Jez wasn't sure what his reaction meant, but she knew then that if Noah ever was forced to watch her have sex with someone else, she wasn't sure *she* could go through with it.

Damn, Jezebeth. Get a grip, he's a human.

Her inner voice made sense, but she shoved it aside and concentrated on the comforting cocoon of warmth that filled her, the warm pressure from Noah, and the deep sleep that beckoned to her.

"Night, Jezebeth," was the last thing she heard from Noah as she drifted off to sleep.

12

As consciousness slowly filtered back to Noah, he noticed he was spooned against a very warm and very naked woman. He took stock and found he was still fully dressed.

A deep breath filled his lungs with the tantalizing pomegranate and honey scent that always clung to Jezebeth, and his cock hardened inside his jeans at the realization that it was her supple body that lay just in front of him.

Liquid warmth filled his chest as he listened to her deep, even breathing, and he allowed himself a few minutes to enjoy the wonderful sensation of being close to her.

When Jezebeth was awake he was constantly reminded that she was a succubus, but like this it was easy to imagine that she was just a woman. A very attractive, desirable woman who was a constant surprise, keeping him on his toes and never doing what he expected.

He smiled as she murmured in her sleep and shifted more comfortably against him. She pulled his arm tighter around her stomach and relaxed back with a deep sigh. Her soft hair against his face was like warm silk, and he rubbed his nose against the soft mass, breathing deep.

What was his big hang-up with her being a succubus anyway? It wasn't as if he'd ever cared that the women he dated were virgins or not. True, several millennia of sex with others, and not just humans, was probably part of what pricked at his pride. But if she didn't sleep with them, she'd die, so did his moral hang-ups really apply in this situation?

He sighed and enjoyed one more long moment of just holding her close, her comforting warmth seeping contentment into him with every slow breath.

Noah forced himself to open his eyes and chase back the last vestiges of sleep.

He found they were still inside the Djinn's cave lying on some type of soft mattress. No pillow sat beneath his head, but whatever they lay on was covered in purple satin.

He wasn't sure where the Djinn had gone, or if they were vulnerable to attack, regardless of the Djinn's promise. But he was reluctant to move and not only wake Jezebeth but end their time spooned together like this.

He decided to compromise. He'd look around, but before he did, he gave in to the urge to place a quick kiss against the back of Jezebeth's left shoulder. Her skin was silky and tempting against his lips, but he forced himself to pull back and not linger.

He sat up slowly, pulled his arm out from under her, careful not to jostle her.

She murmured again and then rolled onto her stomach, revealing the most perfect shapely ass Noah had ever seen. Her back was smooth and lean, her long, dark hair spilling around her as she leaned her cheek on her forearm. She looked like a beautiful sculpture come to life, and a sudden urge to kiss his way over every inch of exposed skin surged through him.

He tightened his hands into fists against the compulsion. He wasn't sure if she'd push him away or not, but he still wasn't entirely sure he wanted to find out. He still needed to work out his misgivings over her being a succubus before he started anything.

He swung his legs off the mattress, stood, and turned in a circle to look around him. The rust-red color of the walls was dimly lit by what appeared to be the glow of moonlight that filtered in from somewhere high above him. The cave seemed entirely empty except the queen-sized velvet purple mattress that sat in the middle of the floor with Jezebeth still sleeping soundly on top.

Something shimmered on the far side of the cavern, catching his attention, and he glanced at Jezebeth to make sure she was all right before he went to investigate. Her back rose and fell in even intervals and one hand was curled under her chin, a childlike gesture that made him smile.

He walked slowly toward the far wall alert for anything that might jump out at him. It was a bit too late to wish he'd thought to ask the Djinn to bring all their gear when it had whisked them out of the truck. Not that Noah had known what to expect then anyway.

He scanned the cave for anything out of place, but other than the shimmering near the far wall, everything seemed entirely normal. The closer he got in the murky darkness, the more the area looked like oil floating on water, but in midair.

He reached out to touch it and the form suddenly brightened, becoming the Djinn.

Startled, Noah jumped back and stumbled over the uneven floor. As he lost his balance, he reached back to cushion the blow as he fell, and braced himself for the impact of landing on his ass.

When no painful impact came, he glanced back to see the trailing tail of the Djinn wrapped around his feet to cushion his fall.

"Careful, human. I promised Jezebeth no harm would come to you within my territory."

Wary of the Djinn's jovial mood, Noah stood. "My name's Noah, not human. And thanks." He gestured toward the Djinn's tail. "What's your name by the way?"

The Djinn pulled his tail back as if he'd touched something hot. *"Why?"*

Noah held up his hands palm out. "I like to be called by my name and not my species, I just thought you might like the same thing."

The Djinn crossed large ephemeral arms over his chest and glowered down at Noah. *"Anyone who knows the true name of a Djinn may command him."*

"I apologize. I wasn't trying to gain any control over you." He cast around for some way around this particular rule. "How about if I give you a nickname? Would that name give me power over you?"

The Djinn pursed his lips and tapped one see-through finger against his bearded chin. *"No, I think it's only my true Djinn name that has power. What did you have in mind?"*

"How about Max? A nice, generic name. Easy to remember, and it would keep us from having to call you 'Djinn' all the time."

"Max." The Djinn tried out the name several times, saying it different ways until it rolled off his tongue in repetitions so fast that to Noah it sounded like a thousand voices speaking inside his head at once. Finally, the Djinn smiled, the area where his mouth would be was a large gaping hole that allowed Noah to see the wall behind the creature. *"Very well. You may call me Max."*

"Great." Noah nodded. "All right, Max. Can you tell me how

long we've been out and how Jezebeth and I ended up on that mattress back there?"

He nodded his large head once and Noah resisted the urge to make a comment. Didn't anyone in the supernatural community know how to nod more than once? He wasn't sure why that one mannerism irritated him, but it really did.

"When the agreed four hours was completed, Jezebeth was asleep, so I created the mattress and laid both you and her on it. Within a few minutes she'd changed back into her current form." He straightened to an even more impressive height. *"Djinn always keep their word, and I would not violate our time agreement, even though I was reluctant to finish."*

After waking up next to Jezebeth, Noah knew exactly how Max felt. "How long has it been since you've had Djinn companionship?"

Max's entire form rippled as if there were signal interference on a television. *"Nearly three thousand years."* His voice was quiet and pain-filled.

"Wow. I can't imagine being able to endure that. You're a much stronger creature than me."

"A Djinn warrior should use the millennium of solitude from our kind to contemplate how he can best be of service to our race." The words tripped off Max's tongue easily as if he were reciting something he memorized.

Noah wasn't sure what to say to that, so he tried to find something to take them on a different conversational path. "How long ago were the four hours Jezebeth agreed to complete?"

"Eight hours, twelve minutes, and forty-four seconds."

Noah grinned at the very specific answer. This guy would make a great character in one of his books. "Do you know what a writer is in the human realm?"

Max nodded once and Noah bit back his reaction. *"When I was phased with the succubus I saw inside her mind that you write stories to strike fear into others."*

Noah grinned. That was an interesting way of describing it. He'd have to remember to turn that into an author branding statement or byline. "Something like that, yes. I think a Djinn would make a fascinating character in one of my books, but I haven't done much in-depth research on your kind. Would you mind answering some questions?"

Max's ghostly lips curved and he sank down toward the floor giving the appearance of sitting.

"How can I be of service, Noah?"

* * *

Jezebeth woke to the soft sounds of Noah answering the Djinn's voice that whispered inside her mind. By the familiar way they were chatting, she imagined they'd been at it for some time.

"So what's with all the tales of Djinn and genies stuck in bottles? What's the real story with that?"

Booming laughter echoed inside her head, and she winced at the sudden increase in volume. *"It was only a story written to poke fun at a Djinn who had angered a storyteller. Unfortunately, the story caught on and became like a myth. Now no one believes the truth."*

Noah laughed. "Seriously? Talk about the power of the written word. Would you mind if I used that in a story?"

Jezebeth sat up, the soft mattress beneath her shifting with her as she moved. Noah and the Djinn stood near the far wall talking in hushed tones, which echoed back to her inside the cave—and inside her head, thanks to the Djinn.

The Djinn laughed at Noah's comment and reached out one diffuse hand to slap Noah on the back, nearly knocking him off his feet. *"Absolutely! Perhaps between us we can make the truth known once again, hu—Noah."*

"You know, Max, you're a very interesting being. Maybe once all this is done I can come back and we can talk some more?"

Jezebeth frowned and froze.

Max? How in the hell had Noah gotten the Djinn to reveal his true name, and more important, who had ever heard of a Djinn warrior named Max?

"I would enjoy that . . . Noah. I would just ask that you not tell anyone anything besides that I captured the two of you to entertain myself for a while. Djinn in seclusion are not allowed to fraternize for pleasure of any type."

Jezebeth held her breath, afraid Noah would question the Djinn beliefs, which would be tantamount to an insult of epic proportions.

"No worries, Max. You did capture us, remember?" Noah patted the Djinn's arm, laughing when his hand pressed halfway into the arm before stopping. "After all, we both have reputations to keep up, right?"

A booming laugh echoed inside her head like a rubber pinball on overdrive, and Jez winced until the sound finally died away.

"Jezebeth."

She glanced up to find Noah watching her, his stormy gray gaze like a physical touch against her skin.

Awareness sizzled between them, tightening her nipples and sending a rush of silky moisture between her thighs until she realized she was still naked and he was fully clothed. For some reason that made the tension ratchet even higher.

She concentrated and clothed herself in jeans, a comfy cotton pullover, and a light sweater to protect against the chill of the cave that she hadn't noticed until just now.

"I thank you for your company, Noah. And you, Jezebeth, for honoring our bargain."

She knew the Djinn hadn't meant to imply that succubi didn't honor their bargains, but that in his own way he was thanking her for the comfort those four hours provided. Jezebeth smiled. His words had softened but not alleviated the tension that had sprung up between her and Noah. "I can see why Djinn would crave such a thing. I don't think I've ever experienced anything quite so comforting."

A knowing chuckle tickled inside her brain. *"If I'm not mistaken, the comfort you and Noah shared when our time was done looked no less comforting than the Djinn way of things."* His form rippled with his amusement.

A blush flowed up Noah's neck and into his cheeks, something she could only see because of her succubus night vision.

Jezebeth didn't remember returning to her favored form during the night, or even ending her four hours as a Djinn. Disappointment filled her that she also didn't remember cuddling with Noah. She strongly suspected it was an experience she would've enjoyed.

Noah cleared his throat. "Glad you're awake. Max can take us back to the truck whenever you're ready."

"I must scout the area first to ensure your safety when I return you. I'll return soon." The Djinn vanished leaving her and Noah alone, the tension flooding back like a tidal wave.

"How long have we been asleep?" she ventured when she couldn't think of anything else to say.

Noah laughed, but the sound was strained, a reminder of the sudden awkwardness between them. "Don't ask Max—he'll give it to you down to the second—but over twelve hours since you turned into a Djinn."

She swung her legs off the mattress and stood to walk toward Noah. "Max?"

Noah shrugged, a self-conscious grin pulling at the sides of his lips. "He said he couldn't give me his real name because that would give me power over him, but he let me give him a nickname."

Amusement spilled through Jezebeth. Leave it to Noah to find a way around that barrier and get himself on a first-name basis with a soon-to-be-powerful Djinn warrior. "So you named him Max? I like it." Her gaze locked with his for a long, sizzling moment, and she dropped it deliberately, not sure what to do next other than change the subject. "I should've offered comfort to Max long ago. I always seemed to be too busy, and he's right, I wouldn't have gotten any energy out of it, and it wouldn't help me meet my quota, so I always blew him off. It seems pretty selfish now."

Noah placed his index finger under her chin and tipped her face up until their gazes locked again. His eyes were a dark, swirling gray with tiny blue flecks in them and Jez felt like she was falling inside them the longer she stared.

"Don't beat yourself up, Jezebeth. He needed you now, and you were here." Noah smiled and she couldn't resist reaching out to brush her fingers lightly over the slight stubble that had grown on his cheeks.

He stilled as she touched him, but kept his finger under her chin as he leaned forward, slowly closing the distance between them until he hovered just a hairsbreadth away from her lips as if giving her time to pull back.

Jezebeth held her breath as heat and anticipation curled inside her.

This was the first time she'd ever craved for someone to kiss her, not because of how much energy she'd receive from the contact, but purely because she wanted to know how Noah's lips would feel against hers and how he would taste. She wanted this connection because Noah would be the one she was kissing.

His lips were firm and warm, and she opened for him. He took his time, slowly delving inside her mouth as if she were a delicacy to be savored. He didn't touch her beyond his index finger under her chin and their lips, but Jezebeth felt like he held her tighter than she'd ever been held before.

She gave herself up to the slow exploration of the kiss, reveling in the new and wondrous sensations swirling inside her. Her arms hung limp at her sides, and she wasn't sure if they would even respond to her demands at this point.

What seemed like a languorous eternity later, Noah pulled back from the kiss, but remained so close she could feel his warm breath feathering against her lips.

Her eyes remained closed as she struggled to find firm footing in a suddenly shifting world. She was definitely aroused, which was nothing new to her, but there was more. Much more. Liquid warmth curled through her veins and she opened her eyes to prove to herself she hadn't dreamed the entire episode.

Noah's storm-cloud gray gaze searched hers and she smiled. "Wow." The word was said on a soft sigh, and Noah huffed out what sounded like a relieved breath before he pulled her against him and captured her lips again.

"My apologies for interrupting, but there's a problem."

Jez gathered reality back around her as she tried to distance herself from the lingering effects of Noah's kiss. "What's wrong, Max?"

The Djinn scowled. *"There are demons stationed around your transportation."*

"Damn. All the supplies are there too." Noah pinched the bridge of his nose and paced away and back as if it helped him think.

Jez cocked her head to the side and studied Max. "How far away from the truck can you drop us?"

"Five hundred point six miles."

Jezebeth shook her head as frustration spilled through her. "And we only have one more day until the location of Uriel's house moves to Greece."

Noah laid a comforting hand on her arm. "We'll figure it out."

13

Lilith stepped inside Uriel's large brick three-story and, not bothering to close the front door, hurried up the steps to find the elusive Archangel. She rounded the corner of the hallway and stepped inside his room just as he walked out of the bathroom.

He stood gloriously naked, drying his long multicolored hair with a black towel.

She sucked in an involuntary breath as she drank in the sight of his bronzed body—his broad shoulders, the smooth hairless chest, trim hips, and muscled thighs . . . and especially the large cock that lay limp against his thigh.

"Lilith." He froze for a long moment before he shook out the towel and wrapped it around his hips, tucking it together, which did nothing to hide his sudden erection. "I apologize. I didn't realize you required more sustenance already. I'm usually more attuned to your needs."

Lilith resisted the urge to snort at his blatantly false statement and instead met his gaze in challenge. "If that were true you wouldn't have materialized out of my chambers without telling me anything at all."

He dropped his gaze, as if unable to look at her as he spoke. "I had urgent business. I apologize for upsetting you."

"Don't give me that bullshit, Uriel." When he didn't move, she stepped forward, edging into his personal space. "Look at me, damn it."

Uriel raised his swirling silver gaze to hers, but his eyes were shuttered, his expression a mask.

"Tell me what was in the journal."

He studied her for such a long time, she thought he was refusing to answer her, so when he spoke, his soft words surprised her. "I ask for your trust and your discretion, Lilith."

She stepped back and took a seat on his black leather couch, toeing off her shoes and tucking her feet beneath her. "You have both." When he raised his brows she added, "Regardless of our disagreement over the state of our relationship, Uriel, you always have my trust. And I have always kept your secrets."

He smiled as he pulled a black silk robe from his closet and slipped it on, dropping the towel only after he'd tied the robe. "You speak as if I've had many secrets."

It was her turn to raise her brows. "You may think I don't know any, Uriel, but you forget how my kind survives. My succubi and incubi are privy to all types of information that finds its way back to me."

Uriel paused on his way toward the couch where she sat. "I suppose I've been naïve to think you're so sheltered in your life, Lilith. I think our relationship will always be colored by how we met." He slowly lowered himself onto the other end of the couch and draped his arm along the back.

"The journal?" she reminded him.

He nodded. "There are apparently four journals in circulation—

well, three other than the one I have—that contain the prophesies for *Har məgiddô*."

A heavy lead weight settled inside Lilith's stomach. "Is the time at hand? Or is this someone trying to jump-start the end?"

"The time is not of His choosing, according to Michael, so this is most likely someone else trying to hasten the end."

"Lucifer?"

He shook his head. "Lucifer has the most to lose by bringing on Armageddon, no matter what stories all the humans have concocted. If there is no world, there is no playground for the fallen ones and all their minions since they aren't welcome in Heaven."

Jezebeth winced as he reminded her that not only wasn't she welcome in Heaven, she wasn't even welcome among the rest of those who weren't welcome either.

He reached out and laid a large, warm hand on her knee. "Lilith, I'm sorry. I always seem to say the wrong thing around you. It's always been so."

She thought back to how he'd treated her after he'd refused to kill her when he'd expelled her from the Garden on God's orders. He'd been polite and gruff, and it had taken him several thousand years to even be able to look her in the eye when speaking to her. Him—an Archangel who was a warrior for God. She smiled at the memory. "Take my word for it, you've improved with time."

One side of his lips quirked, but that was the only sign of amusement he showed. "You haven't asked me why my letters to you would be included in prophesies regarding the end of the human realm."

His words were like a punch to the solar plexus, and she caught her breath as a thousand possibilities, all more horrible than the last spilled through her mind at high speed. "Tell me," she finally managed on a strangled whisper.

"Apparently the succubi are instrumental in these end prophesies. We aren't sure how yet without finding the other four jour-nals, but so far they seem to center around the four sisters who helped you cage Semiazas."

Lilith waited for surprise or even fear, but somewhere inside her gut, she'd apparently known the incident with Semiazas would come back to haunt her. The politics of the nonhuman realm were always fraught with pitfalls and were never what they seemed for long. "I've sent messengers and guides to bring all four of them home, so they can petition Lucifer to re-imprison Semiazas."

"I know. And so does everyone else."

Lilith frowned as anger and a protective spurt of fear sizzled through her. "No one is supposed to know. I can't be seen as helping them." She huffed out a breath and raised her gaze to his. "Can *you* help them?"

Uriel's face remained a mask. "I am forbidden, not officially, but I've been warned to not interfere with their paths. Whatever hap-pens with the succubi has to play itself out as it is meant to or we risk changing what is supposed to be."

Not only were the succubi and incubi like Lilith's children, they were also an extension of her and helped maintain her energy and her power. Even losing one would physically and powerfully hurt Lilith. Losing four—especially four of the original succubi created—would lessen Lilith's energy flow and require her to seek out Uriel's sessions even more often than she did now.

Frustration, sadness, loss, and grief swelled up inside her, threat-ening to overwhelm her. The nearly weekly sessions were always torture, and especially after the last one with Raphael and Gabriel, she didn't expect them to get any easier.

Uriel surprised her by pulling her forward into his arms and gently laying her head on his shoulder.

She sank into his offered comfort and let her tears flow.

"It's all right, *nassah*. I'm here. I've sworn to care for you, and I always shall." He rocked her softly, rubbing her back as he spoke nonsense in low, soothing tones until her tears were gone.

Finally, Lilith sighed against him, feeling empty and broken. The tears hadn't helped the situation, and she definitely didn't feel any better. It seemed so unfair that God had created her specifically as temptation for Adam and Eve, and yet it felt like she was continually being punished for fulfilling that very role.

Uriel brushed her hair back away from her face and gently wiped the tears from under her eyes with his thumbs. "You're low on energy, *nassah*. Let me summon someone for you. What do you wish?"

When she stared into his silver eyes she felt nothing but a heavy ache inside her.

"Raphael?"

Lilith thought about the threesome she'd had with Raphael and Gabriel and imagined Uriel watching the scene again. She cringed. "I'm sorry I hurt you, *ahuvi*." She laid her palm against his smooth-shaven jaw and brushed her thumb lightly back and forth over the warm skin. "Can you summon Gabriel to meet me at my quarters?"

He pulled back as if she'd slapped him. "Only Gabriel?" he asked slowly. "You don't wish me there?"

She sniffed back the last of her tears and stood. "I must maintain energy or die, but I don't have to continue causing us both pain in the process. I'll work out an arrangement with Gabriel long term."

A myriad of emotions flowed across Uriel's features including confusion, hurt, pain, and even panic. He began to speak and she silenced him by laying her fingers over his lips.

"Please, *ahuvi*. I can't bear this between us anymore." Lilith savored the feel of his soft lips just under her fingers and then forced herself to drop her hand.

She wanted to tell him she loved him and beg him not to let her make this decision for the both of them. She wanted him to argue and tell her he would never let himself be cut off from her. But instead, she stepped away from him.

"Good-bye, Uriel." As soon as the words slipped past her lips, she turned and ran.

* * *

As soon as Lilith rematerialized inside her chambers she realized she'd forgotten her shoes back at Uriel's house. She sighed and dropped her cloak onto the ground at her feet. "Evelin!"

The girl rushed inside Lilith's quarters smelling faintly of burnt cinnamon and dropped to her knees in front of Lilith.

Lilith waved impatiently, irritated at the show of supplication when her life was falling apart around her. "Get up," she snapped.

Evelin rose to her full height, which fell several inches short of Lilith's own five foot nine. The girl had milk-pale skin and long red hair—the coloring of her home country of Ireland. The soft lilt in her voice had faded over the centuries, but she was still as lovely as the first day Lilith had seen her.

Evelin kept her gaze down and nodded once, waiting for further directions from Lilith.

"Who has had access to my marble trunk, now, or in the past?"

Evelin raised her intelligent green gaze to Lilith's. "Other than yourself, my queen, me, Lord Uriel, Xander, or the cleaning servants." She paused and then quickly added, "Or anyone else you have invited in."

Lilith sighed. She'd restricted access to her personal chambers and very few of her subjects had ever set foot inside—but there had been a few, including the four succubi sisters who were now firmly embroiled in Armageddon prophesies.

She sighed. She'd have to be more careful about who entered her quarters from now on.

"Until further notice, no one enters my quarters unless I accompany them. That includes the cleaning servants. They can clean while I'm here from now on." An inconvenience, but better than ending the existence of her kind because she couldn't keep her personal items hidden.

A stray thought that she should destroy Uriel's letters flashed across her mind, but she shoved it away. If she was never to be with Uriel again, then the letters were all she had to remember him by.

Evelin dropped her gaze and nodded once, but not before Lilith saw the girl wince. She took her position seriously and would most likely see this as a sign that Lilith didn't trust her. Over the centuries, Evelin had proved more than trustworthy, but with recent events Lilith wasn't in the mood to trust anyone right now.

"Is there anything else you require, my queen?" The girl's voice was pleasant as always, showing no sign of her thoughts about Lilith's sudden announcement.

"No. Leave me. I'm not to be disturbed."

"Yes, my queen." Evelin's gaze remained glued to the ground as she retreated out the door, never turning her back on Lilith—a silly tradition the girl had picked up from human royalty.

When she was gone, Lilith stripped off her dress and tossed it aside as she headed for the large hot spring that sat in the corner of her quarters. She'd heard human women took hot baths when life became too strong. In this, Lilith had to agree with them—things usually looked better after a long soak in the hot springs.

She twisted her long hair into a quick knot and fastened it on top of her head with a clip she kept near the spring for just this purpose. With a sigh, she stepped down into the hot, swirling water and immediately sank to her neck with a hiss and then a long sigh as her body adjusted to the sudden change in temperature.

"Apparently being queen has its perks."

Lilith's head snapped up at the sound of Gabriel's soft voice. The woman stood just at the edge of the spring, her long, silver blond hair spilling around her, making her look every bit the powerful Archangel she was.

"Uriel said you wished to see me. I hope I'm not intruding?"

Lilith raked her gaze over the Archangel's supple body and a zing of arousal surged through her. Maybe this arrangement wouldn't be so bad, especially if Uriel wasn't watching—a constant reminder of what she couldn't have. "Would you like to join me? I actually have a proposition to discuss with you."

Gabriel smiled, her ice blue eyes sparkling with amusement and curiosity. Without answering, she unbuttoned her white fitted shirt, peeled it off, and dropped it to the floor next to Lilith's dress. Her peach-colored nipples puckered as the cool air hit them, and Lilith traced an appreciative gaze over the woman's full breasts, smooth skin, and trim waist.

Next, the Archangel toed off her shoes and stripped off her pants to reveal a tiny white, lace thong that she slid down her trim hips and dropped on top of the pile of clothes before stepping forward into the churning water. "Mmm, I don't know what it is about hot water, but it's one of my favorite vices." Gabriel lowered herself into the water until she was completely submerged and then surfaced with a laugh as she wiped water out of her eyes.

Lilith sat on the smoothed ledge that ran underwater around the back edge of the spring where it flowed inside her quarters. "I know exactly what you mean. I spend a lot of time in here. Especially after my visits to Uriel." Bittersweet memories flowed back to her, tightening her throat with so many emotions she gave up trying to name them all.

Gabriel watched her quietly for a long moment. "Uriel chose these caverns for your lair, didn't he?"

Lilith swallowed back her emotions. "Yes. After the Garden he wasn't sure what to do with me, so he found this place." She glanced around, remembering the first time she'd stepped inside her quarters and seen all the thought Uriel had put into making sure she was happy.

"And he petitioned God to create followers for you so you would have a family of sorts, didn't he?" There was no judgment in Gabriel's voice, her words were matter of fact. "And when certain humans were found to have a bent for temptation, didn't Uriel find a way for you to convert them into succubi or incubi, extending their lives and expanding your family?"

Lilith sighed and looked at Gabriel with new appreciation. She'd not had much cause for interaction with God's anointed messenger over the centuries—Gabriel usually delivered the message and then let the other angels take over during the implementation phases. But Gabriel was proving to not only be beautiful and smart but very intuitive as well as a good listener.

"True," Lilith finally agreed.

Gabriel met Lilith's gaze so intently that Lilith expected vertigo to slap at her as the Archangel looked inside her soul, but the intense gaze remained solid and ice blue. "Uriel may not be able to act on it, but he does care for you deeply."

A small, bitter laugh escaped and Lilith closed her eyes for a long moment. "I have no doubts he cares for me." She brushed away a tendril of long hair that had fallen out of her clip to dangle over her right eye. "It just gets frustrating that he's found a way for me to be with pretty much everyone but him."

"As odd as it sounds, he's following the rules we're all subject to." Gabriel spread her hands wide. "But sometimes it does feel as if the people we truly want to be with are the only ones we can't. Free will takes a part on both sides, even for the Archangels, but sometimes I do wonder if it's part of God's plan to test our endurance and ability to adapt." The expression on Gabriel's face made Lilith wonder who the Archangel had loved and lost.

A long silence of understanding fell between them as the hot waters swirled around them.

"Sometimes I envy the humans."

Gabriel's soft words surprised Lilith. "But you're a powerful Archangel. You're the messenger for God. You're immortal. How can you envy them?" Lilith had envied them often enough for their ability to love whom they pleased without edicts from God to the contrary. But she'd figured that was because even as Queen of the Succubi, she was very low on the supernatural totem pole. In God's esteem, humans were actually on top.

"I envy them their mortality." Gabriel's ice blue gaze slid to Lilith's. "After all, they only endure their pain for the span of a human lifetime, but you and I will endure this theoretically forever."

Lilith hadn't ever thought about it quite in those terms. But presented like that, she had to agree. "And to think they probably envy us our longevity."

Gabriel pursed her lips. "Don't get me wrong, I enjoy quite a few parts of being immortal, as I'm sure you do too." She tipped her chin to the side, a knowing smile curving her lips. "Now what did you want to discuss with me?"

Lilith chuckled. "I nearly forgot that's why I asked you here."

A slow grin spread across Gabriel's face, making her look like a mischievous pixie.

"What?"

"I think we're actually becoming friends." Gabriel grinned. "I don't think I've ever had a friend outside of the Archangels, and they're more like family."

Lilith liked the idea of having a friend. She'd had companions, servants, followers, lovers, and many other things, but in her long life she'd never had someone she considered a friend.

Not even Uriel—especially not Uriel.

What would it be like to have someone to call when things weren't going right, or she just wanted to talk or not be alone? And not because the other being wanted favor in her eyes, but just because they enjoyed her company? Yes, having a friend sounded like a wonderful and novel experience. "I think I'd like that."

Gabriel skimmed her fingers across the top of the swirling water. "So will that interfere with what you were going to ask me?"

Lilith considered for a long moment. "I don't think so." She sat up straighter, the line of churning water bubbling around the tops of her breasts. "Would you be willing to provide me with sustenance on a regular basis?" The words sounded so formal and contractual after their previous discussion, but she wasn't sure how to ask other than outright.

"Just you and I, without Uriel or Raphael?"

Lilith tensed, not realizing until now how much she wanted Gabriel to accept her offer. "Yes, just you and I. I . . . think it will hurt less if Uriel isn't always watching. And it will hurt him less as well."

Gabriel moved forward until she was just inches away from Lilith, the Archangel's pale breasts bobbing gently as the fast-moving water teased the tempting flesh. "Are you sure about this? My offer of friendship will still stand if you change your mind at any time on this point."

The warm words teased against Lilith's senses and she found her gaze drawn to Gabriel's shapely lips. She thought about all the millennia of meeting with Uriel every time she needed energy—the longing for him, the disappointment, and the aching emptiness that always consumed her for up to several days after she left him.

Even the overwhelming joy she'd experienced that one brief

night in Uriel's arms was followed by an endless litany of painful heartbreak. She took a long, slow breath as she met Gabriel's patient gaze. "I'm sure. It's time for me to start standing on my own, making my own choices that aren't fallout from Uriel's guilt."

Gabriel's lips curved and she came forward to kneel between Lilith's thighs, her breasts brushing against Lilith's and sending arousal and energy sparking through her. "To a fresh start and a fresh friendship." She reached up to lay her palm against Lilith's cheek; the sensation of the wet, hot flesh against hers sent a shudder through her.

Lilith enjoyed the anticipation that curled inside her as Gabriel slowly closed the distance between them until the Archangel brushed her lips across Lilith's in a gentle caress. The cool lemony taste that was unique to Gabriel combined with a scent that reminded Lilith of the fresh, crisp smell after a snowstorm filled Lilith's senses, and she sank into the kiss.

She parted her lips as she reached out to pull Gabriel closer so they were breast to breast and mons to mons.

Energy immediately sparked between them and flowed into Lilith in a steady stream, her body regenerating with the strength of the power it fed off of. Within seconds she was fully sated.

She expected a hard slap of arousal, but instead, comfort and contentment curled through her like bright rays of sunshine thawing places inside her she hadn't realized were frozen.

Gabriel skimmed her fingers down Lilith's back to caress the sensitive skin at the top swell of Lilith's ass.

Lilith slowly ended the kiss and pulled back on a long sigh. "Would you like to stay the night? Not necessarily for sex, but just to spend time together and to fall asleep together?"

Gabriel brushed a gentle kiss across Lilith's lips before pulling back with a smile. "I haven't slept in centuries. I think I'd love it."

14

Noah took a deep breath, pulled his backpack over his shoulder, and nodded to Jezebeth and Max that he was ready, even if he still didn't entirely understand the plan they'd hurriedly discussed and decided on. Unfortunately, they both had more supernatural experience than him, so he'd deferred to their combined experience.

Jezebeth's form diffused back into a Djinn and she slowly floated forward to surround Noah like a large blanket. He had a long moment of panic as he became accustomed to the sensation and weight of her, and then as he sensed her familiar energy, he relaxed.

"I'm okay," he only partially lied. "Ready for stage two."

Just as they'd discussed, Max rose into the air and slowly edged downward through Jezebeth's head, neck, shoulders, and torso to merge with her, careful not to merge inside Noah since the human body couldn't survive that type of joining.

Noah clenched his fists against the first stirrings of claustrophobia and hoped they could complete this quickly. "Damn, this is like being inside a thick vat of humidity." Noah's words were muffled and he sensed rather than heard grunts of agreement from Jez and Max.

"*Hold on,*" Max's voice warned inside his head just as the world tipped sideways and Noah's stomach threatened to permanently lodge inside his throat.

Noah swallowed hard and fought not to throw up inside his suit of two large Djinn as they materialized next to what was left of the truck.

In the soft light of the full moon he could make out that the charred frame had what appeared to be bite marks out of it in several places, and the only sign of their supplies were a few shredded scraps underfoot of what Noah thought might have once been his clothes. He hadn't expected much more than that once Max had told him the truck was surrounded, but he'd hoped to find at least something. It made him very glad Jez had shoved his backpack into his hands before Max had taken them.

An eerie silence surrounded them. No traffic noise, crickets, or even the sound of the light breeze that Noah saw flutter through the brush that edged the freeway reached him through the thick layer of Jezebeth and Max that covered him.

Just as Noah had decided that the area was deserted, dark shapes moved at the edges of his vision.

Several demons of all shapes and sizes rushed forward, most likely drawn by the scent of human and succubus, even overlaid as they were by Djinn.

The instinctive fear that was imprinted on each human's DNA scratched up Noah's spine as the demons advanced, and Noah prayed Jezebeth and Max knew what they were doing.

A loose circle of writhing bodies formed around them and still Max stayed frozen and quiet.

Finally after several tense minutes, a large specter demon that had no features and only looked like a large dark shadow stepped forward and reached out a hand toward them. "What have you got there, Djinn?" His voice was cajoling and reminded Noah of nails scratching over glass. "Are you willing to share?"

As soon as the specter touched Max, his dark hand sinking slowly inside the Djinn, other demons rushed forward. Never a species to trust that the first one there would share any of the prize, they pressed their hands inside Max's form to try to reach both Jezebeth and Noah.

Noah's heart began to race as a solid wall of demons pressed around them, all reaching for him, their claws inches away from his flesh, their eyes glowing in the darkness.

Just as claustrophobia and panic threatened to overwhelm him, the diffuse air around him solidified and growls and high-pitched squeals filled the air.

"Got you!" Max's echoing laughter rebounded inside Noah's head like a Ping-Pong ball as the vertigo threatened to rip him in two again.

A long minute later Noah found himself lying flat, his cheek pressed against the cold floor of the cave. Jezebeth crouched beside him with dark smudges under her eyes as she rubbed comforting circles over his back.

"Noah? Are you all right?"

He forced himself to nod and then sit up, even though his stomach roiled threateningly and he tasted the sharp tang of bile on the back of his tongue. "Did it work?"

Before she could answer, high keening squeals of anger sounded from the other side of the cave.

"You can't trap us here, Djinn! You've no right." Noah recognized the voice of the specter demon.

Max giggled, the sound echoing inside Noah's already aching head. *"I can and I have. I trapped you fairly and now you will all entertain me until I grow weary of you."*

"Semiazas is waiting for us to report back." The grating voice of the demon sounded pleading. "When we're missed he'll send others to find us."

"If you truly believe that you are anything other than disposable to Semiazas, then hold on to your hope, demon. But you and I both know you're my new plaything."

Noah opened his mouth to ask Jezebeth what they were going to do next when an even larger wrenching sensation buffeted him. When the world righted itself, Noah groaned and rolled over onto his back, sucking air into his lungs until he was sure he wouldn't lose his long-ago breakfast all over the first person he saw.

It took him a long moment to realize that the movement of the ground beneath him meant they were inside a vehicle of some sort, and not due to all the Djinn transports he'd had in the last fourteen hours messing with his perception.

"Noah?"

The exhaustion in Jez's voice was obvious and without thinking he pulled her down beside him and tucked her protectively against his side, her head on his shoulder. "I'm all right." He rested his chin on the top of her head; the pomegranate and honey scent of her filled his senses and brought a smile to his lips.

A comfortable silence fell between them, and Noah remembered waking up this morning with Jezebeth spooned against him. The feel of her in his arms spilled contentment through him, and he sighed into the sensation. "Where are we?"

"Not sure." Her words were heavy with exhaustion. "Max disappeared just after we all appeared here, so I think we edged outside of his territory."

"What's he going to do with all those demons?"

She made a sound of amusement deep in her throat as she laid her hand on his chest. "By Djinn law he has to be alone, but that doesn't count other beings he traps and uses as pets. Which, by the way, he could've done to us if Semiazas hadn't come gunning for him."

Noah leaned his cheek against her hair, enjoying the sensation of the silky mass against his face. "Or do you think he let us go because of the comfort you offered him?"

"Or the fact that you gave him a nickname?" she countered with a quick laugh.

He shrugged. "Could be either or both I suppose. Any idea which way we're headed?"

"No. Only that we're safe for now and we both need to rest and regroup."

He pulled back far enough to meet her gaze. "You're low on energy from all the shifting." The dark circles under her hazel eyes as well as the exhaustion inside them confirmed his suspicions before she spoke. He couldn't resist reaching out and gently tracing the soft skin under her eyes with his fingertip.

"I just need to sleep for a while, and then I can find someone to feed from once we stop." She yawned. "Some real food would be great too."

The thought of someone else kissing and touching Jezebeth tightened Noah's stomach, and before he could change his mind he leaned forward to brush his lips over hers. "I have all the energy you need." Territorial instincts he didn't know he had rose up inside him, and he knew the next time she needed energy, he'd gladly provide it.

Confusion darkened her hazel gaze, and she started to protest.

Noah smiled as he slowly captured her mouth. Pure male satisfaction surged through him as she slowly melted against him, her hand skimming up to his cheek as she returned his kiss.

A slow tingling flooded him and he had the impression that some of his energy was being slowly siphoned into Jezebeth. He waited for a sensation of vertigo or weakness, but when none came, he rolled them over, still supporting Jezebeth's head on his arm as he took his time exploring her mouth.

When he finally reluctantly pulled back, her eyes fluttered open, and she smiled up at him. The dark circles were gone leaving her skin smooth and unblemished, but she still looked sleepy. "Mmm. Can we do that again after a nap?"

Noah chuckled as he lay down beside her again and pulled her close. "Absolutely."

* * *

Semiazas materialized next to the gutted skeleton of the truck. The site was deserted, and not even small animals or insects made any sounds as he circled the site.

The stink of burning ozone sat heavy on the back of his tongue, and he scowled.

Djinn.

The damage to the truck was definitely from demons—various types from the differing damage left behind. But all those demons suddenly vanishing could definitely be explained by Djinn interference. They were quite secretive as to their territories, not to mention very suspicious of outsiders and extremely powerful.

They'd been around since before the creation of man and lived both on earth and in other realms, so humans had revered them throughout the ages. But if they thought they could meddle in Semiazas's business without repercussions, they'd find out very differently.

"Djinn!" Semiazas roared into the gathering sunlight. He circled, alert for the creature's appearance.

When a shimmer began to warp the air in front of him, Semiazas waited while the Djinn slowly materialized.

"I see another demon infesting my territory. Need to extermi-

nate more often." The large gray Djinn wavered in time with the booming laughter that echoed through Semiazas's head. From the power signature, this was a baby Djinn completing his seclusion. Still extremely powerful, the Djinn had always reminded Semiazas of baby rattlesnakes—even more dangerous than the fully grown models.

"I'm not just any demon, you bag of gas. I'm Semiazas. I've come for information on the succubus and the human."

The Djinn puffed up, his form expanding, most likely in response to both the insult and the commanding tone Semiazas had used while addressing him.

"*I have no use for a succubus or a human, especially now that I have several demon playthings to entertain me.*"

Semiazas couldn't care less about the loss of demons—they were easily replaced and very expendable—but making sure the Djinn feared him and his powers was mandatory. He wasn't sure if the Djinn had seen the succubus and human or not, and there was truly no way to force the information from him, so all that remained were two of Semiazas's favorite tools—trickery and manipulation. "You'll return my minions or I'll petition the Djinn council to extend your seclusion."

"*You should know better than most, demon spawn, that the Djinn care not about the affairs of those who revolted against God.*"

Semiazas laughed, getting into the role. "I know you've been out of touch, boy, but with Armageddon coming, the rules are changing rapidly."

A quick flicker of interest flashed across the Djinn's face before he leaned forward to leer in Semiazas's face. "*Petition all you like. Humans or no, the Djinn will thrive and survive as we always have. Take your bluff and begone.*"

Semiazas sneered as he tried to find a way to twist this situation to work for him. "When I find her, she's in for an eternity of torture as my personal pet. She and her sisters will service my every whim until the end of time."

Rich Djinn chuckling echoed inside Semiazas's head, making him wince. *"That will serve you right, demon. I can see Jezebeth spending every second of that eternity tormenting you and making you wish you'd been a wiser being."*

White-hot anger surged through Semiazas, and he reached for the Djinn only to have his fingers close on empty air, the taunting laughter still echoing inside his head.

* * *

Jezebeth woke when the truck they rode inside trundled over a cattle grate, the vibration and high-pitched grinding noise slicing through her until she gritted her teeth against the insistent noise.

She still lay on Noah's arm, curled close to his body.

Fast asleep, Noah's breathing was heavy and slow, and he reluctantly let go of her as she sat up to look around. Boxes and large crates were stacked and lashed to the walls around them, all the way up to the metal ceiling. She and Noah lay directly on the floor of the truck bed, which seemed to be made entirely of two-by-fours laid side by side and bolted to the metal frame of the truck. She must've been tired not to notice *that* last night.

When she stood and stretched, several vertebrae in her back popped in protest to the night spent on the hard wooden floor.

"Any idea where we are?"

At the sound of Noah's sleepy voice she glanced down at him and smiled. His sandy blond hair was tousled, and his sexy stubble had turned into the spiky beginnings of a beard. "Absolutely none. I just woke up."

The cheese grater sound that signaled the truck passing over another cattle grate vibrated through the car making Jez grit her teeth. "But I wish that would stop. I have to go to the bathroom, and I'm starving." She bit her tongue before she said "in more ways than one."

Jez still wasn't sure what had happened between her and Noah last night, but now wasn't the best time to explore it.

"We're slowing down." Noah's words ended just before the truck took a sharp turn and Jez was tossed to the side. He caught her before she landed on her ass, and she wound up on his lap as the truck stopped and the ignition was turned off.

Noah pushed Jez off his lap and scrambled up beside her. "Come on. Hide. We don't know who's gonna open that door." He gestured with his chin toward the back sliding door of the truck.

Jez wanted to argue. After all, she could become whatever the person facing her most wanted. But before she could say anything Noah pulled her behind a stack of crates, tucking her body close to the side of the truck. She assumed so he would be found first by whoever entered the truck.

While Jez appreciated the chivalry, she hated not being able to see around him. It made her feel vulnerable and out of control—two things she hated.

The sound of the cab door opening and footsteps through gravel told her there was no changing around at this point. No need to make a lot of noise and alert anyone to their presence before they had to. She held her breath to better hear any sounds coming from outside the truck.

Rattling at the back door of the truck made her squeeze Noah's arm in a death grip as tension and her fight or flight response pumped adrenaline through her system.

More footsteps on gravel sounded, but they moved away from the truck, plunging them in an eerie, tense silence.

When no other sounds came for several minutes, Noah slowly peeled Jez's death grip off his arm. "Think you can have shorter fingernails next time you take this form?"

With her gaze glued to the door and her ears attuned to any sound from outside, it took her a long moment to register what Noah had meant. "Sorry." She smiled self-consciously as she examined the deep crescents she'd left in the skin of his arm. "So what do we do now?"

Jez walked toward the inside back door of the truck and felt around the edges to see if she could find some type of release lever.

"There isn't one."

She glanced over her shoulder, but she didn't stop searching. "Why wouldn't there be? There's always some type of safety release, like when you get stuck in walk-in freezers."

Noah shook his head. "Actually, no. Not on these types of cargo trucks. They aren't built to hold people, just cargo."

"How do you know that?"

He shrugged, an irritatingly smug and all-too-adorable smile on his handsome face. "I'm a writer; I do research."

"So there's no way out until someone lets us out?" She smacked the door with her palm and turned to face him.

"Not sure. I just know there isn't a safety release on those types of doors, so maybe we can concentrate on something else." He blew out a long breath and scrubbed a hand over his stubbled cheeks. "Too bad they don't have Triple A service for succubi. We could just call someone for help."

Jezebeth frowned as something tickled at the edge of her memory. Something she'd read, recently. "Your phone!" She rushed forward. "Do you still have it?"

He nodded and fished it out of his pocket. "I was really just joking. Who are you going to try to call?"

Jezebeth took it from him and flipped through his pictures until she found the one from the *Har məgiddô* journal. She scanned down the page past the mention of Lilith and Uriel, filing away her curiosity about their relationship for later. Finally she found mention of Raphael. She'd seen the incantation before, but hadn't bothered reading it since she hadn't thought it relevant at the time.

She scanned the words, a flicker of hope spearing through her. She would owe the Archangel for summoning him, but if he could help them toward their goal in any way, the price would be worth whatever she had to do.

Her lips curved in a slow smile as she glanced up at Noah. "I think I've found us a way out."

"Which is?"

"Did you translate the part about summoning Raphael, the healer?"

Noah frowned and then understanding lit his stormy gray eyes. "Yeah. But after my experience with summoning Lilith I didn't want to press my luck."

Jezebeth grinned. "Well, then I'll press mine."

"Wait. What are the risks with this?" He laid a hand on her shoulder. "Doesn't it say you'll owe Raphael for his assistance? You have no idea what price you'll have to pay."

She nodded. "Nothing in the supernatural world is free, Noah. Nothing. I'm used to it."

He sighed. "I'm not. Maybe we should just wait until whoever is driving the truck comes back."

Her temper flashed and she paced away from him before turning back. "And how long should we wait? Until Uriel's house has moved to Greece? Until we starve to death back here?" A rising sense of panic slowly built inside her chest and moved up to constrict her throat. "Until Semiazas tracks me down and tortures me for eternity?" The last sentence was a thick whisper that brought tears to her eyes.

Noah stepped forward, and she stiffened against the fight and the arguments to come.

Instead, he surprised her by wrapping his arms around her and just holding her tight.

Jez stood in his embrace stiffly for a long moment before giving in to the seductive warmth of the comfort he offered and letting her hot tears flow silently down her cheeks as she wrapped her arms around him.

She hadn't realized how much she'd buried her fear of being found by Semiazas for all this time until just now.

Not only had she been separated from her sisters but she'd been mostly cut off from her kind for the last seven hundred years since Semiazas had been imprisoned. She hadn't even been able to return to Lilith's lair in all that time.

Semiazas was a powerful demon with many friends and connections before he was imprisoned by Lucifer, and just like powerful human criminals, his imprisonment didn't necessarily stop his reach.

She'd lived in fear for the better part of a millennium, and she was tired and ready for it to be over. After everything they'd gone through to make it this far, she wanted to make it to Yuma, step through to Lilith's lair, and deal with familiar problems like succubi/incubi infighting and squabbles. All the things she used to hate but found she missed once she could no longer go home.

When she'd cried herself out, she realized Noah was rubbing small circles on her back and murmuring soft nonsense words to her. Both inane and ridiculous in their own right—and the absolute most wonderful thing anyone had ever done for her.

She took a deep shuddering breath against Noah's chest and sniffed back the last of her tears.

Time to put the big girl panties on and deal with the situation, Jez.

"Are you all right?" Noah lifted her chin so her gaze met his and then gently wiped away her tears.

She nodded and stepped back, suddenly uncomfortable with the foreign sensation of having someone else to lean on. "I'm good. Sorry. Must still be tired."

The back door of the truck trundled open surprising them both and Noah shoved her behind him as bright light spilled into the truck to blind them for a long moment.

15

Noah raised his arm to block out the glare of the sun and give his eyes a chance to adjust so he could see who was on the other side of the truck door.

"What the hell?" The man's voice sounded angry and annoyed as Noah blinked and his features slowly came into view.

He was a middle-aged man with a large pot belly and small beady eyes. His dark hair was streaked with gray and cut so short to his scalp that it only accentuated his deeply lined face. He wore a blue-and-gray flannel shirt tucked into well-worn blue jeans.

As Noah scrambled for something brilliant to say to extricate them from this mess, the man's expression morphed to one of surprise and then a slow smile spread across his face.

"You look just like . . ."

Suspicion curled inside Noah's gut and he whirled to find Jezebeth in full Kate Beckinsale form behind him, complete with the boots and the tight-fitting outfit right out of *Van Helsing.*

Noah bit back the urge to both roll his eyes and groan. Were they destined to meet every man in the country whose fantasy woman was Kate Beckinsale?

"Hello." Jezebeth stepped past him in her new form and headed toward the door of the truck. "I'm really sorry to intrude. One of my mates locked us in here for a joke."

"Are you really . . ." He studied Jezebeth critically with a frown.

"Yes, sir," Jez said with a sexy British accent as she sat on the back edge of the truck, her legs dangling toward the ground as she held out her hand to shake.

The man stumbled forward to take Jezebeth's hand, his face a picture of adoration. "I'll be damned! The guys will never believe this."

"*I* don't believe this," Noah muttered under his breath as he hopped off the end of the truck to stand near Jezebeth. Jez's Kate form was definitely growing on him, but watching men slaver all over her was definitely bringing out his territorial instincts. "I'm Noah." He held out his hand to shake. "Can you tell us where we are?"

"Don," he said as he shook Noah's hand in a too-firm grip. "You guys must've really tied one on for them to be able to lock you up like that and me not notice. I haven't opened the back since Odessa." He glanced at Jez one more time, shaking his head in disbelief. "We're in Tucson."

Noah slowly blew out a breath at the confirmation that they were closer and not farther from their destination. He turned to grab his phone off the bed of the truck and glanced at the time display to find that it was nearly one P.M., which meant they had eleven hours to get to Yuma, assuming Uriel's house would switch over to Greece at midnight local time.

His Arizona geography was a bit rusty, but he guessed it was only a four- or five-hour drive to Yuma from here. But that assumed they'd evaded all the demons and other beasties gunning for Jezebeth along the way—which seemed unlikely.

There were way too many assumptions in those last few thoughts for Noah's comfort. Things to this point had been relatively easy, which scared him all on its own.

Jez cleared her throat. "I'm gonna run into the gas station and use the loo. I'll be right back." She winked at the man. "And then I'll give you an autograph for being so nice and not pressing charges for us being passed out in your truck."

Noah had almost forgotten Jezebeth had said she had to go to the restroom even before the truck had opened. He started forward to follow her when out of the corner of his eye he noticed Don's eye color ripple.

"Jez!" He darted forward and shoved Jezebeth out of the way as he whirled to face the man who was now convulsing, his arms held wide.

"Run," he said over his shoulder. When he didn't hear any footsteps, he cursed under his breath but kept his gaze on the man, whose eyes were now so black they looked like deep pits of tar.

"Hello, follower of Lilith." The gravelly voice that came from between the man's lips sent primal fear scurrying through Noah and he had to lock his knees to keep from running away as fast as he physically could.

His research had shown demons that could possess mortals weren't strong enough to have their own earthbound forms, but one of their abilities to help compensate for that weakness was the ability to cause unreasonable fear in mortals.

Since he knew it wasn't real, he forced himself to shove the fear aside, and he stood his ground even when the being turned its gaze on him.

"Human," it said with a sneer.

"Who the hell are you?" Jezebeth demanded in her Kate form as she tried to push past Noah. He held out his arm to prevent her from going around him.

"I'm the one who will be collecting a very lucrative reward from Semiazas for your capture." The demon shot forward so quickly, all Noah saw was a blur before his air supply was cut off as the demon's fingers closed around Noah's throat in a tight vise.

Noah barely had time to claw at the tight grip before he was lifted off the ground and found himself flying backward until he slammed against a nearby car. Pain shot through every inch of his body as bright silver flashes of light popped in his vision. He tried to blink back clarity as an evil laugh floated from the demon's lips and it advanced toward Jezebeth with slow steps.

Jezebeth crouched into a very competent-looking fighting stance, and fear coursed through Noah, goading him to shake off his disorientation and push himself off the ground. He lurched forward to stumble in between Jezebeth and the demon.

"Noah, stay out of this. You're hurt." The very American inflection of the words coming from Kate Beckinsale's mouth was a bit jarring, but Noah pushed it aside.

"Bite me, Kate." He scowled at the slurring of his own words and the demon grinned.

A sharp pain lanced through Noah's chest a split second before he found himself flying backward again to slam into the side of another car. Several loud cracking noises rang inside Noah's ears as pain lanced through his back and chest before he crumpled into a heap on the ground next to the front fender.

He opened his mouth to suck in a breath and nearly threw up as renewed pain spiraled through him.

After a few long moments, he figured out how to take short, shallow breaths so he could at least breathe.

He forced himself to turn his head to look for Jezebeth, ignoring the wrenching vertigo and the black dots that edged his vision as a result of the movement.

When his vision finally cleared he saw the demon shoot forward toward Jezebeth. She dove to the side to roll out of its path, hitting the gravel hard.

Jezebeth found her feet a split second before the demon grabbed her by the neck and lifted her off the ground until her feet dangled and kicked.

Noah tried to roll over, to make it to Jezebeth, but he ended up scooting only a few inches in the dirt as unconsciousness tried to close in.

"What the hell is goin' on? Put her down!"

Noah blinked and realized he'd blacked out for at least a few seconds. A group of men now stood ranged around the demon where it held Jez. They'd probably come out of the gas station behind them as their arms were full of beer and munchies.

When Noah glanced toward Jez, she was still in her Kate form, but with larger breasts and a low-cut top. Her gaze met his, and even though she showed only stubborn defiance in the face of being strangled by a demon, he had enough fear for the both of them.

"Stay out of this, boys." The gravelly voice of the demon cut through the crowd of men.

A few of them stepped back—most likely because of the wave of fear that had increased to neck-ruffling, gut-wrenching levels—but several set down their groceries and slowly advanced on the demon.

The leader looked like a linebacker, and he stepped forward, his hands out in front of him. "Look, man. Put her down and we can work this out."

Jez still clawed at the hand constricting around her throat, her feet kicking uselessly in the air. Noah tried again to force his body to move, but a slow numbness had set in as his body began to distance itself from the constant pain.

The demon's head snapped around to glare at the man who had stepped forward. "Stay clear of this, human. This one is mine."

"Human?" The man stopped, his brow furrowed as he stared at the demon. "Nice eyes there, sunshine. Borrowed a body, did ya?" He pointed a threatening finger at the demon. "I've seen this kind of thing on that show, *Supernatural*. Let the girl go."

Apparently the burly leader was sensitive. Noah wondered if the man had known that fact before now or not.

The demon's eyes narrowed. "This is your last warning before I kill you all." He shook Jezebeth like a rag doll. "So stand clear."

"Joe," the leader called over his shoulder. "Get salt and lots of—" His words were cut off when the demon's arm shot out to slam against the man's chest, tossing him backward as if he weighed nearly nothing.

The man's body slammed into the side of a semitruck parked near the car Noah lay in front of before he crumpled to the ground, totally still.

The sounds of the fight in progress reached Noah before his fuzzy brain could register that the rest of the men had attacked the demon.

One man crouched near the leader and rolled him over to lay his fingers against the large man's throat. He sighed with what Noah thought was relief.

Tiny granules of white flew everywhere like a sudden snowstorm, which only increased the sounds of the ongoing battle. Noah blew the tiny granules out of his face and tasted salt.

"Kosher salt," Noah forced out. "It has to be kosher."

Another man flew by to land in the dirt near Noah. His body

bounced a few times before he groaned and pushed himself back up to stumble back into the fight.

The friend who crouched near the leader shuffled over to Noah. "Are you all right, man?"

Jezebeth slid next to him as if she'd crouched in midrun; dirt and gravel sprayed against Noah's legs as she slid to a stop. Relief coursed through him that she was still alive. "Jezebeth . . ."

"Your phone. I need your phone." She laid a gentle hand against his cheek as she shoved her other hand into his front jeans pocket and pulled out his cell phone.

Noah tried to make sense of what she was doing, but his vision had slowly turned gray and he couldn't keep his eyes open.

Movement and the sound of Jezebeth's surprised cry made Noah force his eyes open in time to see the demon leaning over him, black eyes boring into his until he could no longer feel the hard-packed dirt underneath him.

* * *

Jezebeth completed the incantation to summon Raphael, dry pain scratching up her throat with each word. She swallowed hard, her throat still raw and aching from the death grip the demon had had on her.

Movement in front of her made her snap her head up, just in time to be batted to the side by the oncoming demon. Pain lanced along her side and Noah's phone flew from her hand as she landed hard on her back. Dust puffed up around her to choke her as she tried to suck in a breath.

She rolled over in time to see the demon loom over Noah a split second before they both disappeared.

"Noah!" She scurried on all fours over to the spot Noah had just been as panic clawed up her throat.

A small glimmer began in the air in front of her and she swallowed a sob. She would have time for reaction later, right now was about finding Noah and getting them both safely to Lilith's lair.

The glimmer in the air reminded her of a diamond catching the light, but then it grew and morphed into a blazing glow until Jez had to shield her eyes and turn away.

She huddled over the empty spot where Noah had lain, waiting for Raphael to materialize—too late to save Noah. Hot tears welled and spilled down her cheeks at the unfairness of the situation even though she tried to keep them at bay.

"Damn it. I don't have time to cry."

Noah had been taken because he'd been here to help her. She would gladly give herself up in his place, even if it meant an eternity at Semiazas's mercy.

A sudden silence fell as the oppressive presence of an Archangel buzzed against Jezebeth's senses.

Jez glanced up, careful not to meet Raphael's gaze, to find the entire scene frozen. All around them in a wide circle men lay broken and bleeding from the fight with the demon.

Raphael walked forward, his black steel-toed boots filling Jezebeth's teary vision. "Please . . . the demon took Noah." She heard the desperate edge to her voice and fisted both hands to try to gain control of her galloping emotions.

"We meet again, little succubus. You do seem to attract trouble." He walked toward her and knelt.

Jez resisted the urge to look up at him as memories of their last meeting filled her mind sending a shudder through her.

He chuckled. "Still haven't forgiven me for that accidental soul gaze, I see. I give you my word that I will warn you before that ever happens again."

"You can't just promise me it won't?" she bit out; the words scratched along her throat and were out before she could think about what she was saying. After all, she was hoping for his help. Irritating him probably wasn't the best plan.

Raphael laughed, a good-natured sound that clashed both with Jezebeth's raw emotions and with the scene of badly injured men strewn around him like broken matchsticks. "I sometimes need to look inside souls for what I do, so I can't promise it will never happen again. But I *can* promise to warn you first." He spread his hands wide. "That's all I can offer."

Jez slowly raised her gaze to look at the dark, clean-cut Archangel with the smiling hazel eyes. "I suppose I'll take what I can get. Can you help rescue Noah?"

Raphael smiled, turning him from handsome to devastating. "Is that why you summoned me?"

Jez swallowed hard and nodded once. The time to pay up had come. "I had summoned you to save him. He was injured and close to dying . . . but then . . ." Her throat closed up as a sob escaped.

Raphael slowly reached out and placed his fingers around her neck as the demon had done, the scent of musky night deep inside a forest surrounded her as warmth tickled along her skin pushing back the raw pain. Tension slowly left her body and her emotions slowly calmed—an effect of proximity to one of the heavenly host.

Anger snapped through her, and she bit it back. She felt like she was betraying Noah by letting those emotions lessen, but she knew that wasn't logical. After all, just a few minutes ago she was cursing because the emotions hadn't stayed buried. Damn, she was losing it.

When Raphael dropped his hands, she swallowed experimentally and sighed as no pain knifed through her.

"Thanks." She rubbed her neck. "Can you find Noah?" She craned her head back to meet his gaze. "I'll pay whatever price you ask. Please."

"And if I do find him and retrieve him from the demon, then what?" His words weren't mocking, but only held a calm request for information.

"We have to get to Yuma as soon as possible."

Raphael's brows slowly rose. "Interesting. I don't recall any portals in that area of Arizona."

Jez closed her mouth and rolled her lips between her teeth as she tried to figure out how to respond. Obviously Uriel hadn't shared the "pass to his place" information with Raphael. Jez hoped she hadn't screwed up by sharing too much with the Archangel. Not that she would be able to lie to him anyway—Archangels could sense lies. Besides, if he agreed to help Noah, she'd tell him anything he wanted.

Way to open your mouth, Jezebeth.

Raphael stepped forward into her personal space and smiled. "When did Uriel visit you?" He held up his hands in front of him. "Wait, don't tell me. Better if I don't know."

Jez wasn't sure whether to be relieved or still worried by Raphael's cryptic remark, but they were running out of time for small talk. The current scene might be frozen, but somehow Jez doubted time for the entire planet was frozen. "So can you help us?"

"I've been ordered to not interfere in any manner with you and your three sisters."

A heavy weight settled firmly in the pit of Jez's stomach, and she opened her mouth to beg him to help her anyway.

"But there was no mention of my helping your companion." He pursed his lips as he studied her. "Do you trust me, little one?"

She boldly met his dark hazel gaze, looking inside herself for the truth since she knew any lie, even one to herself, would be detected by the Archangel. Finally she slowly nodded.

"You and your sisters are tangled in something larger than you know. Watch your backs—on all sides."

When she frowned, he laid a comforting hand on her shoulder. "I can only promise to do my best to locate him."

Hope filled Jezebeth's chest like a warm burst of helium, making her feel suddenly lighter. "Thank you," she whispered.

"In the meantime I think you need to head toward your rendezvous point as quickly as you can." He laid his index finger under her chin and smiled. "Stay low, stay safe, and I'll do the best I can on this side."

"What's my payment for summoning you?"

He grinned, a playful nearly wolfish smile. "You said you'd pay whatever price I asked."

She nodded once, dislodging his finger from under her chin. "I will. Name it."

"Even if it's forbidden?" His tone was teasing.

"Yes," she immediately answered, meeting his gaze boldly, but only hazel eyes filled with amusement stared back at her.

He cocked his head to the side as he studied her. "You would risk everything for this human you've only known a few days, little one?"

"Noah. His name is Noah, not human. And why does everyone always call me 'little one'?" She huffed out a breath, fluttering her bangs, and held the Archangel's gaze, daring him to refute her. "And, yes. I told you to name your price, and I meant it."

Raphael's soft laughter confused her, and she frowned and stepped back, only then realizing she was back in her comfortable nonhunting form. Probably an effect of Raphael's healing. "I have some cleanup left to do here before I can look for Noah. You'd better go."

Jez frowned. "What about payment?"

Raphael turned back from examining the fallen leader. "I'll find you when I require payment."

After a long moment of digesting the surprise that surged through her system at the Archangel's sudden dismissal, Jez turned and ran.

16

Noah opened his eyes as he was suddenly slammed down hard against something cold and metal. He found himself strapped to some type of rack, spread-eagled and naked. Shackles bit into the skin at his wrists and ankles holding him tight against the unforgiving circular frame.

Pain still surged through him with every labored breath and he held on to consciousness by a thin thread.

He tried to glance around despite the searing pain but found he couldn't move.

Anger snapped through him. He needed information, and he needed it now. "Where is Jezebeth? Did she escape?"

"I think 'escaped' is too hasty a term at this point. Let's just say I haven't acquired her . . . yet." The cultured, male voice was almost conversational, and slow footsteps echoed around Noah as he waited to see who the voice came from.

A tall man with a medium build, dark hair, and calculating blue eyes edged into Noah's line of sight, and Noah couldn't miss the dark power pouring off the man in waves.

"What are you?" Noah clenched his teeth against the pain as his vision grayed and vertigo swirled through him.

The man chuckled, sending a shudder of pure revulsion through Noah.

"What indeed. I think you know me better as 'who' for this discussion." His eyes glittered with evil amusement. "I am Semiazas."

Noah clenched his jaw as he studied the demon in front of him. Semiazas was rumored to have been Lucifer's right-hand man, so to speak, for the rebellion against God. Maybe that's why he'd been given enough freedom to start the Black Plague even though it was against his new master's best interests.

"I see by your reaction that you know of me." Semiazas smiled and bowed with a flourish as if they stood inside a seventeenth-century ballroom. "I'm glad. That will make our time together so much more enjoyable." He stopped and cocked his head to the side. "At least for me."

Noah's first reaction was relief that the demon didn't know how to find Jezebeth; just behind that was cold, hard fear. Not of the torture itself—he was absolutely terrified about that. After all, he'd never been big on pain, and didn't think of himself as the He-Man, Rambo type. He was more scared of not being able to withstand the torture and ending up betraying Jezebeth.

The demon walked around Noah in a slow circle. "Now, why don't you make this easy for me and tell me where the succubus is headed, and we'll kill you quickly. We both know you've been caught up in something larger than you're able to handle." He laughed. "Imagine my surprise that Lilith assigned a writer of trite horror fiction to escort one of her prized whores as opposed to a warrior."

Noah remembered his own surprise at the assignment, but somewhere along the way he'd stopped looking at this as some punishment for summoning Lilith, and instead as an opportunity that allowed him to meet Jezebeth.

Semiazas continued in his calm, amused voice. "I have had millennia to perfect the art of torture, and I'm more than willing to show you all my expertise, but I think it would be much easier, and quicker, on both sides if you just went ahead and gave me the information I need. So how about it, Noah. I can call you Noah, can't I? I think once I've seen someone naked, it gives me the right to use their first name."

Noah mustered all his strength to return Semiazas's gaze. Steel-hard determination slid through him and his fingers tightened together into fists as he prepared to do the stupidest thing he'd ever done in his lifetime. "No."

Semiazas raised dark brows. "No, I can't call you Noah, or no, you won't tell me the information I need?" His voice was sweet and cajoling and made Noah wish to drown the damned demon in a vat of holy water.

Noah licked his dry lips. "Both."

Semiazas sighed dramatically. "Then I guess we'd both better get comfortable." He gestured and the demon still inhabiting Don's body stepped forward.

"Did he refuse?" it asked with a hopeful note in the gravelly voice.

Semiazas nodded. "Let's see what you can do. I'd like quick and thorough results."

"Yes, sir," came the gravelly reply as a very sharp-looking knife with a hooked end appeared in the demon's left hand. "This is going to be fun."

A brief thought of memorizing what the knife looked like for a future book spilled through Noah's mind, and he chided himself for thinking like a writer when he was about to be tortured.

Then the demon advanced on him and stabbed the knife deep into Noah's thigh.

Crippling pain shot through him and then dulled until he was floating. Calmly bobbing in a sea of blackness that lulled and comforted him.

He had a moment to wonder where he'd been whisked away to when he gagged. Something thick and hot was being poured down his throat. It tasted almost metallic and he tried to cringe away from the flow, but found he couldn't move.

Panic grabbed at him, and his lungs began to burn as they ached for breath. Finally, he swallowed and sucked in a quick breath before his mouth was filled again with the odd liquid. He swallowed again and then greedily sucked in a large breath of air even as his stomach roiled, threatening to bring back up everything he'd swallowed.

Waves of burning spread through his body in searing waves until he thought this would be his constant state of being.

What seemed like hours later, all the pain receded and his awareness returned in a rush. He found himself still strapped naked to Semiazas's circular metal rack with Don the demon standing in front of him with the now blood-soaked knife he'd stabbed him in the thigh with.

"Welcome back, human. I hadn't realized the extent of your injuries from our fight. You nearly died. You'll have to thank Semiazas for gifting you with some of his blood and fully healing you. Now we have plenty of time to start from scratch and see if you're willing to tell us where the succubus is headed."

Noah cringed as he remembered swallowing the thick, metallic liquid. That was Semiazas's blood? His stomach clenched and he tasted bile on the back of his tongue at the thought that he'd just drank blood.

Not that he could argue with the results. He was fully refreshed and healthy, but a quick glance up at the dripping knife made him wish he could've died. If they could heal him this fully, they could conceivably keep him here forever. If he had to endure torture for eternity, could he? Even for Jezebeth?

True terror spilled through him, and he swallowed hard.

Please, God, let me not betray her . . .

*   *   *

Lilith woke as Gabriel bolted upright in bed.

"Gabriel?"

Gabriel turned a sleepy smile on Lilith. "My apologies. I've been summoned. I must go, but I'll return later?"

Lilith nodded and raised up on her elbow to meet Gabriel halfway. As their mouths came together Lilith parted her lips and welcomed Gabriel's gently probing tongue inside. She reveled in the slow, deep kiss until Gabriel reluctantly pulled back.

"I enjoyed our time together."

Lilith couldn't keep the smile from curving her lips. "Me too."

Gabriel dissolved away and Lilith sighed, running her hands over the warm spot on the bed the Archangel had just vacated.

She hadn't spent a night only sleeping with anyone ever. In fact, the only time she'd slept through the night with someone in her bed was back with Adam and Eve, and there was always sex involved.

And the night with Uriel—well, there had been no sleeping done at all that night.

She flopped onto her back and laid her arm over her forehead as memories of Uriel tried to surface. She ruthlessly pushed them away and pulled the warm sensations of being with Gabriel around her.

Loud knocking sounded against her door, and she closed her eyes tight, wishing the awful sound away. When it came again she huffed out a breath and sat up, the sheet pooling around her waist, leaving her bare nipples to harden in the cool air. "Come in."

"My queen, I'm sorry to disturb you so early." Evelin slipped inside the door, closing it softly behind her. "There is a guest who refuses to leave until he sees you."

Lilith frowned. Why would someone want an audience with her this early? Her internal body clock told her it had to be around four A.M. Whoever it was, the matter must be urgent. "Who is it?"

"My lady . . . it's Semiazas."

Lilith stiffened as different scenarios of what the demon wanted flitted through her mind. He couldn't hurt her here in her lair, although she'd be damned if she let him anywhere else besides the throne room, which existed in both dimensions. Giving him access to other parts of her lair would give him the location so he could find her and pop in on her at any time. However, the throne room was sort of a halfway point between the human realm and the other side.

Even inside the throne room if Semiazas tried to harm her in any way, Uriel through his vow would rain down all kinds of retribution on the demon, and would bring the full force of Heaven with him. But there were a million other ways Semiazas could make things difficult or uncomfortable for Lilith and her followers, so there was no reason to totally snub his request for a meeting.

She sighed and pushed her hair back away from her face. "Tell him I'll see him in the throne room."

"He wishes to see you right away, my lady, and asks for an audience wherever you currently are."

"I'll just bet he does," she mumbled under her breath. Lilith stood, shivering against the cold air after being so warm in bed next to Gabriel all night. She cut Evelin off with an impatient gesture. "If he seeks an audience with me in the middle of the night, he should expect to let me have time to dress. If he does not, then he's a fool." Showing any kind of weakness or fear in front of the demon wasn't an option. Lilith had learned well over the centuries that it was often attitude and confidence that carried the day even over competence.

Evelin bowed her head once. "Yes, my lady. I'll show him to the throne room. Should I offer any refreshment or sustenance to him during his wait?"

Lilith stopped in midmotion of selecting a dress from her wardrobe. The idea of giving any of her followers—even the humans—to Semiazas for his pleasure even for the duration of the time it took Lilith to ready herself sent revulsion churning through her. "No. He isn't an invited guest. Show him to the throne room, and he'll damned well wait until I arrive."

Evelin bowed again and backed out the door, closing it behind her with a click.

Lilith closed her hand around a simple, elegant black dress, and paused. Even with Semiazas here, her mood was still buoyant from her time spent with Gabriel, so she skimmed her fingers over to a soft, yellow dress with a tight bodice and a long, flowing skirt instead. She smiled as she pulled on the dress, making a mental note to find some lingerie for the next time Gabriel came to visit. Lilith had never bothered with undergarments of any type since her body would stay firm and supple for the entirety of her existence, but she was in the mood to try something new and seductive with Gabriel.

She buttoned up the bodice of her dress, slid her feet into comfortable leather shoes, and brushed her long, dark hair until it flowed over her shoulders in silky waves.

Last, she stopped, feeling naked without her jewelry, she ran her fingers over the places they had sat for millennia—the ring, the necklace, the bracelet, and the earrings. She'd done the same thing every day since she sent the four imps to warn the succubi sisters about Semiazas.

"I'll have them back soon, safe and sound," she reminded herself, although she wasn't sure if she referred to the jewelry, the succubi, or both.

A quick walk down the hallway took her to her personal entrance to the throne room, and she laid her hand over her stomach to try to quiet the herd of butterflies that had suddenly taken up residence. She squared her shoulders, raised her chin to a regal height, and stepped forward into the lion's den.

Semiazas lounged on Lilith's throne, his back leaned against one arm while his legs draped over the other, his feet kicking idly. He glanced up as she entered, his smile feral and predatory. "Lilith," he said, not bothering to move. "How good of you to join me."

She kept her voice calm as she approached him. "You're in my way."

He smirked. "Oh, is this *your* chair?" Semiazas made a showy production of sitting up. "I would've thought as queen of the whores, you'd have a bed or something tasteful like a gynecologist's chair, instead."

Lilith had long since become immune to the taunts of others, so she ignored the comment and raised one brow, accompanied by an intense gaze.

He smiled slowly and stood, gesturing with a flourish for her to sit.

As she brushed past him, he turned toward her and sniffed at her hair. He grabbed her roughly by the shoulders and pulled her close. Burying his face into the crook of her neck, he inhaled deep.

Lilith reacted instinctively, planting her left foot and raising her right knee with all the force she could gather in this close-quarters position until it connected hard with the demon's balls.

Semiazas made a strangled sound in the back of his throat and crumpled, loosening his grip and allowing her to slip away.

"I've been manhandled many times since my creation, Semiazas. But to seek an audience with me first is not an act of a peaceful meeting request." She clenched her fists, holding her panic and anger at bay until she could make it back to her quarters.

Semiazas stood with his hands on his knees, sucking in large breaths of air before he slowly straightened to face her. "I apologize. You surprised me, Lilith, and that's not easy to do."

She knew she should leave but curiosity made her turn back. There had to be a reason he'd come to see her, after all, and she'd rather know what it was than find out about it later when it was too late.

"Gabriel has been here."

It wasn't a question, so Lilith didn't bother to answer.

Finally Semiazas took one step forward with a small wince. "Gabriel and I were once very close. I knew when I spoke to her a few days ago that she'd taken a female lover; I just didn't realize she'd gone for the most experienced one she could find." His smile was anything but friendly.

"Do you have a point?" Lilith forced herself not to cross her arms in a protective gesture.

Semiazas seemed ready to snap back at her, but slowly composed himself, the anger and hatred in his expression leaking away to be replaced by a mask of charming calm. The only thing that stayed to remind her of his previous expression was the cold calculation in his blue eyes.

"I wish to offer you a deal, Lilith. You have something I want, and I have something you want."

"I can't imagine you having anything I would want."

"How about the ring Adam made you?"

Semiazas's words were like a sucker punch to the gut. Everyone assumed Adam had made her the jewelry, but those pieces she treasured had actually been from Uriel. She kept her composure and raised her brows.

If he had the ring, did that mean he had Jezebeth as well? And what of her sisters? "If you have my ring, show me."

Semiazas pursed his lips. "I don't have it with me. The human who was wearing it wouldn't give it up so easily."

Which meant Semiazas had found out the hard way that the ring had to be willingly removed. He wouldn't even be able to cut off the human's finger to retrieve it, since his intentions would be known and the inherent Archangel energy in the ring would thwart any such attempt. Most beings assumed the jewelry gained such powers because Adam had made them during his time living in the Garden. Since Uriel had given the set to her the night he'd broken his vows, neither of them had ever bothered to dissuade people from their assumptions. And with Adam and Eve long since dead, the story had become "well-known" lore.

"You'll have to do better than that to keep my interest in this discussion." She turned to walk toward her personal entrance to the throne room.

"I've seen Uriel's downfall."

She froze and turned to face him. Semiazas was many things, but his visions were always accurate, and even though Lilith knew it would be a twisted account, she couldn't walk away without hearing it. "You have my attention . . . for the moment."

"I'm not ignorant of your plan, Lilith. You sent those four bitches to petition Lucifer to cage me all those years ago, and now that I've escaped, you're looking to do the same thing again. I won't allow it." His voice was a low hiss of warning.

"You've now lost my attention." She shrugged with a smile and started to turn away again.

"Uriel will fall. He will join our ranks of those who rebel against God, and all to protect you, queen of the whores."

"You're late to the party, Semiazas. Uriel has already carried out that revolt back when he refused to kill me at the Garden."

"So you mistakenly think repeated violations won't try God's patience?" Semiazas laughed. "Where will you end up when the end comes, Lilith? You're a being without a side, which means you'll be left standing alone when the music stops."

She didn't miss his clear reference to Armageddon, and she narrowed her eyes. "What are you trying not to tell me, Semiazas?"

"Uriel will betray God again, and it will be for you, and the world will fall."

Lilith's blood ran cold, but she tried to hide any visible reaction from the demon. "Uriel's choices are his own."

Impatience snapped in Semiazas's gaze. "Give me the four succubi and I'll ensure you have a place in the new hierarchy once the humans are no longer an issue." He smiled and stepped forward. "You have plenty of other followers. What will these four matter?"

"This entire meeting has been a waste of my time. I am officially banning you from visiting even my throne room, Semiazas, follower of Lucifer. Be gone."

With a snarl, he rushed forward but vanished well before he reached her.

She hoped it was worth it. She'd just pissed off Semiazas for a small measure of safety that he couldn't return to her throne room. Lilith shuddered and vowed to sink into her hot springs as soon as she found some breakfast.

17

Semiazas stumbled forward as he rematerialized back in Hell, at the portal point he'd used to visit Lilith's throne room.

The fucking whore had banished him!

He clenched his fists and looked around for something to kill to work off his anger and frustration. Unfortunately, all the demons and other residents of this part of Hell were all staying well hidden. He supposed his reputation preceded him—which could both be good and bad.

He currently stood in the administrative section of Hell, which resembled tightly packed office space, so he settled for pounding his fist against one of the large lava stone walls that separated this section from what was affectionately referred to as "the pit."

Pain lanced through his hand and down his arm, but his blow didn't do anything to mark the wall. Inside Hell and even inside Lilith's lair since neither was in the human realm, he wasn't impervious to pain, but at least the sharp dose of pain had helped to evaporate his immediate anger.

He wondered if the humans would see the irony that a large portion of Hell resembled corporate America so closely that they could be interchangeable. He shook his hand, trying to shake away the remaining pain.

He'd hoped Evelin could get him past the throne room of Lilith's lair, but he should've known the queen wouldn't allow it. The bitch hadn't survived this long by taking stupid chances—or at least too many.

He would almost respect her if he didn't owe her and the four succubi for locking him away for the last seven hundred years.

Damned politics! He couldn't attack her directly because he'd bring down the wrath of the Archangels on his head, and by extension, God.

Even though Semiazas had no respect for the ineffective deity, Lucifer would have his head if he brought that kind of attention to himself.

Unlike the denizens of Heaven who had thousands of rules of morality to adhere to, the demonic realm seemed to thrive on the principle that as long as it didn't cause Lucifer any trouble, then they were all free to do as they wished. Just one of the many reasons Semiazas knew he'd made the right decision on who to follow.

But at times like this he wanted to curse Lucifer's one rule, which prevented Semiazas from getting what he wanted.

He took a deep breath to regroup and dematerialized back to his torture chamber.

He quickly rematerialized in between the two vertical circular racks that spread-eagled his two current residents so he could torture them at will.

Unfortunately the man had been so near death when he arrived that Semiazas had been forced to give the man a blood transfusion to heal and survive. He'd need it to withstand the torture. After all, his human body wouldn't be damaged in Hell, but the human mind would make the pain and suffering the soul experienced very real, and too much could shatter the mind beyond redemption. Not that Semiazas would mind giving the human a free lobotomy, but he needed him for leverage, especially since his bid to get Lilith to give him the four succubi bitches hadn't panned out.

He'd tried using a soul gaze on the man, but someone had gotten there first so his wasn't effective. That's when Semiazas had found the human wearing Lilith's ring, although all efforts to remove the damned thing had proven unfruitful.

He'd tried cutting off the human's finger, hand, arm, or anything else he could to remove the ring, but it was as if the thing was charmed so that the wearer could only remove it willingly. And apparently, torturing the man to make him "willing" wasn't fair game either, since that hadn't worked. The human had weathered the pain of his limbs being severed, but when it was over, both the limb and the ring remained where they'd started.

Semiazas ground his teeth in renewed frustration.

He'd given several of his most creative demons free reign with the human male with the admonition not to break his mind. But the man had only given up the information that he owed Lilith and that's why he accompanied the succubus—Jezebeth—wherever she wanted to go. Either the human didn't know the portal location the succubus was headed to or he was very strong indeed.

That left persuasion of another kind.

Upon learning that the demon who had inhabited the man to capture the human male in the first place had failed to get him to talk, Semiazas had banished it, which left Semiazas with another male subject to play with while forcing the succubus's companion to watch. Humans were so sentimental.

"And how are my guests doing tonight?" Semiazas leaned close to the man's face, irritated when the human didn't even open his eyes. Semiazas slapped Noah hard across the face, using all the supernatural force he could muster. The human's head snapped around on his neck, and his eyes fluttered open, but his gaze remained defiant.

"Oh good, you're awake. Just wanted to thank you for all the information you've given me."

The man hung limply on the black metal rack, his naked body gashed and bleeding in several places, the way he'd been for several hours since Semiazas had left him to stew over his situation. The great thing about torture in Hell was that the man could hang here for eons and still be in this same condition. Semiazas couldn't see the damned human maintaining his stubbornness and composure for quite that long. Unfortunately, that kind of time was a luxury he couldn't afford right now.

Semiazas turned away from the man and stalked toward the second man, the one who had been possessed by the demon.

The tangy scent of fear filled the air and Semiazas breathed deep, enjoying the heady aroma. "Now that's what I'm talking about." He turned back to Noah. "I can sense your fear, but it's buried deep. His is right here on the surface where I can enjoy it." Semiazas slapped the man hard, his head snapping to the side and a low whimper escaping as he closed his eyes tight as if that would remove him from the reality of what was to happen.

"Stop. Leave him alone." The human's voice was raspy and dry as if each syllable scratched up his throat like a razor blade.

Semiazas turned back with feigned surprise. "I'm sorry, did you say something?" Without turning back to face him, Semiazas grabbed the man around the neck and began to squeeze. The older man cried out, probably more from surprise than pain.

Noah's gaze narrowed, and he ground his teeth.

"One little word, human, and I'll let him go." Semiazas shrugged.

Humans were a dime a dozen. All he cared about right now was finding those succubi and completing his revenge. He grinned as his long-range plans spilled through his mind like promises for the future.

"Your word?"

Semiazas laughed. "You would trust that? I think not." He grinned. "Let's do it this way." He waved at the rack the man hung on and he disappeared. "He's back where I found him in the first place." Semiazas left out the part that he was entirely naked. "But I can get him back, or another human in his place, if you don't hold up your end. Fair enough?"

Noah nodded and swallowed hard as if evaluating his options. "Greece."

Semiazas raised his brows. "Greece? And why were you two on a road in Arizona if you were going to Greece?"

"I didn't have all the details, but there will be a portal opening in Greece."

Semiazas narrowed his eyes and studied the man. His soul gaze might not work on this human, but he'd had practice reading the meat sacks since this pitiful excuse for a species began. As unlikely as the answer sounded, it held some truth. There was still something the human held back, but at least this was a step in the right direction. "Fine. Then it looks like you and I are taking a trip to Greece, my boy. I hope you brought your sunscreen to enjoy our trip, because if you've lied to me, it'll be an eternity before you see the sun again after this."

* * *

Gabriel rematerialized near where Raphael was busy healing several humans who looked like they'd been tossed around like rag dolls. The immediate scene was frozen, Raphael the only movement within the area besides herself.

He glanced up to meet her gaze, his expression grim.

She hurried forward, icy dread curling inside her stomach. "What's wrong, Raphael?"

"I was just summoned by one of the four succubi sisters."

Gabriel frowned and glanced around at the frozen scene of destruction. "Was she responsible for all this?"

Raphael shook his head. "No. A demon possessed a human, smashed everyone up, and then dematerialized with the succubus's companion."

Gabriel frowned. There was something more she was missing. "The companion sent by Lilith?"

Raphael nodded. "I promised to help look for him."

"We were ordered to stay clear—"

Raphael stood, cutting her off with an impatient gesture. "Not officially. And even then, we were told only to stay clear of the succubi sisters themselves. Michael never said anything about the companions Lilith sent to help them find their way back to her lair."

Gabriel shook her head. "True," she slowly admitted.

"I could use some help finding him. Any ideas where to start?" He waved a hand in the air and the scene resumed around them with the men slowly sitting up, disoriented, but healed and healthy.

Gabriel avoided Raphael's hazel gaze. She had no reason to feel guilty for her previous relationship with Semiazas, but that was logical, and emotions seldom listened to logic. "Why do you think I would know more than you about where to find him?"

"You know I'm not passing judgment, Gabriel." His words were soft and gentle.

She raised her gaze to his and searched his face, finding the truth of his statement.

"You two were very close before he made his choice to follow Lucifer. You know him better than he knows himself."

She sighed.

Raphael laid a hand on her shoulder and met her gaze with a small smile.

"I wouldn't ask if I didn't need help."

Gabriel studied Raphael and pursed her lips as she thought of where Semiazas might take a human hostage. "His old stomping grounds we used to spend time at are now all part of Hell, but there are a few likely places."

"Should we find Uriel first?"

She nodded. "Three would be better than one, or even two, especially when it comes to Semiazas." Pain sliced through her as it always did when she thought of Semiazas—something she'd had to do too much of since his recent escape from incarceration.

She turned away from Raphael and then stopped. "Why do you think Lucifer hasn't done anything to recapture Semiazas?" She had her own theories but wondered what Raphael's take on the situation was. Gabriel had never been close to Lucifer, even before the fall, and definitely hadn't spoken to him since.

"Lucifer is arrogant and thinks the universe revolves around his needs. He incarcerated Semiazas only because the plague was beginning to cause an imbalance in power that would rain down the wrath of Heaven upon his head. Since Semiazas has escaped, my guess is, the demon hasn't done enough to warrant Lucifer's attention."

She nodded, not surprised that Raphael's thoughts mirrored her own on the situation. "But that also means he won't interfere with us until our actions actually affect him." Gabriel turned back to look at Raphael over her shoulder.

"Exactly."

"I'll meet you at Uriel's."

* * *

Jezebeth walked until her legs ached and her skin felt tight and dry over her bones. She'd hitched rides on and off throughout the day, even stealing a few deep kisses here and there from willing men along the way to keep up her energy—the succubi version of a snack. She'd had time and opportunity for more, but for some reason hadn't felt comfortable while Noah was captive somewhere.

Night had fallen hours ago, and she'd nearly given up trying to find someone to hitch another ride with. Eloy, Arizona, wasn't exactly a hotbed of weeknight activity. But with time dwindling until Uriel's lair moved to Greece and worry about what was happening to Noah eating at her insides, she had no choice but to continue to force one foot in front of the other toward her destination and trust that things would work out in the end.

She rubbed her hands over her arms, a futile attempt to keep the chill night air at bay. Thoughts of her kiss with Noah flashed to the forefront of her mind, and her body warmed, not just with arousal but with something stronger and more comforting. She held the image of him healthy and whole inside her mind and kept moving forward.

Raphael would find Noah, and Noah would be fine. He had to be.

Jezebeth didn't have the energy right now to contemplate any other outcome.

Headlights flashed behind her, illuminating the dark night, and she turned and stuck out her thumb, trying to look both sexy and harmless in her own form since she had no extra energy to change to a different one.

The small, compact car slowed and finally stopped several feet ahead of her. Jezebeth breathed a silent prayer of thanks and hoped the driver was someone with an abundance of energy to share as she jogged forward to lean down and look in the open passenger car window.

A teenage boy who was still growing into his features raked a concerned gaze over her. "You need a ride?"

Disappointment arrowed through her. Even if she were near death, she wouldn't take energy from an underage innocent. After all, even succubi had morals. She forced a smile, and it felt like a very tired gesture. "I'd really appreciate a ride. I broke down hours ago. How far are you going?"

"I'm headed to Somerton."

Jezebeth relaxed when she only sensed genuine concern from the boy—pure female intuition, not anything supernatural at work. She'd turned down a few rides earlier in the day because her instincts had told her to run rather than get inside those cars. As a succubus, she'd learned to follow her intuition to survive. She might not be worried about rape like human women, but being shot, chopped up, or otherwise hurt could weaken her to the point where something supernatural could kill her. "Is Somerton anywhere near Yuma?" she asked, recognizing the hope inside her voice.

The boy smiled. "Very near. Hop in. You look like you've been walking for a while. It's not safe for a—for someone to be out here alone at night."

She opened the car door and slid inside, smiling that he'd almost said it wasn't safe for a woman to be out here alone at night but had changed it at the last minute in case he offended her. "I really appreciate it. I'm not sure I could walk another mile, let alone all the way to Yuma," she said, trying not to let her teeth chatter from the cold.

The boy rolled up the power windows and turned up the heat. "No problem at all. I know you're not supposed to pick up hitch-hikers, but if it was my mom out here walking alone at night, I'd hope that someone willing to help would stop."

She smiled and huddled against the seat, wondering if he realized he'd just made a reference to her age—or at least the age she looked, which she'd been told was mid- to late twenties. Probably not. "I'm Jezebeth, and I really do appreciate this."

"Darian."

"Great to meet you, Darian." She tried unsuccessfully to stifle a yawn. "I'll put in a word for you to get back double good karma for helping me." She was only half joking. After all, she did know quite a few low-level angels she'd done favors for over the years who could do something nice for the boy.

He laughed and shook his head. "That sounds exactly like something my mom would say. Just reinforces the idea that I did the right thing by picking you up." He edged the heater up another notch and reached into the back seat for a coat. "Here you go. You look beat. Go ahead and sleep. I'll wake you when we hit Yuma."

Too tired to argue, Jezebeth smiled at him through another yawn and then curled under the coat and leaned her head against the passenger window. She wrapped the memory of her kiss with Noah around her like a mantra for everything to turn out well in the end and let sleep take her.

* * *

Uriel materialized inside Lilith's throne room, not sure if he was welcome in her quarters any longer. The large black cavern looked much like he remembered it, although he hadn't been here in centuries. In fact, before the previous day he hadn't visited Lilith's quarters since the day he'd given her this lair.

Memories flooded back hot and bright, and Uriel shoved them aside to concentrate on his current mission.

Evelin, one of Lilith's servants, scurried forward wearing a gauzy red harem outfit. Her head was already bowed before she reached him, so he couldn't see her face. "My lord, Uriel. How may I be of service?"

"I wish to see your mistress."

Evelin glanced up, confusion evident in her expression. "My lord?"

Uriel ground his teeth. This is what he got for trying to respect Lilith's new boundaries within their relationship. "I wish to see Lilith, Evelin. Please tell her I'm here in her throne room to see her." His words were cutting, and Evelin managed a single nod before she turned and ran toward Lilith's quarters.

Uriel waited impatiently, pacing the length of the large black cavern, wondering if he should've just gone straight to Lilith.

Several long minutes later, Lilith rushed into the room wearing only a black silk robe which stuck to her still-wet skin to outline the full curves of her body.

Uriel's cock instantly hardened inside his slacks and he had to force his gaze up to Lilith's face.

"Uriel?" She rushed forward until she stood so close he could feel the heat of her body—or maybe it was only his raging hormones.

He cleared his throat in a futile attempt to push back the thick lust that currently surged through every vein in his body. "Have you heard anything from Jezebeth's companion?"

"The human?" Her dark brows furrowed, and he read the confusion in her gaze.

"Yes."

She shook her head. "Is Jezebeth . . ."

"I don't know." He couldn't resist reaching out to lay a hand on her shoulder, but instantly regretted it as the moist warmth of her skin hummed against him—a blatant temptation, which described Lilith perfectly. "Raphael has seen her and she was on her way to Yuma to use my property as an entry point to your lair."

Lilith blew out a slow breath and the strain in her features softened. "And her companion?"

"Taken by a demon. We've searched for him but can find no trace."

Lilith cocked her head to the side, studying him, and as always seeing him much more clearly than he liked. "And why are Archangels looking for the human companion of a succubus?" Her voice was soft, but devoid of any emotion.

Uriel sighed, tempted to turn away so she couldn't see his eyes, but instead, he held her gaze. The two of them had been through too much together, and he'd hurt her too much of late to lie to her even more. "Your four little succubi are deep in the middle of something that concerns the Archangels, although I can't divulge what. I need to know if there's any way to track the human."

Lilith nodded slowly, once. Her expression was resigned, giving him the impression she accepted the limitation, but she didn't like it. "Each companion carries one piece of jewelry you gave me."

Uriel frowned as surprise hit him hard in the gut.

He'd assumed Lilith had stopped wearing his jewelry because of the recent unpleasantness between them. He should've realized she would be more practical than that. Those items imbued with her essence after so many years of her wearing them would render their wearers impervious to the effects of a succubus, enabling them to not only be protector but energy source as well.

He smiled and, before he could think better of it, leaned forward to brush a kiss across the soft skin of her cheek. "Thank you, *nassah*," he said as he dematerialized to find Gabriel and Raphael.

18

Semiazas materialized in Greece, the human draped over one arm like a very large garment bag. The tang of warm, salty air felt divine against his skin after his time spent back in Hell, and he vowed never to be sent back to seclusion again.

Those seven hundred years spent locked alone in a deep, dark pit of Hell had been torture. No sun on his skin, no companionship, no food, no pleasures or comforts of any kind. Only time for his anger to simmer and his plot for revenge to fully form.

He dropped Noah on the ground where he landed with a pained-sounding oof.

Only when several passersby stared did Semiazas realize the human was entirely naked and the humans only saw the man appear suspended off the ground and then drop to the dirt. Most humans couldn't see anything supernatural, and the thought of what stories they would tell to explain this sight away amused him for only a second.

The man moaned and slowly sat up, probably just now realizing the damage from the torture done in Hell didn't translate to his physical body.

A quick wave of his hand and the human was dressed in the clothes he'd been captured in. "All right, human. Here we are in Greece." Semiazas turned in a slow circle enjoying the vivid colors and the soft sounds of laughter that carried on the breeze. "Where is your pet succubus?"

"I don't know *where* in Greece." The man stood slowly as if not sure to trust his body to support him or not.

"All right. You're lucky I enjoy this place. Let's do a little sight-seeing, shall we?"

* * *

Awareness slowly came back to Jezebeth, and she forced her eyes open as memories flooded back. She sat up straight, the coat Darian had given her falling down onto her lap as she glanced around. She still sat in the passenger seat of the car, but the boy was gone and the car was parked outside the Fairfield Inn Yuma.

The sleep had recharged a little of her energy, but she needed sustenance soon.

Urgency pricked at her and she fumbled for the door handle and finally managed to open the door of the car and step out into the chilly night.

A prickling along her right side made her turn, but all she could see was a darkened parking lot and the landscaped greenery that surrounded the property. She took one step forward and the prickling increased, centralizing in a large bubble inside her chest.

Uriel's pass.

The pass he'd given her and Noah was pulling her toward his property.

Excitement urged her forward, and she let out a cry of triumph as adrenaline surged through her and she started to run.

She dodged buildings, climbed fences, and even jaywalked through traffic, all in an effort to follow the invisible path before her.

Finally, she rounded the corner of a shopping center and noticed a silver shimmer along the back edge of the darkened parking lot.

Without thinking, she ran forward, anticipation and near relief warring inside her as she raked her gaze over the parking lot looking for any sign of Noah or Raphael.

When she was still a hundred yards away, the shimmering began to dim, and panic shot through her as she realized it was about to shift—to Greece.

"No!" Jezebeth ran as hard as she could and finally jumped and dove forward, her arm reaching out to touch the elusive shimmer.

Her body in midair, hurtling forward, the shimmer died away and disappeared completely.

Anger and denial hit her hard a split second before she impacted with the unforgiving blacktop, her air whooshing out in a painful rush.

She rolled over onto her back, ignoring the pain of her abraded skin, her bruised ribs, and anything else as searing disappointment and loss won out. Tears flowed down her cheeks unchecked, and she let the sobs come, almost resigned to dying here.

After everything she and her sisters had been through, everything Noah had endured for her, and she'd missed the portal by a second. She slammed her fists against the blacktop, railing at the unfairness of the situation.

A tsking sound made her snap open her eyes and look up. A beautiful man with long, flowing blond hair, green eyes, and a powerful presence that was both Archangel and demon stood looking down at her. "Giving up so easily. How disappointing."

Jezebeth sat up and scrambled to her feet as she realized she stood facing Lucifer. "What do you want?" She waited to feel fear, but all she could muster was a wary curiosity. Her adrenaline had already begun to wane, leaving her hollowed out, aching, and raw inside. She simply didn't have the emotional bandwidth to deal with the Prince of Darkness right now.

He smiled, the movement making him even more stunning, except for those cold, dead eyes. "I'm sorry I had to delay your entry into the portal. There are things to discuss. I want you and your sisters to hold up your side of the agreement, little one. Even if I'm the only one of the fallen who realizes it."

Jezebeth stepped forward, realizing too late that she'd just advanced on the Archangel who had rebelled against God—probably not a great idea in hindsight. "What do you mean? My sisters and I never made any agreement. But you did. You locked up Semiazas, and now he's escaped; so what are you going to do about it?" she asked carefully, not wanting to push her luck too far.

He studied her for a long moment before answering. "Ahh, so there is some spunk left in you. I'd thought by that display of self-pity I came across, you might not be worth my time."

She swallowed hard, suddenly angry he'd witnessed her mini breakdown. "You didn't answer my question."

"No, I didn't, and don't plan to. Come along, little succubus, if you'd still like a chance to save your human and keep your side of our bargain." He held out his hand.

Irritation surged through her and she snapped, "What bargain?"

When Lucifer only looked at her with a calm expression she huffed out a breath. "And if I don't come with you?"

His smile was sad this time, the first genuine emotion that had shown inside those eerie green eyes. "Then your human will die, along with all the others. None of the four can fail. I'm constrained to the agreements I've made, just as we all are, little one." He gave a Gallic shrug. "So, what will it be?" He held out his hand again. "The devil you know? Or the Hell you don't?"

Confusion and panic edged up the back of Jezebeth's throat

with the sharp tang of bile and she swallowed hard and followed her gut.

*   *   *

Noah found himself sprawled on all fours on sandy soil. Warm sun beat down on his back and with a huff of relief, he realized he was once again dressed. It would've sucked to be plopped down in the middle of nowhere bare-assed naked, but if it was that or Semiazas— he would've taken naked.

He glanced around quickly before pushing up to stand.

There was no sign of Semiazas, but Noah didn't for one minute think the demon had given up and let him go. Although if Noah wasn't mistaken, he now stood on one of the islands in Greece.

He wasn't sure which one, but apparently Semiazas wanted Noah to do the legwork and find the portal in Greece. Yeah, like that was going to happen.

A salty breeze teased his hair and cooled his skin, and for the first time he realized that even after all the torture he'd endured at the hands of Semiazas, he felt great. Apparently, the tortures inflicted in Hell didn't translate to the human realm.

He said a quick prayer of thanks to whoever might be listening. Noah had never been sure of the existence of God—that was until he'd accidentally summoned Lilith. Now, he figured it couldn't hurt to remain open-minded since he'd already met demons, Archangels, succubi, and Djinn. It couldn't be too much of a stretch to believe in God after all of that.

Noah glanced around wondering how long Semiazas would play with him before the demon decided to kill him outright. Or worse—took him back to Hell and put him through another round of very creative torture.

The only way Noah had survived those long hours of pain was by treating it like research and filing away his reactions for future books—sick and twisted, but it had worked. He refused to betray Jezebeth. Even if the deadline passed and Uriel's property suddenly appeared somewhere in Greece, Jezebeth would still be safe back in Yuma, Arizona, on the other side of the world.

The best lies had large grains of truth in them.

Noah thought about running, but where to? It was obvious he couldn't outrun the demon, and he was sure Semiazas was tracking him somehow. He had no intention of looking for the portal, but maybe he could find some kosher salt, holy water, or something else that would help. Semiazas was obviously a high-level demon, so most of those would only be a minor nuisance to him, but something was better than nothing at this point.

Noah started down a steep, winding road as he scanned the lush view for any possible escape or defense against Semiazas. He wanted to keep the demon away from Jezebeth, but that didn't mean Noah was resigned to die yet. He had plenty of life left to live and he wasn't going to let one vindictive demon take it from him.

A huddled form materialized in front of him, and Noah's steps faltered as icy fear and foreboding sliced through him.

The huddled form slowly straightened, and his worst fears were confirmed.

Jezebeth.

Her clothes were dirty and there were dark circles under her eyes, but she seemed to be all right.

He knew the second she saw him—relief filled her expression, and she pushed to her feet to run toward him.

Despite his earlier thoughts, Noah grinned and ran toward her, picking her up and swinging her around as he enjoyed the sensation of having her safe in his arms again. When he sat her on her feet, she ran her hands over him, searching his face with her hazel gaze. "Are you all right? How did you get free?"

The reference to Semiazas sent ice skittering through Noah's veins, and he took Jezebeth by the shoulders and looked into her eyes. "Jezebeth, you have to get as far away from me as you can. He let me go, but I'm sure he's tracking me. As long as we're together, you're in danger." He frowned as he realized she should be in Arizona. "Wait. How did you get here?"

She sighed. "Lucifer."

"Damn, and I thought Semiazas was the biggest thing we had to worry about. What happened?"

Jezebeth stood on her tiptoes and brushed a kiss across his lips before she pulled back and smiled up at him. "Let's get moving and we can fill each other in on the way. I have no idea where the portal is, but now that we're both here, we may as well make a good run for it."

Unable to resist holding her and reassuring himself she was safe, Noah squeezed her into a tight hug, resting his chin on top of her head as he breathed in her pomegranate and honey scent. "I'm so glad you're all right, but you need to run, Jez. Staying with me puts you at risk."

She wrapped her arms around his waist and pressed her cheek against his chest. "There's no way I'm leaving you again, so you can either get your ass in gear and help me find the portal, or we'll stand here and wait for Semiazas to find us. Your choice."

Noah tightened his grip on her, his protective instincts warring with respect for Jezebeth's stubborn courage. He blew out a breath in defeat and opened his eyes. A beat-up pickup sat farther down the steep hill by the side of the road. There wasn't anyone in sight nearby. "Fine. Let's go. I think I just found us some transportation."

Jezebeth followed his line of sight and smiled. "You work fast—"

Noah cut off her words with a kiss, enjoying the way she melted against him, and even the slight tingling sensation that told him his energy was siphoning into her. When he finally slowed the kiss and pulled back, the dark circles were gone from under her eyes, and she smiled at him sending warmth curling inside his gut.

He cleared his throat, not sure he could speak through the swirling emotions filling his chest. "Let's go."

A few minutes later they sat in the cab of the truck and Noah did something he hadn't done since he was a teenager—hot-wired a vehicle.

The ignition chugged to life and he slammed his hand down on the steering wheel in celebration. "Yessss!"

"Done this before, I take it?" Jez clicked her seat belt into place and grinned over at him.

"It's been a while, but I guess once you have the touch, it's easy to get it back." Noah put the truck in gear and pulled out onto the road. "I have absolutely no clue where we're going, but we'll find it quicker by looking than sitting still." He navigated down the steep hill, riding the brake as gravel skidded under the front tires.

"Noah, how did you get away from Semiazas?"

He scowled, but kept his eyes on the road. "He let me go, which is why I wanted you to get far away from me. He's got to be tracking me. I'm sure he's going to pop back in on me at any moment."

She nodded absently. "Lucifer let me go as well. He made me miss the Yuma portal by a mere half a second and he brought me here." She shook her head. "I'm still not sure why. There's something going on . . . something I feel like I should know, but I just can't seem to remember." She rubbed her forehead with her fingers and scowled. "But I still think we should stay together. At least that way we aren't left wondering what happened to each other."

Jezebeth's words mirrored his own thoughts and he opened his mouth to tell her. But as they navigated one of the many bends in the road, Noah saw an ancient-looking church at the bottom of the hill with a fountain in front complete with a waist-high basin.

Holy water. Blessed by the priests so the masses could anoint themselves with it on their way to and from services.

He straightened as hope curled inside his stomach. Finally, maybe they had something to defend themselves with.

About halfway down the hill to the church Noah noticed a slight shimmer that overlapped the church, larger than the building, but shaped differently. He frowned as he tried to get his eyes to make sense of what he was seeing.

Without warning the truck bucked beneath them and the entire world began to spin.

19

As the world slowly righted itself, Jezebeth shook her head, trying to find her equilibrium. It took her a long moment to piece together that she hung upside down in the truck cab, held in place by the seat belt.

She tried to turn her head to look for Noah but stopped when sharp pain lanced through her and a warm gush of blood told her she had something lodged in her neck. After a few deep breaths to chase back the black dots that tried to infringe on her vision, she raised her hand to gingerly explore her injury.

Her fingers closed over a thin piece of jagged metal.

A warm grip closed gently over her fingers, pulling her hand away. "Hold still and take a deep breath. This is going to hurt."

At the sound of Noah's voice, relief poured through her and tears burned at the backs of her eyes. She hadn't realized how scared she was that she'd never hear his voice again after the demon had taken him.

White-hot pain slashed through her neck, ripping a surprised gasp from her throat and threatening to make her black out as a gush of hot blood flowed down her shoulder.

Something soft pressed against her neck, which slowed the flow of blood. She opened her eyes to find Noah's upside-down face just in front of hers. She giggled. She had to be unconscious or close to it if she was hallucinating.

"Jezebeth. Stay with me." Light stinging slaps against her cheeks jarred her back to reality and she frowned since she didn't remember blacking out. Noah's lips pressed against hers and the spark of his energy flashed between them before it trickled into her through their connection.

She didn't have the energy to move her lips against his, so instead, closed her eyes and savored each touch and nuance.

If she was to die soon, she wanted to have these last memories of Noah to treasure. Since she wasn't an actual demon, she wasn't immortal, and had no idea if succubi were allowed an afterlife or merely ceased to exist. Once her present form was killed . . . well, she wasn't sure. But she didn't think she'd get to poof back to Lilith's lair and hang out and wait for another incarnation.

Right now, all she cared about were Noah's lips against hers, firm but soft. The sexy stubble on his jaw lightly abraded against the soft skin of her face, and she could taste his fear as his energy trickled inside her.

She tried to raise her hand to his face, and only then realized she still hung upside down, her arms drooped limp and lifeless over her head not answering her demands for control.

"Damn it, Jezebeth. Open yourself up and take my energy. Take whatever you need. Just take it now!"

She blinked open her eyes and her gaze locked with his. Reality sharpened as she recognized not only concern in his gaze, but something else. Love?

No, Noah couldn't love a succubus. He'd been more than clear how he felt about her and her kind. But there was definitely some type of caring she saw there in the depths of the storm-cloud gray eyes.

It was enough.

Joy surged inside her, warming her and chasing back the cold that had pervaded her. She leaned forward to press her lips against Noah's, opening herself wide to receive his energy.

This time his rich, life-giving energy flowed inside her like a river, filling her cells and bringing her back to life.

As her body converted the energy into healing, she was finally able to bring her hands up to cup Noah's face while she continued to kiss him. Something wet pressed against her cheeks and she pulled back expecting to see tears in Noah's eyes. But when she looked at him, his eyes were dry.

She touched her own cheeks and her fingers came away wet. Jezebeth stared down at the moisture in wonder.

She was the one crying?

"Are you strong enough now to move?" Worry filled Noah's voice, and Jezebeth forced a smile onto her lips as she realized how close to death she probably had been. In fact if it wasn't for the silver ring Noah wore that made him immune to her succubus powers, he'd probably be dead right now from all the energy she'd taken.

She nodded once. "Please. I'm tired of hanging upside down."

Jezebeth braced herself as Noah released her seat belt and she fell headfirst into his arms. He slowly righted her, and Jezebeth blinked against the wave of vertigo that threatened to turn her stomach inside out.

Apparently even with all the energy she'd taken from Noah, she was still a long way from totally healed. She reached up to trail her fingers over the wound in her neck and winced as pain shot through her. The skin had closed so at least she wouldn't bleed to death. Small favors.

"Come out, come out, wherever you are."

The singsong voice sent ice skittering through Jez's veins.

Semiazas.

"I've found you fair and square, you little succubus bitch. Time to come out and die for stealing seven hundred years of my life from me."

Noah's arms tightened around her just before the truck split apart, the ruined bottom pulling away from the top of the truck cab where they huddled. With a loud groan of metal, the twisted wreck above them was lifted away to fall a few hundred feet away with a loud crash.

"There you are." Semiazas's cultured voice matched the handsome features that easily showed he used to be an angel. He had all the ethereal beauty of that race, all except for the calculating evil shining in his piercing blue eyes.

Jezebeth grabbed Noah's hand and threaded her fingers with his as they slowly stood. She refused to die cowering before Semiazas.

Noah pulled her behind him in a protective gesture.

"Well, well. The little horror writer is willing to give up his life for a succubus? This would truly be a touching scene in one of your books." Semiazas laughed, the sound slightly too high and a little crazed. "I think you writers call it the big black moment? Too bad no happy ending will come out of this one." He gestured behind him at the glittering patch of air that marked the portal to Uriel's property. "I think this is what you've come looking for?"

Anger speared through Jezebeth. They'd come too close to fail now. Only a few more feet and they would be safely inside Uriel's home, and only a few steps beyond that, they could be at Lilith's lair. She refused to miss two close chances at the portal twice in the space of an hour.

"I won't let you hurt her." Noah's voice rang with authority, and Jezebeth tightened her grip on his hand, trying to silently tell him not to provoke the fallen angel.

Jez had no doubt in her mind that she would die today, but if Noah continued to live, it would be enough for her.

Semiazas laughed. "I like you, human. It's too bad we didn't meet under other circumstances. Your soul isn't quite tainted enough to come play with us once I kill you." He shook his head with mock sadness. "If only we had more time."

He sighed dramatically and gave a Gallic shrug. "Oh well. Time to get on with this. I have three more succubi to kill." He stepped forward and grabbed Noah by the throat, lifting him until Noah's boots dangled several inches off the ground.

Semiazas tossed Noah aside to smash against the hard, dusty ground in a heap and then he stepped forward to grab for Jez.

Jez dove to the side, Semiazas's fingers grazing her arm as she fell. The impact against the hard-packed dirt knocked the breath from her, but she ignored the discomfort and continued to roll, trying to keep out of the demon's reach until she could figure out a plan.

She expected pain to burst through her at any moment, but when none came, she figured Semiazas wanted to kill her with his bare hands rather than bothering with something dramatic like an energy blast.

She flipped over and found her feet in time to see Noah jump onto Semiazas's back, his arms wrapped around the demon's throat.

Semiazas roared, his face contorted with rage as he easily broke Noah's grip and tossed him like a rag doll.

Noah's body landed hard and bounced once before falling into a limp pile.

"Noah!"

The air crackled with power, and Jezebeth glanced up to see the glowing form of an Archangel standing behind Noah, a shining, silver broadsword held in his left hand. Michael was built like a Greek god—fitting considering where they were. The Archangel stood several inches taller than Noah's six foot four with dark, clean-cut hair, green eyes, mocha-colored skin, and features that could only be described as ethereally beautiful.

The Archangel dipped his long sword in the holy water from the fountain and the wet blade gleamed in the morning sunshine. Jezebeth thought she heard him murmur, "Bless this tool of Your might, Lord, to help guard against evil intent."

"Semiazas," the newcomer said conversationally, the power from his voice crackling against Jezebeth's skin like persistent heat waves out of a hot oven.

Noah groaned and slowly stirred, trying several times before he was able to push himself up to a sitting position.

Jez slowly edged out of the truck toward where Noah sat on the ground.

Semiazas walked forward, but kept well back from the Archangel. "You have no claim on a succubus, Michael, and you know it. Your side is all about noninterference last time I checked."

Michael shrugged. "I'm only here to watch the show and make sure all the rules are observed."

Rules?

Jezebeth whipped her head toward the Archangel, ignoring the flash of pain in her back and neck from the sudden movement. Both Semiazas and Noah seemed similarly surprised.

"Rules?" Semiazas laughed. "There are no rules in this game we all play, my friend. It's winner take all as it's always been."

Michael's mocha features hardened, and he slowly pointed toward Semiazas with the tip of the sword.

Semiazas stopped in midstride, holding his hands out to his sides. "Be careful where you point that thing, my old friend. We can work this out between us to find an equitable solution."

Michael's brows drew together and the air around him crackled with lightning as the sky darkened like there was a sudden storm. "Don't ever call me 'friend' again, traitor."

The menace in those few quiet words made Jez's insides churn, and she took a step back before she realized she'd done it.

Semiazas chuckled. "Still upset that the only way you rose to the top of the ranks was that Lucifer gave up his spot?"

Michael's expression remained hard, but by the single tick in his jaw, she knew the jab had hit home.

Three other Archangels materialized behind Michael—Uriel, Gabriel, and Raphael—just as Jez reached Noah's side to assess his injuries.

Noah grabbed her hand and squeezed. "I'm all right," he whispered. "What's going on?"

Jez could only shrug and turn back to watch the unfolding show in front of them.

Semiazas smiled. "Well, the gang's all here, I see. Did you miss me, Gabriel?" he called out toward the female Archangel. Semiazas's tone had taken on a taunting quality. "Are you ready for a nice, thick cock after these eunuchs have left you so high and dry you've had to go and find pussy instead?" He grabbed his crotch and thrust his hips against his hand.

Michael frowned and glanced back at the three Archangels behind him.

"You didn't know?" Semiazas laughed. "Gabriel and Lilith are fucking. Really, Michael, you'll have to get all your Archangels on a social networking site so you can keep better track of them."

"Enough." Michael's voice left no doubt there was no room for negotiation.

"Give me the succubus, and I'll leave."

"I told you, I'm here only to ensure the rules are followed." Michael's response was so soft, Jez wasn't sure at first he'd heard it at all. But then everything happened at once as the world seemed to slow to a crawl.

Semiazas darted toward her with supernatural speed and grabbed her arm yanking her forward away from Noah.

Raphael, Uriel, and Gabriel suddenly appeared in a loose circle around them, the power of the circle of Archangels crackling against Jez's skin in a nearly painful rush. She tried to wrench her arm out of Semiazas's grip, but he held on tight.

As Semiazas snarled at the Archangels, Jezebeth took advantage of his distraction and raked the nails of her free hand down his arm and kicked, bit, and fought like a woman possessed.

He scowled down at her and shook her hard enough to kill her if she'd been human. The black dots returned, threatening to make her black out again if she wasn't careful. She sucked in breath after breath, fighting to stay conscious as she fell limp in his grip.

"Be still." Semiazas pulled a silver knife from his pocket and slashed it across her cheek. Pain blossomed along with impotent anger just before a warm rush of blood spilled down her cheek from the wound.

"No!" Noah lunged toward her, but she knew he'd be too late as she watched Gabriel dart toward Semiazas as well.

Semiazas whipped around, surprised, the bloody knife still in hand.

Gabriel's momentum carried her forward until the silver knife impaled her through the stomach.

Noah's steps faltered and Jez's breath died in her throat as the female Archangel's expression turned to surprise and then swiftly to pain.

Semiazas's features twisted in agony as realization of what he'd done hit. He caught Gabriel and slowly, almost lovingly, lowered her to the ground. "Gabriel?"

20

Sharp pain lanced through Jezebeth's head as she watched Semiazas slowly lower Gabriel to the ground.

She winced as a large buzzing inside her mind joined the pain as if something was trying to burrow its way out of her brain with a blowtorch.

Gabriel clutched her stomach as thick, red blood poured out. Since no ordinary knife could hurt an Archangel, something more sinister was at work here. But Jez didn't know what.

Jez glanced past Semiazas's shoulder to find Noah running toward her. She wanted to call out for him to stay back, to stay away from danger, but then motion around her caught her attention, chasing back the pain enough for her to think.

Uriel and Raphael rushed forward just as Michael raised his sword high over his head. "Betrayer!" Michael bellowed, causing the ground beneath Jez's feet to rumble with the force of his words.

With supernatural speed the Archangel plunged the sword downward toward Semiazas's exposed back.

Pain shot through Jez's brain again, bringing with it the sudden knowledge that if Michael killed Semiazas like this, all was lost.

She couldn't explain it, but she also couldn't let it happen.

Urgency gripped her with sharp talons. Everything depended on the rules being followed to the letter. She and her sisters had sacrificed too much to fail now.

"Michael, no!" She stood, stepping into the path of the already descending sword, and then closed her eyes as she waited for pain and oblivion.

A hard, unexpected blow from the side made her stumble, and as the gravel from the road bit into her knees and shins she heard Raphael's soft curse just above her.

She opened her eyes and looked up to see the Archangel hunched over her protectively, the shining silver tip of the sword of Michael protruding from his chest and pain etched across Raphael's handsome face.

She scrambled out of the way as his legs buckled and he fell to his knees.

Deafening silence descended around her as if the world had taken a collective horrified gasp.

"No!"

"Raphael!"

She couldn't tell who the shouts came from and she didn't care. Denial slowly curled through her and an overwhelming urge to make everything right swept over her like a tidal wave. "No! No more."

She stood and shoved Michael back away from Raphael before she grabbed the hilt of the large silver sword with both hands. The pommel was so large, she had a sudden insight into how children must feel when handling adult-sized tools.

"Hold, daughter of Lilith." Michael's voice held a hard warning as the scene froze around them, just as it had when Raphael had appeared to her and Noah back in Tucson. "If you remove the sword before Raphael is dead, you will negate the sacrifice he made to save you from punishment for treason. You interfered with my execution of Semiazas, and for that you gained his fate."

Jezebeth didn't hesitate. Using all her strength, she pulled the sword free and dropped it to the ground.

Even if she hadn't owed the angel for finding Noah and healing her, she knew she would've gladly taken his place. She couldn't watch him suffer. He'd helped both her and Noah and then rushed forward here to save her again.

She sent one final glance toward Noah, who was frozen mid-step. Longing and regrets spilled through her. She'd wasted so much time . . . she wondered if she had it to do over again if she would be smart enough to change her actions. Too late to find out now.

She sighed and turned to face Michael, her fingers clenched into tight fists. "I'm ready to take the consequences for my actions."

"Why?" Michael's expression seemed almost amused.

Jez frowned. She'd expected a quick death, not a quiz. "Why what?"

"Why did you try to save Semiazas?"

Jezebeth opened her mouth to answer and then stopped. She remembered the sudden knowledge that Semiazas must not die at the hands of Michael . . . it would break the rules, and the rules *must* be followed.

It was imperative.

After all, she and her sisters had given their word . . .

Her head began to throb and she rubbed at her temples with her fingers. "What rules, damn it? I think I'm losing my mind."

Michael smiled, the contrast between his mocha skin, white teeth, and amused green eyes making him even more striking. "A creature of honor. Apparently, we've chosen well."

The knowledge of everything Michael meant stayed just outside her reach, tickling along the edges of her consciousness but refusing to sharpen into focus. "I don't understand."

"Which is part of the agreement, I assure you. And yet, even without the details, you followed your inner knowledge of what needed to be. Most creatures much more powerful than you wouldn't have had such insight, little one. I would venture to say I'm proud, but I fear it would make me sound condescending."

Jezebeth shook her head as she gave up trying to pull all the details together. "You make it sound as if I've passed some type of test."

"You have. But only the first and easiest of many to come, I fear." He reached out and laid a gentle hand on her arm and knowledge and memories came rushing back, crashing over her in crippling waves.

She found herself inside Lucifer's lair, a gilded room full of opulence and self-importance—totally unlike the caricature of Hell she'd expected to find.

Power prickled against her skin, stealing her breath until she braced against it and forced herself to suck in a full breath and blow it out slowly.

"Welcome, ladies."

Jez started at the respectful greeting and glanced to the side as her hands were clasped from both sides in a silent show of comfort and support.

She squeezed each hand lightly recognizing the familiar presence of her sisters. Galina stood on her right and Reba on her left. Amalya stood just on the other side of Reba.

Jez swallowed back the fear of an audience before Lucifer and said a silent thanks that she was here with her sisters, and not by herself. She wasn't sure if she'd have the strength on her own to do this.

"That is something we'll soon find out, Jezebeth."

She started as Lucifer's gaze met hers sending an icy chill of foreboding through her.

He smiled as if he enjoyed making her uncomfortable. "Yes, within my lair, I can pick up strong thoughts from others." He motioned off to his side. "Michael, join us."

Jez barely had time to be shocked that Lucifer had read her mind before the name he'd spoken registered.

Michael? As in *Archangel* Michael?

Holy shit!

Jez's mouth went dry and she gripped her sisters' hands tighter. What had they gotten themselves into?

A large Archangel with a muscular, sleek build, mocha skin, and piercing green eyes joined Lucifer. Standing side by side, their eyes were identical, even though the rest of their features were very different. They were a study in dark and light, but while Lucifer's power bit at her, making her resist the urge to shudder and cringe away, Michael's power flowed over her in a seductive, enticing warmth. With power like that, someone would willingly walk off a cliff for just the privilege of basking in its warm embrace.

"Greetings, followers of Lilith." Michael's deep voice washed over Jez, calming her and chasing back her fears. When her sisters' grips on her hands loosened, she knew they were experiencing the same thing.

Jezebeth steeled herself against her reaction to the Archangel and clenched her jaw before she cleared her throat and gathered her courage around her like a cloak. "We have come to ask—"

"We already know why you're here." Michael's voice was kind, but Jez refused to succumb to the supernatural calming effect of his words. She needed all her wits about her for this meeting.

Lucifer paced a slow path back and forth in front of them giving the impression of languid, slow movement, while still seeming impatient. He moved like liquid sin, and Jez was sure succubi and incubi everywhere wished they could move half as well. But the eerie energy pouring off him was enough to remind Jez that for all his beauty, there was something evil lurking beneath that handsome exterior. "Ladies, we are well aware of Semiazas's activities, and they will be curtailed . . . for now." He stopped in midstride and met each of their gazes in turn.

Jez swallowed hard. If there was ever a time for them to be diplomatic and not piss someone off, now was the time. But with the volatile and vastly different personalities of her sisters—including herself—Jezebeth wasn't so sure she could bank on such a thing happening. "Why only for now?" she ventured.

Lucifer cast her an impatient look, and the edges of Michael's lips quirked as if he were trying to hide a smile.

"Semiazas will be imprisoned for his crimes, but there are more powerful forces at work here, ladies." Lucifer raised one eyebrow at her as if making sure she wasn't going to interrupt again.

Jez clamped her lips closed, resisting the urge to do just that.

"Prophesy," Lucifer said slowly. "Armageddon prophesy to be exact."

"Fuck."

Jez snapped her head toward the sound of Reba's quick curse, but since she agreed with the sentiment, she didn't bother to shush her, not that shushing Reba ever did any good.

Lucifer laughed. "Very eloquently put, Reba. From the expressions on your sisters' faces, I'd say they agree with your very astute assessment."

Reba scowled, and Jez sighed. She needed to move things along before one or more of them said something to set off the powerful demon or Archangel in the room, which meant all of them would end up dead. "Do you think we could move past the dramatic theatrics and get on with why exactly we're here, since I don't think it's for the reason you agreed to meet with us?"

Lucifer's green eyes narrowed, and this time it was Michael who laughed, the warm sound echoing through the large room like a sudden wave of spring. "Calm yourself, brother. They have every right to know what they are agreeing to."

Lucifer didn't look like he would agree, but finally he nodded. "All right, ladies. Here's the situation. Armageddon could be at hand."

"Could be?" Amalya's voice held an icy slap that made Jez wince, since pissing off the Prince of Darkness and God's right-hand warrior wasn't exactly a good idea under any circumstances.

Michael smiled. "Yes, *could* be. If it comes to pass is up to you four." He held up a hand to stop Lucifer from speaking, and once Lucifer gave a small nod, Michael continued. "The four horsemen have been imprisoned in Atlantis at the bottom of the Aegean Sea since before the beginning of your recorded time. If they are released, then Armageddon begins, and the outcome is decided at the expense of untold human suffering."

"The horsemen?" The words scraped out of Jez's throat as she tried to make sense of Michael's words. "As in Pestilence, Death, War, and Famine? *Those* horsemen?"

"Exactly." He nodded as if she were a prized student.

"Excuse me, my lord," Galina interrupted politely—the only one of them so far to remember the respectful address. "But what do Armageddon and the horsemen have to do with us? We only came to warn you of Semiazas's activities before he kills off the entire human race on earth."

Lucifer snorted. "No one wants Armageddon to come about, not me, not Michael, and certainly not our Father. This world is a playground for those of us who rebelled and a grand naïve experiment for those who didn't."

Michael cast Lucifer a long-suffering look, but remained silent. This seemed like a familiar argument between them.

"Don't you see?" Lucifer continued. "Rather than flip the switch and risk the entire thing, we want to exercise the loophole and use a test group, as it were, to prove the world is worth saving."

"And *we're* the test group?" Jez's last word ended on a squeak.

Michael held up a hand. "You have to willingly take on this responsibility, and the contest would be between you four and Semiazas. He will be imprisoned for his crimes and as soon as he is free, he will hunt the four of you down to seek revenge, which is the beginning of the Armageddon prophesies."

Jez swallowed hard. "What happens then?"

Michael exchanged a glance with Lucifer before continuing. "We will separate the four of you to protect you the best we can until the prophesy begins, then only our Father, Lucifer, and I will know of the contest. The four of you will have to make your way to safety, find each other, and prevent Semiazas from releasing the horsemen, however you can."

Reba snorted. "Yeah, that sounds like a walk in the park. Can't we just do something easy like turn the world inside out or get Lucifer to make up with Daddy?"

Jez's gaze snapped toward Lucifer as she waited for all four of them to be killed where they stood, so she wasn't sure how to react when he laughed and slowly clapped his hands. "Bravo. That's just the kind of spunk and fire all four of you will need to win." His heavy gaze settled on Reba, and he raked a sensual gaze over her from head to toe. "Perhaps when this is decided, little one, you'll come back and pay me a visit."

"Not likely," she bit out, making Jez cringe.

Lucifer only smiled and exchanged a look with Michael that told Jez there was much more they weren't being told. "There is always a way to win, ladies, but . . ." He held up a finger. "There is a catch that I think you missed."

Silence descended, and Jez gritted her teeth, waiting for another comment from her sisters that thankfully never came.

Finally Lucifer smiled, making him resemble a hungry predator looking at his next meal. "None of you will know about this test. You might find clues along the way, but your choices must come from free will and selfless actions. Any allies you make along the way can help you, but neither Michael nor I can directly interfere other than to enforce the rules."

"Rules?" Jezebeth found herself asking.

Michael nodded. "If any of the four of you fail—Armageddon begins. Any of the four of you can kill Semiazas if you can, but not before all four of you have stopped the horsemen. And Semiazas can not die at the hand of anyone else. Otherwise—"

"Armageddon begins . . ." Jezebeth didn't realize she'd spoken until she heard the words. "And you said we have to willingly sign on for this. What if we don't? What if we refuse?"

Lucifer spread his hands wide. "Armageddon begins."

Jez snorted. "So we have no choice." She exchanged a glance with her sisters, seeing the same frustration she felt mirrored in their expressions.

"There is always a choice," Michael said softly. "You may not like the options, but there is always a choice."

A wrench of vertigo pulled Jezebeth nearly in two and she sucked in a breath to keep from throwing up as she realized she was back standing in front of Michael where he'd frozen the fight scene with Semiazas.

"Crap. I think I liked it better before I remembered any of that."

Michael smiled, but the expression was sad. "Your memories will fade again, little one, at least most of them. Anything you've learned on your own will remain with you. You have much left to do, and your sisters must pass their own trials before this is done."

Jezebeth sighed as weariness settled over her, and a fresh longing for her sisters twisted inside her. "Why did you try to kill Semiazas? Isn't that against the rules?"

"He mortally wounded Gabriel—which supersedes that agreement and earns him death. As the right hand of God, it is my duty to avenge her." He shrugged. "You intervened, which transferred the sentence to you. However, you have preserved the contest, and saved Raphael in a selfless manner, so we seem to be back where we began."

"So you're not going to kill me?" She winced at the small sound of hope in her words.

"No, little one. As I said, you preserved the contest so we are for all intents and purposes back to where we began."

"Okaaaay." She shook her head trying to figure out where that left her and her sisters, not to mention everyone else. "What's going to happen to Gabriel and Raphael . . . and Noah?"

"Without intervention they will all die. My sword was coated with holy water, which bought Raphael some time, but Semiazas's knife was made from the same holy fire as my sword. Semiazas stole it from Lucifer, who imbued it with his blood." His gaze cut to Gabriel's still form. "It isn't within my power to know her fate."

"And Noah?"

"If things resume and nothing changes, he will fight Semiazas to save you, and he too will die."

Jez shoved her hair out of her face and glanced past Michael to see the glimmering that marked the edge of Uriel's property. A small glimmer of hope curled inside her gut and she snapped her gaze back to Michael's. "Wait. Whenever I went back through to Lilith's lair, I was healed from any injuries. Something to do with the other plane healing me back to my original form; won't that work for Gabriel and Raphael?"

Michael straightened and smiled before he stepped back and disappeared as the scene resumed.

Raphael crumpled to the side, clutching his chest, and Semiazas's bellow of pain echoed around them, rattling the earth beneath their feet and churning the blue waters of the sea at the bottom of the hill.

Noah ran forward, shoving past Semiazas to step in between her and the demon.

"Wait." Jez held out her hands wishing she could freeze the scene as Michael had done. "We need to get Gabriel and Raphael through to Lilith's lair before they die."

Semiazas pierced her with a hate-filled gaze, and Jez resisted the urge to recoil.

"She'll die if you do nothing, Semiazas. Is that what you want?"

Uriel stepped forward and knelt near Gabriel's still form. "She's right. The portal to Lilith's lair contains healing energy left over from the Garden. It may save Gabriel."

Semiazas ran his fingers gently over Gabriel's cheek before he stood and stepped back. "Save her, and I'll spare you." His gaze bored into Jezebeth. "If she dies, I'll torture and kill everyone you've ever cared for before I come for you. Understand?"

Noah shuddered in front of her, and she reached forward and laid a gentle hand against his back hoping he took the silent hint and didn't antagonize the demon.

Jezebeth nodded once, more to say she understood the threat than she agreed—not that Semiazas needed her buy-in for that particular plan.

Raphael groaned, and Uriel seemed to snap to attention. "Noah, carry Gabriel: I'll get Raphael. We need to take them through the barrier, quickly."

Jez kept her gaze on Semiazas, resisting the primal instinct to run as she watched Noah gently pick up Gabriel's limp form.

Jez slowly backed away from Semiazas, the raw pain on his face scaring her more than anything had so far. But finally, a slow tingling bit at her skin and her foot found thick, soft grass instead of dirt.

"Follow me," Uriel's command was soft, but laced with steel as Jez glanced around at the sudden Utopia they'd stepped into.

He hefted Raphael's form higher in his grip and started across the expansive lawn that sat in front of the large brick three-story.

Noah followed quickly behind Uriel with Gabriel tucked gently against him as the cool, salty breeze ruffled his sandy blond hair.

A large weeping willow sat against the far corner of the yard, and as soon as Uriel reached it, he ducked behind it and disappeared.

Jez cast a quick glance back at the portal where they'd entered, which now was only a pristine ocean beach, and then scanned her gaze over the brick three-story house and the lush lawn of Uriel's property. Too bad they hadn't come here under better circumstances. She, like Noah, would've loved to look around and gain more insight into Uriel.

She nearly ran into Noah's back before she returned her attention forward and quickened her pace to stay close as they followed in Uriel's footsteps.

So much had happened since the pestilence demon had found her, and now thanks to the memories Michael had returned, she realized how much had happened even before that. She wanted to tell Noah everything before her memories faded as Michael had warned, but one look at Gabriel reminded her discussions would have to wait.

Gabriel's limp arm hung down past Noah's waist, her dark blood soaking into the front of his shirt, and Jez darted forward to lift the Archangel's arm and gently tuck it across the woman's stomach.

Noah stopped and captured Jez's gaze, the storm-cloud gray of his eyes boring into hers. "Everything will work out. You'll see."

She didn't know if she believed him or not, but she forced a smile and watched as he stepped past the weeping willow and disappeared.

21

Jezebeth stepped forward, and sudden tingling seared through her entire body in a breathless rush, causing her to stumble. When she caught her balance and glanced up, it was into a scene of pandemonium.

Noah was in the process of gently lowering Gabriel onto the floor of the giant underground cavern that made up Lilith's lair. Uriel had stripped off Raphael's shirt and was examining his still-closing wounds from the sword.

The cavern was filled with echoing noises of several beings speaking at once while incubi and succubi bustled around in what appeared to be confusion and chaos at the interruption of their morning meal.

Jez raised her fingers to her neck, not surprised to find the jagged wound from the truck accident totally gone and in its place, smooth, unbroken skin. There weren't even any remnants of blood left behind on her neck, although her clothes were another matter.

She walked toward Noah, relieved to see the bruises that had marred his face and neck were now totally gone. He had peeled Gabriel's shirt away from her wound and was examining the now-closed wound and remaining severe bruising with wonder. Jez frowned as she glanced down into Gabriel's pale face. The Archangel's eyes were still closed, although her breathing was deep and even. She'd held out hope that once through the portal, both Archangels would be fully recovered. Apparently some injuries were more than even the portal could handle.

Noah glanced up, his gaze imploring. "Jez." He took her hand in his and warm comfort curled through Jez's gut. "The wound is closed, but there must be more internal damage she's going to have to heal with time."

Jezebeth forced a smile and began to answer when words directed her way stopped her in midmotion.

"Welcome, Jezebeth. It's been a long time . . . sister."

Jez glanced toward the sultry voice to see a redhead who reminded her of a harem girl complete with the *I Dream of Jeannie* outfit, only in scarlet red rather than pink. A possessive instinct roared through Jez and she stepped closer to Noah. "Evelin." Jez stiffly bowed her head before meeting the calculating green gaze of the woman who stood before them.

"What have you brought with you?" The distaste was evident in both Evelin's tone and in her gaze as it raked over Noah.

Noah slowly stood until he towered over the newcomer's smaller form. "I'm Noah, on a special assignment for Lilith. So if you'll just be a good messenger and let her know we're here, I'd appreciate it."

Jezebeth tightened her grip on Noah's hand as if to warn him about being too forward with the snide woman in front of them.

Evelin's full lips curved, but the smile never reached her eyes, which flashed with barely suppressed fury.

He raised his brows as he met Evelin's gaze unflinchingly—an action that filled Jez with a surge of pride and satisfaction. Even in the midst of injury and death, Evelin had come to play political games, but Noah had done his research. If he hadn't corrected Evelin's phrasing that Jezebeth had brought *him*, his position as her protector and champion would've been in danger, and Noah would've been free game for any succubi or incubi, including Lilith herself.

Damned politics.

Jezebeth glanced down at Gabriel's still form and anger snapped through her veins. "You're done here. Move along, Evelin. Now."

The woman's green eyes narrowed and an evil smile barely curved her lips, but she nodded once and turned to go.

"Silence!"

All sound and movement inside the cavern stopped suddenly, and Jez glanced up to see Lilith emerging from the entrance to her private chambers. Her face was pale, her features drawn.

The queen's gaze was locked onto Gabriel's still form as she darted forward through the throng knocking people aside in her hurry. When she reached the Archangel's still form, she dropped to her knees, running her hands over Gabriel to assess the extent of her injuries. "Jezebeth, what happened?"

Jez nodded her respect to the queen as she spoke. "My queen. Semiazas accidentally stabbed her. We brought her through the portal in hopes it would heal her injuries."

Lilith nodded and glanced back toward Raphael, who was now sitting up, but still looking unsteady. Surprise flashed across her face as if she'd just noticed him there. When her gaze met Uriel's she stiffened and swallowed hard.

Jez burned to know what history lay between the queen and Uriel, but knew better than to even hint at asking.

"Human, please bring Gabriel to my chambers. Uriel, Raphael too. I can tend them both better from there."

A murmur of shock rippled through the crowd echoing Jez's sentiments. As long as Jez had been in existence, she never remembered the queen playing nursemaid to anyone—let alone two Archangels who were forbidden to consort with their kind.

Jez was even more shocked when Noah didn't comment on being called human, but picked up Gabriel gently and followed after Lilith's retreating form. "Wow. A day for surprises," Jez murmured under her breath as she trailed behind Noah, staying close and making her claim on him obvious for any other incubi or succubi who might have thoughts about trying anything like Evelin had.

How sad that she had to worry about such things when Gabriel could still die and Raphael might still be in danger. Some things never changed.

"I can bloody well walk, Uriel." Raphael's voice echoed around the still-silent cabin and Jez glanced back quickly to see Uriel pick up Raphael and toss the Archangel over his shoulder to the accompaniment of more weak protests.

"Paybacks are hell, Uriel. Remember that," Raphael warned in a halfhearted threat.

Uriel laughed. "When you can kick my ass for this, then I'll know you're back to normal."

* * *

Lilith swallowed back both her fear and the urge to run her hands over Uriel like she had with Gabriel to ensure he hadn't been harmed. She stepped inside her chamber and held the door wide— tacit approval for those following her to enter.

The human came through first with Gabriel cradled in his arms, followed by Jezebeth, and then Uriel with Raphael slung over his shoulder.

"My bed. Put them both on my bed." Glad her voice had come out strong, she pulled back the comforter and top sheet as memories of her and Gabriel cuddled together sleeping rose up to taunt her. Raw emotions filled her throat and threatened to spill out, but she ruthlessly swallowed them back and stepped aside to allow Noah to gently lower Gabriel onto the soft bedding.

When the human took the time to arrange Gabriel's head more comfortably on the pillow and pull off her leather boots before stepping back, Lilith had to swallow back a surprised sob. When Noah Halston had first summoned her, he'd looked at her as if she were the lowest creature on the planet. She burned to know what had changed, but that would have to wait for later.

Uriel slowly lowered Raphael onto the other side of the mattress, careful not to jostle Gabriel's still form. Raphael winced but allowed Uriel to position a pillow behind his back before he relaxed back against it.

"I told you I'm fine, Uriel. I just need to lick my wounds for a few days and I'll be back in the game."

Uriel huffed out a laugh. "Only if that game involves dominos. Don't be so stubborn; there's no reason not to let yourself recover a bit more before you limp off to lick your wounds."

Lilith nearly smiled at the familiar banter between the Archangels. At least it had helped lighten the mood and had chased back her tears. Eager to tend to Gabriel, Lilith turned to the human. "Thank you . . . Noah." She nodded once as a further sign of respect. She couldn't address him as such in front of her subjects, but here, in private, she could show him how much she appreciated what he'd done. It would have to be enough.

Jezebeth cleared her throat. "My lady, if there is anything I can do to help tend them, please ask. I owe Raphael my life, and probably Gabriel as well."

Raphael made a disparaging noise in the back of his throat. "We're even, little one."

Jezebeth seemed ready to argue, but then confusion swam across her features and she fell silent.

Lilith studied the succubus intently, but couldn't sense anything wrong with her beyond fatigue and a need for sustenance.

"That goes for me too," Noah added, breaking Lilith's perusal of Jezebeth. "Anything I can do to repay their kindness, just let me know."

"Xander will show you to your quarters." Impatient to tend to Gabriel and evaluate Raphael's condition, Lilith gestured toward the doorway where the incubus stood lurking. "And will provide anything you both might need. I'll summon you later." She turned her back, not bothering to watch to see if her orders were carried out. Xander was power hungry and could be snide, but she was confident he knew better than to directly disobey his queen.

When the door closed softly behind Jezebeth and her human companion, Lilith began to gently strip off Gabriel's clothing, careful not to press too hard on the Archangel's stomach. Dark bruising marred that area where Lilith had explored very recently, and made Lilith more determined to see it back to its pristine pale beauty.

She pressed her hand against the area as if she could will health back into the still woman in front of her.

On the other side of the bed, Uriel was helping Raphael disrobe as well, even though the injured Archangel cursed and winced with nearly every movement. "Damn it, Uriel. Remind me to be unconscious next time this is necessary."

"Stop whining, Raphael. This can't be as painful as taking Michael's sword through your back."

Lilith froze in midmotion and turned to stare at the two men. "Michael's sword?"

Neither of them acknowledged she'd spoken. Instead, Raphael lifted his hips so Uriel could slide off his leather pants, revealing dusky skin that Lilith remembered well from the night at Uriel's. "That happened fast—one sharp pain."

Uriel shook his head but remained silent.

"We'll get them into the hot spring, which should speed their healing." Lilith gently lifted Gabriel to pull the tattered shirt away and drop it on the floor next to the bed before she reached for Gabriel's pants. "Now, tell me what happened." Lilith didn't care which one of the Archangels answered her, as long as one of them did. She caught Uriel's gaze and held it until he relented and glanced away.

Uriel cleared his throat and quickly filled her in on everything that had happened.

"Then Michael just disappeared?" She snapped her gaze to Uriel's to make sure she'd heard correctly.

"Yes."

When he didn't elaborate, Lilith catalogued all the information inside her mind to go over later, but for right now, all that mattered was making sure Gabriel and Raphael were fully healed.

Lilith pinned up Gabriel's hair before stripping off her own dress and clipping her hair on top of her head. She gently lifted the female Archangel, cradling her against her chest, trusting Uriel would bring Raphael.

Lilith stepped into the swirling hot springs, careful to keep Gabriel's head above water, even though the Archangel didn't need to breathe to survive. As the hot water swirled around them, Lilith began to rock slowly back and forth with Gabriel in her arms as she said a silent prayer for the Archangel.

Life couldn't be so unfair as to have robbed her of first Adam, then Uriel, and now Gabriel. Did God even listen to the prayers of succubi? Or was she considered beneath His notice?

Raphael laid a gentle hand on Lilith's shoulder. "He hears all prayers, Lilith."

She snapped her gaze to his as embarrassment spilled through her. "It's impolite to listen to my thoughts."

He laughed, but the sound was weak. "It wasn't a thought but a prayer, Lilith. And those we hear regardless." He patted her shoulder before letting go.

Uriel stood next to the springs, still fully dressed. "She'll be all right, Lilith." He gestured to Gabriel with his chin. "Your little succubus suggested taking us through the portal to your lair, and damned if she wasn't right. They aren't fully healed, but I think the springs will speed them along."

"She's a smart one," Raphael added. "And her human is worthy of her."

Gabriel murmured and snuggled closer against Lilith's chest. "Gabriel?" Lilith heard the raw hope in her voice, and for once didn't care who heard. "Can you hear me?"

When no response came, Lilith refused to let it dampen the small light of optimism that had warmed her. She felt the weight of Uriel's gaze and glanced up in time to see the raw pain in his silver gaze before the normal mask he showed the world slid firmly into place, locking her out.

Pain sliced through Lilith at his reaction. Even though she'd been the one to tell him they should no longer see each other, her heart still railed against the unfairness of it all. She slowly sucked in a breath and raised her chin. She had found a small measure of budding happiness with Gabriel—something Uriel refused to offer her—so she refused to let guilt steal that possibility from her as well.

"I must go and clean up any damage done in the human world." Uriel turned and then stopped. "Raphael. Call me if you need anything, and let me know how Gabriel fares."

"I will," came Raphael's soft reply from beside Lilith.

When Uriel dematerialized, the tentative dam Lilith had shackled over her emotions broke and sobs wracked her as she held onto Gabriel like a lifeline.

Raphael's strong arms closed around her, and she allowed herself to wallow in the comfort offered as she cried.

22

Jezebeth stepped outside Lilith's room as Noah pulled the door closed behind them. Memories prickled at the edges of her consciousness, and she had the distinct impression that she'd forgotten something important, but no matter how hard she tried, she couldn't catch those escaped thoughts.

Wasn't there something she wanted to tell Noah?

"I greet you, Jezebeth." Xander's words broke her out of her thoughts, scattering even the wispy tendrils of memories she'd tried to capture. He accompanied his words with a blatant up-and-down perusal of Jezebeth—something she knew was done purely to irritate Noah. There had never been much affection between her and Xander, and he'd paid her very little sexual notice in the past.

"Xander." She kept her voice noncommittal. Not that Xander wasn't attractive; he definitely was. In fact, he resembled a Greek god come to life with dusky skin, dark hair, and bedroom eyes. He wore silk pants that had always reminded her of something to be worn inside a Persian harem, which left his impressive, muscled chest bare.

However, Xander was the epitome of a manipulative social climber, and anyone who trusted him did so at their own detriment.

Noah took a quick step forward placing himself in between her and Xander. Noah's eyes were narrowed, his lips thinned into a hard line.

Xander raised one questioning brow. "And greetings as well to your human, Jezebeth." As the man's dark gaze raked over Noah with the same thoroughness he'd done with Jezebeth, Noah scowled, and Jezebeth sighed. She really hated succubi/incubi politics and power plays. Even though they'd been a constant part of her life since her creation, that only meant she'd tired of them long ago.

"My name is Noah, not human. And you are?" Noah pierced Xander with a steady glare.

"Xander." The incubus smiled, completely unruffled by Noah's aggressive stance. "I am an incubus, so am at your service as well, hu— Noah," he amended when Noah growled under his breath. Xander's lips quirked as if unsuccessfully trying to hide his amusement.

Jezebeth started to answer, but Noah distracted her by reaching behind him to pull Jezebeth closer. "Your services aren't required by either of us, *Xander*. Why don't you just show us to our room?"

Xander nodded in a small bow, his lips still quaking as he continued to unsuccessfully hide his amusement. "As you wish."

The hair on the back of Jezebeth's neck prickled, and she made a mental note to remind Noah to watch his back while he was here. He might still have Lilith's ring, but she wasn't sure what protection that would offer him here among her own people. After all, now that his assignment was at an end, any one of them could try to twist him for their own purposes.

Jezebeth smiled at Noah before she followed Xander down the hallway with Noah close beside her, his palm warm on the small of her back. She couldn't remember when exactly he'd begun treating her with this level of intimacy, or when she'd begun to enjoy it, but being back here steeped in her old life reminded her that no matter how much she would miss it, she'd soon have to live without it, and him.

Jez swallowed hard against the thick wave of loss that tightened her throat and instead concentrated on savoring each moment with Noah while she still could regardless of the curious glances Xander kept tossing back at them over his shoulder.

Noah's touch remained gentle, but his gaze swept around them in a continuous sweep as if he were alert for an ambush. Since Xander still walked with him, she didn't explain to Noah the subtle nuances of succubi/incubi political intrigue. This place was worse than the English court at the height of King Henry VIII's reign, which had to be quite a shock to Noah after the human world.

Xander stopped in front of a doorway a corridor away from her own and turned the doorknob and pushed open the door. "This is your room . . . Noah."

To Noah's credit, if he was surprised by Xander's proclamation, he didn't show it. "Where is Jezebeth's room?"

Xander frowned and cocked his head to the side. "Your role as Jezebeth's companion has been completed, I—"

Jez cut Xander off midsentence. "He's my *protector* and has not yet officially been released by Lilith."

Noah opened his mouth to add something, and Jez gave him a subtle head shake, which luckily he picked up on and closed his mouth. Having Noah declare any type of attachment for Jezebeth without Lilith's express consent would be disastrous for him. After all, Jez was Lilith's creature entirely and irrevocably as much as she'd begun to wish it were otherwise.

Xander studied them both before slowly nodding. "These will be your quarters when you are through inspecting Jezebeth's to ensure her safety, as per your agreement with the queen."

Jezebeth noticed the quick look of calculation in Xander's eye and decided to take control of the situation before it got out of hand. "I appreciate your hospitality, Xander, but I can find my way to my quarters and I'm sure Noah can find his own way back to his."

A quick flash of irritation flowed across Xander's chiseled features as he looked between her and Noah. "I'll ensure both of you are sent nourishment." He nodded curtly before turning to walk back down the hall, the way they had come.

Before Noah could ask a bunch of questions that should never be asked inside an open hallway in Lilith's lair, she pulled the door to his quarters shut, grabbed his hand, and pulled him down the hall, around the corner, and down to the end of the hall where her own quarters were located.

Once inside, she closed the door and leaned back against it with a relieved sigh.

"What was that all about?" Noah seemed genuinely curious rather than angry as she'd expected. But then Noah surprised her at every turn, which was one thing she really loved about him.

"You showing a preference for me without Lilith's express permis—"

Noah stepped forward and placed his finger over her lips. He stood so close, the heat radiating off his body teased her with vivid memories of the first time he'd kissed her back at Max's cave.

Her nipples hardened and her pussy clenched as a warm slickness took up residence between her suddenly swollen labia. She let out a shaky breath against his finger as she lost herself in the storm-cloud gray of his eyes.

Noah smiled as if he knew exactly the reaction he'd caused. "And since I haven't been officially released as your protector, it would show weakness for me to defer to anyone else, or to lessen my guard at all in regards to your safety. Since you are regarded as Lilith's property, the care I take with you is looked upon as the care I extend directly to the queen. Correct?"

Jez swallowed hard and managed to nod.

Noah dropped his finger from her lips to trace down her collarbone and over one hardened nipple.

A hard shudder ran through Jez along with a hard stab of arousal. "I keep forgetting about you and all your reading."

Noah chuckled as he slowly brought his mouth to hers, stopping when their lips hovered only a hairsbreadth apart. His warm, sweet breath feathered against her lips. "Maybe I can make you forget about *everything*."

A loud knock on the door startled them both, and Jez inwardly cursed at the interruption as Noah verbalized his creative curses.

Jez turned and opened the door, surprised to find Xander back after her previous dismissal.

"Noah," he said pointedly, as if he expected a reward for not calling him "human" again. "Lilith would like me to help you find some more appropriate wardrobe choices for the duration of your stay here." The incubus's expression was smug as he watched them both for a reaction.

Jez was tempted to question the incubus, but not many who resided in Lilith's lair were stupid enough to lie and use the queen's name in the process. The punishment for such betrayal was something far worse than death—each instance more creative and excruciating than the last, considering Lilith turned all offenders over to the demons for their sport, and none were ever heard from again.

Jez smiled at Noah as she looked again at his shredded, dirty clothes. "I'm perfectly safe in my quarters. No one except you or the queen can enter without my permission."

Noah nodded. "I'll check in on you before bed." Without waiting for her to answer, he turned and followed Xander.

Jez sighed, her body still humming with awareness from Xander's sudden interruption of her liaison with Noah. It would've been nice for once for her and Noah to have some time alone without the threat of the scariest denizens of Hell breaking in on them at any moment. She couldn't wait to make love with him.

Jez started toward the bathroom and stopped suddenly. "Make love?" The words sounded foreign inside her tiny quarters, and she frowned at how they sounded. She'd never referred to sex in that way, and she'd had *lots* of sex over her long lifetime.

Even if Lucifer agreed to protect her and her sisters from Semiazas, Lilith would have to approve her relationship with Noah. The queen would look at what had passed between them so far as normal behavior for a succubus kept in close quarters with a man who could provide her energy. Otherwise, Lilith wouldn't have provided Noah with the ring to keep him safe from Jez's succubus energy siphoning.

Any continuing relationship with Noah . . . Jez couldn't see Lilith agreeing to it. An ache blossomed inside her chest, and she rubbed at the spot with the heel of her hand. She would miss him.

Uh-oh.

She loved him.

Jez's chest tightened and it became harder and harder to suck in her next breath as churning emotions tightened her throat. The backs of her eyes stung and hot tears spilled out onto her cheeks to slide down her face and drip off onto her shirt.

Jez flopped down onto her bed and buried her face into the pillow as she let the tears come.

*   *   *

Noah followed Xander down the long stone corridor, tense and alert in case anything jumped out at him. Jezebeth was obviously the expert on the world of succubi and incubi, but Noah had done enough research on both Lilith and her minions to have an idea what to expect—especially since his time with Jez had refined his knowledge in this area. Not to mention, he didn't trust Xander at all. The incubus was about as subtle as a hooker at the Vatican.

Xander stopped in front of the door to Noah's assigned quarters and waved Noah forward. "Only you can open your quarters unless you give someone else permission."

Noah remembered Jezebeth holding his hand and pulling him inside her quarters. "Does the same go for *entry* to my quarters?"

When Xander nodded once—a succubi/incubi habit that grated on Noah's nerves—Noah ground his teeth. "Does an invitation to enter extend indefinitely?"

Xander's face tightened and the incubus forced a smile. "Only if the invitation is open-ended."

Such as Jezebeth pulling him inside her quarters. Noah could definitely see how that could be construed as an open invitation. He sifted through the situation in his mind, trying to figure out what Xander was up to, and couldn't. He needed more information to find that out, but in the meantime, he had to sidestep the situational sparring as best he could.

Noah reached forward, turned the knob, and pushed the door open to reveal a spacious room about twice the size of Jezebeth's. He frowned and stepped inside. Even from only the quick glance he'd given Jezebeth's quarters, hers looked homey and comfortable where this room looked more like a sterile hotel room with stone walls, regardless of the larger size.

Along the back wall just next to the large canopy bed stood an open door that Noah assumed led to the bathroom. On the right-hand wall was a large open closet jam-packed with clothes and shoes.

Xander cleared his throat, an obvious attempt to regain Noah's attentions. Noah ignored him and instead took another long moment to look around the room before he turned back toward the incubus. "What are the exact parameters for what I need to wear tomorrow for the audience with Lilith?"

Xander's eyes narrowed, and his lips thinned into a hard line. "Lilith asked me to help—"

"And you will help, by telling me the parameters she requires. I don't need any assistance getting cleaned up or dressed, and there are obviously plenty of clothes in here for me to choose from. So what exactly are the requirements for my dress for an audience with the queen?"

Xander's eyes flashed red for a quick moment before returning to their normal brown color, but he remained silent.

Noah enjoyed the small surge of triumph at catching Xander at his own game. "Are there *any* requirements either implied or specifically communicated to you by the queen as far as my wardrobe for the audience with her tomorrow?"

Xander sucked in a deep breath as if fighting the urge to answer the question. Finally he barked out, "No."

Shock slapped at Noah, making him frown. He'd expected a verbal jousting match, so the total lack of any sparring was a bit jarring. "What exactly did Lilith tell you to help me with?"

Xander again seemed to struggle not to answer, but finally through gritted teeth said, "To help you with anything you might need."

Noah laughed as he realized the extent of Xander's creative interpretation of the truth. After all, if Noah hadn't had any warning about the incubi/succubi political climate or culture, he might have gone readily along with whatever Xander had suggested, thinking it was Lilith's wish. The incubus was still going off what Lilith had told him when she'd dismissed him and Jezebeth back at her quarters.

Noah glanced back at Xander, and the hungry look in the incubus's brown eyes stopped him as some of the missing pieces suddenly fell into place. "So you were trying to score some energy off me? How the hell would that help me?"

This time Xander didn't struggle to answer. "I'm quite skilled at providing pleasure, and you're a very attractive man . . . for a human." His gaze raked over Noah until Noah squirmed under the intense scrutiny.

Discomfort morphed into anger, churning inside Noah's gut like giant snakes. "Yeah, and you'd suck out my energy like a parasite. Is that how Lilith tells you to treat guests?"

Xander took a step back even though Noah stood several steps away. "You've obviously allowed Jezebeth to pleasure you; I hardly see a difference unless you protest pleasure between two men—"

Noah cut him off with a sharp gesture and stalked forward to stand toe to toe with the incubus, who seemed rooted to the spot. "I don't give a damn what you see. Nothing about me is any of your business. Neither is anything about Jezebeth, not as long as I'm her protector. Got it?"

When Xander's eyes only widened farther, Noah stepped back inside his quarters and slammed the door in the incubus's face.

The echo of the slamming door did little to salve Noah's swirling anger. Hell, he'd seen a lot during his time with Jezebeth, and his definitions of sex had definitely been altered, but Xander seriously only saw him as a energy source, where Jezebeth . . .

What did Jezebeth see him as?

He pondered that question as he headed toward the bathroom and a hot shower.

Jezebeth may have looked at people in the same way Xander did when he'd first met her. But even back in the bar when he'd rescued her from the pestilence demon she'd surprised him by coming back for him and risking her safety to make sure he made it out alive.

She cared about everyone regardless of their species and that made her much different from Xander. A vivid memory of her cuddling with Max the Djinn came back to him, making him smile.

His cock hardened as he remembered the way her silky hair felt against his face when she'd been spooned in front of him.

He stripped out of his ruined clothes and dropped them on the floor before turning on the shower full blast and stepping under the hot spray. The heated massage of the water soothed his aching muscles and washed away the top layer of grime from the last leg of their journey, but none of that seemed to help his raging erection. The sensation of the water spraying over his heated cock only brought thoughts of what he'd hoped to be doing with Jezebeth right now if they hadn't been interrupted by Xander's bullshit.

Noah found a bar of soap sitting in a recessed niche in the wall and used it to lather every inch of his body. The scent of pomegranates and honey rose around him, filling his senses and hardening his cock nearly to the point of pain. He smiled through the discomfort as he realized this was where Jezebeth's signature scent had come from. But she'd taken plenty of showers while they'd been trying to make it safely to Lilith's lair, and she'd never lost the enticing scent that surrounded him now.

A vivid mental image of Jezebeth in the shower with him rose up to taunt him. Their soapy bodies sliding against each other, soft, slippery skin against him, driving him beyond control. He allowed his eyes to slip closed as he slid his soapy hand down to cup his aching balls and then up to smooth over his cock.

He envisioned Jezebeth wrapping her legs around him as he slid inside her tight pussy. A long moan escaped him as he braced one arm against the wall of the shower while he stroked his cock in one tight fist.

He squeezed harder as he imagined the sensation of her tight channel milking him as she orgasmed around him, her perfect ass gripped in both his palms as he thrust inside her.

The image shoved him over the edge, and his balls tightened up against his body as his cock jerked.

Noah yelled as his come jetted forward to blend with the streaming water. He continued to stroke until the last of the pulses died away, leaving him only partially soft—a reminder he wanted the real thing and not just a fantasy.

He missed her smile.

He missed her quick wit and sense of humor.

Hell, he missed her.

So what was he doing jacking it in the shower to a fantasy when the real thing was just down and around the hallway?

With renewed purpose Noah found one of the small bottles of shampoo and thoroughly washed his hair before soaping up his body to clean off any traces from his brief fantasy culmination. He shut off the water and quickly dried and fished his money out of the ruined pockets of his jeans before heading out into the main room of his quarters to find something to wear.

A quick look through the choices showed him everything from jeans and T-shirts to something more along the lines of the male *I Dream of Jeannie* look that Xander wore. Noah opted for soft cotton boxers, comfortable jeans, and a simple black T-shirt. A pair of soft leather boots in the bottom of the closet were the closest he could find to his size, but they were better than his ruined boots that still lay discarded on the bathroom floor.

He ran his fingers through his hair and did a quick mirror check to ensure it wasn't all standing on end as he crossed the room in quick strides and pulled open the door.

A stunning redhead stood just outside his quarters, her hand raised as if she'd been about to knock. When she saw him, she dropped her arm as a slow smile spread across her face. "I've been sent to provide you sustenance, human." In a quick move that Noah was sure she'd perfected with repetition, she pulled the tie at her throat and her gauzy black dress slithered over her full curves to pool around her feet.

She looked like a woman who had stepped out of a fashion magazine or off a movie screen—attractive, perfect, desirable—and not Jezebeth.

The erection that Noah had had to carefully tuck inside his borrowed jeans deflated as he looked at her, and he stooped to grab the dress and pull it back up around her. "I'm sorry, but I'm not in need of any sustenance."

She gripped the dress with one hand, keeping it up, although it continued to slip out of her tenuous grip to show tantalizing glimpses of perfect female flesh. "I don't understand. Xander said you were in great need of sustenance after your long trip."

At the mention of Xander's name, Noah's mood darkened, and he bit back the words that popped into his head, instead remembering what culture he was in for the time being, and choosing more carefully. "Tell Xander that while I appreciate his kind gesture, I will let him know of any further help I need and don't welcome any more kind gestures on his part."

"Have I displeased you, human? Would you prefer someone taller, shorter, larger, smaller, or perhaps with different coloring? Lilith's lair can provide any type of companion you can imagine, including male or even another species if you'd prefer."

Noah shook his head. "You haven't done anything to displease me. You're a beautiful . . ." He trailed off, not sure if she was succubus, human, or something entirely different. "What I mean is that I desire no companionship or sustenance at this time from anyone." He latched onto the only argument he was sure would work. "I'm still assigned as Jezebeth's protector and must ensure my focus remains there."

Hurt and confusion flashed inside the depths of her blue eyes, but she slowly nodded. "As you wish. I will convey your message to

Xander." She tied her dress and straightened. "Would you like me to show you the way to Jezebeth's quarters?"

Unlike Xander, her words seemed genuine, so Noah smiled. "I appreciate the offer, but I'm good. Uh, thanks for stopping by."

She smiled and left Noah to feel like a ridiculous ass standing in the doorway watching a woman that most men would give their right arm for walk away.

He smiled, thankful he was a good deal smarter than most men.

23

Jezebeth lay on her bed sniffling. Her tears had run their course and now she was left with a headache, a wet pillow, and a large ache inside her chest. Not much of an improvement from before she'd begun to cry.

A soft knock sounded at her door and excitement and anticipation shot through her like a super dose of adrenaline.

"Noah."

Jez lurched out of bed and wiped her wet face on her arm as she jogged toward the door. She grabbed the knob and pulled the door open ready to jump into Noah's arms the second he appeared. "Hey—" Her words died in her throat as she found Jerome on her doorstep. He was a human who had lost his soul to Lilith in an incantation very similar to the one Noah had performed.

"Welcome home, Jez. I've missed you." Jerome's gaze was possessive as it roamed over her, and for the first time since she'd met Jerome over a thousand years ago, his blatant gaze repulsed her. She and Jerome had very often exchanged sustenance over the years and they'd formed a friendship of sorts, but he definitely wasn't who Jez had hoped to see right now.

Jerome was a handsome man by any standards, and he flashed a deadly smile that would cause human women the world over to give him anything he asked for. But it had no effect on Jez. "Are you going to invite me in, or do you want to do it right here against the door to your quarters?" His voice was low and suggestive, and she wondered how she could've ever thought his banter charming.

Because before you met Noah, Jerome was charming, her subconscious insisted.

Jez bit back a grimace—mainly because that little voice was entirely right. "Jerome . . . I'm not really up for anything tonight." She wasn't sure how to tell him she was no longer interested without giving away the reason, which could endanger Noah if word got back to Lilith.

Jerome frowned as he searched her gaze. After a long moment his expression softened and he smiled down at her, sadness filling his blue eyes. He reached out to run his fingers across her cheek.

"You've found love."

Jez stepped back as if he'd slapped her. Was she that transparent? Did Lilith already know?

Jerome laughed and shook his head. "Jez, come on. I won't say a thing. I'm happy for you." He sighed, and the regret in his blue gaze was enough to convince her he was being honest. "I gave up love for one night with Lilith, remember? I didn't realize that no matter how skilled the lover, without love, it's just a fleeting experience. And now I'm paying with eternity."

Relief slid through Jez like a cool autumn wind, and she relaxed the muscles in her shoulders and arms as she stepped forward to lay her hand on Jerome's chest over his heart. "Thank you, Jerome. I hope one day you find love again. You're a good man."

"For a human?" he asked with a small smile.

She laughed and stood on her tiptoes to brush a kiss across his lips. "For anybody." When she dropped her heels to the floor, her gaze traveled past Jerome to find Noah watching her from a few feet away.

His hair was still damp from a shower, the dark gold ends curling lightly around his collar. He was dressed in clean jeans and a black T-shirt, and she wanted nothing more than to pull him inside her quarters and keep him there with her for eternity.

She stumbled back from Jerome as guilt stabbed at her. "Noah. I was . . . we were just . . ."

Noah stepped forward, effectively cutting off Jez's feeble attempts to gather her thoughts. He faced Jerome, the tension in the air between the two men a palpable thing that beat against Jez's skin like tiny electric shocks. "I'm Noah Halston." Noah held out his hand to Jerome and met the other human's gaze unflinchingly.

Jerome's lips quirked as if he approved of Noah's approach and clasped hands with him. "Jerome."

"No last name?"

Jerome huffed out a laugh. "It used to be MacNiel, but once my soul went to Lilith, there seemed very little use for it here."

Noah shrugged as if that made perfect sense. "Thank you for looking out for Jez through the years."

Jez frowned as she glanced up at Noah. She didn't remember mentioning Jerome. Just how long had Noah been standing in the hallway?

Jerome smiled and nodded once, in the same manner the succubi and incubi did before he leaned in close to Noah's ear to whisper something Jez couldn't hear. He straightened and the men exchanged a glance filled with both understanding and meaning.

Irritation flashed through Jez and she grabbed both men's arms. "Hello? I'm still here, and don't appreciate being talked about as if I'm not."

Sexy smiles curved both men's lips, and Jez glanced toward the ceiling—a silent plea for strength in dealing with males of any species.

"I'll just leave you two alone for a while." Jerome stepped back and winked at Jez before turning to walk away down the hallway, leaving her and Noah alone.

Jez glared after him.

"Are you going to invite me in?" Noah's low, sexy voice pulled Jez's attention back to him, and she glanced up into his storm-cloud gray eyes and answered automatically. "When I led you inside earlier, that gave you an open invitation to my quarters."

He grinned, the action sending sudden shocks of arousal through her like thousands of tiny darts of fire. "I know. But I'd love it if you invited me inside." The dark promise and double entendre shot through her, causing familiar slick moisture to form between her labia.

He stepped forward, herding her backward until he stood just outside and she stood just inside her quarters.

The ache inside Jez's chest had disappeared to be replaced by a growing warmth that seemed to thrive when Noah was around. It was like nothing she'd ever experienced in her long millennia of life. The sensation spread outward to meet up with the growing ache between her thighs.

So it was true. She really did love this man.

Human or not, he'd captured her heart, and there was no going back. Not that she wanted to. Now that she'd identified the emotion, she wanted to revel in it, to wrap herself inside it and explore its depths until reality came crashing back in on them.

Her decision made, she grinned as she reached up and grabbed a handful of the front of his shirt and hauled him inside her quarters, slamming the door behind him.

She turned back to jump into his arms, but Noah surprised her by picking her up and tossing her over his shoulder so her face bumped against his muscled back. "Noah!"

He slapped her lightly on the ass, sending a shot of straight arousal to churn deep inside her gut. "Do you know what I was thinking about while I was in the shower with my hands slick with soap that smelled just like you while I stroked my cock?"

Jez's breath caught in her throat as the vision he described took up residence inside her mind and refused to dissipate. She swallowed hard as he dumped her on the bed, where she bounced lightly against the soft mattress. "What were you thinking about?" Her voice came out barely a whisper, but she knew he heard her by the way his eyes darkened.

He stripped off the black T-shirt and tossed it away to reveal his broad shoulders and firm chest lightly dusted with sandy blond hair. Jez's gaze traced downward to where the line of hair disappeared under Noah's jeans.

As if summoned there by her thoughts, Noah brought his hands to the top button of his jeans and Jez watched fascinated as he undid the button and slowly slid down the zipper to reveal soft-looking black boxers tented by Noah's erection. A small dark spot against the cloth told her the swollen head of his cock was already leaking pre-come.

"I was thinking about *you*."

She snapped her gaze back up to his face in time to see the most vulnerable expression she'd ever seen etched across those handsome features.

"I was thinking about not only how you would feel beneath me, or surrounding me as I slid inside you, but also about how I'm not sure I could ever go back to a life without you in it."

Jez's throat tightened as emotions tore through her like a tidal wave, closing her throat and pressing against her chest.

"I love you, Jezebeth. I don't give a damn that you're a succubus, or that you have to face Lucifer soon, or that Lilith thinks you belong to her. I don't care about any of that, because you and I really belong to each other, and nothing anyone else says or does can ever change that."

Pressure built at the backs of Jez's eyes until her vision wavered from the unshed tears filling her eyes. She pushed up onto her knees and poked her index finger against his chest. "You know that's a dangerous way of thinking, don't you? To fall in love with a succubus? Lilith would kill you, and she's not the only one who would try—she's just the one with the most right to."

Noah kicked off his boots and slid his jeans and boxers off in one fluid movement, revealing his long, beautiful cock with the heavy sac that hung beneath. He crawled onto the bed and wrapped one arm around her waist as he toppled her backward and fell on top of her, bracing his weight with his arms.

He laid between her legs, his cock pressing against her pussy through her jeans. "Look at me and tell me you don't feel the same way."

Jez let herself fall into his gaze, but couldn't bring herself to lie, even to save Noah from himself. No matter what else happened, she wanted him to know the truth. "I can't. Heaven help you, Noah, I love you too, which dooms us both."

A slow, satisfied smile curved his lips as he lowered his face to hers to whisper against her lips. "I can't think of anyone I'd rather be doomed with."

The combination of his warm breath against her skin and his words sent a wave of gooseflesh marching over her, and she shivered under him even as she chuckled at his words.

Noah lowered his weight onto her and she wrapped her arms around him, threading one hand into the hair at his nape while the other hand explored the fascinating ridges of the muscles along his sides and back.

Noah took possession of her mouth, delving inside as if she were a delicacy to be savored. He thrust against her, his cock a teasing hardness and heat through the unwanted barrier of her jeans.

Jez started to pull away to undress, but then Noah skimmed his fingers down her sides and slid them under her shirt. As soon as his fingers hit her bare skin, Jez moaned into his mouth and arched against him.

For the first time, Jez didn't fight for control, but let Noah set the pace, ready to follow wherever he led.

As if Noah sensed her surrender, he growled deep inside his throat and skimmed his lips down her cheek to the hollow at her throat—a spot that drove her wild.

The nibbling kisses and the exquisite friction from Noah's cheek stubble sent arousal skittering down Jez's neck into her torso. Her nipples tightened and her breasts ached, suddenly confined and uncomfortable inside her bra.

As he continued the sensual torture, a slow, steady throb began deep and low inside Jez's belly.

Noah skimmed his hand up higher under her shirt, cupping her breasts through the bra. The warm, possessive touch made Jez squirm and arch against him, but it wasn't enough. She wanted skin-to-skin contact.

As if he sensed her impatience, Noah nipped her neck just hard enough to get her attention and began to slowly unbutton the few still-intact buttons that held her shirt together.

Jez gasped and lolled her head to the side to give him better access to do as he pleased against her neck while she held his head in place with her hand.

"There will be no rushing tonight, Jezebeth. I'm going to unwrap you like a package and savor every second." The husky words whispered against her skin sent a frisson of awareness through her entire body.

Noah made her feel cherished, cared for . . . and beautiful. Jez tried to think of the last time she'd felt truly beautiful—not just in whatever form she'd taken to please someone else, but her true self.

She couldn't remember.

He raised his head to look at her and frowned. "No thinking." He traced his finger over the crease between her brows, smoothing it away as he smiled down at her. "This is all about feeling." Noah ripped away the rest of her shirt, leaving the scraps under her as he popped open the front clasp of her bra and slowly peeled back the cups as if she were a long-awaited Christmas present he wanted to savor.

His expression was filled with a mix of wonder and male possessiveness that made Jez catch her breath. But when Noah leaned forward to suck one tight nipple into the warmth of his mouth, Jez moaned. Each pull of his lips against her flesh sent liquid warmth coursing through her body, tightening the tension slowly building inside her.

When Noah moved his mouth to the other breast, his warm palm cupped the one he'd just left, massaging and gently rolling her nipple between his fingers while Jez bucked her hips against him, wanting him inside her.

Noah made an "mmm" sound deep inside his throat, the vibrations traveling through her breast and along her skin like a whispered caress. She traced the muscled planes of his back and shoulders and then skimmed her fingers down to cup his well-muscled ass in her palms, urging him to grind against her.

Noah pushed up on all fours and Jez immediately missed his warmth. But when she glanced up into his intent gaze, she knew he was far from finished with her.

Anticipation curled inside her gut like a sleeping dragon ready to awaken at Noah's command, and she laid her palm over her quivering belly, willing herself to calm and just enjoy the sensations he continued to create.

Noah picked up her hand and placed a gentle kiss on her palm before laying her arm on the bed beside her. He leaned down slowly, his gaze still locked with hers as he laved the tip of his tongue along the waistband of her jeans.

Jez jerked at the intense warmth of his mouth against her sensitive skin, and Noah only chuckled as he dipped his tongue inside her navel and then blew on the wet patch of skin.

Jez gasped as another march of goose bumps flowed over her, turning her entire body into a live wire. "Noah, please . . . I want you inside me."

He didn't answer and, instead, slowly unbuttoned and unzipped her jeans, thoroughly kissing and licking each newly exposed patch of skin before revealing more.

Sensations buffeted her in continuous waves until Jez was panting and had the sheets on either side of her in a death grip.

Noah continued his assault, slowly edging the jeans down her hips and exploring each newly exposed expanse of skin. When the jeans edged low enough to reveal her smooth mons, he glanced up at her and raised his brows. "I want you as just you, Jez. You don't ever have to put on a costume of any type with me."

Jez bit her bottom lip. She hadn't thought he'd noticed that part of her true form, and most current-day men preferred the smooth mons, and she thought Noah did too. Only one way to find out . . .

She concentrated on Noah and let her gift take over. After a quick second of tingling throughout her body, she glanced down and frowned at what she saw. There were tiny freckles dotting her skin, her stomach slightly rounded, and her mons was now covered with dark brown curls. This was her true form, the one she only took when she was alone. The form she'd decided on long ago that she felt most comfortable in. "This is impossible."

Noah grinned up at her. "You tried to use your shifter magic on me, didn't you?" When she remained silent he spoke again. "You stubborn succubus. I meant it—I want you, as you are. Got it?"

She nodded even though she was still trying to fathom how he could choose this form out of any other in the universe. After all, she could be in any outer form for him and still be her true self on the inside. The last thing she'd expected was for anyone to prefer the same form she did.

A slow grin curved her lips. "Except you," she said, answering her own unspoken thought. "You've always surprised me since the first day we met."

He pulled her jeans and panties off in one quick movement and then crawled back up the bed toward her like a hungry predator. "Good." When he reached her knee, he licked a path up her inner thigh, spreading her legs wide as he positioned his large body between them. "I'll do my best to never stop."

Before she could think of a reply, he buried his tongue between her labia and licked a slow line up to the silky skin just below her clit.

A strangled gasp escaped from Jez's throat as the intense sensations ripped through her.

Noah repeated the action over and over, faster and faster until Jez thought she'd jackknife off the bed from the spasms taking up residence inside her belly.

Noah anchored her to the bed with his large hands and held her still while he devoured her—licking, laving, nipping, and sucking—but only sparing a quick kiss for her clit until Jez's thighs were quivering and her belly was clenched so tight with the need to orgasm that she was afraid she'd never be able to relax again once this was over.

When Noah stopped all motion suddenly and gently sucked the tip of her clit inside his mouth, her world shattered and exploded—a thousand explosions rocking her body while waves of liquid pleasure pulsed through her in a seemingly never-ending stream of ecstasy.

Distantly she heard murmuring and only when her body began to calm and relax did she realize it was Noah. His words of encouragement, love, and wonder buoyed her and supported her back to reality. When sanity returned, she glanced up into his face just as he slid his cock inside her in one slow thrust.

She gasped as he stretched and filled her, widening her thighs and tipping her hips to take him deep. Jez wrapped her legs around him, hooking her ankles around each of his thighs, pulling him tighter against her as he filled her, and relaxing when he slowly retreated before thrusting inside her again.

Noah set the rhythm and Jez held tight to him, her gaze locked with his as her body slowly tightened around him. Each steady movement drove her higher until Noah murmured her name and stiffened over her, the heat of his come spilling inside her.

The first slap of energy stole the breath from her body and a frenzied tingling flowed outward along every nerve ending to rebound on itself and boomerang through Jez's body again. When Noah slumped on top of her and gently stroked her hair, she had to chase back the euphoria of the orgasm/energy combination to let her brain process his words.

"Ride me, Jez. I want to see you come again." His words were slightly slurred, and she smiled to herself as smug female satisfaction spilled through her. As Noah rolled them over, she held on and positioned herself more comfortably on top of him. His cock had softened slightly when he came, but was still hard enough for her to ride him and tempt him back to full power.

Noah grabbed her hips in his large palms as he looked up at her. "Take your hair down and let me watch you, Jez."

She reached back slowly, her breasts rising as she arched her back. Jez smiled when Noah's eyes darkened and his cock hardened inside. She slipped the elastic band out of her hair, tossed it aside, and ran her fingers through the long mass until it spilled around her bare shoulders and edged down to cover the top mounds of her breasts.

"My God, you're beautiful. Even more so, like this."

His words warmed her, and she basked in his gaze as she began to move.

She leaned back, bracing one hand behind her on Noah's thigh as she slowly pushed up onto her knees and then dropped back down, taking him deep. His aura tasted sweet as his energy merged with hers and her movements created an exquisite friction between them.

Noah's moan merged with hers as she increased her speed and let her eyes slip closed and her head drop back. He grabbed her hips, allowing her to set the pace, but pulling her tight against him with each thrust.

A fine sheen of perspiration dotted Jez's body as she continued to move on top of him, the intoxicating scents of musky arousal and sex blending with Noah's unique scent. Jez quickened her pace as the familiar tingling that signaled a full-body orgasm began to buzz deep inside her gut. Her breathing choppy, she rode Noah hard, aiming toward the bliss that hovered just out of her reach.

When he stiffened and cried out beneath her, his hot come shot inside her to be absorbed and turned into energy that washed through her body in a scalding rush. Pure liquid heat spilled through her veins like warmed brandy on a cold night. Jez hovered on top of the exquisite sensation, slowing her movements as the heat drained away leaving behind a wonderful boneless sensation.

She slumped on top of Noah, burrowing against his chest as she waited for his arms to wrap around her.

When nothing happened, a sliver of icy unease stabbed through her previous warmth, jarring her fully alert. Jez raised her head to find Noah pale, his eyes closed, his breathing shallow.

She slid off him, gently laying her hand against his cheek. "Noah?"

His eyes fluttered open, his gaze unfocused as if she'd drained him of his energy.

Panic galloped through her, churning like acid inside her stomach. "But the ring—" She cut her words short as she grabbed Noah's right hand and touched the ring he still wore.

If someone had tampered with the ring . . .

When Lilith's essence tingled against her own, she knew the ring was genuine. But one glance down into Noah's pale face told her that something had gone horribly wrong. "No. Please, no." She covered her mouth with her hand as the consequences of what she'd done spilled through her mind on fast-forward.

"Jezebeth."

Jez jumped at Lilith's soft words and then with one hand laid protectively over Noah's chest, she turned to face her mistress.

24

Noah struggled not to lose consciousness even as black dots danced and teased at the edges of his vision. He forced open heavy eyelids to find Lilith standing next to the bed in a gauzy black dress that showed more tantalizing glimpses of creamy, perfect skin than it left to the imagination. Long, dark hair spilled over her shoulders, and the only thing that kept her from being breathtakingly beautiful was the carefully blank expression she wore.

"Why didn't the ring work?" Jez demanded as she laid one warm protective hand on Noah's chest.

Noah wanted to curl around that warmth and pull it inside his body, but somehow he knew he was already too close to dying to reverse the process. He searched for regrets, and only found two—that he would have to leave Jezebeth, and that even had he lived, he wasn't able to protect her from Lilith and the world she'd been created into.

"In the outside world, the energy in the ring was stronger than your inherent succubus nature, but here in my lair, that's no longer true. The humans I take in here are inherently changed so they live longer and also gather energy in the same manner as the incubi and succubi. Noah is still purely human." Lilith stepped forward, and Jez moved her body to shield Noah.

Curiosity and surprise sparked in Lilith's dark gaze. "This human means enough to you to protect him from me?"

Jez swallowed hard. "I love him." As soon as the words were out, Jez wished them back—especially when Lilith froze in place, a frown marring her lovely features. The tension in the room grew until Jez fought to breathe against the stinging energy emanating from her queen.

Finally, Lilith cocked her head to one side and looked past Jez toward Noah. "But does he love you in return, little one?"

"Yes."

Jez stiffened at Noah's soft word, running her hand along his chest as she glanced up at Lilith to gauge her reaction. When Lilith's expression continued to hold only curiosity, dread tightened Jezebeth's stomach. There were worse things than a curious and very powerful succubus queen, but they were the stuff of Jez's nightmares. This situation was scary even in the light of day.

"We shall see." Lilith's words cut through the chamber like an icy knife as she circled the bed slowly, crossing to the other side before sitting down next to Noah.

As the bed dipped with her mistress's weight, Jez took Noah's hand and laced her fingers with his. She had no way of protecting him from Lilith that wouldn't immediately get them both killed. The knowledge of that weakness burned through her, making her want to lash out in frustration. But she bit her tongue hard until the urge receded and she continued to watch Lilith warily.

"Easy, little one." Lilith met Jez's glare with a calmness that made the skin on the back of Jez's neck prickle. "I only wish to speak to your human."

When Lilith reached out and brushed the hair away from No-ah's graying face, Jez stiffened but held herself in check.

"So you say you love my Jezebeth, Noah Halston?"

Noah swallowed hard and slowly turned his head to face Lilith. The strain on his features showed how difficult even that small movement was for him. "Yes." The word was so faint and weak that a giant hand squeezed Jez's chest. She remembered many times where his words had burned with intensity . . . but not now, not after what she'd unknowingly done to him.

Lilith's lips curved, but the smile didn't touch the rest of her face, or even reach her dark eyes. "You are dying, Noah. Dying from one of my creatures taking too much of your energy. Only I can save you now." She stroked Noah's hair as if he were a small, sick child, and Jezebeth had to check the urge to slap Lilith's hand away from him.

Lilith glanced up and met Jez's gaze, a clear warning to stay quiet and not interfere shone in the dark depths of the queen's gaze. "What is your life worth to you, human?"

Jez tightened her fingers around Noah's and thought she felt a slight squeeze in return, which comforted her at least a little.

Noah licked his lips as if to prepare for the great energy required for him to answer. "Depends. On. Cost."

Lilith laughed—the first genuine thing she'd done since she'd entered the room, and the sudden shift sent a cold stab of fear straight to Jez's gut. "I can see why Jezebeth is interested in you, human. You're not like all the others." She traced her fingers along his cheek and rubbed one thumb over his lips, but instead of open-ing his lips, he kept his mouth unmoving under Lilith's questing fingers.

Jez sucked in a silent breath as she waited for Lilith's eyes to snap with fire—a feat she'd only seen the succubus queen master—or for Lilith's temper to explode, but neither came, which made the tension in the room skyrocket even higher. Jez had the impression of sitting next to an unexploded bomb with a faulty countdown clock.

"What is the cost compared to what I can offer you, Noah Halston? After all, your incantation was what began this entire episode, wasn't it?" Lilith leaned forward so her hair trailed over Noah's bare chest and she brushed her lips over his.

Noah didn't react, and Jez hoped it was from choice and not because he simply didn't have the life force left to respond.

"I offer you the same deal you requested with that incantation, human. One night of ecstasy with me, where I will fulfill any fantasy you can possibly imagine, and in return I'll return your life force, and you'll be my creature for eternity." She sat up straight and looked down at him. "Of course, since I don't like my playthings to be used by others without my permission, you won't ever see Jezebeth again, but that's a small price to pay for your life, isn't it?"

Lilith's words plunged deep until Jez felt like her insides were being slashed apart with a thousand sharp knives. Her gut clenched, her chest ached, and tears filled her eyes. She could no longer imagine her life without Noah, but even worse was a world with no Noah in it at all. As a succubus, she'd survived horrors of all kinds, and though it would be the hardest thing she'd ever done, she would learn to live with the knowledge that he was alive and well— even if he could never be with her.

"No." Noah's quiet word sent skittering panic down Jez's spine.

"What do you mean, no?" Jez took Noah's chin between her fingers and turned his face so she could meet his gaze. "Please, Noah. I couldn't stand it if you died. Please, take the deal . . . and live."

His features softened and he slowly blinked his eyes, as if it cost him even to keep them open. "Not worth life, without you."

At the unexpected resolve and strength in Noah's voice, the

tears that had pooled in her eyes spilled forward to streak down her cheeks to fall against his chest. Jez collapsed onto Noah's chest as sobs wracked her.

"This is your last chance, human. You have only seconds of life left inside you."

Noah's body tensed under her, and then his arm settled over her. He had used the last of his strength to comfort her, and that knowledge only made Jez cry harder.

"Lilith . . ." Noah said against Jez's hair. "Go to hell."

With those words, all hope drained out of Jez, along with her will to live. Lilith had been Noah's last chance and now he was going to die.

Lilith's soft laugh ran over Jez in a skin-tingling rush and then died away with an eerie echo. "So be it." Lilith vanished, her powerful aura receding from the room and leaving dead, still air behind.

"Noah, please forgive me," Jez whispered against his chest as hot tears flowed unchecked. "I love you." Pain washed over her in great waves and Jez gave herself up to it, sobs wracking her body as she vented her pain and anger at the unfairness of the universe.

Finally, she'd cried herself dry. Noah's chest under her cheek was wet with tears and she felt hollow and empty—a sensation she knew she would most likely carry for the rest of her life. Exhaustion filled her like a sudden overwhelming weight from the emotional toll of the last hour, and she sighed and let her eyes slip closed.

A gentle hand stroked her hair and she stiffened, half expecting it to be Lilith gloating as Jez wept over Noah's dead body. Jez wiped her eyes and sat up to find Noah smiling up at her, his face full of color, his storm-cloud gray eyes studying her.

"Noah?" She ignored the waver in her voice as she ran a hand through his hair and over his cheek to reassure herself she wasn't dreaming, and he was very much alive.

"It's still me." He shrugged. "I'm not sure how, but I suddenly feel great." He slowly sat up and flexed his arms and fingers as if making sure everything still worked as it should.

"What happened? You were near death. You turned Lilith down." Thoughts raced through Jez's mind, tripping over each other as she tried to make sense of the fact that Noah was alive and well and sitting in front of her.

Noah grinned at her, and the vise around her chest loosened and fell away. "Maybe she had a change of heart?" he asked hopefully.

Jez held back the sarcastic laugh that threatened to bubble out of her throat and dropped her gaze to her lap. There would probably be a price to pay for this miracle, there always was—but she would gladly pay it just for the sight of Noah alive, well, and happy in front of her.

Noah lifted Jez's chin so she met his gaze. "Yeah, I don't really believe that either. But I'm definitely not going to complain about the outcome right now."

Jez couldn't help but smile at Noah's playful tone. She couldn't think of any other being, human or otherwise, who would be so accepting of his own near death. "I'm sorry, Noah. I had no idea the ring wouldn't work here, or—"

Noah cut off her words by laying his fingers over her lips. "Hey, if I have to die, that tops my list as one of the ways I'd prefer to go out."

Jez glanced down at his naked body and grinned. "Well, I guess when you put it that way, I'd have to agree." She reached out to lay a hand against his chest, and joy leapt inside her as his heart beat steady and strong under her palm. "How would you like to spend the night with a succubus? No sex," she added quickly. "I don't think I can handle nearly killing you twice in one night—but just some spooning and a nice, long relaxing night of sleep?"

Noah cupped her face in his palm, and she leaned into the offered comfort as she drank in his gentle, loving gaze. "As long as you're the succubus in question, then sign me up."

* * *

Lilith returned to her rooms to find Gabriel sitting up in bed, sipping something hot from a ceramic mug. She raked her gaze over the hot springs and the rest of her quarters, but they were alone.

"Raphael just left." Gabriel shoved damp tendrils of her silver blond hair away from her face and gave Lilith a weak smile. "He said to thank you for your hospitality, but that now that the tough part was done, he could finish recuperating on his own."

A sound escaped Lilith—a combination sigh and a huff of a laugh. She wasn't sure why she should be surprised. "I guess he can take care of himself. He's been doing it for this long."

"I think he also realized I'd like to be alone with you."

Surprise and joy twined through Lilith's stomach, chasing away all the conflicting emotions swimming through her for the past several hours. She sat on the edge of the bed near Gabriel, the soft mattress gently dipping with her weight. "I was really worried. You came through the front portal looking just short of death."

Gabriel sipped from the mug and frowned as she lowered it to her lap. "I was." Her tongue darted out to wet her bottom lip. "Not that I excuse Semiazas's actions, but I know it was accidental."

"Accidental?" Lilith snapped. "Semiazas doesn't do anything accidentally."

A slow, sad smile curved Gabriel's lips. "There's a long history between Semiazas and me. Until recently I'd held out hope that he could . . . that he *would* change back to the being he used to be." She shook her head. "Now I know that won't happen, and I've made peace with it." She shrugged. "He would've gladly gutted anyone in that clearing . . . except me. I saw the surprise and pain in his eyes even as it blossomed inside my belly."

Lilith had heard rumors about a relationship between Gabriel and Semiazas back before the fall, but she hadn't given them much credence until now. A slow curl of jealousy worked its way through her. "So what will you do now?"

"I hope to finish my tea, take another dip in those healing hot springs with you, and then we can discuss someone inside your lair who has been betraying you."

25

Comforting, soft warmth and the sweet scent of pomegranate and honey tempted Noah back to consciousness.

He opened his eyes to find Jez spooned in front of him wearing the T-shirt and sleep shorts she'd pulled on so they could avoid the temptation of skin-to-skin contact throughout the night. Surprisingly, that hadn't been an issue—after the emotional near-death episode, they'd both fallen asleep quickly and Noah had slept hard.

He nuzzled his face against the back of her neck, enjoying the sensation of waking up with her in his arms, her soft hair sliding against the stubble on his cheeks.

"Mmm. Keep that up and you'll be back on death row." Her voice was heavy with sleep and Noah's cock hardened instantly against her ass.

He couldn't help but smile and pull her tighter against him even as he ignored the urge to roll her over, strip off her clothes, and plunge inside her—death sentence or not. "I agree. But this is going to be very hard . . . er . . . difficult."

She chuckled and then stretched before turning over in his arms to face him. "You look great." Her smile faded as she reached out to run her fingers over his stubble.

"What can I say? Alive is a good look for me." He grabbed her hand and laid a kiss on her palm before laying it flat against his chest.

Her smile returned, but it was almost sad. "We still have to audience with Lilith this morning. She could choose to kill us both for our relationship and be done with it, you know."

"She could. But I wouldn't have traded one minute of last night or this morning for anything, no matter what happens. Would you?"

Jez cocked her head to one side, a mannerism he loved. "No. We're probably both insane for thinking that, but you're right. I wouldn't trade it away."

An hour later, Noah guided Jez out the front door of her quarters, his hand resting possessively on the small of her back as they headed down the hallway toward the throne room. One perk of last night was they no longer needed to hide their attachment from Lilith or anyone else. If Lilith decided to kill them, there wasn't anything either of them could do about it, so Noah chose to live whatever time he had left as he wished.

The hallways were strangely deserted, but Noah sensed people watching them from the shadows and just beyond doorways, even though he couldn't see anyone.

When they stepped inside the main cavern where they'd entered the day before, Noah glanced up to see glittering multicolored stalactites covering every available inch of ceiling space, the glow of light emanating from the crystals strong enough to illuminate the entire cavern. The ceiling gave way to smoothly polished black walls dotted with niches recessed at various heights along the walls— each filled with thick candles, glittering gems the size of Noah's fist, or erotic silver statues.

Surprise made him slow to study some of the contents more closely until Jezebeth tugged on his arm, reminding him Lilith waited.

Evelin, the tiny redhead who had exchanged verbal sparring with Jezebeth yesterday, stood just outside two double doors that were high enough for a semitruck to easily drive under. The woman paused as they approached and then nodded to the two small demons who reminded Noah of dog-sized gargoyles.

Each tiny gargoyle grabbed a large steel ring attached near the bottom of the doors and pulled the doors wide to reveal Lilith's throne room.

The throne room was smaller than Noah had expected, more the size of a large living room than the huge expanse the doors implied. The soft glow from the ceiling here set a more intimate mood than the brighter lights in the outer cavern.

Lilith's throne sat on a raised dais, the large chair covered in various colored silks and pillows. A wide runway led up to her throne, and on either side were sunken areas filled with large cushions and pillows. Lilith herself wore black, her long hair curving around her as if it possessed a life all its own. She lounged comfortably on the chair and yet seemed tense at the same time.

The sudden charged silence in the room made Noah glance around to realize that Jezebeth and Evelin lay prostrate on the floor on either side of him while he stood gaping. He glanced back toward Lilith expecting to see her displeasure at his social gaffe, but surprise shot through him when her expression struck him as more amused than angry.

Lilith met his gaze and her lips curved slowly into a sensuous smile of invitation. "Evelin, come before me." Noah started forward, but froze when Evelin stood in one graceful movement. Only then did his brain catch up and he realized Lilith hadn't spoken to him.

Jezebeth stayed in her submissive position next to him and Noah remained quiet, not sure what to expect as Lilith broke their gaze, her expression turning to boredom as she turned her attention to Evelin.

Evelin swept forward down the runway that led to the throne like a dignitary expecting praise. She bent low before Lilith, holding the uncomfortable pose for a long moment before speaking. "My queen. What is it you wish of me?" She sounded so smug that Noah wanted to shake her until her eyes rattled around inside her head.

"Rise and face me, Evelin."

Evelin rose, her satisfied smile making her look like a sated predator.

Lilith returned the predator's smile and foreboding spilled through Noah in a warm, slow rush. From his limited dealings with Lilith, her current expression couldn't be good.

"How soon can I expect Jezebeth's sisters?" Lilith's voice easily carried to the back of the throne room where Noah stood and Jez still lay prostrate on the floor.

The smile drained from Evelin's face like melting wax. "My queen?"

"Did you not hear me?" Lilith's voice was deceptively mild, but Noah heard the steely threat underneath the softly spoken words and was very glad it wasn't aimed at him.

"Yes, Lilith. I—"

"Let me save you time, Evelin. You betrayed me and your sisters for Semiazas's lies."

All color drained from Evelin's face, and she swallowed hard as her fingers tightened into fists. "No, mistress. I would never betray *you*."

Lilith raised one dark brow, and Evelin lifted her chin in defiance. "I am your most loyal subject, my queen. I would do anything for you."

"But not for your sisters? That which injures my succubi and

incubi injures me. It depletes my energy and my power, which threat-
ens my survival."

Evelin swallowed hard but didn't drop her gaze from Lilith's.
"What proof do you have, my queen, of this slander?"

Lilith raised her right hand and a shimmering form appeared
next to her throne. When the form solidified, Noah sucked in a
quick breath.

Gabriel.

She seemed fully healed; the energy pouring off her was a thousand times what Noah felt from Lilith when in her presence. Tall
and lanky, she had athletic curves that were well showcased in her
white formfitting clothes. Long silver blond hair spilled over her
shoulders and down to her waist, her ice blue eyes making her seem
like a winter fairy suddenly come to life. A marked contrast to the
injured Archangel he'd carried through the portal just yesterday.

She met his gaze and smiled as if aware of his thoughts and
observations. She nodded to him once, surprising him before she
turned her attention toward Lilith.

"Welcome, Gabriel." The intimacy in Lilith's voice and the way
she raked a possessive gaze over the woman surprised Noah, and
he glanced toward Jezebeth to gauge her reaction, but then realized
Jezebeth's forehead was still pressed to the floor since Lilith hadn't
yet addressed her.

When Evelin gasped, Noah turned back toward the dais in time
to see Gabriel kissing Lilith.

Wow. Immortals gone wild . . .

He froze as he stared at the two women, his cock hardening
inside his jeans and his balls pulling up tight against his body.

Gabriel's hand was braced on the arm of the throne, her palm
cradling Lilith's cheek gently while a tender kiss bloomed between
them.

This was no female/female kiss like Noah had seen on porn flicks or between two women trying to get attention in a bar. The scene in front of him was so intimate and caring—two stunning women exchanging a kiss, as if they'd been not only lovers but friends, that Noah couldn't help but stare.

Finally Gabriel broke the kiss and ran her thumb over Lilith's bottom lip before stepping back.

Lilith's tongue darted out to wet her bottom lip, and Noah wondered what taste Gabriel had left behind. The two women's gaze lingered on each other for a long moment before Lilith smiled and turned back to look at Evelin. "Your accuser is the Archangel Gabriel. Do you dare call her a liar?"

Holy shit.

Jezebeth's head snapped up and she glanced up at Noah with a "what the hell" expression filling her features.

"My apologies, Jezebeth." Lilith's light laugh softly echoed around the room. "Rise and stand next to your protector while we finish this unpleasant business first."

Jez unfolded from the ground and slowly stood as if expecting Lilith to change her mind at any moment. Noah captured her hand in his, lacing their fingers together.

Evelin's skin had taken on a sickly gray color, each movement jerky instead of graceful like when she'd greeted them and escorted them to Lilith.

"In light of your silence, succubus, stand and be judged, before God." Gabriel stalked forward and Evelin flinched as if expecting to be struck. Instead, Gabriel stood just in front of the succubus, close enough to invade the woman's personal space but not close enough to touch her.

Evelin stiffened, her gaze suddenly fastened on the floor in front of her.

Gabriel reached out slowly and stroked Evelin's long red hair. When Evelin flinched again, Gabriel laughed and brought the hair close to her face and inhaled. "Do you know what I smell, little one?"

Evelin whimpered as her entire body began to shake.

"Burnt cinnamon and guilt."

The words echoed through the chamber like a death knell.

Evelin's gaze snapped up to Gabriel's, and the tiny woman froze as their eyes met.

The soul gaze.

Noah shuddered as he remembered what that had felt like when Uriel had done the same to him. He rubbed at his chest, the remembered sensation of his raw, aching insides coming back to him fresh and new.

When Gabriel finally broke the gaze, Evelin sagged, but remained standing.

Gabriel glanced toward Lilith. "We were correct. Even if I hadn't smelled her scent on Semiazas in Central Park, what I've just seen confirms our suspicions."

"Suspicions?" Evelin stiffened. "You had no proof?"

A sharp gesture from Lilith silenced the woman's words. "I pulled you from a horrible human existence and gave you an extended life and all the gifts that come with being a succubus, and yet you chose to betray me. You'll get no leniency here, Evelin. You have no idea what you could've done here."

"What will you do with her?" Gabriel asked softly.

"She is yours to do with as you wish." Lilith's gaze filled with a thousand unsaid things Noah couldn't decipher, but apparently, Gabriel could, because the Archangel wrapped one arm around Evelin's neck and blew a kiss to Lilith before she dematerialized, leaving only Lilith, Noah, and Jezebeth to stare at the place where they'd been only moments before.

Noah tightened his grip on Jezebeth's hand, unsure what the display they'd just seen meant for the two of them.

Lilith laughed, the sound more amused than threatening. "There is no need to fear, human. That business was concluded with you here only to reassure you both that Evelin's interference will no longer be tolerated." She motioned them forward. "Step forward, both of you."

Noah glanced over at Jezebeth to find she was also looking at him. Her look seemed to say, "What have we got to lose, we've come this far?" He shrugged and started forward, but he swept his gaze around them, alert for anything.

Lilith chuckled as if she knew exactly what he was thinking, but he didn't give a damn at this point. They'd been attacked by demons, kidnapped by a Djinn, beaten up, tortured, and several other things he didn't want to remember in his nightmares. He was damned well going to keep his eyes wide open for anything that decided to pop out at them.

When he reached the front of the dais just in front of Lilith's throne, Jez dropped to her knees, but at least didn't prostrate herself again. Noah glanced down at her, but refused to show the same deference for Lilith. After all, she'd gotten them both into their current circumstances—he refused to pretend he was thankful.

"Rise and come to me, my daughter."

"My queen," Jez murmured as she rose and stepped forward.

Lilith dipped her hand between her generous cleavage and pulled out a black cord attached to a red amulet with intricate markings. "Wear this at all times until you and your sisters approach Lucifer."

At Jezebeth's flash of surprise, Lilith nodded. "Evelin has tried to do her damage, but I have faith that the other three will find their way home to us." She gestured toward the red amulet. "It will protect you and will also grant you access to Hell, not to mention it will show Lucifer that you have my blessings in your request."

Jezebeth accepted the amulet and slipped it over her head, settling the amulet under her shirt between her breasts.

Lilith's expression darkened. "Now. About last night."

"I ask that you are lenient with Jezebeth." Noah said the words quickly before Jezebeth could interrupt. "I'll take any punishment you have in mind for the both of us."

"Noah!" Jez hissed from beside him.

Lilith surprised him by dipping her chin in acknowledgment, a small smile playing at the edges of her lips. "You continue to surprise me, human. And as much as I would never admit this in a larger audience, I think I enjoy being surprised after all this time."

"Will it cost me anything to ask you why?"

Jezebeth stiffened in his grip. He ran his thumb back and forth over the soft skin at the back of her neck and she stilled and relaxed against him.

Lilith pursed her lips as if considering his request. "I suppose since you've met the requirements of the incantation, I have no choice but to honor my part of the bargain."

Jez stiffened again as Noah scrambled to make sense of Lilith's words.

Lilith's laugh echoed around the cavern, and she finally walked over to her throne and sank down, tucking her feet under her like a small girl rather than an ancient queen. "The rest of the incantation that you apparently didn't read said if you resisted my temptation three times and showed yourself worthy, you would receive three gifts that are within my power."

The meaning of Lilith's words spilled through Noah as possibilities blossomed inside his mind.

Lilith waved away her words. "Since you were rather indisposed last night, I hope you'll forgive my presumption in returning your life force as your first gift."

Jez gasped from beside him and surprise flashed across Lilith's features. "You think I'm so callous as to wish you pain, Jezebeth? You may not be my creation, but you're my creature, and I care for your welfare."

Noah glanced down to see Jez's small frown before she replaced it with a blank mask.

Lilith sighed. "I suppose it's difficult for you to understand, but even though the succubi and incubi aren't demons, by our very nature as acting as one of the temptations for the world, it's easy for all of us to fall prey to some of the very temptations we offer the humans." She raised her gaze to Noah's. "As for you . . . Noah. I owe you two more gifts. You may ask for anything within my power, and I'll happily grant it." She nodded once—the annoying succubus habit. And for a split second, he was tempted to ask for that mannerism to be abolished.

She grinned as if she'd heard his thoughts. "Choose wisely. For there are only two that remain." She gave a Gallic shrug. "And I think the nod is something I've done for too long to change at this point anyhow."

Jez frowned at the exchange since she obviously hadn't heard Noah's thoughts, but to her credit, she remained silent, since this discussion was between him and Lilith.

Noah mentally braced for Lilith's reaction as he decided to ask big and see what happened. "I'd like to use my second gift to free Jezebeth from the revenge of Semiazas."

"Noah, you can't—" Jez's words faltered as Lilith held up her hand, palm out.

"As much as I wish I could, unfortunately, that is not within my power. I have helped Jezebeth and her sisters as much as I'm able under the current circumstances already." Lilith paused, her expression a mixture of concern and sadness. "To do more would endanger us all."

Noah hadn't expected a different response, but disappointment tasted bitter on his tongue anyway. "Damn. It was worth a shot, right?"

Jez turned in Noah's arms, her palms against his chest as she looked up at him. "Noah, don't waste your gifts on me. No one has ever resisted Lilith's temptation; you've earned those gifts. There are wondrous things within her power to grant you. Take some time and think through what you can ask for. There isn't any time limit, and—"

This time Noah cut Jez off with a kiss. Her lips were soft and plush against his, and after a quick second of shock, she melted against him, returning his kiss before pulling back and casting a wary glance toward Lilith.

"These are my gifts, remember?" He chucked Jez under the chin with his fingers. "Trust me to use them well, okay?" Besides, life without Jezebeth would be anything but wondrous.

She nodded, but didn't look happy.

Noah pulled her close, holding her gently by his side as he turned his attention back to Lilith. "If Jezebeth is amenable, can you make her human? Release her from her succubus life?"

Lilith slowly shook her head. "Being a succubus isn't something that was chosen for her, it's something she *is*." Lilith spread her hands wide. "I don't hold the power of creation, so that is also something beyond what I can grant." She laughed. "Believe me, if I had possessed that power, there were many times over the countless millennia that I would've availed myself of it."

Disappointment arrowed through him, even though he hadn't expected any different. He'd asked on the off chance that some loophole would allow her more powers in this instance. But from everything he had read and understood about Lilith and her world, he at least now knew what he could ask for and reasonably receive.

"All right. Then, if Jezebeth is amenable, I'd like to be allowed to remain here with her as her mate, and for my immunity to her powers to be permanent and universal so I can provide her sustenance as she needs it—without me dying."

Jezebeth turned to gape at him, and he grinned before turning to see Lilith's reaction.

Lilith studied Jezebeth curiously. "Since your consent is included as part of his request, are these things you would wish?"

Jezebeth dug her fingers into the front of his shirt as she searched his face. "Noah, are you sure? I could be dead soon, and even if you stayed here and were immune . . . I'd still have quotas to meet."

Jez's words hit him like a fist to the gut. Quotas meant she'd still have to tempt and seduce other men . . . or even women.

Could he live with that?

Every possessive instinct inside him roared like a beast brought suddenly awake to protect its mate. *Mine!* it screamed, and even Noah's logical side agreed with the instinct.

"It's part of who and what I am. If Lilith can't release me from my succubus nature, then I will still be required to fulfill the same duties I have since my creation."

Noah pulled Jez tighter against him. "I hadn't realized what keeping myself immune would mean. But there has to be some way to work this out. I love you. I can't just go back to my old life and forget. My heart would always be here with you. But I also don't think I could stand by and watch you . . . fulfill your quotas."

"Would you be willing to entertain a side bargain?"

Noah stiffened at Lilith's seductive words. Verbally sparring with the succubus queen was always a dangerous proposition, but if there was a way to work this out, Noah would take it. "What type of bargain?" he asked carefully.

Jezebeth's fingers tightened on Noah's arm, and he placed his hand over hers and squeezed it, hoping she would trust him to navigate any verbal traps Lilith might lay for them.

"You have two wishes remaining. Allowing you to stay here as

Jezebeth's mate is one, and granting you immunity from the effects of her succubus nature is another. However, if you remain here, I assume you would want to continue your writing and your research?"

Noah winced as he remembered how some of his research had gotten him into this mess with Lilith in the first place. As for writing, that was his passion, not just a job he could walk away from. The stories that took shape inside his head would find an outlet one way or another.

He searched through Lilith's words for a verbal trap or alternate meaning and found none. "Yes, I would want to continue both," he finally answered, alert for anything she might throw his way.

She pursed her lips, and then fell silent so long that Noah had started to think she wouldn't speak again. When she finally did, her words were conversational and soft. "I occasionally have need of a liaison whom I could trust. This person would carry important messages for me and receive my guarantee of protection. I can only assume a position like that would allow you to meet those for research who you would never normally meet—at least without getting yourself into further trouble."

A messenger? The last thing Noah needed was to spend all his time running around the world on errands for Lilith, especially if they were all as complicated as the assignment he'd just completed.

Lilith smiled, confirming his suspicions that she could at least some of the time pick up his thoughts. "That's not what I had in mind. I sometimes need to send specific and sensitive messages to one of the Archangels, or certain denizens of Hell. I have others to deliver low-level summons and all the rest, but I need someone quick-witted and intelligent whom I could trust for these special projects. And as these messages are infrequent, your off time could be used as you choose." She shifted on the throne, as if settling herself more comfortably. "If Jezebeth agreed to serve in this capacity with you instead of her normal duties, she could guide you and could translate or liaise as needed, which would remove her from any requirements of her current succubus quotas."

Noah's bullshit meter went off, and he cocked his head to the side as he studied Lilith in a new light. She had found a way that he and Jezebeth could be together while still allowing Noah to research and even write. "Why would you offer this to us?"

Lilith sighed. "I do have concern for those under my care and wish them to be happy." She shrugged, and he saw a flash of something unsaid in her expression. "I also know what it's like to be denied that happiness." She sat up straighter, squaring her shoulders and raising her chin as if throwing off the vulnerability she'd dared to show them for a fleeting moment. "Not to mention that when Semiazas forced you to drink his blood, he extended your life and gave you a certain amount of protection from his own powers."

Noah and Jez exchanged a startled glance. This was definitely news to him.

"Do you accept my offer of liaison? And are you sure those are the two gifts you'd like to request?"

He dropped his chin to gauge Jezebeth's reaction. Disbelief swam in the hazel depths of her eyes, but there was also hope.

"Do you think you could put up with me full time?"

She laughed. "You mean give up hunting and make love only with you, and only when we wanted? Travel with someone I care for and actually have Lilith's protection when I do?" She laughed. "I suppose I could learn to live with that if you could."

Joy spiraled through Noah, and he leaned down to capture Jez's lips with his own.

"If you'll save the celebrating for a moment longer, we can make this official."

At Lilith's words, Noah stepped back from Jez like a guilty child as heat burned up his neck. Jez's face was also tinged pink, and a soft laugh escaped from her.

"Sorry," he said as he faced Lilith but still held Jezebeth's hand.

Lilith cocked her head to the side, studying them. "Don't be. Take what happiness you can in the time allotted. There is much before us that is unknown for now."

Noah frowned, not liking the sound of that.

"Step forward, Noah Halston, and receive your gifts."

Noah squeezed Jezebeth's hand before releasing it and walking across the remaining expanse of runway until he stood before Lilith.

"Kneel and remove your shirt."

Unsure what was about to happen, Noah slowly knelt as he pulled the black T-shirt off and held it loosely in one hand.

Lilith pulled a golden dagger from her skirts and crouched in front of him. As she raised the dagger, the wicked-looking sharp edge caught the light and Noah clamped his teeth together as the first spurt of unease surged through him.

"Be very sure you want this, Noah Halston. Once this is done, it cannot be undone."

Noah thought of Jezebeth's smile, her laugh, the way she constantly surprised him, and the way she felt curled against him when he'd woken this morning. When he imagined spending the rest of his life with her, a sense of rightness settled firmly inside him, and he smiled as he met Lilith's gaze. "I'm very sure. Let's do this."

Without warning, Lilith slashed out with the dagger.

Sharp burning pain across the left side of Noah's chest pulled a gasp from his lips and he glanced down to see a wide, bleeding cut across his left pectoral.

Lilith slashed the dagger across her palm with a hiss and then laid her bleeding hand against his chest wound.

The contact stung as her cool fingers closed against his skin, and Noah let out a slow breath of relief. "There for a second I thought you were going to turn me into an incubus." He laughed. "I thought this was going to be something much worse than—"

Crippling pain lanced through Noah stealing his words and bowing his body backward until he thought his spine would snap in two.

Distantly he heard Jezebeth's cry of concern as blackness closed around him.

He waited for the blackness to smother the pain and steal his awareness . . . but his world became only the constant waves of throbbing agony.

26

Michael materialized just outside the tiny pub in Ireland, unnoticed by the small groups and couples who huddled inside their coats against the chilly evening as they went about their business. The smell of peat was strong in the air as well as various scents from the foods being cooked inside. Raucous laughter sounded in bursts over the Irish reel being played by a live band.

Lucifer's energy rolled out of the pub in an invisible wave of power, and Michael ducked through the door and scanned the packed tiny tables and the group of bodies clustered around the bar for the fallen one.

Lucifer sat against the back wall, a pint of Guinness in his hand and an amused expression painting his patrician features. He must've sensed Michael's presence because he glanced up at that moment and motioned the Archangel over.

Michael sat, and a barmaid placed a pint of Harp on the table in front of him before slipping back into the crowd. "So much for going unnoticed during this time."

"You know as well as I that only those who are sensitive will even give us a second look. However, it does help to get enough notice to be served." He raised his Guinness in a mock salute before taking a drink. "After all, we must enjoy all the pleasures the human world holds in case it's not around much longer."

Michael bit back a growl of impatience. Lucifer had a way of grating on his last nerve—something all brothers seemed to have, but over the millennia, Lucifer had perfected it to an art form. "You asked me to meet you here. I'm assuming there was a reason?" he prompted.

Lucifer motioned toward the motley crew of musicians who had begun to play a sad, slow ballad. "All work and no play. You really must learn to take time for yourself, Michael. After all, eternity can be boring if you never stop to smell the roses." He reached for his beer again, and Michael reached out to stop him.

"Spare me the temptation routine, Lucifer. I have neither the patience nor the time."

Lucifer met Michael's gaze, the fallen one's green eyes burning with intelligence. "On the contrary," he said softly. "You have eternity, regardless of what happens here in the human world."

Michael cocked his head to one side and raised his brows. "Ask me."

Lucifer's lips slowly curved into a smile, and his expression suddenly lost all artifice, reminding Michael of the Archangel before he'd betrayed their Father and been banished from Heaven. Michael bit back a sigh of old memories and regrets and waited.

"All right." Lucifer drained the rest of his beer and set the empty glass on the table, waving away the waitress who had come forward with a refill. "What are His thoughts on all of this?"

Michael had expected some form of the question, just as Lucifer asked every time they met. Lucifer, the son, had rebelled and would wait for eternity for their Father to extend forgiveness and ask him back into the fold. What Lucifer still didn't understand was that his actions had been forgiven as soon as they had been made. Lucifer only needed to repent and he would be welcomed back. Michael was beginning to think the standoff would last indefinitely. He'd seen the pattern repeated in the human world again and again— fathers and sons really were patterned after their divine creator. He shook his head and sighed.

"He simply said all will be as it should."

Lucifer's green eyes flashed with annoyance, and he clenched his jaw. "Which says nothing."

"And everything." Michael stood. "Is there anything else?"

"The last two journals have yet to be placed, and the next succubus has been found."

Michael nodded.

*   *   *

Awareness trickled back slowly.

The first thing Noah noticed was the lack of pain. He'd become so used to the white-hot agony over the past countless hours that his nerve synapses seemed almost confused by the total lack of discomfort.

He took stock and realized he was warm, comfortable, and lying on something soft. All his toes and fingers worked and seemed to obey his commands.

So far so good.

The soft scent of pomegranate and honey teased his senses, and Noah fought through the last of the languid haze holding him to force open his eyes.

The sight of Jezebeth's smiling face looming over him was the most beautiful thing he'd ever seen, and cool relief slid through him.

"Noah!" She rained wet kisses over his face, murmuring words he couldn't quite catch as he realized she was crying.

He wrapped his arms around her and in a quick move, rolled them both over, gaining a laughing squeak from Jezebeth as he captured her mouth with his. She tasted sweet and warm as she returned his urgent kisses, wrapping her arms around him as if afraid he would suddenly disappear.

Noah's cock hardened as he realized he was naked. The erotic sensation of his bare skin brushing against Jezebeth's jeans and thin top sent heat roaring through his veins. He buried his fingers in her silky hair, pulling off the band that held it back in a ponytail and tossing the small elastic ring aside while continuing to kiss her with frenzied need.

He stripped away her clothes, baring her until there was nothing between them but skin and the red amulet that Lilith had given her, that she wore around her neck. Her heat burned into him like an erotic promise, and he shifted on top of her so he could slide his cock inside her tight warmth.

The exquisite friction seared through him as he slid deep and his pelvis pressed snug against the soft lips of her labia.

He broke the kiss as a long moan sounded in his ears. It took him a moment to realize the sound hadn't just come from Jezebeth, but also from him.

She arched under him, her nails digging into his back—sharp stings that only increased his urgency as she captured his mouth again. She nipped at his lips, and he began to move inside her.

She moved with him, tightening her thighs around him with each thrust and loosening to let him pull out until he drove inside her again and again. With every movement his chest pressed against her breasts, the teasing hardness of her nipples stroking him in time with their movements.

Urgency built between them as Noah lost himself in the sensations between them. Jezebeth's scent surrounded him, her soft skin and warm heat enveloping him, teasing him, soothing him. As she slowly tightened around him, her breathing came in sharp pants in between the small, urgent sounds that spilled from her throat and into his mouth, driving him faster and harder.

When she cried out, her teeth clamping down on his shoulder, the liquid warmth of her orgasm spilled around him and he pistoned inside her, the extra slickness driving him over the edge to his own release.

He spasmed inside her, his balls squeezing tight against his body as his release jetted forward, sending shooting fire along every nerve ending with a backwash of pure liquid warmth.

When reality returned, he was still on top of her and inside her, bracing his weight off her with his forearms.

She smiled up at him, a languid smile stealing across her expression. "Still alive I see."

He laughed as he realized he hadn't stopped to ask if Lilith's gift had kicked in yet before he'd rolled Jezebeth over and slid inside her. "I suppose so."

She brushed his hair away from his forehead, her cool fingers skimming gently across his skin. "You were right."

He frowned and cocked his head to the side, trying to understand what she meant.

"You said alive was a good look for you . . . and you're right."

Noah laughed again and nuzzled his face into the crook of her neck until she squirmed and laughed. "Only good?" he said against her skin, enjoying the sensual shudder that ran through her.

She gently scraped her fingernails down his bare back, sending a quick line of gooseflesh marching over him, and he raised his head with a laugh. "Don't get greedy. I'm just glad you're all right. You really had me worried there for a while."

A raw memory of the ongoing searing pain flashed back to

Noah and he winced. "What happened?" He swallowed hard and then finally asked the question he'd been avoiding thinking about since he'd woken. "Am I an incubus now?"

Jezebeth's lips curved and she shook her head. "No. Totally human. Although with both Semiazas's and Lilith's blood inside you, you'll have some immunity to both incubi and succubi as well as some demons, not to mention the extended lifespan—although no one is sure by how much."

Noah blew out a slow breath, relieved for some reason that he'd retained his humanity. The lifespan question didn't bother him. After all, he'd never known exactly what his original lifespan was, so who was he to quibble over a longer one? "If I get to spend it with you, then I don't care how long it is. I'll treasure every minute." He leaned down to brush his lips over hers.

When he raised his head, tears glistened in Jezebeth's eyes. "I never thought I'd fall in love, let alone with a human." She absently ran her fingers over his bottom lip and he kissed her fingertips, making her laugh.

"I'm glad you waited for me."

"I don't think you can wait for something you don't know is coming. But I do think we were meant to find each other."

He smiled and nodded. "So, what happens now? How soon will your sisters find their way here?"

She shrugged, an odd motion since she was lying on her back beneath him. "The faster the better. But I think Lilith has some errands in mind for us while we wait."

He shifted, and his cock hardened again inside her.

Jezebeth gasped and tightened her thighs around him, pulling him tight against her.

"Do you think those errands can wait for a while? I'd like to enjoy my newfound immunity."

A low, smoky chuckle rumbled out of Jezebeth's throat. "I think you'd better. I'm a succubus in need of sustenance from my, what did you call me back in Lilith's lair? Your mate?" She nodded, answering her own question. "Yup, 'mate,' that was it."

She grinned up at him as she threaded her fingers in his hair and pulled him close until his lips were so close to hers they shared breath. "I need sustenance from my mate." She brushed her lips over his. "I love you, Noah."

He answered her with a kiss that made her head spin as their energy twined together between them. Only when she was breathless and panting did he pull back to look at her. "I love you too, Jezebeth. My very own succubus." Noah grinned.

Turn the page for a preview of Cassie Ryan's
next Sister of Darkness novel . . .

The Demon and the Succubus

Coming soon from Berkley Sensation!

"Not what I expected. But a lovely prelude to our relationship."

Sunk deep in a relaxing hot bath, Amalya glanced toward the doorway to find a stunning stranger in a very expensive Italian suit devouring her with an amused, hazel-eyed gaze. Irritation and surprise warred inside her and she bit them back. "I'm sorry. Did we have an appointment, Mr.—" She remained in her reclined state with her head resting back against the bath pillow and her arms resting along the sides of the ridiculously large claw-footed tub, waiting for him to fill in the blank as she mentally reviewed her calendar.

There were no appointments for today, and the Madame hadn't informed her of any pop-ups, which was why she'd slept in this morning and was now lounging in the tub.

After all, even succubi liked to relax on their days off.

"Levi." His rich voice, with its definite upper-crust British accent, softly echoed around the spacious bathroom as he walked forward uninvited. He grinned as he crouched and reached out to rub some strands of the long blond hair she'd pinned on top of her head in between his fingertips. "Soft and lovely." His inflection told her he meant more than just her hair.

Surprised at the man's bold actions, Amalya resisted the urge to define her personal space. Instead, she mentally shifted into work mode.

She cocked her head to the side and reached out to touch his hair in the same manner he had hers, smiling when he raised his brows as if she'd surprised him. His hair was soft to the touch, the color of rich milk chocolate, clean-cut but longer on the top where it fell over onto his brow. She traced one finger down his sideburns, which were long and ended even with the bottom of his earlobes.

He was definitely good-looking, attractive, with a strong jaw and rich hazel eyes that sparked with amusement.

He intrigued her.

A glowing aura of nearly white energy surrounded him like a pulsing mist. Amalya wasn't in need of energy, having just entertained a client last night, but this man's presence tasted human with an undertone of something exotic she couldn't quite place. Her skin began to ache—the succubus equivalent of a stomach growl, telling her he would give her a surge of energy better than any she'd had lately among the stream of humans and lower-level supernaturals. Not to mention he intrigued her, and she had a feeling she would very much enjoy spending some time with this mystery man.

Everything that made it well worth working on her day off.

"So, what did you expect . . . Mr. Levi?" she asked with a small smile.

"Levi is my given name." His gaze devoured her face as silence fell between them as if he were trying to put his thoughts into words. "Perhaps someone older?" His lips quirked up at the edges.

A lie.

Amalya bit back a smile. Each succubus had a gift, and hers was being able to discern truth from lies. Not the most powerful gift among her people, or even her three sisters, but one she'd grown to rely on over the millennia—and millennia was how long she'd lived.

From the way Levi's eyes sparkled, he knew it.

His grin widened as he slowly stood and reached into the inside pocket of his jacket. "The Madame gave me this." He held up a black old-fashioned ladies' fan, and a spurt of surprise threaded through Amalya that she hoped hadn't shown on her face.

Each different color of fan represented what the client had paid for and what they expected from their time with her. It was a very simple tool that kept all talk of money out of the bedroom, and part of a philosophy that had made The Sinner's Redemption one of the most profitable legal brothels not only in Nevada, but in the world. The black fan meant this man had paid with an open account and he had deep enough pockets to cover whatever he wished to go on inside this room or out.

"My apologies, Amalya. I've caught you off guard." He bowed from the waist as if they were in Victorian England, but the intense gaze that bored into hers held no apology, only delight, intrigue, and anticipation.

"Not at all," she lied, glad most others didn't share her gift. "I must not have received the Madame's message to expect a client. If you'll give me a moment, I'll get ready." She sat up and braced her hands on the side of the tub so she could stand.

"Don't." His voice sounded like more of a request than a statement, and she stilled and glanced up at him.

He laid the fan aside and crouched again next to the tub, making the room feel very small as he loomed next to her. "Please don't be angry with the Madame, she didn't know of my arrival until just a few minutes ago, and I asked her not to disturb you." He smiled— the first genuine smile she'd seen from him—which made him look younger and more vulnerable. Now that she'd seen the real man behind the mask, he'd never be able to fool her with his masked expressions again. "And now I'm glad she didn't."

Amalya sensed no danger—no special succubus talents needed. Pure female intuition honed over a long life. Not to mention that Jethro, her longtime friend and the bodyguard at The Sinner's Redemption, wouldn't have let Levi through if he were any danger to her.

Amalya had been in Hell's version of the witness protection program for just over seven hundred years. She couldn't afford to let down her guard when the demon she'd helped lock away still had plenty of contacts within the human realm and would relish the chance to torture her and her sisters for the rest of eternity.

She searched Levi's face, finally meeting his deep gaze squarely. Pure logic told her there was something more to him than a rich playboy who wanted some time with her. "What can I do for you, Levi? Really."

"It's what I can do for *you* that brings me here."

The truth of his cultured words hit her like a slap before he stood and took off his suit jacket. "Do you mind if I join you? It seems a shame to waste a perfectly good bath, don't you think?"

Amalya wanted to make him explain his odd statement, but figured he'd get around to it in his own time. Years of isolation from her sisters and her own kind had taught her patience.

She studied Levi and debated saying no. She'd never let anyone join her in the bath before—for her, baths weren't sexual. It was a silly distinction for a succubus to make since she'd had partners in just about every other scenario, location, and position before. But there was definitely something about this man that intrigued her and made her want to share even this private sanctuary with him.

She mentally shrugged and relaxed back against the tub. "By all means. There are extra towels just behind that door."

He smiled and opened the door to her spacious walk-in closet, pulling a large green towel off the shelf and hanging it on the hook next to hers. He toed off his shoes and loosened his tie. "You know, I don't think I've bathed with anyone since I was a child. Baths have always been my private thinking time."

She smirked at the irony of his statement and raised one brow, earning a short laugh from him.

"Touché. Apparently, we are very similar creatures, Amalya. And for interrupting both your day off and your private time, I promise to make it worthwhile."

Amalya didn't bother to censor the laugh that bubbled up from her throat. "You're very sure of yourself, aren't you?"

He stilled and met her gaze directly. "Yes. I have no doubt I can give you everything you need."

She frowned at the strength of the truth in those few words. They hadn't been said as a boast, but almost as a sad fact.

Pure instinct made her add, "I have no doubt you already know I'm a succubus and everything that entails . . . " By which she meant that time spent with her would drain some of his energy.

He smiled slowly. "I'm well aware, and not worried in the least, my beauty."

A weight lifted from her and she sighed as anticipation slid through her. She hadn't realized what a relief it would be not to have to hide what she was. Even supernaturals tended to try to forget to some extent what she was during their time together.

What would it be like to just be herself with no secrets for a while?

Intrigued by the man in front of her, Amalya allowed herself to relax as Levi continued to undress.

He draped his suit jacket and tie over the closed toilet lid before turning back to her and unbuttoning his expensive designer shirt.

A surge of delight tripped through her. He seemed eager to be with her—not the well-known courtesan from The Sinner's Redemption, but her. She knew it was probably only her imagination, but she held on to the sensation anyway.

Each opened button of his shirt revealed a new tantalizing glimpse of firm skin dusted with crisp, dark hairs, and Amalya, riveted in place, couldn't seem to look away.

Arousal slid through her like fine cognac, a slow warmth that built in intensity until her nipples hardened under the hot water and familiar slickness formed between her labia. Apparently, her body wholeheartedly agreed with her decision to suspend her day off.

When both sides of Levi's shirt hung loose to reveal a strong line of firm male flesh, his hands quickly moved to the button of his slacks.

Amalya tightened her fingers on the porcelain to keep from pushing out of the tub and taking over the simple task. Apparently, his hurried movements weren't even fast enough for her. She smiled and mentally chided herself for acting like a teenager in a backseat after prom.

So much for all her hard-earned patience.

Levi lowered his zipper and she found herself moistening her lower lip with her tongue as impatience snapped through her to see what was hidden underneath the fine, dark fabric.

When she glanced up into Levi's face, he was smiling.

Heat seared into her cheeks as she realized she'd been caught staring.

"There's no need to be embarrassed for looking, Amalya. I fully plan on returning the favor once you're not hidden in all that water." He hooked his thumbs in the waistband of his slacks and slid them off, along with his dark silk boxers, in one fluid motion.

Amalya frowned as Levi bent over to pull the slacks off each foot, blocking her view of his newly revealed body. The rest of him was magnificent, and she was impatient to know if his cock matched the rest of the package.

She huffed out a small breath of frustration, laughing at herself in the process. How long had it been since she'd been this anxious to see a man's cock? Three thousand years? More? She couldn't remember, which was answer enough.

Levi straightened and tossed his slacks on top of his other clothes, then slipped off his shirt and gave it the same treatment.

Amalya sucked in a breath as her gaze devoured him.

His entire body was a study in male beauty. He was fit and trim with long legs, muscular thighs, a flat stomach, and a long, thick cock that stiffened to attention under her perusal. He wasn't circumcised, which was rare in this day and age—especially here in the United States where the bulk of her business came from, but since most of her existence had been spent during times when that practice was rare, she appreciated the fine art of pleasuring a man with foreskin still attached.

Her mouth watered as she imagined taking his hard length between her lips and running her tongue over the taut skin while she sucked him.

As her vivid mental fantasy continued, she ran her gaze over every inch of him within her sight while Levi stepped into the water, settling his large body against the other end of the tub and tangling his legs with hers.

The water level rose to within an inch of the top edge of the tub, and a large sigh escaped Levi as he relaxed back and grinned at her.

Suddenly self-conscious for the first time she could remember, Amalya mentally shook herself and pulled out her full work arsenal. "You mentioned there was something you could do for me, Levi." She traced her toes up his inner thigh until she gently brushed against the heavy sac that hung just under his cock. "Why don't you show me?"

Levi's hazel eyes darkened to nearly black, and his balls tightened against his body, making a small surge of triumph snake through Amalya. She'd hated the sensation of being off balance. She liked being the one in control when it came to sex, and she knew exactly what men wanted and how to give it to them.

Without warning, Levi reached out and pulled her across the tub until she straddled him, his hard cock caught between them, nestled against her stomach and burning into her skin like a dark promise. She glanced up to find herself so close to him she could see the small scar that ran just over his right eyebrow. Her heart beat thickly inside her chest as his energy aura pulsed against her in a tempting thrum. Before she could gather her wits and think of something seductive to say, he pulled her firmly against his chest and captured her mouth with his.

The faint taste of warmed whiskey filled her senses as did the scent of something exotic, musky, and very male.

Amalya melted against him as he captured her lips in a slow but surprisingly firm caress. His arms came around her, holding her close, but rather than crushing her to him, gave the impression that she was someone to be treasured.

He sucked gently at her bottom lip, nibbling and teasing without breaking the sensual dance of their kiss.

Surprised and impressed to not be the one doing the leading, Amalya sighed against his lips and laid her palms flat over the muscled male chest in front of her.

He settled her against him more firmly, gently caging her hands between them as he explored her mouth and reactions with lips and teeth and tongue, then artfully repeated those actions that pulled an unwitting sigh, gasp, or shudder from her.

He slowly and expertly kissed her into breathlessness as she enjoyed the sensations of his mouth against hers and his hard body beneath her. She gave herself up to the unexpected arousal he ignited, twining her arms around his neck and spearing her fingers into his silky hair as he continued to kiss her.

One of his large, warm hands cupped her cheek, his thumb feathering a slow, wet line back and forth across her cheek as he thoroughly explored her mouth. She gasped as the first wave of his strong, clean aura knifed into her, absorbing into her pores and converting into usable energy inside her.

Amalya closed her eyes tight against the wave of light-headedness that assaulted her from the sudden influx of strong energy—the succubus equivalent of brain freeze—and greedily kissed him back, wanting more.

Her pussy ached and she ground against his cock as the scent of their arousal perfumed the air around them, overpowering the strong aroma of vanilla and lavender from the bath salts.

Levi growled low inside his throat and in a quick motion cupped her ass in one of his large hands, lifted her, and impaled her.

A long moan ripped from Amalya's throat as her body stretched to accommodate his generous girth. She slowly sank down on him until they were pelvis to pelvis and he filled her completely.

Levi stilled, and Amalya appreciated the moment to allow her body to adjust. It showed consideration for her as a person and not just a warm body to fuck—something she didn't often find in her profession.

She brushed a quick kiss over his lips before she leaned back and began to move. Not wanting to waste the exquisite full sensation he gave her, she ground against him, rubbing her clit against the crispy hairs that covered his pelvis while her sensitive nipples rasped against his chest with each movement.

Levi's hands gripped her hips, but he let her lead, keeping her gaze as she rode him and he hardened further inside her.

Amalya set a slow, steady rhythm, refusing to move faster when their breathing became raspy and Levi's fingers tightened against her hips. She continued to move, torturing them both until the world fell away and only this one room and the two of them existed for her.

Curling heat of arousal snaked through her limbs as Levi's dark gaze bored into her own.

When the first drop of pre-come leaked from Levi's cock and came into contact with the inner walls of her pussy, a hard blast of energy surged through her and she stiffened on top of him. Her pussy clenched around him as her body absorbed the life-giving energy he offered.

As her borrowed power surged through her, she faltered and Levi moved his grip to her ass, guiding her to continue the same movements she'd begun, which drove her hard toward a peak that seemed to surge forward in a dizzying rush.

The sound of his harsh breathing merged with hers inside the small room, blending with the sounds of sloshing water and the rushing that sounded inside Amalya's ears from her blood rocketing through her body.

She tried to speed her movements, to meet the urgency of that edge that stayed just out of her reach, but Levi held her firmly, keeping the pace she'd started and torturing her until small whimpers of need spilled from her throat and she dug her nails into his shoulders in a silent protest.

"Patience, my beauty." His words were a harsh rasp as he began thrusting up inside her with each movement. A small scream of surprise ripped from her throat as the tip of his cock firmly made contact with her cervix again and again until Amalya was sure her body would break apart from the intense pleasure shooting along every nerve ending and threatening to overload her brain.

When she was sure she couldn't take any more, a hot surging

warmth began deep inside her and spilled out into her body, seductive and enticing, until it engulfed her, blanking her mind and leaving her euphoric and boneless.

Almost distantly she heard Levi's soft cry of completion and felt the hot spurt of his release as he came inside her.

Her body absorbed Levi's essence, feeding the spreading warmth.

Tiny aftershocks quaked through her. Each one equaled an ordinary orgasm, and they continued to rock through her until they blended together to become surreal in their intensity. She lost track of time as the sweet bursts spread liquid ecstasy through her veins until she was sure she'd never be able to move again.

When awareness returned, she was slumped against Levi's chest, her face buried in the crook of his neck, her arms bonelessly draped over his muscled shoulders.

She sighed against his neck and tried to make her brain cut through the fog of endorphins and the tiny aftershocks of great sex that still twitched through her whenever she moved. The only real movement she could manage was tracing her fingers over his shoulder. When her fingers found a metal medallion on a chain, she stilled.

Amalya frowned, unable to raise her head yet. She didn't remember him wearing a necklace when he'd undressed, but her attention had definitely been on other things. She wasn't surprised she'd missed it, especially since the medallion had hung down his back rather than over his chest.

She closed her fingers over it, tracing the etching and wondering what it said.

When the sharp essence of her mistress, Lilith, the Queen of the Succubi and Incubi, tingled against her fingertips, shock stabbed through her and she forced herself to sit up and meet Levi's dark gaze.

She pulled the medallion around to the front where she could see it, and ice churned through her blood, chasing away the boneless euphoric sensation of just a moment ago. The medallion was sterling silver with faded ancient Hebrew characters inscribed on it that roughly translated to the current-day equivalent of "temptation"—fitting for a succubus.

However, the last place she'd seen this necklace was hanging around the neck of her queen.

Why did Levi have this?

Dread pooled inside her stomach, and she swallowed hard against all the horrible possibilities that flashed through her mind like a macabre old-time silent movie.

Movement from the doorway made Amalya snap her head around to find Jethro standing in the entranceway, a fully packed duffel in his hand.

"Is she fully energized?"

Fully energized? If she were any more energized, she'd blow the roof off the entire building!

She glanced between the two men. Anger and irritation snapped through her as she realized Jethro was talking to Levi and not her. She stiffened, and with as much dignity as she could maintain while still sitting impaled on Levi's cock, she demanded, "What the hell is going on here?"

Levi met her gaze. "I think it's time for the second part of what I can do for you, my beauty."

Amalya scrambled off Levi's lap, not caring if she snapped off his cock in the process. She stood at the other end of the tub, the water dripping off her as she turned to face Jethro. "What's going on?"

Her friend met her gaze squarely and she thought she saw a flash of guilt before the familiar calm mask fell across those deep blue eyes—which definitely didn't bode well for the situation.

"Jethro," she said in a low tone of warning.

"Get dressed, Amalya," Levi said smoothly as he stood, "and we'll explain everything."

Amalya held out a hand to stop Levi's words and stared at Jethro, piercing him with her steady gaze until he nodded.

"Semiazas has escaped his prison. Levi has been sent by Lilith to bring you back to her lair." He sighed. "I had hoped to let you get to know him a little first, but I just received reports of two bounty demons moving this way. One pestilence and one famine. We have to go. Now."

Amalya took several long seconds to absorb the shock of Jethro's words.

She'd known this day would come. Semiazas would either serve his entire term, and then hunt down her and her sisters, or he would escape early with the same result. She'd had no illusions that this would end otherwise, but that didn't make it any less terrifying. She raised her chin as she stepped out of the tub, grabbed a towel, and began drying off in rough motions. "My sisters?"

"No word." Jethro sounded apologetic.

"How close?" Levi stepped out of the tub and Amalya pointedly turned away so she wouldn't have to see his muscled body or remember what he had felt like moving inside her.

Jethro set down the full duffel and stepped inside Amalya's closet as he spoke. "We've got maybe ten minutes, give or take. They must have someone on the inside because we had no early warning on this." Anger vibrated just under the surface of his deceptively calm voice. He came back into the bathroom holding a full set of Amalya's casual clothes, which he gently pushed into her arms. "Get dressed quickly." He met her gaze for a long moment and then brushed a warm finger over her cheek before he turned to face Levi. "Meet me at the side entrance when you're done."

Amalya hurriedly dressed in the flowing skirt, tank top, and white tennis shoes Jethro had chosen for her, then pulled the clips from her hair, letting her long blond hair spill around her shoulders. She finger-brushed the tangles out as she turned to find Levi already dressed and watching her.

"Amalya," Levi began, "we needed you at full strength for the trip ahead, and this was the best way to get it done quickly."

"It?" Anger and embarrassment twined through her, both fighting for dominance. She stiffened and glared up at him. "You mean you both decided that the poor, weak succubus couldn't be trusted with very important information that concerns her, so you took matters into your own hands to trick me into sex, supposedly for my own good?"

Levi picked up the duffel off the floor, seemingly unaffected by her words or her anger. "Would you thinking I paid a lot of money for the privilege of fucking you sit better than Jethro and I making sure you would be ready before we begin this very dangerous journey?"

His reasonable tone grated against her nerves and she stared at him with all the hatred and revulsion she could muster as the full slap of betrayal surged through her. This man had given her the best orgasm of her entire life, she'd shared her private time with him and even her real self, and it had all been an act, a job assigned to him by Lilith.

"Regardless of what you may think of me, Levi, I'm neither a fool nor a woman who is ashamed of what she is or what she does. So fuck off." She started to step away and then stopped short. "That was a freebie; however, the fuck in the tub will definitely cost you, no matter what you thought when you got into this."

Levi's smug chuckle echoed gently around them. "I have very deep pockets, my beauty. Don't worry about that."

She glanced back over her shoulder as she hurried down the hall to find Jethro. "I never said it would cost you money, now did I?"